V
DH
RK
JR

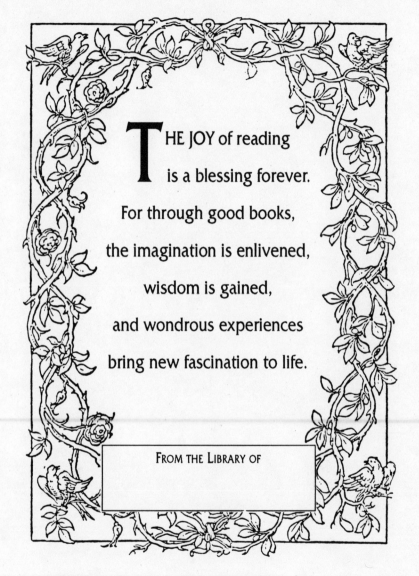

THE JOY of reading
is a blessing forever.
For through good books,
the imagination is enlivened,
wisdom is gained,
and wondrous experiences
bring new fascination to life.

FROM THE LIBRARY OF

AN EXCLUSIVE FAMILY BOOKSHELF
2-IN-1 EDITION

A SILENCE IN HEAVEN

✪ ✪ ✪

A TIME TO HEAL

GILBERT MORRIS

AND BOBBY FUNDERBURK

✪ ✪ ✪

COMPLETE AND UNEDITED EDITIONS

Family
BOOKSHELF
Since 1948, The Book Club You Can Trust

Library of Congress Cataloging-in-Publication Data

Morris, Gilbert.
    A silence in heaven / Gilbert Morris and Bobby Funderburk.
        p.   cm. — (Price of liberty : #5)
    ISBN 0–8499–3511–3
    1. World War, 1939–1945—Fiction.   I. Funderburk, Bobby, 1942– .   II. Title.   III. Series: Morris, Gilbert. Price of liberty ; 5.
    PS3563.08742S5   1994
    813'.54—dc20   93–50157
                                                                    CIP

Printed in the United States of America

456789 LB 987654321

First combined hardcover for Christian Herald Family Bookshelf: 1995

A SILENCE IN HEAVEN

GILBERT MORRIS AND
BOBBY FUNDERBURK

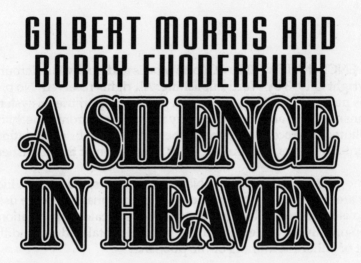

A SILENCE
IN HEAVEN

WORD PUBLISHING
Dallas·London·Vancouver·Melbourne

Library of Congress Cataloging-in-Publication Data

Morris, Gilbert.
    A silence in heaven / Gilbert Morris and Bobby Funderburk.
      p.   cm. — (Price of liberty : #5)
    ISBN 0–8499–3511–3
    1. World War, 1939–1945—Fiction.   I. Funderburk, Bobby,
1942– . II. Title. III. Series: Morris, Gilbert. Price of liberty ; 5.
  PS3563.08742S5   1994
  813'.54—dc20
                                            93–50157
                                                CIP

Printed in the United States of America

456789 LB 987654321

To Jim Wilsford—

A man of honor and integrity.
A true friend.

—Bobby

CONTENTS

Part 1

THE BLITZ

1

DIANA

*T*he wine glass began to dance across the rose-damasked tablecloth, teetered precariously at the edge, then plunged to the floor, shattering into paper-thin, crystal shards.

Diana Marlowe's blue-green eyes narrowed slightly as though she had been touched briefly by the merest shadow of pain. She listened intently to the distant crunching sound of the first bombs striking the warehouses and wharves of London's East End. *It seems I would get used to it.* For a moment she appeared to stare at something beyond the blackout curtains that led onto the balcony. Her long dress, the color of summer plums, flowed smoothly over the swells and turnings of her body in marked contrast to the childlike quality of her face. *It has only been a few weeks though. Maybe in time . . .* She took a white linen napkin from the table and bent to clean up the mess.

Seeing Diana tremble slightly, Dale Banning knelt next to her, sweeping the glass fragments up with another napkin. "The bloody Krauts will have us all drinking out of pewter mugs at this rate. I'll have to post a letter of reprimand to *Adolph* as soon as I get back to the field!"

She glanced over at Banning, then laughed softly, taking comfort in the familiar sight of his strong chin and the half-smile that lit his dark brown eyes. She thought he looked especially dashing in his flight officer's blue uniform. "You could always make me feel better, Dale. Even when we were children."

The sight of her blonde hair, shimmering in the lamplight, and the rose glow of her skin sent a rush of pleasure through him. "It's

11

my calling in life, I'm afraid. Don't really have any choice in the matter."

"It seems such an awful time for an engagement party." She glanced about the hotel suite at the glasses and cups and plates of the guests who had gone to their homes or to shelters before the bombing intensified. Like most parties since the war had begun, it was far too noisy to suit Diana. She was enamored of things old and familiar and longed for the sedate murmurings and the slow grace of pre-war gatherings. "It was lovely, wasn't it?" Staring at the red stain on the napkin as she finished wiping the floor, a fragment of a poem flashed across her mind—"the wine-dark sea." *I remember reading that in "The Odyssey."*

"Not bad. Considering the things falling out of the sky these days, it's a wonder we had any turnout at all."

Sir James Marlowe, knighted after World War I for valor at the Battle of Belleau Wood, ambled over from the door where his wife, Doreen, still chatted with the last guest. "It'll take more than a few German bombs to keep us from lifting our glasses with kith and kin. You can be certain of that! The little unemployed paperhanger in Berlin made a big mistake when he lost his temper and attacked London." Marlowe moved his tall, almost gaunt frame with a peculiar sliding gait, legacy of a German shell fragment that had sliced away part of his pelvic bone.

"I'm afraid I don't understand, sir," Banning frowned. "Seems he's doing a proper job on our factories and warehouses."

Marlowe snorted. "Winnie's duped him."

"Mr. Churchill's the prime minister now, Father," Diana chastened him good naturedly. "Don't you think it a bit improper to call him 'Winnie'?"

"He was 'Winnie' on the parade ground at Sandhurst and the polo field in India, and he's still 'Winnie' at 10 Downing Street." Confronted by confused stares from his daughter and Banning, Marlowe swirled the dark liquid in his brandy snifter and gulped some down. "Now where was I?"

"Winnie duped the paperhanger, sir."

"Ah—quite. The bombing that destroyed the Church of St. Giles and knocked poor John Milton's statue off its base was pure accident, although our *prime minister*," he nodded his head at Diana, "would have us believe otherwise. Just two pilots who lost their radio beam and got off course. They were supposed to bomb the aircraft factories at Rochester and Kingston with the rest of their squadron." He took another swallow of brandy. "But Winnie's used it as an excuse to bomb Berlin. Make Hitler so mad he'd change his basic battle strategy."

"How did you discover this, Colonel?" Banning met the steady eyes of the old soldier who had served with Churchill in the Fourth Queen's Own Hussars.

"I still have a few contacts, my boy. Besides, I know what goes on behind that sly old bulldog face." Marlowe eased into an overstuffed chair, sitting at an odd angle as he crossed his long, bony legs.

Banning poured some brandy and lowered himself in a chair next to Marlowe. "I've spent so many hours in the cockpit of my Spitfire the past four months, I haven't had time to think much about strategy—but I don't see how goading Hitler into bombing London will help us win this war."

"You still have that Spitfire and an airdrome to take off from, don't you, my boy?"

"Of course, but—"

"Chances are you wouldn't have either one for long if the Germans had stuck to their initial plan—the destruction of Fighter Command—which would have left not only London, but this entire green island defenseless."

Banning nodded his head slowly as he began to understand. "Precisely. Sometimes it's hard to take the long view of things with a Messerschmitt on your tail, trying to dump you into the Channel. Those reprisal raids on Berlin *were* a stroke of genius. I'm just surprised Hitler fell for it."

"Took four raids before his pride got the best of him. It's hard to look like the invincible führer with British bombs dropping on your capital city." Marlowe polished off the brandy. "Hitler's a madman anyway. That'll be his ruin in the end."

"Well, we can thank Churchill for saving Fighter Command. We lost a fourth of our pilots in three weeks' time after they really began to come at us in the middle of August. When they started hitting the city, it certainly took the pressure off us." Banning's eyes lost their focus in thought. "That was only a month ago. Seems like it's been a year—longer than that."

Diana took Banning's hand in both of hers, sitting on the edge of his chair as she turned toward her father. "Are you and Mother going back to the country tomorrow?"

"Haven't decided yet." He gave his daughter a fond smile. "You two coming down to the shelter with us? That is, if your mother ever finishes this interminable farewell."

Diana glanced at Banning, waiting as usual for him to make the decision for both of them.

He squeezed her hand. "I think we'll stay here for awhile. It's the first night we've had together in weeks and I don't want to spend it hiding in some dark cellar."

Marlowe eased painfully from the chair, keeping a hand on its back to steady himself. "Just as soon stay with you myself," he mused. "But Doreen wouldn't hear of it. Always was a cautious woman."

Doreen Marlowe closed the door that led into the hall and returned to the sitting area, her high heels ringing dully across the oak floors of the suite. Her eyes were an exact replica of her daughter's, as was her hair, except that it was touched with gray and swept up on her head. Outwardly she was all charm and feminine vulnerability, but she had a granite core that had kept her family on solid ground while her warrior husband traveled the remote parts of the world protecting the British Empire. "Well, shall we adjourn to the shelter before the cots are all taken?"

"We're staying up here for awhile, Mother."

"Nonsense! Don't you hear that dreadful noise outside? We're going where's it's safe."

"It's perfectly all right, Mrs. Marlowe." Banning had a reassuring tone to his voice. "There aren't any military targets near here. We're in no danger."

"Dale Banning, you wouldn't recognize danger if it walked into the room whistling 'God Save the Queen.' I think your poor mother spent more on iodine and bandages for you than she did on food when you were growing up. Besides, I don't trust these *Aryan supermen*. What if they decide to bomb hotels?"

"What if you fall down the stairs on your way to the shelter?" Banning put his arms around Diana's waist and gave her a quick hug. "Believe me, I'd never put your daughter in harm's way. Who else would marry me?"

Doreen knew they needed some time to themselves, but gave her husband a pleading look.

He merely shrugged his shoulders. "Can't live the young folks' lives for them, Doreen. If anything happens to my daughter though, Dale, my boy, the Messerschmitts will be the least of your troubles." Kissing his daughter on the cheek, he turned and walked toward the door.

"Well, don't be long," Doreen sighed. She hugged Diana, kissed Banning on the cheek, and went clicking off across the wooden floor after her husband.

Dale listened to her murmuring to her husband as they left the suite. "I think your mother liked our relationship better when we were ten years old."

Diana slipped into Banning's lap and lay her head against his shoulder. "She's just a worrier, that's all. She thinks the world of you."

Outside the suite, the Marlowes had entered the service stairwell that led down to the basement. The banister trembled slightly under their hands from the bombing as they descended in the murky shadows.

"I'm afraid for Diana, James."

"Whatever for? She's the absolute picture of happiness. I've never seen a more devoted couple than those two." Marlowe gave his wife a puzzled frown.

"That's the problem. She's far *too* devoted to him."

"Isn't that the way it's supposed to be for young people in love? My word, Doreen! The longer I live with you, the more of an enigma you become."

Doreen stopped on a landing and stared up at her husband. Through a high window, the yellowish-orange light from a hundred fires started by the bombing flickered across her soft features. "If something happened to him, I just don't know if she could handle it. She's looked to Dale for her strength since she was a child. With you gone so much, he was the only man in her life."

Marlowe felt a pang of guilt. His dark eyes seemed haunted in the half-light of the landing. The dull thudding of the bombs outside took him back to the battlefields of France, when he was young and unaware of the war his own wife was waging at home against that most relentless of enemies—loneliness. "I think you underestimate our daughter, Doreen. She's so much like you, she must have gotten some of your strength."

Doreen thought suddenly of her daughter's kitten, killed by a fox in the glade behind their house where she always played. Diana, twelve at the time, had become hysterical and couldn't sleep for weeks without having a light on in her room. She glanced about at the shadows dancing across the walls, then back into her husband's eyes and understood what he needed to hear. "Perhaps you're right."

"That's my girl! No need to worry. Lord knows we've got enough *real* problems these days." He took his wife's face in both hands and kissed her firmly on the lips.

"Such passion!" Doreen teased, pulling back.

"It's the danger. Always affects me that way."

Doreen smiled mischievously at her husband. "You must have been the scourge of the French milkmaids, soldier boy."

Marlowe's laughter echoed in the stairwell, the burden he had felt for Diana already lifting. He lay his arm around his wife's shoulders to steady himself as they continued their slow journey down to the shelter.

*   *   *

A Heinkel medium bomber roared straight down the Thames, its exhaust trailing behind like a pale ribbon against the night sky. A half mile behind it, where it had dumped its lethal cargo, two explosions, followed closely by a third, ripped into the wharves. The first two looked like huge flaming golden balls billowing upward—the third a balloon of fire encased in black smoke.

"What was that?" Diana stood on a high, darkened balcony above the city, breathing deeply the chill autumn air.

Banning leaned against the railing with one hand, his arm about Diana's shoulders. "The first two were high explosives. The third was an oil bomb. Blow the building apart—then burn it to the ground."

Diana had a view of one third of the entire circle of London. The whole horizon of the city was lined with huge fires—scores of them—lighting the heavens and the earth. Some were close enough so that she could hear the crackling flames and the yells of the firemen.

16

Little ones grew larger. Big ones died down beneath the firemen's watery onslaught, only to break out again later. The vicious, bitter firing of the anti-aircraft guns seemed insignificant in the face of such devastation.

She remembered seeing the peaceful silver curve of the Thames from this same balcony before the war; the graceful bridges that spanned it; the ornate and majestic buildings. Yet somehow this ancient city had never been as magnificent as it was this night. Something deep inside her stirred, on the verge of awakening from its dry and stony sleep. She shuddered. "It's horrifying—yet there's something about it so strangely beautiful."

"You want to go inside?"

Diana stared with rapt fascination at her city, circled and stabbed with fire. "No—not yet."

Banning saw the change reflected in the face of this girl he had known all his life. He saw fear, but also something undefinable that he couldn't touch, like trying to find a light switch in a strange and midnight room. The faces of some of his fellow pilots had mirrored that same gleaming in the eyes before battle. "You're certain you're all right?"

"Perfect."

Banning turned her toward him, circled her with his arms, and pulled her close. She lifted her face to him and was again the Diana he had always known. He kissed her deeply as she responded with a passion he hadn't expected. Moments later they pulled apart breathlessly.

"My goodness!" Diana breathed deeply. "I believe I missed you more than I thought."

"Almost makes it worth being away from you so long," Banning said hoarsely, feeling the constriction in his throat. "Want to try it again?"

Diana smiled and her eyes were warm with emotion as she pressed her face against his chest. "I'm afraid I'd swoon. Oh, I do love you so, Dale! If anything ever happened to you . . ."

"Don't be a foolish girl." Banning held her tightly. "We'll live to spoil our grandchildren."

After a few moments, Diana stepped backward, her eyes holding his. "Do you remember that huge old oak behind our house where we played all the time?"

"How could I forget it?" Banning laughed. "It was our Camelot and you made such a fetching Guinevere."

"And you always rescued me from the Black Knight or a fire-breathing dragon or the troll that lived under the bridge that crossed that lovely little brook."

"Ah, yes! I certainly *do* remember that troll. Never did kill the little rascal. Too quick for me." Banning pursed his lips and sighed, rubbing his chin with a forefinger. "Often wondered why they always live under bridges. Must be in the bylaws of the troll charter. You certainly won't find any in the forests. The fairies and wood nymphs have cornered the market there. And I've never seen one living in a shoe; that old woman and all those—"

"Will you please hush and kiss me again? I think all that flying is turning your brain to porridge!"

Banning chuckled softly, took her face in his hands, and did as she asked.

A new wave of bombers thundered overhead dropping batches of incendiary bombs as the couple stood on their balcony and held each other, looking out on their city. The incendiaries flashed brightly as they hit the buildings and streets, then simmered down to pinpoints of dazzling white. Some went out immediately as alert firemen and civilians smothered them with sand—some leaped into yellow flame as they caught buildings on fire.

The streets below were dimly lit from the glow. Just above the fires, the sky grew red and angry. Higher still, like a vast ceiling covering all the city, stretched a cloud of pink smoke. Inside the cloud flashed the brilliant dots of light that were the anti-aircraft shells bursting. After each flash came the sound.

High above the flaming buildings, the barrage balloons stood out as clearly as bright day, except that now they were colored pink instead of silver, as though some giant circus clown wanted to add gaiety to all the destruction.

Directly in front of the balcony, the largest fire sent great flames whipping toward the sky and spawned a cloud of white smoke. As the wind gradually thinned the smoke, the gigantic dome and spires of St. Paul's Cathedral took shape like a print coming to life in a developing tray. It was surrounded by fire, but as untouched as the bottom of the Thames.

Diana finally looked away. She burned with shame that she

could have taken pleasure in such a dreadful scene. Yet she couldn't deny its singular attraction or forget its haunting beauty. She didn't resist as Dale led her back inside.

Banning was troubled at the mood that had come over Diana. All her life she had been frightened of even the smallest things; shadows at the window, creakings at night in her old house, and even the wind that howled around its eaves. Now, in the midst of wanton destruction, she was flushed with excitement. He poured a sherry for her, another brandy for himself, and sat down beside her on the hideous Victorian sofa someone had perpetrated on an otherwise well-appointed room. "Here. You look like you could use this."

Diana smiled wearily, as though she had just reached the end of a long journey. "You know I don't drink. Besides, the only thing I need is you." She kissed him warmly on the lips, curled her legs up on the sofa, and lay her head in his lap.

Banning set their drinks on a marble-topped table. He thought she looked like a child again as he brushed the tips of his fingers along the silken curve of her throat; let them trail through the bright soft sweep of her hair—exactly like she did when they played together all those long and peaceful, green English summers that seemed like a hundred years ago. He felt he could hold her forever, lose himself in the softness and the scent of her. *Three months until the wedding. Seems like an eternity away.*

The telephone jangled harshly. Banning knew who the caller was before he answered.

"Yes, this is he. Right away, Sergeant."

Diana sat up sleepily. "Who was it?"

"The duty officer." Banning rose, slipped into his greatcoat, and grabbed his cap.

"But this is the first night we've had in weeks!" Diana stood up and clasped his hands. "This is our engagement night, darling. It's not fair!"

Banning gazed into her eyes. "Did you know that your eyes are the exact color of the sea on a bright day? I just realized that. Lord knows I've spent enough time over it lately!"

"Please don't go yet."

"There's another wave of bombers reported over the Channel—and more expected." He gave her a quick, hard kiss. "I have to get to the field right now."

Quick tears brightened Diana's eyes. She brushed them away and held to Banning with a trembling hand as he led her down to the shelter and her waiting parents.

*　*　*

As Banning stepped from the elevator into the lobby a white-haired man, who looked like a banker or a member of Parliament, bumped into him. On his uniform, he wore the wings of a British flyer above a triple line of service ribbons.

"Sorry, sir." Banning immediately recognized the man as Air Chief Marshall Arthur Harris, head of RAF Bomber Command.

"My fault, Lieutenant," Harris replied crisply. "Afraid I'm in a bit of a hurry."

"So am I, sir," Banning added. "Just got the call."

Harris took him in at a glance. "What's your squadron?"

Banning told him.

"Not far out of my way. Let me give you a lift."

"Wouldn't want to put you out, sir."

"Nonsense!" Harris clapped him on the back, almost pushing him across the lobby. "Got to take good care of you fighter pilots. You know what the prime minister said, 'Never have so many owed so much to so few.'"

"He must have been talking about our liquor bill, sir," Banning quipped as he hustled along to keep up with Harris.

"Jolly good, Lieutenant," Harris laughed. "Glad to see our fighting men still have a sense of humor."

"We may have to use it in our fuel tanks instead of petrol if the Germans keep up this bombing." Banning trotted down the hotel steps after Harris to a Bentley convertible parked at the curb.

"We're giving it back to them bomb for bomb, Lieutenant." Harris said this out of years of trying to build confidence in men, knowing it to be a lie. "They'll run out before we do." He stopped next to the car and extended his hand. "By the way, what's your name?"

"Banning, sir. Dale Banning."

"I'm Arthur Harris. Hope you don't mind riding with someone in Bomber Command. We're not nearly as glamorous as you fighter chaps." Harris climbed into the Bentley.

"Not at all, sir," Banning smiled, sliding into the passenger's seat.

Harris pushed the engine into life and roared off into the flame-brightened streets. "What do you fly, Lieutenant?"

"Spitfires, sir."

"Splendid aircraft! Heard it described once as, 'pretty and precious-looking as a cavalier's jeweled rapier.'"

Banning laughed at the comparison.

"From what I've seen, there is a sense of honor and fair play up there, almost like the gentlemen swordsmen of another age." Harris passed a speeding fire truck at breakneck speed, pulling back just in time to miss an oncoming car.

"Perhaps." Banning clung tightly to the door handle to keep from being thrown about the car. "But an honorable death lasts just as long as any other kind."

Harris gave him a sharp glance, then hit the brakes hard as a policeman waved him down. The car skidded to a halt, the left front tire up on the curb.

The bobby stalked over toward the driver's side, a scowl on his broad face. The buttons of his uniform gleamed in the light from distant fires. Noticing for the first time the sticker on the front fender, exempting the driver from the speed limit, his attitude changed abruptly. "Sorry to have stopped you, sir. I didn't notice your sticker at the speed you were traveling."

"Just doing your job, officer. Now, if you don't mind, we'll be on our way."

"Do be careful, sir," the bobby warned in his most official tone. "You might kill somebody."

"My dear man," Harris snorted. "I'm *paid* to kill people!" He sped away from the curb to the smell of burning rubber and the screeching of tires.

When they reached the outskirts of the city, Harris looked back over his shoulder at the monstrous beauty of London in flames. "If we make it through this, it very well may be 'our finest hour.'"

2

THE WINDY CLIFFS
OF FOREVER

*B*eneath a pewter sky, the soft yellow fog curled in wisps around the trees and flattened out over the runways and ramps of the airdrome. Rain dripped from the leaves and outside the brick officers' quarters, a nightingale welcomed the morning, in spite of its drab beginning.

Located in the countryside east of London, the base was virtually undetectable from the air, as were the dozens of others scattered about the area. With the use of paint and secret camouflaging materials, the buildings, airdromes, and gun emplacements had been blended to look like farm plots, pastures, hedges, and haystacks.

Junker 88s had hit the area during the night, shaking the buildings to their very foundations. The sharp reports of the anti-aircraft batteries punctuated the bomb blasts and the roar of engines. With the relentless pounding ending shortly after 1 A.M., the pilots had gotten a few hours of much needed sleep.

An hour before dawn, a runner from officers' mess awakened Banning and George Papworth, his roommate, with the usual cup of tea.

"Bloody Krauts! Never give a man a decent night's sleep!" Papworth sat on the edge of his cot, his coarse black hair still combed in waves back from his forehead as though he had held it in place while he slept.

Banning sat across from him, elbows on his knees, staring at the thick white mug he held with both hands. "Four hours isn't bad, Pappy. You forget those nights when we got none at all."

"I jolly well haven't forgotten." Papworth sipped his tea, eyes still closed. "It's just that I don't understand how they expect us to have a decent go at the bloody 109s when we're all walking around like a bunch of flippin' zombies."

Taking a swallow of tea, Banning stood up and looked out the window. "Another lovely East Anglica morning," he said sarcastically. "They must think it'll break off soon though."

Papworth still sat with his eyes closed, sipping the tea slowly. He would only force himself out of his dozing half-sleep when it became absolutely necessary.

Banning opened the window. The damp morning air flowed over him, washing most of the cobwebs from his mind. He decided it was not cold enough for the fur-lined Irving suit. Slipping into his thick silk undersuit and fireproof sidkas, he pulled on the heavy boots and stuffed his maps into them. With his helmet, Mae West life vest, and gloves under his arm, he headed downstairs for breakfast. Papworth, his eyes mere slits in his dark face, followed Banning's motions like a mirror image running twenty seconds behind schedule.

In the dimly lit dining hall, most of the pilots were engaged in animated conversation, trying to ignore their weariness. Some were elated that another nightmare of waiting was now behind them and the actual battle at hand—some forced themselves woodenly through the motions because it was expected of them—and some truly loved rushing along the edge of death's deep chasm at 350 miles an hour.

"Kippers, eggs, scones, and heavy cream for the tea," Papworth mumbled. "Looks like we're in for a rough one. I'd settle for toast and jam if we could just coast for one sweet day."

"You worry too much, Pappy." Banning chewed a huge mouthful of kippers and eggs, washing it down with the rich, steaming tea. "Got to take life one day at a time. Enjoy the simple pleasures like I do."

"How can I enjoy anything when my stomach feels like a ruddy toilet!"

Banning grinned and continued to wolf down the hot food, talking between swallows. "Eat. That's your problem. Get some hot food in you. Make you feel like a different man."

"I already feel like a different man. One forty years older than I was six months ago."

"Think about your wife and kiddies then. That always makes you feel better." Banning sipped his tea thoughtfully. "I can still see Diana the last night we had together."

"Your engagement party, right?"

"Right you are. Always makes this bloody mess bearable when I think of her."

Papworth poured more of the rich cream into his tea. "When's the wedding?"

"Christmas." Banning smiled at him. "I think even the Jerries might slack off a bit for the birth of our Lord."

"Don't know about that," Papworth mumbled dejectedly into his cup. "You might have a better chance if it was the ruddy führer's birthday."

"Cheer-o. Mind if I join you?"

Banning looked up at the man who had spoken, standing next to him holding a tray of food. He wore new flight gear, a new haircut, and a very old New York Yankees baseball cap. Short and chunky, he flashed a smile that was as bright as the freckles that covered his round, pale face.

"Suit yourself." Banning pulled a chair out for him.

"Dimitry Stetsensko." He placed his tray on the table, holding his hand out to Banning. His voice was thin and reedy, almost like that of a twelve-year-old boy.

Banning introduced himself and Papworth.

"What's that name again?" Papworth peered around Banning at the man, a perplexed look on his face.

"Dimitry Stetsensko."

"I think you made a wrong turn at Helsinki, Bucko. Moscow's that way." Papworth pointed east.

Stetsensko gave Papworth a patient smile. He had heard it all before—many times. "I was born twenty miles from here."

Papworth took a bite of scone, able to eat now that he had found something to keep his mind off the imminent mission. "Stet—that's a Russian name, what?"

"Quite. My father left Georgia during the revolution. There wasn't a lot of tolerance for White Russians and he saw things were only going to get worse." Stetsensko spooned sugar into his tea, sipping it with obvious relish.

"You don't look Russian."

"Mother's Irish."

"Give it a rest, Pappy. You're not the bloody Gestapo." Banning grinned at Stetsensko. "Glad to have you with us."

"I hope so," Stetsensko mumbled into his breakfast. "I've been assigned to your section."

"Where'd you come from?"

"Hornchurch. I was there for six months."

"Well, we've got one big problem," Banning mused, rubbing his chin with thumb and forefinger.

Stetsensko shook his head slowly. He had come to accept the fact that some people would give him a rough time, but hoped he could avoid it when the stakes were life and death. "What problem is that?"

"Your name."

Stetsensko stifled a curse. "What's the matter with it?"

"Dimitry Stetsensko. We have to look out for each other up there. Banning pointed toward the unseen sky. Watch each other's backs. By the time I got your name out, the bandits would have smoked you."

Stetsensko gave a sigh of relief. "Is that all?"

"This is serious. Hmmmm. What did they call you at Hornchurch?"

Stetsensko smiled. "Dimi."

"Dimi it is."

"One more thing." Papworth wore a puzzled frown. "Where'd you get that flippin' hat?"

"It's not a hat. It's a New York Yankees baseball cap," Dimi laughed. "My father brought it back to me from the States years ago. Baseball's my one true passion. Ted Williams is my favorite. I'd give a hundred quid for a Red Sox cap!"

"It's bloody unpatriotic, that's what it is!" Papworth was incensed.

"What is?" Banning frowned.

"Baseball! Any Englishman worth his salt plays cricket." Papworth stood up from the table abruptly. "Baseball! Bloody barbarism!"

* * *

The pilots filed out of the mess hall and across a dew-wet, meadowlike area in the murky, gray light of dawn. The Spitfires had been moved from the boundary of the airdrome, where they were kept as a precaution against the bombing, over to the hangers where the ground crews waited.

"Morning, Sergeant." Banning dropped his parachute onto the Spitfire's wing where he could grab it quickly and glanced around the field. The fog was already breaking up, wisps of it still hanging like wet cotton in the treeline.

"Morning, sir." Sergeant Walter Landor looked more like a butler than a mechanic in the RAF. His gray-flecked dark hair was always neatly combed and his thin face freshly shaved. "Some fireworks last night, what?"

"Don't see any damage," Banning replied, after his quick survey of the field.

"No, sir," Landor grinned. "But they bloody well wrecked a dozen or so paper and wood Hurricanes at the dummy airfield down the road."

Climbing inside the cockpit, Banning set his gunsights for thirty-two and one-half feet, the wing span of a 109, the aircraft he was most likely to encounter. He climbed down and walked around the Spitfire, making a final inspection. As he headed for the airdrome office, Papworth and Stetsensko fell in beside him.

"Think we'll go up soon?" Papworth chewed on a thumbnail as he spoke.

"Didn't get the Jerries' latest bombing schedule in the post yesterday, Pappy." *He's going to cave in on me if he doesn't get a hold on himself.* Banning let the two men enter the office ahead of him. He waited while they both signed the "700 sheet," checked it to make sure all the ground crew's names were there, then signed it himself.

"See you in the dispersal hut," Papworth called over his shoulder as he left, Stetsensko behind him.

Banning picked up the phone and called Operations. "Blue section now in readiness." He left the office, walking toward the dispersal hut, located almost at the edge of the ramp. *Maybe they'll come soon.* And they did!

After a few minutes of cards and dominoes and reading, the flat, metallic voice of the controller sounded over the loudspeaker.

Seven-oh-one squadron, Blue Section. Scramble! You will receive further orders in the air.

"I love it when a man gets so excited about his job," Banning quipped while he ran across the tarmac, pulling on his helmet and gloves.

As if verifying the remark, the emotionless voice continued. *Seven-oh-one, take off as quickly as you can, please.*

The Rolls-Royce Merlin engine of his Spitfire was running smoothly as Banning grabbed his chute and slipped into the harness.

"She's hot and ready, sir." Landor stood next to the Spitfire, patting the cowling proudly.

Banning climbed aboard and fastened the Sutton Harness loosely so that he could lean forward to fight off blackouts. He attached the oxygen tube to the tank, plugged in the radio cord and, with his feet on the brakes, revved up the engine. As he released the brakes, the Spitfire leaped forward as if aching for an aerial brawl.

Gaining speed down the runway, Papworth and Dimi on his wingtips, he flipped the magneto switches, adjusted the propeller at full fine, and set the carburetor boost. They lifted off together, going into a steep climb against the gray ceiling of clouds.

"Battle Control, Blue Section airborne." Banning spoke clearly into the mike.

In two minutes, as the section was still circling for altitude, Control came back. *Hello, Blue Leader. Battle Control calling. Are you receiving me?*

"Hello, Battle Control, Blue Leader answering. Receiving you loud and clear. Over."

"Blue Leader. Vector 250. Is that understood?"

"Battle Control, Blue Leader answering. Understood vector 250. Listening out."

At 17,000 feet, they broke through the cloud cover into a world of bright and dazzling beauty. Below and all around them stood the cottony mountains and whipped cream valleys of the upper atmosphere. The sunlight glared painfully into their eyes in this dreamlike battleground.

Operations came on again. *Angels two five. Bandits.*

Banning set his oxygen dial to 25,000 feet, pulled the auxiliary throttle, and pulled back on the stick. The three Spitfires moved into single file, each plane to the right of the one in front. At 23,000 feet, they leveled off, and flew into another cloud bank. When they broke through, there they were! Below them fifteen dull green Junker 88s flew in three stepped-up, line-astern formations. The Spitfires would have to run a gauntlet of machine gun and cannon fire from all three levels of the bombers as they attacked.

Turning on the gun sight, Banning basked for a second in its comforting glow. He set the button in firing position and took several deep breaths of the oxygen. His stomach felt hollow and, as always before battle, the palms of his hands burned.

Feeling a chill at the back of his neck, he glanced upward. An even dozen Messerschmitt 109s followed them overhead like sharks in an airy ocean. Black crosses stood out boldly on the underside of their square-cut wings. He knew they would dive as soon as he did, but there was no way out now!

Suddenly Banning's fear disappeared like a wisp of cloud in a high wind. He pulled the throttle wide open, pushed the stick forward and dropped toward the bomber formation in a sixty-degree power dive. "Tallyho!"

As he came out of his dive, Banning lined up his gun sight on the front bomber of the top formation, knowing that one of the front aircraft was the flight leader, following the radio beam. If he got the leader, the rest of the formation would be flying blind and head for home. As the 88 loomed larger and larger in the gun sight, he started the Spitfire into a roll. Flashes of light winked at him from the top turret as the gunner fired at him.

Suddenly the stick began to shake in his hand. The sideways motion told him bullets from somewhere were hitting an aileron. He couldn't tell if they came from a 109 or another section of the bombers. Too late now. At 300 yards, he squeezed the firing button. The tracers streaked out too far in front of the pilot's cabin. As he tried to pull the nose of his Spitfire around to bear on the pilot, it responded sluggishly, the right wing dragging. *Must have shot the fabric off.*

Wrestling his damaged aircraft into position, Banning sent a hail of tracers into the nose of the Junker, shattering the plastic cabin. As he rocketed upside down beneath the bomber, he caught a glimpse of the blood-spattered cockpit and the faceless, limp form of the pilot. The big aircraft began to slowly roll over, like a great wounded beast with its brain shot away.

Now Banning became the prey! As he started his breakaway, he caught sight of three Messerschmitts in his rear-vision mirror. When he looked forward he was almost on top of another 88. Giving it a quick burst at point blank range, he dropped away into a sickening dive.

With the blood draining rapidly from his head, he heard a sharp, *Crack!*, as a cannon shell from the bomber ripped through the hatch, just missing his head and showering him with glass and shell fragments. Wind screeched through the cockpit. His head and shoulders became unbearably heavy. The force of the dive pulled his jaw down, even with the chin strap of the helmet supporting it. He could no longer hold his eyelids up as he lapsed into a howling darkness.

As he fought his way back to consciousness, Banning saw the sky around him filled with screaming, diving planes. A Spitfire tumbled past in flames. He recognized the call letters on it as Papworth's. A stab of grief went through him, but there was no time for mourning.

Pulling his aircraft gradually out of the dive, Banning felt it shudder as tracers from a Messerschmitt slammed into his starboard wing. Still groggy from the dive, he had almost forgotten them. How could one still be on his tail? Yet there he was! Gunning the throttle, he banked over into another steep dive. The bandit wouldn't turn loose as his heavy tracers drummed into the fuselage.

Banning twisted and turned with all his skill, but the winking lights of the 109's machine guns stayed directly behind him. *Galland! It must be Adolph Galland. Only he could stick with me through all that! Only one thing left to do—go into a spin. I might not pull out of it in a damaged plane, but it's better than sitting here letting him blow me apart.*

Pulling the throttle, Banning jerked the stick viciously back toward him. The wings abruptly lost all their lift. At 300 miles an hour the Spitfire stalled, whipping over and down into a shrieking spin. As he blacked out again, Banning glimpsed Galland's 109 zoom by overhead.

Banning gradually fought his way back from the darkness, sick at his stomach, his head buzzing loudly. The Spitfire was still in the spin with the altimeter at 3,000 feet. He shoved the stick forward and reversed the controls. Nothing! The altimeter read 2,500 feet!

Holding tightly to the stick, he gunned the throttle and the plane gathered speed. Gradually the controls began to firm up. The spin slowed, then stopped as the speedometer climbed to 250 and on up to 300. He eased back on the throttle, bringing the stick back slowly on the left side to keep the damaged starboard wing from dropping. The altimeter now read 500 feet!

Twenty minutes later Banning taxied along the ramp, stopping next to the hangar. As he climbed wearily out of the cockpit, Walter Landor walked toward him.

The sergeant ran his amazingly clean hand along the bullet-riddled wing as though he were inspecting a room in prep school. "Bit of a ruckus up there, sir?"

"A bit, Sergeant." Banning peeled off his gloves and stuffed them into his helmet. "I'm sure you'll have her ship-shape in no time."

"Right you are, sir."

Dimi fell in beside Banning as he walked toward the hangar. He started to mention Pappy, but thought better of it. "New Spit for you, eh, Lieutenant?"

Banning kept walking, his eyes fixed on some spot beyond the hangar. "Just until Landor gets mine back in shape. I'm rather fond of the old girl." He knew he could be back in the air in a matter of minutes and always felt uneasy about his first combat in a different fighter.

After checking out his new aircraft, Banning walked over to the airdrome office with Dimi where they made out their combat reports. Then they notified Operations that they were in readiness again and headed toward the dispersal hut.

Suddenly, Banning stopped. He glanced toward the officers' quarters. "See you in a bit. Got something to do."

"Mind if I tag along?"

"Suit yourself." Banning started toward the brick building at a brisk pace.

When they were in the room, Banning immediately began picking up Papworth's belongings and stacking them neatly on his cot and the floor next to it. On the wall next to the pillow hung a black and white photograph of a pretty, blonde-haired woman holding an infant. She sat in a straight-backed chair in the small brick courtyard of a rowhouse. Next to her, squinting into the sunlight, stood a boy of about four.

"Pappy looked at this picture the first thing every morning and the last thing every night." Taking the picture off the wall, Banning sat on the cot and stared at it for a long time. The mid-morning

31

sunlight streaming through the window cast the left side of his face into shadow. A deepening sorrow troubled his eyes and his bright-dark features seemed to carry the weight of age.

Dimi sat down opposite him. "It's rough when you have a family."

Banning stared over at him. "You want his bunk?"

Taken off guard, he stammered, "Why—why I suppose so. Are you sure?"

"Why not?"

"That would be splendid," Dimi beamed. "I'm not settled in yet. I'll collect my things tonight."

The loudspeaker boomed through the partially open window. *Seven-oh-one Squadron, Red and Blue sections. Seven-oh-one Squadron, Green and White sections. Scramble!*

"You'd think they'd give us time for a bloody cup of tea!" Banning lay the picture face down on the bed and rushed from the room, Dimi in his wake.

*   *   *

The sky above the Channel was alive with Messerschmitts, Dornier 17 heavy bombers, Hurricanes, and Spitfires. Farther out, toward the shores of France, other clusters of planes were moving steadily through the golden, misty distance.

After crippling one Messerschmitt, Banning broke loose from the wave of German fighters who continued on toward England. Spotting a lone Dornier sailing low over the water toward home, he banked the Spitfire over into a steep, screaming dive. *Must have an engine on the fritz. Let's just see if I can add to his troubles.*

As Banning drew nearer, pulling out of his dive, the Dornier dropped closer to the sea, leveling off thirty feet above the choppy waves. Now if he dove on the German, he would plunge into the water. He pulled astern, the only option left, hoping to blast the top turret gunner and then go for the pilot. Pulling steadily closer, he was careful to avoid the propeller backwash which would send him tumbling out of control.

The German opened fire, sending a line of tracers at the Spitfire. Banning moved the stick right then left, alternating foot pressure on the rudder to keep the gunner in his sights. He saw the man's face clearly in the bright afternoon sunlight. It was distorted by fear, his teeth clenched as he desperately twisted the twin cannons back and forth.

Banning pressed the firing button with his thumb, showering the plastic blister of the German gunner with explosive, ball, incendiary, armor-piercing, and tracer bullets. The muffled roar of the guns drowned out the shriek of the wind as the Spitfire vibrated and slowed from the recoil.

The German gunner lay sprawled out backward inside the shattered blister, arms outstretched over his head as though grasping for something to keep him from the inexorable pull of death. Two minutes later, after Banning had sent a hail of machine gun bullets into the pilot's cockpit, the Dornier's nose dropped slowly and it exploded into the surface of the sea, sending up great geysers of blue-white water.

As Banning slipped up and to the side of the Dornier, climbing in an almost vertical bank, he caught sight of nine planes in three V formations roaring at him from the direction of Calais. At full throttle, he rushed toward the clouds. A black curtain dropped over his eyes and as he began to level off, the Spitfire shuddered as though a giant hand were shaking it to pieces.

Coming out of the darkness, Banning felt a flowing warmth down the left side of his face and neck. The stick jerked violently in his hand. He fought to remain conscious. In his rear vision mirror, he saw the Messerschmitts, like three avenging angels, closing in for the kill.

Got to make it to the coast! My only chance! As he hit full throttle, the big Merlin engine shuddered; streams of black smoke flowed from under the cowling. He reached for the hatch, trying desperately to slide it open so he could bail out—but it was jammed shut, damaged by the hail of bullets from the Messerschmitts.

Banning gazed down at the Channel, blue-green and sparkling in the afternoon sunlight. Ahead of him lay the shining coast of England, the white wind-swept cliffs rising from the sea.

How lovely it all is! How I hate to leave you, Diana!

3

THE WHITE BREATH OF EVENING

*D*iana let her fingers trail across the keys of the Baby Grand as the final notes of Beethoven's Piano Sonata No. 14 in C-sharp Minor drifted on the dark air of the drawing room. *"Moonlight." How aptly named.* She glanced out the French doors. A misty, gray rain was sweeping down across the meadow toward the woods where the brook ran. *There'll be no moonlight shining on the meadow tonight.*

Three leaves blew down from the big elm, tumbling and drifting on the wind until they disappeared behind the stone wall. *The last leaves of autumn*, Diana thought, staring up at the tree's limbs, taking on the appearance of a dark filigree against the clouds. *"Winter's bittersweet herald."*

She rose from the piano bench, taking her cup of tea with her, and walked over to the fireplace. Her mother's soft, high-backed chair next to the hearth, always her favorite place as a child, accepted her like an old friend. Her thoughts turned to Dale as she placed her tea on the sewing stand next to the chair and curled her legs beneath her tartan-plaid, wool skirt. She pictured him at the altar in his dress flight officer's uniform, flashing her his best smile, as she walked down the aisle on her father's arm.

Rain whispered against the windows. Flames crackled and popped in the massive stone fireplace, sending shadows flickering along the walls. Diana snuggled deeper into the chair, pulling her sweater around her shoulders. As she lifted the cup to her lips, the door of the drawing room opened.

"Diana, dear. Would you come here a moment, please?" Doreen Marlowe stood in the door, her face pale and her eyes holding an unbearable truth.

Beyond her mother, Diana could see Dale standing in the hallway. She recognized his uniform, although the diffused light from behind him cast his face into shadow. He glanced nervously about. It was a movement Dale had never made—not exactly like that!

Diana stared at her mother—at the familiar face that had been drained of comfort; at the graceful hands that had lost their ability to soothe away hurt.

At the sound of a voice, the man in uniform turned his head to the left. He took two steps and was lost behind the doorframe. *This isn't Dale! This is someone . . . !*

Suddenly, with an almost audible sound, a wall of silence fell about Diana. She seemed to be looking through a pane of glass covered with a thin film of moisture. The room took on an infinite strangeness as though it were too insubstantial to be real—as though she had only imagined it.

"Diana?"

She heard her mother's voice faintly as if she were calling from a high clifftop.

"Diana, you have to—"

"No!" Diana jerked away from the touch of her mother's hand and fled toward the French doors—toward some safe place where she wouldn't have to hear the words of that fearful messenger, the words that would forever rob her of . . .

"Diana! Come back!"

Grabbing the brass handle of the door, she flung it open. The wind gusted into the warm drawing room, a cold spray stinging her face. Without hesitation, she ran across the flagstone surface of the terrace, gleaming wetly in the tin-colored light. She tugged the piked iron gate open, ran underneath a towering elm and out into the open meadow.

The tall, wet grass, waving in the wind, brushed at her bare legs and skirt. The cold rain soon had her soaked to the skin. She became unaware of the outside world—felt nothing but a deepening emptiness welling up inside and a weight like a cold stone pressing against her breast.

Just inside the edge of the woods, she stopped, breathless, her chest heaving as she tried to draw air into it. She leaned against a tree, its rough bark cutting into the soft flesh of her face. As she walked blindly along a familiar path, her shoes splashing muddily, she came to the great, friendly oak of her childhood. It stood next to the brook that was swelling and turning to a rich brown color in the downpour. The wooden bridge that crossed it, rails and flooring darkening in the rain, ended at the opposite bank where a path led on into the woods.

The huge root, worn smooth from their countless playtimes, invited her to rest. Diana sat on its wet, dark surface, once again remembering the shining knight that Dale had always been in their childhood fantasies. And then she seemed to see him—looking the same as he had all those years ago!

He appeared on the opposite bank, as he had many times in that time so long ago, in his blue cape fashioned from a cast-off curtain from his mother's kitchen. He drew his apple-crate Excalibur from its cardboard sheath and brandished it at the make-believe Black Knight who guarded the bridge. With a shout, he rushed across the bridge at his enemy.

Diana saw the sun flashing on Dale's sword as the battle was joined. He slashed and dodged and parried, and, as always, when the foe was slain, lay his colors at her feet. Down on one knee before her, his smile brightening the air around them, Dale took her hand and gently pressed it with his lips.

Diana felt at peace in this cloudless land where she had fled from the tall stranger in uniform whose words she could not bear to hear.

At that moment, Doreen stepped to the edge of the glade, staring at her daughter. Diana's hair hung in dark, wet tendrils about her face and ears and neck. She was staring at something directly in front of her—at something only she could see. And a placid smile lay like a lover's kiss on her pale face.

"Diana!" Doreen draped her coat about Diana's shoulders and held an umbrella above the two of them. "Come on along now. Come on home!"

Diana, gazing now out into the glistening trees, didn't respond to the sound of her mother's voice.

"You must come with me, Diana." Doreen tried to keep her voice calm.

Glancing up into her mother's face, Diana's voice had a quality of tautness about it like a violin that had been strung too tightly. "Of course, Mother. Is something wrong?"

Doreen had never seen madness before—not close and personal—not in someone she loved! Diana's eyes were turned on her, but they were seeing something incredibly far away from this rainy glade—if they saw anything at all! Doreen prayed that this would soon pass—that Diana would not remain out there somewhere in that unimaginable void.

Putting her arm about her daughter, Doreen held the umbrella and led her out of the woods and across the meadow. The rain was slackening, settling down to a steady drizzle that would last for a long time.

* * *

Doreen sat on the edge of the tub in the steam-filled tile bathroom. With a soft cloth, she bathed her daughter's face and neck and arms, staying with her—helping her as she would a child. She steeled herself against weeping as she stared at the flat, dull glaze that shock had left in Diana's eyes.

Later, in her antique-rosewood bed, Diana lay propped up against her plush satin-covered pillows, while her mother added sugar and lemon to the tea.

James Marlowe stood in the shadows of the room, feeling useless. He had never run from a fight—always in the forefront of the battle, leading his men. But this was—different!

"Here, drink this, child." Doreen offered her the steaming tea, the sharp tinkling of the cup against its saucer betraying her own nervousness.

"Thank you, Mother. It smells marvelous." Diana's movements were slow and deliberate, as though she had just begun to learn them.

Doreen allowed her daughter to drink the tea, studying her face for some kind of outward sign that would reveal the nature of the inner struggle she was enduring. Hoping for some indication that she would soon respond normally again. *Oh, God! Don't let her stay like this!*

When Diana finished the tea, she handed the cup and saucer back to her mother. "Thank you so much. It was just what I needed, Mother."

"Diana?" Doreen pushed ahead, trusting that her daughter had the strength to handle the tragedy. "Do—do you understand what's happened?"

Diana looked away, but she had come a long way back from that make-believe land where she had been down at the brook. "Something awful's happened to Dale. That's all I want to know for now. It'll be all right later. I just know it will. I have to believe that."

"There's no way to make it any easier, child. The sooner you accept it the better off you'll be."

"I don't want to hear any more now." Diana's voice was calm, but sounded dry and brittle, as though it could snap at any moment. She clasped her hands together tightly.

"For heaven's sake—leave the poor child alone, Doreen!" James Marlowe stood behind his wife, holding a flask of brandy and a heavy, squat glass. "She's endured enough for one day."

Doreen stood up and whispered urgently in her husband's ear. "We have to make her understand, James. She *has* to accept what's happened."

"Tomorrow." Marlowe poured the glass half full of dark brandy. "Here, sweetheart. This will help you sleep."

Diana took a swallow of the brandy as her father held the glass to her lips. It felt like liquid fire, burning her throat and all the way down into her stomach where it sparked briefly before settling down into a warm glow. The glow began to spread outwardly into her breast and arms, finally bringing its dull and blunted comfort to her face, coursing darkly through her brain.

"See? She feels better already." Marlowe held the glass for his daughter as she slowly sipped all the brandy. "That's my girl. Now you get a good sleep." He kissed her on the forehead and left the room in his awkward, sliding gait.

Diana felt as though the liquor were slowly spinning and tumbling through her body. Through half-opened eyes, she saw the sharp corners of the room gradually round themselves off. The harsh colors and textures lapsed into things benign and friendly. Her wheeling thoughts slowed, settling into patterns that were calm and quiet and safe.

Doreen turned the lamp off, took her daughter's hand and sat with her in the darkened room. Outside, the October rain murmured on the stones, settling down for the long night.

* * *

Diana endured the memorial service in the little stone church with its ancient graveyard full of forgotten names. She wore her grief like a mantle of hope, never allowing one tear to break free of her icy hold. She greeted old friends and strangers all the same, with a clear eye and a fit and proper smile.

With a final hug for Dale's mother, Diana glanced at her parents. "I think I'll walk home," she said brightly. "It's such a lovely day. I shan't be long."

Doreen gave her daughter a troubled stare, recognizing something artificial in Diana's manner. "A bit chilly though. You'll catch your death."

"Oh, Mother, it's perfect!" Diana shook her hair free of her coat collar and it glittered like dark gold as the light struck it. "I'll take the path through the woods." She walked briskly away through the murmuring, scattered groups of people that were leaving the churchyard.

Diana walked along the path beneath the oaks and elms and yew trees wearing their tattered autumn coats of bronze and scarlet. October sunlight, thick as honey, flowed down through the trees and lay in pools about the woodlands. From a high tree, a Raven's hoarse cry split the still air.

If only they had found his plane! All I know is that it was lost at sea somewhere off the coast of Dover. "The wine-dark sea." The words struck Diana like a blade. She remembered that last night with Dale on the darkened balcony high above London—remembered the angry red sky filled with bombers and the deadly bright winking of anti-aircraft fire—and the feel of Dale's arms around her, circling her with a safe, abiding joy. *Oh, God! Help me! Please stop this awful pain!*

Diana left the woods and walked across the meadow toward her house. The gold and blue and white wildflowers waved gaily in the breeze. Their beauty was lost to her as she opened the iron gate, crossed the terrace, and went in through the French doors.

Inside, her mother called much too gaily from the kitchen. "That you, Diana?"

"No, it's the Queen Mother come for tea." No smile crossed Diana's face as she spoke. She tossed her coat on a table and slumped into her mother's chair.

"Here you are." Doreen handed her a cup of tea. "I'm going to take a quick nap. Then I'll fix us some lunch."

"Splendid," Diana muttered, staring at the bright flames as they danced across the logs in the fireplace.

"This is hard on us all, Diana. You're not the only one who loved Dale." Doreen's voice carried a hint of impatience which she tried to hide. She waited a few seconds, staring at her daughter, then quietly left the room.

A dark anger welled up in Diana as she stared at the fire, at the light and shadow of the room with its high windows and portraits of dead relatives lining the walls. Her gaze came to rest on a bottle of brandy resting on a cabinet in a corner near the fireplace. She drank half of her tea, walked quietly to the cabinet, and filled the cup to the rim from the brandy bottle.

As she sat sipping her brandy-tea before the fire, Diana felt the sharp-edged uncertainties of the day begin to fade and disappear. She felt an unexpected ease flow through her—felt a renewed confidence that she could accomplish whatever she desired, but she desired only to sit and enjoy these splendid new feelings. She was giggling quietly to herself when her mother returned from her nap two hours later.

Doreen shook her head sadly as she walked past her daughter. *Poor thing. What'll she do next?*

* * *

As the weeks slipped by, Diana adapted readily to the indolent guile of the secret drinker. Waiting until her parents were asleep, she would creep down to the cellar and the riches of her father's rows and rows of wines and liquors. She created a patterned and proficient method of thievery that left the missing bottles undetected.

All through the house, she carried her teacup full of liquor in her nocturnal ramblings that sometimes found her bundled against the cold, out roaming the moonlit meadows and the shadowed woodland paths. At dawn she would lapse into unconsciousness until the late afternoon sun splashed across her face. The hidden bottle in her room gave her courage to go down and face the dying end of each day.

* * *

"I think I'll visit the city. Stay in the hotel suite for a while." Diana looked across the terrace and the sere brown meadow toward the woodlands where she could almost see Dale's sword flash in the dark air, almost hear his battle cry ringing through the trees. Her hair was dark and oily from neglect—her gray slacks rumpled and her slip-over sweater stained from several spills.

Doreen gazed with a thinly layered smile at her daughter's disheveled appearance. Doreen's dress hung loosely and the skin on her face lay closer to the bone. She knew of her daughter's drinking. It was obvious after the first few days, but she never could bring herself to confront Diana with it. "I don't think you should, dear. The bombing may get worse and there are—other dangers there. Why don't you just stay here until you feel stronger."

"I'm fine, Mother," Diana lied. Lying quietly in the shadowed areas of her mind, the seed of self-destruction was being watered by every cup she filled.

"Come sit with me."

Doreen took her chair by the fire while Diana sat on a thick Persian rug on the floor, her knees bent, hands clasped around her legs.

Taking a deep breath, Doreen let it out slowly. "You have to come to terms with his death, Diana. You simply must! You're ruining your life—and your health!"

Diana stared up at her mother, still youthful looking in her crisp blue house dress. "I know you're right, Mother. I can see what I'm doing to myself." Her blue-green eyes brightened with tears. She brushed them away. "I just don't seem to have the will to go on anymore. Dale was my whole life. I don't even know who I *am* anymore."

Doreen slipped from her chair, knelt next to her daughter, and cradled her in her arms. Diana broke, allowing the pain of all the long nights pour forth. Her body wracked with sobs, she clung to her mother like a child. They stayed that way and after a long while the sobbing stopped.

42

Still Diana held to her mother, feeling the comfort she gave—yet knowing that it was not enough, that it would never be enough to heal her fearful wound—the waking nightmare of Dale lying at the bottom of the Channel. She saw him in her wanderings in those early dead hours of morning—with seaweed wound like garlands about his body—with hands floating upward toward the light-drenched surface of the sea—saw the empty, desolate eyes. And knew that the mermaids would never sing for him.

"I have to get away." Diana took her mother's handkerchief and wiped her face. "Maybe it's what I need. To leave all these memories behind."

"Perhaps you're right. You can visit some of your old school chums. Go shopping." Doreen wanted to believe that the change would be good for her daughter. "Maybe you could do some volunteer work."

Diana saw the concern on her mother's face. "I'll be all right, Mother. This has helped me so much. You've always been there when I needed you."

* * *

"Give us another round!" The British seaman bellowed over the din in the pub. His beefy face was red from drink and the long days on the deck of a ship.

"Nothing for me, thanks." Diana slipped off her stool. She straightened her skirt, tugged at her wool jacket. She wore too much makeup to try and hide the hollow darkness of her eyes. "It's late. I have to be going."

The seaman gave her a surprised look that turned slowly to a frown. "Not so fast, girlie. I didn't spend five quid on drinks to have you running off on me now, did I?"

Ignoring him, Diana turned to leave.

"You deaf, girl?" The man grabbed Diana by her shoulders, spinning her around roughly.

Diana lost her balance, going down on one knee. The rough wooden floor of the pub was sticky with spilled liquor and smelled of stale tobacco and filth tracked in from the streets. She felt nauseous, her vision blurred, and she struggled to get up.

"That's enough, mate!"

43

Managing to stand erect, Diana saw a snip of a man no taller than she, facing the bulky seaman. His dark hair was parted in the middle and plastered to his thin skull. He wore a white shirt, black armbands above the elbows, and red suspenders. Hands clasped behind his back, he said in a surprising baritone, "You heard me, mate. Let the young lady be!"

The big sailor merely smirked and, without a word, quickly drew back a massive fist. Before he could swing it forward, there was a blur of motion from the little bartender. His right arm whipped around from behind his back, a sawed-off billiard cue in his hand. The bat landed with a sickening thud just above the left ear of the seaman. The light in his pale eyes went out like a snuffed candle. His knees buckled and he struck the floor like a bag of sand. Two of his shipmates got up from their table, dragged him over against the wall, and returned to their drinking.

The little bartender turned to Diana, noticing her wilted appearance and hollow eyes with their dark circles, and said in his big voice, "This ain't no place for the likes of you, Miss. You'd best be on your way. The blokes in 'ere ain't used to fine ladies like yourself."

Brushing herself off and straightening her clothes, Diana stammered, "I—I just came in for a quick drink. I don't remember how he came to be at my table."

"It's right as rain now, Miss. You just toddle on 'ome and leave the drinking to them what can handle it."

Diana felt her face grow hot with shame. "I'm sorry if I caused you any trouble."

Retreating from the bartender's knowing smile, Diana hurried out into the street. The Germans had finished one of their endless night raids only minutes before. She stumbled along the darkened streets in the flickering glow of the fires. Anti-aircraft batteries began cracking sharply in the distance at the leaders of yet another bomber formation roaring in over the city. Shrapnel began to clatter on the rooftops.

Diana knew she should find shelter, but it somehow seemed unimportant to her. Life had become a burden that bore down heavier on her with each day that moved along at a snail's pace. Sometimes in the stale hours just before dawn, she thought about laying it down.

Walking unhurriedly along as though she were strolling through the woodland paths of her home, she watched fires break out through huge gaps in the bomb-ravaged buildings. The twisted tracks of the trams and the tangled overhead wires looked like the outsized works of a demented sculptor.

An elderly man wearing the flat-brimmed helmet, long wool coat, heavy leather belt and cross strap of the Home Guard walked directly across the street toward Diana. "Come along now, Miss," he said in a grandfatherly tone. "We can't have you walking around, with the Jerries throwing everything at us but their blinkin' laundry."

Diana looked at him with a blank stare.

He took her gently by the arm. "Let me just escort you to a shelter."

Diana noticed that his white mustache curled up at the tips exactly like the one in the portrait of her own grandfather. She followed his lead.

"Here we are, Miss. You might just catch a performance if you hurry."

Looking up, Diana saw they were at the entrance to Aldwych Station in the theatre district. "What kind of performance are you talking about?"

"Oh, the very best there is, Miss. Splendid, indeed! Saw one or two meself, I did." Looking at the puzzled expression on Diana's face, he hastened to explain. "The stars come down to the station platforms of an evening when their plays are over. Perform for the common folk, they do."

"Sounds interesting," Diana said with little enthusiasm.

"Good evening, Miss." The man bade her farewell like a member of the palace staff, tipping his hat and walking briskly away amidst the sound of explosions.

Diana descended on the escalator into the Underground, or the "Tubes," as most Londoners called them. This subway system whose tracks ran deep beneath the city and the River Thames became the most common shelter during the Blitz.

As Diana moved through the twilight world of the Underground, she saw a lone figure on the station platform, surrounded by a throng of people, all bundled against the cold. Pushing closer, she recognized the tall, elegant figure of Laurence Olivier. Wearing a long gray cape, he assumed a theatrically noble posture and began to recite for his audience:

Once more unto the breach, dear friends, once more,
Or close the wall up with our English dead.
In peace there's nothing so becomes a man
As modest stillness and humility
But when the blast of war blows in our ears,
Then imitate the action of the tiger,

Enthralled by Olivier's voice and stage presence, Diana didn't notice the man standing next to her until she smelled his foul cigar. Then he spoke.

"Splendid performance, what?"

She turned to see the black bowler hat perched over his square bulldog face. He wore a polka dot bowtie, a pin-striped suit, and a heavy topcoat. Diana was speechless as she looked into the face of the prime minister. She had heard that he walked the streets of London during the raids, but thought it only another war rumor. Here stood the man who was almost single-handedly holding the nation together—the man whose will had become one with the will of his people.

"You're fond of Henry V, or are you only in love with Olivier like half of English womanhood?" Churchill clamped down on his cigar, a wry smile on his cherubic face.

Collecting her wits, Diana said in a raspy voice, "Mr. Prime Minister! I never expected to see *you* here!"

"Splendid time for a walk—when the bombs are falling. Makes one feel the essence of life."

"I'm surprised the government would allow you to put yourself in such danger."

"Ives tried to stop me—once! My valet—a Royal Marine." Churchill chewed happily on his cigar, relishing the sound of his own voice. "Hid my bloody shoes."

"What did you do?"

"Made him produce them, of course. Told him that, as a child, my nursemaid could never prevent me from taking a walk in the Green Park when I wanted to do so. And, as a man, Adolf Hitler certainly won't."

Diana could almost see the prime minister stalking about 10 Downing Street, searching for his shoes. She laughed softly. Then they formally introduced themselves.

46

"Would you care to join me?" Churchill offered her his arm, a sly disarming smile on his face. "Sounds like it's over up there for the moment."

Diana took his arm and they made their way to an elevator and up to the streets.

"What's that fellow doing?" Diana pointed to a man who was crawling over the wreckage of a bomb-blasted building. He poked his nose here and there, snuffling into the debris like a dog.

"He's a 'body sniffer,'" Churchill informed her. "When the rescue gangs don't hear any groans or movements under the rubble, they call them in. They can smell the blood."

"Fresh blood down 'ere, and still flowing!" the sniffer cried as if verifying Churchill's statement.

The rescuers covered the spot, digging frantically with picks and shovels. From a few yards away, another sniffer shouted, "Blood 'ere." Then he bent closer to the stones and splintered timbers, sniffing harder. "Don't bother, blood stale, this one's a stiff."

"Oh, how awful!" Diana muttered, holding tightly to Churchill's arm.

"War is that—and much, much more, my dear. Still, there are some things worth dying for—I suppose."

"Like democracy. My fiancé used to tell me that."

"Democracy is the worst system of government," Churchill complained.

Diana stared at him, her eyes wide with surprise.

". . . except for all the others," he continued, the glint of humor in his eyes. "Whether it's worth dying for is an entirely different matter. We *are* caught up in this business though, aren't we? And I don't fancy a diet of sauerkraut and sausages myself."

"Nor do I," Diana agreed. She felt a new confidence in the presence of this charming and intelligent man. *Maybe I could learn to accept things as well as he seems to.*

"Have to run, my dear. I see my nursemaid coming." Churchill tipped his hat and was gone.

Diana watched him walk away with the tall, Royal Marine at his side. In Churchill's absence, the bitter loneliness moved back in. Diana walked the streets, looking at the destruction wrought by the bombers. The emptiness of her life passed before her like a tapestry of grief. In the distance, she saw a wrecked sign hanging above a dimly lit doorway. She made out the words *Sword and Dragon Pub.* Her pace quickened.

* * *

"Yes, speaking. What's that, you say? Are you sure?" James Marlowe spoke in a sleep-drugged voice. "Yes. Of course. I'll be there directly."

"James, what's the matter?" Doreen sat up in bed, her face clouded with fear.

"It's Diana. She's at the police station in London. She's not hurt—just had too much to drink and passed out in a pub. Bloody bad show!"

Quick tears sprang up in Doreen's eyes. "Thank God she's all right!"

An hour and a half later, Marlowe escorted his daughter down the front steps of the police station. He drove her to the hotel where they kept a suite, parked in back, and took her upstairs. She soaked for a long while in a hot tub, then put on a gown and robe and went into the living room to face her father.

Marlowe paced back and forth on the gleaming hardwood floor. He wore house slippers and a gray wool topcoat over his pajamas. "You must get a grip on yourself, Diana. You're ruining your life—and your poor mother's as well."

"I'm sorry for that, Father. But it *is* my life after all, isn't it?" Diana stared through the glass panes of the door that led onto the balcony.

Marlowe scowled fiercely at his daughter. "You bloody well better change your ways or it won't be anybody's life, young lady! You'll end up in some alley with your throat cut! The constable told me what kind of pub they picked you up in. What if some of our friends had seen you?"

"It was convenient. That's all."

Enraged now, Marlowe opened his mouth to speak, but Diana interrupted him. "I'll pick nicer places to drink in from now on." She spoke coldly, her eyes growing hard. "That seems to be your primary concern."

Marlowe took a deep breath, trying to control his anger. He paced the room for a few moments, then came back to where Diana stood gazing out the window. Finally he sighed wearily, "Your mother and I are terribly worried about you, Diana. What can we do to help?"

She looked into her father's dark eyes and remembered all the years he had never been there when she needed him . . . and remembered with a shudder of pain, Dale, who had been. "It'll take time, Father. I'll be all right. You'll see."

Marlowe forced a smile, relieved to set the matter gratefully at rest for now. In the deepest part of him, he knew Diana was only giving lip service, but he couldn't let himself confront it. *I can't order her to become her old self again.* After a few minutes of small talk, he said without conviction, "I must get back to your mother now. Let us know how you're doing. She never can catch you at home, you know."

"I will, Father," she murmured, knowing she would continue to live just as she had since Dale's Spitfire went down in the Channel—believing that nothing would change.

Marlowe kissed her quickly on the cheek and left, the door closing behind him like a final curtain.

Diana stepped out onto the balcony, gazing as she always did at the graceful, silver curve of the Thames—remembering as she always did the feel of Dale's arms around her on that final night—feeling again the warmth of his kiss. She stood there for a long time as the fires burned below her.

Part 2

CAT KILLER

4

NICE GUYS FINISH

*A*nd now the final and most prestigious award for this senior class of 1937—the winner of the 'Why I'm Proud To Be an American' essay contest." Alvin Ditweiler's broad face beamed as he held the red, white, and blue striped envelope aloft, then opened it. Although he looked like Babe Ruth, farming, not sports, was his one abiding passion. Being principal of Liberty High School paid the bills, but his heart was always among the tomatoes and purple hull peas and corn rows behind his barn. "And this year's winner—I don't have to remind you that he or she gets a trip to Washington to meet the president—is . . . "

"C'mon, get it over with!"

"Don't drag it out!"

The auditorium rang with catcalls and the disgruntled yells of students who had been cooped up too long on a beautiful spring morning.

Mark Courtney straightened his tie, brushed back his thick auburn hair, and leaned forward eagerly in his seat.

"Larry Gatewood!" Ditweiler stepped from behind the podium, motioning for Gatewood to come up on the stage and say something to his classmates. Leaning toward the microphone, he added quickly, "And the runner-up is Mark Courtney."

Larry, looking slightly embarrassed, grinned at Rose Delano seated next to him. He had loved her since the third grade and the smile that lit her eyes over his victory was worth more to him than the award *and* the trip to Washington.

"I'm so *proud* of you!" Rose, the school's beauty queen and head cheerleader, was applauding along with the rest of her classmates. Leaning toward her, Larry whispered, "Wish I didn't have to go up there to get it. I'm no good at this."

Giving Larry a peck on the cheek, she pushed him gently toward the front. "You'll do fine."

Trotting down the aisle, Larry bounded up the steps to the stage and shook Ditweiler's meaty hand as he received the plaque. "Thank you, sir."

Ditweiler motioned him toward the microphone.

Larry cleared his throat and took a deep breath. "I think maybe the greatness of this land can be measured in small things—" he began, after adjusting the microphone to stop the shrill feedback. "Things like someone from my upbringin' winnin' this award." A half-smile lit his tanned face. "Ya'll know me. I come up poor as Job's turkey like half the rest of you. In some countries that would have been the end of it—some place where only the bluebloods can get ahead. Now I'm not very smart, but I meant every word I wrote in that essay . . . "

Mark Courtney wore his best smile as he listened, the one he had charmed his teachers with throughout his school years. *Save the Abe Lincoln rail-splitting, studying by the fireside speech, Gatewood! You pulled some strings somewhere—that's the way it's done. I don't know how, but you did it.*

Gatewood was concluding his brief acceptance speech. ". . . and I especially want to thank my English teacher, Mr. Gifford, for his encouragement. Back in September, the first theme I handed in started, 'See Spot run.' He's brought me a long way from that."

A smattering of laughter wafted up from the audience as Gatewood thanked Ditweiler again and returned to his seat.

Courtney glanced back over his shoulder at the beaming face of Rose Delano, her eyes glued on Gatewood. *That's another riddle. What does she see in you? Must be more to it than being captain of the basketball team. If she'd played her cards right, she could be going to the prom with me.*

After standing and singing the school alma mater, the students headed for the doors of the auditorium in a drone of conversation and scuffling of shoes on the polished hardwood floors.

Gazing out over his charges from the podium, Ditweiler pulled a large white handkerchief from his back pocket and swiped at the sheen of perspiration on his forehead. *Whew! What a year! Now the summer's all mine! Plenty of sunshine and honest sweat. Fresh tomatoes and fried okra and cornbread. And all the watermelon I can eat! Hot dog!*

Standing near the rear door of the auditorium, Leslie Gifford spoke his farewells to some of his students as they filed out:

"Thanks, Ben. Glad you enjoyed the books. Looking forward to having you in my class in a couple of years."

"Have a good summer, Mike. And be sure to stay in shape. We're counting on you for at least a hundred yards a game next season."

Gifford waited until the last student had filed past him. Then he limped slowly down the aisle toward the side exit, his right foot making a slapping sound as it hit the floor. His left arm, damaged by the polio that had ravaged the muscles of his leg, swung loosely from the shoulder. *What a fine year we had! I'm sure going to miss these kids this summer.*

Ignoring the smell of the new clover and the warm May sunshine, Courtney walked across the schoolyard among his classmates, noticing none of them. He enjoyed the company of people and fancied himself a good conversationalist, but it was a luxury he couldn't afford under the circumstances.

His mind was searching frantically back and forth for a solution to his problem, like a good rabbit dog in a briar patch. *There's still got to be a way to get that trip to Washington. I was countin' on that picture with Roosevelt to use later on in my first political race. Something like that would be better than $10,000 in campaign funds!*

"Tough luck, Mark. Maybe next time," Keith Demerie smirked, clapping him on the back. "But then there won't be a next time for you, will there?"

His concentration broken, Courtney stared at the chunky tow-headed boy in front of him. He forced a smile. "That's right, you dumb little freshman punk."

Caught off guard by the remark, Demerie relaxed when he saw Courtney smiling brightly at him. "Well, you've won just about every other talkin' and writin' award in school. Can't have everything, I guess."

"I guess. See you later, Keith. Be sure and give my regards to your father." *If your ol' man wasn't a state senator, I'd tell you exactly what I think of you! You pampered moron!*

"Sure thing, Mark. Have a good summer." Demerie jogged clumsily off toward a blonde-haired girl with great, round blue eyes and an expression of perpetual astonishment. "Hey, Debbie, wait for me!"

* * *

Heaven is in your eyes, bright as the stars we're under. Maebelle Watts was no Frances Langford, but she had as pleasing a voice as any waitress in the country and the week-end gigs helped supplement her paycheck at the Liberty Hotel's restaurant. She sang into the microphone in the school gym beneath the sparkling globe lights. With her eyes closed, she pretended she was the *new* girl singer for Tommy Dorsey's band instead of the same *old* girl singer with this band one of their members had dubbed the "Front Porch Swings."

A clerk at the hardware store played piano, a truck driver was on drums, and a twenty-year-old member of the county maintenance crew blew a soulful rendition of "I'm in the Mood for Love" on his saxophone. The Liberty High Senior Prom of 1937 would be history in a matter of minutes. The final long note died away on the sax. Couples began drifting off the dance floor. Some remained, embracing, gazing raptly into each other's eyes, wanting the moment to last forever.

"Aw, c'mon, Larry!" Courtney clapped Gatewood on the shoulder. "It's our last night as Liberty 'Rebels.' For old times' sake, let's go out and lift a few."

Gatewood watched Rose Delano walking across the gym floor toward the ladies' room with Becky Smith, Courtney's date. Then he turned to stare at Courtney—at the frosty white tuxedo jacket, the even tan he got from lying in his backyard thirty minutes a day, the dazzling teeth. He saw, as Courtney straightened his tie, that even his fingernails were better kept than most girls he knew. "You're just too perfect for Liberty, Georgia, Mark. You oughta be behind a big desk on Wall Street."

Mark relished the compliment, but shrugged it off. "Knock it off! I'm not interested in that stuff. How 'bout it. You wanna have one last fling?"

"Gotta take Rose home and—you know."

"Yeah. What I know is that it's not gonna take long. Ol' man Delano will have you moving on after ten minutes on the front porch with *his* little angel."

Gatewood chuckled. "Don't I know it!"

"All right, then." Courtney glanced around at their classmates, some leaving hand-in-hand, some wandering aimlessly about the gym. "I'll meet you down at Rudy's tavern at one."

"You gettin' serious about Becky?"

Courtney spied his date walking with Rose back across the hardwood basketball floor, its gleaming waxed surface scuffed and smeared now from four hours of healthy teenagers' jitterbugging to the latest swing tunes. "Naw. All fluff and glitter. She makes a nice appearance, but nobody's home upstairs." He pointed to his head and gave Gatewood a blank stare.

"I think she's OK."

"If you say so. You goin' to Rudy's or what?"

Gatewood smiled across fifty feet of perfumed air at Rose. "OK. See you at one o'clock. Unless the ol' man takes his shotgun to me before then."

"Good deal," Courtney beamed. "We'll play the ol' Christmas tree decorating game."

"Christmas tree game?" Gatewood gave him a puzzled look.

"Yeah, you know. Really tie one on!"

Gatewood chuckled, holding his hand out to Rose.

Courtney took Becky by both hands and kissed her quickly on the mouth. "Ah, love of my life!" Then turning to Rose, he continued, "Smartest girl this side of Atlanta. Made me what I am today."

* * *

Rudy's real name was Joseph Palermo. Everybody called him "Rudy" because someone once said he looked like Rudolph Valentino, and the name stuck. But that was a long time ago and any resemblance to Valentino had disappeared into his heavy, dark jowls and the even heavier layers of fat that encircled his midsection, lapping over his wide leather belt like candle wax just beginning to melt.

"Rudy, my man. How about a whiskey?" Courtney slid onto a barstool, tapping a Camel out of a pack he took from his inside jacket pocket.

"Hey, Courtney! Long time, no see. How you doin'?" Palermo's twenty-year tenure in the deep south had thinned his Brooklyn accent, but it occasionally slipped through the slow, forced vowels of his adopted land.

"Growing up, Rudy. Just trying to grow up." Courtney flicked a match with his thumbnail, squinted his slate gray eyes while it flared and lit his cigarette.

"The usual—just a touch?"

Courtney nodded, glanced over his shoulder at the sound of someone entering the bar.

Palermo flavored a tall glass of ice with whiskey and finished filling it the rest of the way with water from the tap. "Looks to me like you're slippin' a little."

"How's that?" Courtney took a deep drag on the Camel, letting the smoke flow out through his nostrils as he had seen Bogart do in a movie.

"I don't see no young lady on your arm. You used to wear 'em around like lapel buttons."

"Guess that's part of growing up, Rudy. Women aren't nearly as important as I thought they were." Courtney set the cigarette in an ashtray to let his throat cool. "Supply and demand you might say—and there's a big surplus of 'em in my life right now."

Palermo smiled knowingly. "Rose Delano in that big surplus of yours?"

"You heard about that, huh?" *This guy's smarter than I thought. Something to be learned here. Don't get too comfortable around anybody!* Courtney was a young man who constantly evaluated people—their strengths and weaknesses—how he might be able to use them or how they might be able to harm him. His relationships were based on an economy of favors—who owed him and who he owed favors to. The former tab he kept much more accurately than the latter. "Can't figure out what she sees in Gatewood. Looks like Icabod Crane to me."

"Maybe so," Palermo mused, "but looks ain't the most important thing to a lot of women, Courtney. You might wanna jot that down somewhere." He wiped the spills from the bar with a large white towel. "Guess Gatewood ain't exactly your best friend right now, is he?"

"I don't hold grudges," Courtney lied. "Let by-gones be by-gones. That's my motto. Why I like him so much, I'm gonna play a little practical joke on him. And you know I only do that with my best friends."

"Why am I havin' trouble believing you? Must be my suspicious nature."

"See for yourself." Courtney pointed to Gatewood, entering the door and looking around. "Hey, Larry! Over here."

Gatewood threaded his way between the tables and chairs of the long narrow tavern, stepping over sprawled out legs, coughing in the thick smoke. "What a joy *this* place is!" He blew his breath out and sat down next to Courtney.

"If you want someplace really nice, try Shorty's Saloon out on the highway," Palermo snarled. "It's got a dirt floor and there's a dead cat under every other table."

Gatewood raised his eyebrows at Courtney as he nodded over at Palermo. "Is he always this much fun?"

Courtney ignored the question. "Give him a whiskey, Rudy," he winked. "Maybe he'll see your place in a different light if he's wrapped around a little sour mash."

Rudy placed a highball glass half-full of ice on the bar, filling it from a square bottle off a shelf behind him.

Gatewood lifted the glass, turning it in his hand as the light from a Pabst Blue Ribbon sign on the wall glinted on the whiskey, turning it a warm amber color. "It's pretty, all right, but I'd be a zombie ten minutes after I finished it."

"You afraid of a man's drink, little boy?" Palermo drew a beer for a customer and slid it down the bar.

Gatewood grinned at Courtney. "What about it? Reckon I can handle it?"

"One way to find out." Courtney held up his watered-down drink, clinked it against Gatewood's, and downed it in one long swallow. "Brrrr! A renegade Indian wouldn't drink that stuff!"

"Here's to the class of '37," Gatewood offered, turned the glass up, and drank it in several swallows. A spasm of coughing took him as he set the glass down.

Courtney gave Palermo a sly grin. "Let's get a table and do some serious drinking—and reminiscing about the high times and hallowed halls of good ol' Liberty High."

"Can't stay long," Gatewood gasped. "Gotta get things ready for my trip. I leave for Washington on Monday."

"OK, then. A couple of drinks and we'll call it a night. C'mon, I see a booth open."

Gatewood's brown eyes had a slight glaze to them from the triple shot of whiskey. "Remember, only a couple. I'm in Daddy's Buick. He'd skin me if anything happened to it."

"Yeah, I saw you driving it to the prom with Rose. We *certainly* wouldn't want anything to happen to that car." Courtney motioned to Palermo, then turned back to Gatewood. "You go play something on the jukebox. I'll bring us some more drinks."

Gatewood walked across the crowded floor, dropped a dime into the jukebox, and leaned on it with both hands. The din of the tavern and the thick smoke made him queasy. He had only been in a bar once before and now he remembered why he avoided them. The whiskey still burned in his stomach, but was starting to relax him. *What's the harm? You only graduate from high school once.* Pushing the buttons on the jukebox, he went to join Courtney.

Bing Crosby began crooning "June in January" in his smooth baritone as Gatewood slid into the booth opposite Courtney. Several of the men seated at the bar turned around and scowled at the jukebox.

"What a pitiful tune. Couldn't you play something with a little life in it?" Courtney scowled.

"He's my mother's favorite. Besides, I like that song." Gatewood's guileless eyes drifted away for a moment. "Kinda how Rose makes me feel. You know, like all the days are good ones no matter how bad the weather is. She makes January just as pretty as June."

Courtney rolled his eyes. "Oh, Lord! One little drink and the boy turns to mush! Here, maybe another one'll stiffen your backbone a little."

With a sheepish grin, Gatewood grabbed the drink Courtney handed across to him and took a long pull on it. "Whew! That's powerful stuff!"

"Speaking of powerful stuff, that was a mighty powerful essay you wrote to win the contest." Courtney noticed that Gatewood's drink was two-thirds finished. He drank some of his own, his gray eyes narrowing to a wolfish gleam. "How'd you manage to pull that off?"

Gatewood felt like his mind was draped with cobwebs. A slight roaring filled his ears. Puzzled at the question, he mumbled, "What do you mean? I just did a lot of research and wrote it."

"C'mon, Larry. This is just between friends—off the record and all that. You can give me the straight dope." He leaned forward conspiratorially. "Did Gifford write it for you? I know you were one of his favorites."

"He edited it for me. You know, grammar—punctuation. But he helps his students out like that every year. Told me my paper showed a—let me remember now—a unique and genuine respect for the American way of life. Said that would go a long way with the judges." Staring at the gleam in Courtney's eyes, Gatewood felt a slight chill, as though someone were sneaking up behind him with a knife.

Courtney gave him a sly smile. He half expected Gatewood to break down and confess.

"You're accusing me of cheatin'! What kind of friend are you anyway?" He downed the rest of his drink, slammed his glass down and got up to leave.

"Hold on, partner! Can't you see I was just having a little fun with you?" Courtney stood up, tried on his most reassuring smile, and put his hand on Gatewood's shoulder. "What's the matter? Lost your sense of humor?"

Gatewood tried to grin, but it didn't work. He gazed at Courtney's bright, friendly face. *Maybe he was just kiddin'.* "You really had me goin' for a minute or two." But a slight chill remained at the back of his neck.

"Let's have another one."

"Naw. I gotta be goin'. I ain't never drank this much in my life."

"Well, you certainly can't tell it, partner. Guess you're one of those people who can really hold his liquor," Courtney reassured him merrily.

"I think I better . . . "

"One for the road," Courtney beamed and was off to the bar before Gatewood could respond.

"The Music Goes 'Round and 'Round" blared from the juke-box, as though it were imitating what was happening inside Gatewood's head.

* * *

"Better git up, boy! You gonna have to go over to the court-house in a few minutes." Ring Clampett leaned against the cell door, one bony hand clasped around the bars. He wore khakis and scuffed brown cowboy boots. A big shiny badge pulled down on the left pocket of his shirt like the insentient weight of the law.

Larry Gatewood smelled something awful while he struggled back from the nether world of alcohol stupor. As he sat up on the rough concrete floor, he realized he was smelling himself. His clothes were caked with his own vomit. "W—what happened?"

"A boy trying to drink like a man—best I can figure." Clampett spat a brown stream of tobacco juice into a Campbell's Tomato Soup can he held in his free hand. "Then there's the little matter of the tore-up picket fence."

"How did I get here?"

"You was lucky there. I got to you 'fore you could do any real damage with that big Buick of yore daddy's." Clampett spat again, a small brown stream trailing down from the corner of his lip. "Some good citizen called and said he saw a drunk driving out of Rudy's parkin' lot—on the wrong side of the road!"

At the back of Gatewood's mind, bits and pieces of memory from the night before flickered like an old movie on a faulty projector.

"Good thing for you that feller, whoever he was, called me. You coulda had a bad wreck."

"Where's my daddy?" Gatewood leaned back against the wall. Through the narrow window in the concrete block wall, he could see a bright trapezoid of blue.

"He come here real early. You was so knocked out he couldn't wake you up. When he saw you was all right, he went on to church. Said he hadn't missed teaching his Sunday School class in fifteen years and didn't see no reason to start now." Clampett took the soaked wad of tobacco from his bulging cheek with a thumb and forefinger, dropping it with a *plop* into the soup can. "I don't think he was too happy about that dent in his Buick, though."

Gatewood groaned. *Oh, Lord, not Daddy's car! Anything but that!*

"He called J.T. to come over here and git you out. You prob'ly gon' have to go before Judge Stone." Clampett chuckled obscenely at his own words.

"What's so funny?" Gatewood moaned.

"You'll find out soon enough. They don't call him the 'Hangin' Judge' for nothin'."

J.T. Dickerson entered the town marshal's office five minutes later. He brushed the thick cascade of brown hair back from his forehead with his left hand. His brown eyes were a little too bright and his smile too wide. The navy pin-striped suit he wore needed pressing. He had miscounted when he buttoned the open-throated white shirt and the extra button at the top waved about on display like a family secret.

"'Bout time you got here, J.T." Clampett sat in an ancient ladder-backed chair, his feet propped on a battered gray table. "Yore client's feelin' right poorly."

J.T. gazed down at Gatewood. "'Wine is a mocker, strong drink is raging: and whosoever is deceived thereby is not wise.'"

"The boy don't need no sermons, J.T." Clampett barked. "What he needs is somebody to keep Judge Stone from lockin' him away in the caliboose."

"It's the Lord's day and I feel anointed to bring His Word to this viperous pit of forgotten souls." J.T. continued to stare with his too-bright eyes at Gatewood, his stertorous voice ringing off the concrete block walls of the little room. "'Be not among winebibbers; among riotous eaters of flesh: For the drunkard and the glutton shall come to poverty.'"

"Ain't *you* the one—preachin' about *drunkards*," Clampett guffawed, cutting another plug of Brown Mule with his rusty pocket knife.

Turning around slowly, J.T. turned a steely gaze on him. "I'd like some privacy with my client, *Ringworm!*"

The smile faded from Clampett's face. "I told you not to never call me that no more! My name's *Ring Clampett!*"

J.T. took the three steps over to Clampett and slammed his briefcase down on the table. "I want privacy for my client *now*, Ringworm!"

Clampett glanced down at the sawed-off Louisville Slugger he kept against the wall by his chair.

"Try it," J.T. said icily.

Clampett thought back to their days in high school when J.T. played quarterback and defensive safety; remembered his panther-like quickness and the crushing tackles he had made on even the biggest fullbacks who had the misfortune to make it through the defensive line. "If this wudn't Sunday, you'd be in big trouble, J.T.," he said piously. "I respect the Lord's day." He eased himself out of his chair, keeping his eyes on J.T., then scurried across to the door and out of the small office.

J.T. smiled sadly, took the seat Clampett had just vacated, and opened his briefcase. Then he stared directly into Gatewood's blood-shot eyes. "'Awake, ye drunkards, and weep: and howl, all ye drinkers of wine.'"

Up until now, Gatewood had remained silent, nursing his splitting skull. "What's gonna happen to me now, Mr. J.T.? Ring thought it was real funny 'cause I was gonna have to go before Judge Stone."

"He would." J.T. opened his briefcase. "First thing is to get you out of here."

"I don't think Ring's gonna go for that."

J.T. placed a legal-sized sheet of paper on the table. "He doesn't have to go for it. This is an order signed by Judge Stone authorizing your release."

Gatewood smiled broadly, although it hurt him to do so. "How'd you manage that?"

"Plea bargained."

"What's that?"

"I gave the judge something—he gave me something." J.T. rubbed the back of his neck. "It wasn't easy to get your charges dismissed."

A worried frown crossed Gatewood's face. He could remember almost nothing that happened after he left Rudy's.

"Last night you not only destroyed the judge's fence, you also ran over his cat. Well, actually it's worse than that. The cat belonged to his wife."

"Oh, Lord!" Gatewood closed his eyes and placed both hands over his face, shaking his head slowly. "What do I have to do to make up for all of that?"

"Well, it's more like what you *don't* have to do, Larry," J.T. said sadly. "You don't have to go to Washington."

Gatewood jerked his head around toward J.T. "You mean I lose—everything?"

"'Fraid so. Ditweiler met me at the Judge's home this morning. Stone told him we couldn't have a drunk cat-killer represent Liberty High at the White House."

Suddenly, it hit Gatewood like a freight train. "That's why he bought me all those drinks! For old time's sake—for the old alma mater! That dirty skunk! He set me up!"

"What *are* you raving about, Larry?"

"Mark Courtney, that's what. He got me drunk last night so I'd mess up somehow and lose my trip to see the President."

J.T. propped his chin on his folded hands. "You're a big boy. I don't think he could *force* you to drink anything."

Gatewood was up pacing the tiny cell. "You don't understand how he—*uses* people! How he gets them to do *just* what he wants! I didn't either 'til right now."

"Why would Mark want to hurt you?" J.T. asked thoughtfully. "I thought y'all were friends."

"He doesn't know what friendship *is*! And he don't care whether he hurts me or anybody else! He just wanted that trip to Washington—and now he's *got* it!"

"You lost me, boy."

"Mark was runner-up in the essay contest," Gatewood spat furiously, pacing the cell. "The runner-up gets to go if something happens to the winner—and he made something happen to me! How *stupid* can I be?"

J.T. had seen hundreds of people in trouble over the years—most of them looking to blame somebody else. "You need to stand up and take this like a man, son. You can't go through life blaming other people for your mistakes."

"But he's worse than a snake! He don't care about anybody but Mark Courtney. I know he's the one who called . . ." Gatewood sat down, putting his face in his hands. "What's the use? He's too slick—he can make people believe *anything*!"

J.T. closed his briefcase, the chair scraping loudly on the bare concrete as he stood up. Walking over to the cell, he stood gazing down at Larry Gatewood, dejected and helpless. J.T. had never known him to act like this before—blaming someone else for his mistake. "Maybe you're right, Larry. Maybe Mark Courtney *is* that smooth and cunning."

Gatewood looked forlornly up at him. "He is."

J.T. knew that the words carried the flat, unadorned ring of truth. "Sounds like ol' Mark might make a fine politician!"

5

THE CANDIDATE

Governor, this is Mark Courtney. Mark's my new administrative assistant." Arnold Cooper had the "country bumpkin" look that endeared him to his rural Georgia constituency. But he had shed the practiced axioms that went along with it, in favor of a more conventional idiom—traded his off-the-rack suit and five-year-old necktie for tailored clothes and fifty-dollar Italian shoes. Today he had come to court the governor for his expertise in planning the strategy for his re-election campaign as State Representative.

"Nice to meet you, young man. Arnold here's told me some good things about you. Degree in Political Science from the University of Georgia, Phi Beta Kappa, Who's Who in American Colleges and Universities—outstanding record." Powell, his pale eyes sharply intense between the white bushy brows and amiable smile, regarded Courtney thoughtfully. He sized him up at once. *Ambitious. Bright. Polished—Dangerous!*

"Thank you, sir. I'm very grateful that a man of Mr. Cooper's stature would take me aboard." Mark mentally tried the governor's chair on for size and found that it suited him perfectly. "He's taught me a great deal already."

"I'm sure he has, son. Cooper here's been a state representative for more years than he cares to remember. Been through some tough political battles. Survived them all so far. Right, Arnold?"

Cooper sat back in the plush, brown leather chair and crossed his short legs. His broad face had a sunburned glow about it that reached up into his thin, reddish hairline. "Nobody's shot me out of the saddle yet, Beau. Been winged a couple of times though," he chortled.

Powell smiled. "Happens to the best of us." He glanced over at Courtney. "How's Courtney here at covering your flanks when the action gets hot?"

"The best," Cooper beamed. "You should see how he handles newspaper reporters. Even the toughest questions they hit him with—you've been there—state-awarded contracts, campaign funds, state jobs. By the time Mark's finished with them, they all want to go out and start tacking up campaign posters for me."

Courtney smiled broadly at Cooper, then assumed a humble posture with Powell. "He gives me too much credit, Governor. With a record of service to the people like Arnold Cooper has, it makes my job easy."

"Well, you won't always have it easy in this business, son." Powell grew philosophical. "There are some real snakes in this arena. Sell their own mothers out in a second."

"I haven't had much experience at it yet, but I can sure believe you, Governor." Mark looked around at the trappings of office—the memorabilia of decades in public service: black and white prints of ribbon-cuttings, speeches before great throngs of the common people and small gatherings of the power brokers, handshaking with dozens of others, including two ex-presidents. He loved it all—craved it as he had nothing else in his life—was already addicted to it. "You've had some career."

"*Have*, is the word, son. Not *had*. I'm still very much in the thick of the fray."

Mark could have kicked himself. *Watch what you say! Choose every word carefully—words are life and death for a politician.* "Sorry, sir. I'm sure you know what I mean."

Powell's mouth smiled, but his eyes burned with a cold fire. "No, I'm afraid I don't, son. I only know what you *say*."

Cooper broke the tension that was beginning to charge the air. "Well, now that the formalities are over, how about a little campaign strategy?"

Powell's eyes softened. He again looked like everybody's great uncle. "You ought to have it all down pat by now, Arnold. You've been in the trenches long enough."

Courtney took a slim, leather-bound notebook from his inside jacket pocket and began to write as the two older men discussed the upcoming campaign. He knew it would be out of line for him to offer advice at this stage of his career, so he merely nodded agreement occasionally and continued to write, allowing part of his mind to drift.

He imagined himself as governor: scores of underlings at his beck and call; being driven to all parts of the state in a chauffeured limousine; flying to Washington to meet with the decision makers of the nation. And the women—he had already become acquainted with that certain type of woman who is mesmerized by the mere proximity of power, victimized by the extravagant charm of the limelight.

The late afternoon light slanted in through the high windows that gave onto the western lawn of the mansion. Dust particles danced and drifted in the air like wingless moths.

While Mark took notes with a rigorous dedication, his mind was constantly collecting facts, picking and choosing the bright and colorful ones he needed for his collection. When he had just the right balance, he impaled them, still wriggling, on a board behind a glass case—waiting for the right moment to put them on display.

* * *

STATE REPRESENTATIVE INDICTED. Arnold Cooper held the newspaper out in front of his flushed face, punching the headlines viciously with a stubby forefinger. "Look at this! If you don't do something, I'm ruined! You've got to help me!"

Beau Powell gazed studiously at the bold lettering of the headlines, his chin resting on his clasped hands. "Nothing much I can do now, Arnold. Once the newshounds plaster it all over the state for everyone to see, it's out of my hands."

Cooper's bloodshot eyes pleaded with his old political crony for some kind of special dispensation, some miraculous exercise of governmental authority that would take away the guillotine hanging directly above his neck—some secret trick that would make things right with the world once more.

Trying to regain control, he spoke in a voice that was little more than a whisper. "You've *got* to do something, Beau. This is my whole career we're talking about here—my whole life! Besides those funds for the new health unit went into your *nephew's* construction account. You've *got* to do something to help *him*."

"He's a grown man. He can take care of himself," Powell said absently. "Who sold you out—tipped that investigative reporter off?"

The question shocked Cooper. He couldn't find a place for it in his world that suddenly had room for only one thought, *Get me out of this!* "What difference does it make?"

"Probably none—to you."

"I don't know. We all make enemies along the way. You know how it is. Could have been anybody."

Turning his chair slowly on its swivel base, Powell looked out the window at the groundskeeper. A black man of indeterminate age, slim and erect, he raked the few scattered brown and rust-colored leaves that had begun to fall from the massive oaks. *Not a very good year for color. Too much rain.* "You see that man out there, Arnold? His name's Obadiah."

"What—what in the world are you talking about?"

Powell remained silent.

Cooper walked over to the window and looked out. "So what? Just an old black man raking leaves."

Powell turned his pale eyes on Cooper. They held an unfathomable sadness. "He may be the happiest man I've ever known."

"Why are you talking like this? Don't you understand what's happening to me?"

"Obadiah prophesied the utter destruction of Edom. Not this pleasant and happy Obadiah down there raking leaves, to be sure." Powell leaned forward on his elbows. He could almost see himself as a small boy, sitting on a slab bench in the old brush arbor that served as a church—could almost hear his father's voice ringing in the cold night air as he preached God's wrath down on the sinners and the infidels of their county. "You see, Arnold, the Edomites treated the Jews rather badly. They also thought their own strongholds were completely invincible. I guess you'd say pride was their downfall."

Cooper thought his old friend had gone mad. He collapsed into a chair and stared blankly at him.

"Of course, Jerusalem was destroyed and the Jews dispersed—but they always came back to their land. You know what happened to the Edomites?"

"No. What happened to the Edomites?"

"Their cities were destroyed too." Powell looked out the window again. "But with a difference. They disappeared completely from history. Not a trace of them left."

* * *

Cooper finished the letter, folded it carefully, and put it into an official Georgia House of Representatives envelope. His office was dark except for the yellow glow of the desk lamp. He struck a match on the edge of a stone ashtray with the words *Lookout Mountain, Tenn* carved on the base. Touching the flame to the edge of an 8x10 black and white print, he watched the face of the young woman with the long blonde hair blacken and curl and turn to gray, crumbling ashes.

He placed a gold-framed picture of a woman and three small children on the desk directly in front of him. She had shiny dark hair and pleasant eyes and the children looked exactly like he had as a child. His face seemed to sag all of a sudden. The hard lines around the mouth relaxed. His steady heart still pumped the rich, life-giving blood, but his eyes had gone as cold and dead as the depths of space.

A thin smile crossed his face for the first time in days. He stared at the picture and eased the cold barrel of the .38 revolver into his mouth.

* * *

"I've appointed Mark Courtney to serve in the interim period until the legislature can call a special election in the spring." Beau Powell stood behind a barrage of microphones on the back portico of the mansion. Reporters, state and local officials, and passersby gathered before the gallery with its miniature Corinthian columns and brick flooring made by slaves, to listen to this man who could somehow capture an audience with the sound of his voice and his

mere presence, without saying anything of any consequence whatsoever.

Courtney stood at his side, dressed in a conservatively-cut
dark suit befitting the gravity of the occasion, managing to look
humble and confident at the same time. He observed Powell's man-
nerisms carefully, listened to his speech patterns—an apprentice in
the presence of the master.

"It was such a tragedy for all of us," Powell continued, removing his gold-rimmed glasses to wipe his eyes, "losing a man of
Arnold Cooper's dedication and integrity. A man who had spent
his life in service to his fellow man—a man I was proud to serve
with—a man I gladly called *friend*."

Courtney looked at the faces of the people gathered around
this great bear of a man who used the microphones to play the
crowd like a fine musical instrument.

The reporters, with their press cards pinned to their hats or
coat lapels, were stonefaced and bored. They had heard it all before
hundreds of times and were going through the motions to put bread
on the table and shoes on their children's feet.

The rank of public officials showed the proper deference, respect,
and mild sense of awe required of them. They sat in cushioned chairs
in a semicircle in front of the governor. Their crisp white shirts
brightened the shade of the old trees; their shoes, shined to a high
gloss by ten-year-old black boys, gleamed like new armor or old
jewels.

Then there were the people who paid the bills for the governor
and his cushioned accomplices—housed them, fed them, clothed
them, bought their liquor, and paid for new automobiles every
year. They stood randomly about the grounds, singly and in small
groups, watching their actors play out the parts they had given
them in the ballot boxes.

After his introduction, Courtney stepped before the bank of
microphones to a smattering of applause. "Arnold Cooper knew
the people of this state as few other men have—loved them as few
other men have. Arnold Cooper gave me my start in public service.
I was proud to have worked for him—and for you. Now I plan to
continue serving you in the spirit of Arnold Cooper during this interim period until the special election is held."

Courtney paused a few seconds as the semicircle up front applauded him. After a few more remarks he opened up the forum for questions.

"Why do you think Cooper killed himself? Diversion of funds isn't exactly unheard of in this state." A pot-bellied man wearing a brown fedora, a red necktie, and a practiced smirk waited with his pencil poised.

"I think conjecture at this point would be highly inappropriate and inordinately *common*. This family has suffered enough from the speculations of insensitive and callous individuals that your newspaper has already printed." Courtney stared at the man as though the jaded reporter had just committed a blasphemy. "Speculations that serve only the prurient interests of some of your more jaded and insensitive readers."

The man in the red tie merely shrugged and jotted down a few notes.

"What do you have in mind for the flood control problem Cooper was working on?"

"I think a dam would serve the most needs for the least amount of money. Not only would it prevent loss of life and property, it would also provide recreation and be a decided boost to the economy."

After answering questions for twenty minutes, Courtney was about to close the news conference.

"What are your plans for the immediate future?" The reporter was female, young, and had a smile that the Pepsodent company could use in an ad.

Courtney smiled just as brightly back at her. "To take you to lunch if you're not busy."

Genuine laughter ran through the crowd as the reporters scribbled frantically in their notebooks. He had left them with something they would remember.

As the news conference was breaking up, Obadiah Johnson squatted at the base of a sprawling live oak near a quiet street that ran by the mansion. His khakis hung on his spare frame, his thin shanks lost in the heavy work boots. The loudspeakers had carried the sound of Courtney's voice across the expanse of lawn as he gathered an armful of leaves and dumped them into the cart next to him. The expression on his dark face was as placid as a desert sunrise.

Helping him was his fifteen-year-old son, Amos, who had dropped out of school in the fourth grade and worked part-time at the mansion.

"You know, I done worked forty-one years around dis big ol' white house. Started when I was younger than you is."

"Yassuh."

"I seed a lot of folks come in and I seed a lot of folks go out. Dat's fuh sho.'"

Amos dumped an armful of leaves in the cart, leaning on it with both arms as he studied his father's face.

"One thing I learnt about ever one of 'em. When dey ain't got nothin' a'tall to say, they says it to a mikah-phone."

* * *

"More coffee, Mr. Courtney?" The white-jacketed waiter held the glass carafe poised.

Courtney looked up from his schedule book that lay in front of him on the linen tablecloth. "Yes, thank you. Looks like it's going to be another long night. I've got about two month's work to fit into three weeks time."

The waiter was an old-timer at the restaurant. Located a half-block from the State Capitol, it catered to the political crowd. Tips were excellent. "Must've been some news conference at the mansion this morning. I read your comments in the afternoon paper. Did you really do that?"

"Did I do what?" Courtney watched as the waiter poured steaming dark coffee into his thin china cup.

He grinned at Courtney, stopping the coffee level at just the right moment. "Did you take that woman reporter to lunch? You remember?"

Courtney laughed softly as he stirred a spoon of sugar into his coffee. "A gentleman doesn't tell, does he? Not even about luncheon engagements."

"Right you are, sir." The waiter turned to walk away, then stopped and looked back at Courtney. "You know, I think you're gonna do just fine in this town. A lot of 'em can handle it locally, but it's a different story when they come here for the sessions or on special business."

"Well, thank you," Courtney beamed. "I'll consider that an expert opinion."

"Yes, sir. You got what it takes."

After the waiter had gone, Courtney gazed about the restaurant at the handsomely dressed men—the elegant women. He sipped his coffee slowly, let his hand trail over the texture of the linen tablecloth. It had been a fine meal; the food and wine excellent and the service impeccable. And to top off his day, he would be having drinks in one hour's time with the reporter he *had* taken to lunch after the news conference.

The governor was a little guarded with me this morning—but then he's like that with all the young lions, I expect. Afraid one of us will challenge him. The important thing is he appointed me to replace Cooper . . . just as I hoped . . . just as I planned. That anonymous phone call tipping off the press to Cooper was the smartest political move of my career—well, maybe the second-smartest! After all, where would I be today if I hadn't called old "Ringworm" Clampett when—what was his name? Gatewood?—staggered out of the bar that night back in Liberty, headed for home. And the governor will endorse me in the spring election. Yes, sir! What could be better than this?

6

AN INCONVENIENT WAR

*P*ass me not, O gentle Saviour,
Hear my humble cry;
While on others Thou art calling,
Do not pass me by.

A white-haired deacon in his seventies walked stiffly across the platform and handed Rev. Thad Majors a white sheet of notebook paper, folded twice.

Saviour, Saviour,
Hear my humble cry;
While on others Thou art calling,
Do not pass me by.

Majors waited, head bowed, until the invitation was finished. As no one had come to the altar, he unfolded the note, read it, and lay it on the pulpit. Six feet tall, well dressed and with an almost perpetual smile on his face, Majors looked like Roy Rogers disguised as an insurance salesman. At this moment, however, his crinkly eyes had lost their cheerful gleam.

He gazed out at his congregation, some nodding off after the mild gluttony at the "Dinner on the Grounds" to celebrate First Baptist Church's annual homecoming services. Glancing down at his watch, Majors noted the time—3:17 P.M. It remained etched into his memory. He would be able to recall it when he had forgotten the names of his two sons.

Hartley Lambert, who owned the lumber mill and half of the downtown buildings, held his barrel frame erect on the front pew. His blue eyes were trained on the preacher, but his mind probed at the weaknesses of the banker from Atlanta he would meet with on Monday. Seated next to him, his pretty blonde wife, Ellie, was trying to remember where she had hidden the half-full bottle of bootleg hootch just before she passed out at 2 A.M.

Ora Peabody, who looked like Santa Claus's wife but in fact taught American History at Liberty High, worried that her crippled husband, Euliss, who never went to church, would leave the stove on and burn down their house.

The gravel-voiced football coach, Bonner Ridgeway, still fretted about his month-old loss to the Centreville Bobcats in the district championship game.

Just as well there's no service tonight. Majors turned his eyes on his congregation. "I don't know how to tell you this—except just to *tell* you. "The Japs have bombed Pearl Harbor!"

A collective gasp escaped the mouths of the people, almost as if they were one being. Cries of anguish and of disbelief spread throughout the congregation.

Majors waited a few moments as the first shock wore off and an almost palpable silence settled over the church. "The news is still sketchy right now, but it looks like they dealt us a pretty heavy blow. The fighters and dive bombers from their carrier force hit our ships and some of the naval and army air bases located near the harbor."

"Them dirty Japs!" someone shouted from the back of the church. "We'll blow 'em off the face of the earth!"

Affirmations, including a few *Amens!*, rang in the church building.

Majors raised his hands and called for quiet. "Settle down now, folks. I know you're all anxious to go to your homes and listen to further reports on the radio. But before we do, I'd like to close with prayer."

The people rose off their pews almost as one person, their heads bowed.

"Heavenly Father, we come to You in the name of Your Son, Jesus. We ask that You would watch over our men and women in uniform and protect them from this heathen enemy that has so cowardly and viciously attacked them. Give us courage in the days to come and strengthen us for the job to be done. We ask this in Jesus' name. Amen."

J.T. Dickerson, sober now these three days before the homecoming services, which he attended every year, along with the Christmas and Easter services, stood up slowly and placed his hand over his heart. His dark suit was neatly pressed and the necktie with the Harvard insignia that he wore only three times a year was tied with a perfect four-in-hand. An intense light burned in his sad brown eyes. Although his baritone voice cracked slightly in the beginning, it smoothed out after the first few words, becoming stronger.

> God bless America, land that I love,
> Stand beside her and guide her
> Through the night with the light from above.

The rest of the congregation, in a mild state of shock when they saw who was singing, began to sound the old familiar words, tentative at first, then growing louder.

> From the mountains, to the prairies,
> To the oceans white with foam;

Finally they joined as one voice, making a proud and joyful chorus.

> God bless America, my home sweet home.
> God bless America, my home sweet home.

The people of Liberty, some with tears in their eyes, began making their way out of the church, offering their hands and their hearts to each other.

From his pulpit, Thad Majors, who had pastored the First Baptist Church of Liberty, Georgia, for thirty-one years, surveyed his flock with gladness and a deep, abiding love. He was a man of God. Everyone said so—even those who didn't especially like him. They grudgingly admitted that Thad Majors was the same man on Saturday night that he was in the pulpit on Sunday morning—the same man by himself in Atlanta that he was with his family in Liberty.

When the church building was empty, Majors walked slowly off the platform to his office, located just to the rear of the choir loft. Holding his worn and dog-eared Bible, he knelt and prayed. His wife found him there fifteen minutes later, after the last car had left the churchyard.

Morton Spain drove his gleaming black Cadillac out of the church parking lot. His wife, Angela, twenty-eight years his junior, sat over against the passenger door. Her violet eyes and long lashes had clouded his mind to her shortcomings, causing him to make decisions totally devoid of logic. Unfortunately for him, they seemed to have the same effect on a substantial portion of the male population of Liberty. His law practice *and* his health were suffering considerably because of this.

The news of the attack on Pearl Harbor had disturbed Angela. She gazed out the window of the Cadillac with the expression of a faintly annoyed housecat. *I hope Ben wasn't hurt. Such a lovely young man. What a waste that would be!* She remembered with pleasure that rainy night she had invited him into her cozy parlor—and how he had left before they could become—better acquainted. *We'll have to have a talk when he gets home. I'll bet he's learned something more than swabbing decks in the navy.*

* * *

"It's a shame this had to happen now. You were so close to winning that seat in the House," Senator Tyson Demerie, whose grandfather founded the town of Liberty, expounded in his rich bass voice. He sat with his legs crossed in the lounge area of the Pine Hills Country Club, a long, slim cigar clenched between his white teeth. "I don't think anyone else would have even bothered to qualify against you. Not with the governor's endorsement—and my own wouldn't hurt you any either."

From his leather and chrome lounge chair, Courtney gazed languidly at the blue smoke drifting upward from the senator's cigar. His barely touched scotch and water ringed the surface of the polished table next to him. "What a thoroughly despicable thing to do!"

"Agreed. Dropping bombs and strafing ships and airfields can hardly be considered as some of the more genteel pastimes of the human race." Demerie leaned his head back, blowing a circle of smoke. It floated in the almost still air, breaking slowly apart until it disappeared completely.

"Why did they have to pick *this*—of all years—to start their blasted war? The timing couldn't *possibly* have been any worse!" Courtney sat up quickly and slammed his hand down on the table next to him. Several people in the lounge, startled from their reading and conversations, gave him icy glances.

Demerie chuckled behind his cigar. "It was inconsiderate of the little slant-eyed rascals, wasn't it?"

Courtney regained control of himself. "Well, I've certainly got some decisions to make."

"Look on the bright side, my boy." Demerie's face held a conspiratorial mirth. "A good war record is a virtual guarantee of lifetime incumbency. Nobody can beat a man with a string of campaign ribbons across his chest."

"Maybe you're right," Courtney mused.

"No maybe about it. We're going to have the senator *and* representative from this part of the state both living in good ol' Liberty." Courtney glanced at a buxom, dark-haired woman in a tennis outfit as she walked past him toward the glass doors leading out onto the courts. "Always bothered me—Cooper living over there in Centreville. Funneled too much money into that area."

Lifting his scotch and water, Courtney drained half of it. *How stupid can I be! If I play my cards right, I can use this war to coast right on into the governor's mansion—maybe higher!* "You're absolutely right! Now all I have to do is decide what branch of service to join."

"Not much of a decision there at all." Demerie tugged at his right ear, his head tilted to one side so that he gave Courtney an oblique glance.

"Army. Navy. Marines. What else is there—Boy Scouts?" Courtney's eyes sparked with interest. He knew of Demerie's military connections.

Demerie spread his hand and made a looping motion in front of him. "Army Air Force. The only way to fight a war. Beats wallowing around in the mud with the infantry."

"Pilot training? You think I could make it as a pilot?" Courtney asked warily.

"Don't see why not. You've got a good touch with a nine iron. Your tee shots are as straight and true as anybody's I've seen. Timing, coordination, and eyesight. Same thing it takes to make a good aviator."

Courtney was not quite certain of the validity of Demerie's comparing golf and pilot training. But flying sounded a lot better than facing a jungle full of crazed Japs trying to make it to Shinto-land, or wherever it was they went when they died, by slicing his gizzard out with a bayonet. "What did you have in mind, Sena-tor—specifically?"

Demerie stubbed out his cigar, leaning back in his chair. "I have a long time friend, Colonel George Washington Adams. His father greatly admired our first president, and afflicted his only son with the namesake. By the way, never call him anything but Colo-nel, or G.W. if the occasion affords it. Never, never use either of his given names."

Courtney filed the advice away.

"G.W. is playing with heavy bombers right now. I believe that's the latest toy the army's bought for him." Demerie shrugged casually. "Shouldn't be much of a problem to get a bright young man like you in his outfit."

Resting his chin on his clasped hands, Courtney stared out the plate glass window at the dark-haired woman and Chance Rinehart, the only world-class tennis player Liberty ever produced, rallying on the court down by the ivy-covered wall. "Heavy bombers? Sounds like a sky full of Messerschmitts and heavy flak to me."

"Good Lord, boy, we'll make a staff officer out of you! I can't groom you as the consummate statesman after the war—if you don't come *back* from the war!"

"Staff officer? Sounds like a desk job?"

"You're finally seeing the light. What a detective you'd make!" Demerie laughed. "Later, we just might be able to wrangle you a job at the Pentagon."

"What about the pilot part? Seems to me that pilot training would require a certain amount of flying."

"Oh, yes. That. Well, you'll have to fly a few missions, of course." Demerie chuckled softly. "I hardly think the voters would accept you as the daring young pilot who defeated the dreaded Hun—if you never saw any combat."

"When do we get started?"

82

"I'll call G.W. tomorrow morning." Demerie glanced across the lounge. "Look. Here comes my lovely daughter. I think she's got her cap set for you, son."

Oh, yes. That. Demerie stood up to greet Barbara Demerie, his smile as bright as the flash of sunlight on the white tennis ball beyond the plate glass window.

*   *   *

"What's so important about Pearl Harbor?" Barbara Demerie sat across from Courtney in the last booth near the jukebox in Ollie's drugstore. She glanced over at Ollie Caston, then swirled the ice in her cherry Coke with her straw.

Courtney pursed his lips, shook his head slowly, and took a sip of his coffee, staring at Barbara over the rim of his cup. *Nice eyes, figure's not all that bad, but she looks too much like her brother, Keith, to be pretty. If her daddy wasn't a senator . . . The things I suffer for my career!*

Ollie Caston, one ear cocked toward the radio for the latest reports on the war, mopped the floor with his usual energy. "What's that? Oh, Pearl Harbor? It's a great big naval base. Headquarters for the Pacific fleet."

"Oh." Barbara smiled at Courtney and sipped her Coke.

"Don't they teach you people anything over at Emory, Barbara?" Courtney tried to hide the slight edge to his voice.

"Well, it's only my first year."

Caston glanced over his shoulder toward the soda fountain where the last two customers were leaving. "Guess you'll be joining the navy or maybe the army, eh Mark?"

Courtney shrugged, not wanting to get involved in a conversation that would divulge what was going on behind the scenes.

Billy Christmas, his black hair a negative image of the slim blonde girl's with him, dropped two quarters on the marble-topped counter and slid off his stool. He took her hand, helping her down as they started toward the door.

"So long, Billy, Jordan. Y'all come back." As they waved goodbye, Caston spoke under his breath. "Nice couple, but the General's never gonna stand for his son to keep company with a girl like Jordan Simms. Coming from the wrong side of the tracks is bad enough, but being raised by ol' Annie—well, that just puts the icing on the cake. It's a shame too. She's a fine girl."

Barbara answered Caston's question about Courtney for him. "Oh, no! Daddy's already taken care of that! Mark's going to be a pilot. Aren't you, Mark? I think he'll look so cute in that little cap with the goggles."

Ollie leaned on his mop. "That's just great, son! We're gonna need some good pilots to blow them Jap Zeros out of the skies. Make 'em pay for Pearl."

"That's the truth," Courtney agreed, a little uneasy at the direction the conversation was taking.

"Daddy talked to his friend, General Adams, over at the air base. Mark's going to fly bombers." The thought of uniforms and writing long love letters overseas touched the romantic bent in Barbara Demerie's ample breast.

"Bombers. That's a pretty rough job."

"There ain't gonna be any easy jobs in this war, Ollie." Courtney suddenly found himself enjoying the role he had been thrust into. He liked the sound of the phrases as he lapsed into his old high school speech patterns. Now that he felt protected from the uncertainties that most men faced in the war, he assumed a devil-may-care attitude.

"What outfit you goin' with?"

"Nothing's certain right now. The senator says the army is beginning to form up the Eighth Air Force." Courtney almost felt that he was about to risk his all in defense of the flag. *I regret that I have but one life to—Hold it! That's going a little too far, even for you, Mark.* He had to suppress a grin at his own vivid imagination.

"Know what they're gonna fly yet?"

"B-17s, I think."

"The *Flying Fortress.* That's some airplane."

"I think I can handle her, Ollie."

Caston's eyes held a distant light, not quite focused on anything around him. "As long as this country has young men like you to defend her, we've got nothing to worry about. I'm proud of you, Mark."

* * *

Courtney paced in front of the double windows that looked out on the ramp where a half-dozen B-17s were parked. The office was dimly lighted, the only illumination coming from the amber glow of a small desk lamp and the winter light filtering through the Venetian blinds in dreary, gray bars.

The desk showed that its occupant had a decided contempt for paperwork. Stacks of it cluttered the surface, spilling off onto the floor. A World War I bayonet lay next to a partially opened stack of letters. The bottom three inches of a sawed-off, eight-inch shell casing was filled with ashes and cigarette butts. Dozens of photographs in black frames hung on the walls.

Where is he? I haven't got all day to wait around in this freezing office for some petty little bureaucrat!

At that moment, Courtney's head snapped around at the sound of screeching tires just outside the window. He watched a short, round man in an army-green overcoat with gold eagles on the epaulets bound out of his Jeep and hurry around the side of the building. In thirty seconds, the door burst open.

"You must be Mark Courtney. Tyson called me about you. Said you'd make a fine addition to our staff. He right about that?" Colonel Adams held out his hard stubby hand.

Grasping the proffered hand, Courtney thought it felt like a wood rasp. "I hope so, sir."

"Gotta be more than *hope so* in this man's army, son." Adams plopped into the big desk chair, his feet dangling above the floor as he leaned back. "Sit down."

No wonder it's so cold in here! He's built like an Eskimo. "Yes, sir. I think I can be an asset to your staff."

"Asset, huh? Yeah, well, maybe you can at that." Adams picked up the bayonet and began cleaning his fingernails. "We need all the connections we can get with government. You've certainly got some experience there—even if it isn't on the federal level."

Courtney twisted uneasily in the hard gray chair he had taken, hoping Adams wasn't typical of the officers he would encounter in the army.

"You can't get any funds for us, but like ol' Tyson does, you can make life a whole lot easier with the state government. Permits, a road paved here and there. Help with the local courts too. Boys will be boys, you know, and soldiers tend to get carried away more than most. Some real knock-down-drag-outs in them joints just off the base."

Wondering if the whole thing was worth it, Courtney listened as the little colonel rambled on and on.

"'Course, you'll be going off for basic and flight training before long. Then after a few missions, I'll assign you to my staff—something in Operations, most likely. Maybe the flak officer. That's a real plum."

"But when we'll *really* need you is in a year or two. This little fracas with the Japs can't last long and we're gonna count on your help when the shootin' stops. The army ain't treated nearly as good by civilians after we've kicked the enemy's butts." Adams plunged the bayonet into the top of the wooden desk.

Courtney flinched at the sound. The long blade quivered slightly, glinting in the cold, gray light.

Adams spun around in his chair, looking out at the massive bombers just outside his windows. "Yes, sir. Peace is a terrible thing for a fightin' man to endure!"

7

MERRY OLD ENGLAND

*T*he clipped open field, scarred by a dirt trail along its edge, rolled smoothly toward the distant tree line. Dew drops winked on the grass as the light-rimmed east grew brighter, turning from a glowing red to orange and finally gold. Wispy clouds, brushed with the light stroke of a master artist, lay motionless across the pale morning sky.

"Move it! Move it! Move it! Pick up the pace, girls! My ol' granny can move faster than this!" The man with the booming voice wore green shorts and undershirt with high-topped black tennis shoes. His dark hair was an inch long on top and shaved on the sides. Sweat glistened on his heavy muscles. Sergeant Burley Stoddard loved his job.

"How is this gonna help me fly a plane?" Courtney had yet to get an answer to his question, but he no longer had to struggle to keep up with the rest of his flight. His already lean frame had hardened and added layers of muscle. He hadn't counted on physical fitness to be a part of flight training and his first few weeks were roughly equivalent to six month's labor in the tin mines of Libya. "This is strictly for the infantry."

Harlan Carrington III loped along painfully next to Courtney. Although he had never been an athlete in school, he had found out something of what lay ahead in the Army Air Force and had done running and calisthenics for a month prior to his enlistment date. His wind improved, but his muscles still looked pre-pubescent under his milky skin. "I keep telling you. Logic and purpose have no place in the army."

"Stoddard has no place in the civilized world, but there he is," Courtney puffed, nodding to the bronzed sergeant at the front of the sweaty men stretched out in a ragged line along the path.

At the edge of the meadow where the path continued on into the woods through thick brush, bogs, and ravines, Stoddard gave his men a five-minute break. They sprawled in the shade, leaning back against the tree trunks; cursing the army, talking about women and fast cars and baseball and thick juicy steaks—everything but the war that lay somewhere beyond these endless days and nights of training.

Courtney gazed at Stoddard where he lay on his back in the new clover. "The man's a troglodyte."

Carrington squinted at him with his myopic brown eyes. "How do you know?"

"One of the sentries saw him coming out of a cave in the hills just before sunrise Tuesday."

"Doesn't prove anything."

"Sure, it does. You never saw him sleeping in the barracks did you? He has to return to his cave at night, like Dracula back to the coffin." Courtney chewed on a grass stem, breathing evenly, his pulse rate almost back to normal.

"Sergeants don't sleep in officers' quarters. You have to be more objective about this. If you're going to demean a man's character, make sure you have your facts straight." Carrington loved word games almost as much as Stoddard loved to see men throwing up at the end of a long run.

"You're just taking his side 'cause he let you do forty push-ups yesterday while we all watched."

Carrington grimaced. "That was a nice gesture, but it's not the reason. I'm just being logical. Not enough evidence to prove he lives in a cave."

"I have more."

"What?"

"His breath smells like bat dung."

"Now you're making sense!"

"All right, ladies—let's hit it!" Stoddard was already thudding away down the hard-packed dirt path into the woods.

*   *   *

Courtney lay on his bunk in the tiny room he shared with Carrington. His eyes were closed, his hands lying limply at his sides as he dropped off into a state of complete relaxation. Showers and breakfast over, he coveted the few moments of peace and quiet before morning classes began.

But it never lasted with Carrington in the same room. He flicked the knob on the bulky wooden Philco radio his mother had sent him. It sat on the floor against the wall. "Now, that's a song!" he assured Courtney as the sounds of Jimmy Dorsey's band playing "Green Eyes" pulled Courtney back from his reverie. "Bob Eberly and Helen O'Connell—best in the business!"

Courtney grunted and turned toward the wall.

Carrington thumbed through an outdated issue of *Life* magazine. "Now, here's something interesting!"

"Pilot trainee kills pesky roommate," Courtney mumbled into his pillow.

"I'm serious." He sat up on the edge of his cot, the magazine opened on his lap. "Listen to this. 'Camel smokers enjoy smoking to the full. It's Camels for an invigorating lift in energy. At mealtimes it's Camels again for digestion's sake."

"I don't smoke anymore. Give it a rest, will you?"

"Maybe you should take it up," Carrington continued unperturbed. "This is the good part. 'Thanks to Camel's gentle aid, the flow of the important digestive fluids—alkaline digestive fluids—speeds up. A sense of well-being follows. So make it Camels—the live long day.'"

Courtney maintained his silence, hoping the reading session had ended.

"You think there's anything to that?"

Courtney relented and sat up, rubbing his eyes. "I think they're trying to sell cigarettes."

"But look at this." Carrington pointed to a distinguished looking man in a business suit, with a cigarette stuffed between his middle and forefinger. "This sportswriter, James Gould, says Camels are the favorite smoke of athletes."

"You know, Harlan, for a smart man, you sure get stupid when you open up a magazine. I think you'd believe anything Madison Avenue conjured up to make a quick buck."

"You have to admit there's some scientific evidence here," Carrington said huffily.

"No. I don't have to admit that," Courtney yawned. "What I *do* have to admit is that I'm not ready for the aerodynamics test we're having this morning."

Carrington closed the magazine and tossed it under his bed. "The way you fly that 17, you could make an E-minus and still graduate in the top ten percent of the class."

"I do seem to have a knack for it, don't I?" Courtney thought of how easily it had come to him—handling all the massive bulk and weight of the Flying Fortress. He had seen most men wrestling with the controls, trying to manhandle the 17 into submission, but, like any lady, she would not be pawed at. The law of gravity seemed not to apply to him any longer when he slipped behind the controls and drove twenty-seven tons of metal along a highway of air and sunlight and clouds.

"That you do, me boy," Carrington responded, failing miserably at a British accent. "You're going to be blooming mad about Merry Old England."

"We haven't got any orders yet," Courtney frowned. "How do you know where we're going?"

"East Anglica, me hearty. I can already see one of those quaint little pubs. A pint of bitters for me and my friend here—if you please, laddie."

"You're just guessing." Courtney punctuated his statement with a lifted forefinger. "Ah, but it's an educated guess, mate—a bloody fact-filled, genius-inspired guess. Pray, do continue, my good man." Courtney entered the game against his better judgment.

"Simple. Southeast England is the closest Allied controlled territory to the bloody Krauts—to the ball bearing and aircraft factories, the oil storage facilities," Carrington said flatly. "The closest place with air bases, that is."

"I hadn't really thought much about where we'd go when this training is over." *Except for all those daydreams about some plush office in the Pentagon.*

Carrington's brow furrowed in thought. "Of course, there *is* one other possibility."

Courtney didn't bother to ask what it was, knowing the answer would come with or without the question.

"North Africa. There's that slight problem with Rommel, naturally, but Eisenhower and Patton should be able to kick him out of

Tunisia—with a little help from Montgomery, of course." Carrington shook his head slowly. "What a dismal prospect *that* would be! Cold and wet in the winter—hot and dry in the summer. Smelly camels and barbaric Bedouins. Merry Old England—that's the place for us!"

"It all sounds so exotic and—well, simply smashing, old boy!" Courtney found himself affecting the accent in spite of himself. "But I fancy meself in other climes. Washington, D.C. for example. Shangri La on the Potomac."

"Not much chance of that."

"Why, may I ask?"

"You're too good at this job—the one the army's spending so many taxpayer dollars to train us for." Carrington turned on Courtney with a bothersome stare. "Anybody can sit in a swivel chair and prop their feet up on a desk. The country's full of men who can stand in front of a wall map with a pointer."

Courtney began to get a prickling sensation at the back of his neck. "Hold on a minute, Carrington. I'm strictly the administrative type. I can prop my feet up at the drop of a hat—point to a wall map with the best of 'em."

"Don't doubt it for one minute, old chap." Carrington thought of the times he had sat in the copilot's seat watching Courtney—remembered how he had flown the great aircraft using his fingertips. With controlled and unhurried movements, he had put the 17 through its paces as smoothly as the air slipping along its wings. "But there's precious few what can do the job you can with one of those blinkin' big bombers."

"Sorry. Doesn't fit in with my game plan."

Carrington stared out the window, where a B-17 was taxiing into position for take-off. "The game plan is to destroy the Nazi war machine, me bucko. And that means bringing a rather violent conclusion to their means of production. The 17, I'm afraid, is essential to this end. I'm not any more eager to violate the führer's airspace than you are. It tends to be cluttered up with those awful puffs of black clouds—you know, the kind that bite."

"Oh, I'll fly a mission or two, all right," Courtney said with a cheerfulness he didn't feel. "But I don't plan to make any long term commitments."

*   *   *

"Hey! Hold on a minute!" Carrington, his new wings gleaming brightly on the left side of his chest, walked rapidly across the parade ground toward Courtney.

Courtney stopped, waiting for him to catch up. He was in a black mood in spite of the June sunshine and mild breeze. Everybody else seemed to think it was a joyous occasion as they scattered out from the bleachers with their families and friends on their way to celebrate.

As he had stood at parade rest with his fellow officers, the graduation ceremony had gnawed at him like a mouse inside the woodwork. All the speeches about the glorious traditions of America's fighting men; duty to God and country; courage and honor and valor had left him empty and cold. "I can tell by your face you've got some great new revelation," he sighed as Carrington approached. "What is it now? A quart of booze a day increases longevity?"

"It's about the ol' man."

"What about him?"

"He's dead."

Courtney's mind leaped back to that dreary winter day when he had first met Colonel G.W. Adams—his first encounter with the military mind. He tolerated the man at first, having no other choice, then in time came to almost admire his bulldog tenacity in getting things done in spite of the bureaucratic gauntlets thrown up in front of him. In particular, he admired the man's arranging for the assignment of Courtney, Mark E., First Lieutenant to his headquarters staff.

Carrington snapped his fingers in front of Courtney's face. "Did you hear what I said?"

Courtney came out of the fog. "I heard you. What happened to him?"

"Walked right into a prop."

"That's impossible!" Courtney was shocked as well as appalled at the news. "He's been around aircraft for twenty years. It just couldn't happen."

Carrington walked into the shade of an old elm and sat down on a stone bench. "Anything's possible." The years seemed to have clambered over his face, aging him in a few hours' time.

"When did it happen?" Courtney sat down beside him, trying to control his emotion.

"About eight this morning."

"This morning? Why didn't you tell me before now? What's the matter with you?"

"Just couldn't bring myself to do it. Took me awhile to work up the courage, I guess."

Courtney still refused to believe it. "There must be some explanation. It's a mistake of some kind."

"Mark—I saw it happen!" Carrington's face looked drained of blood—his mouth nothing more than a thin, tight line beneath eyes that still held a glaze of disbelief.

Above them, high in the crown of the sun-spangled elm, a thrush sang to celebrate the long summer ahead. Courtney quietly waited.

"I was at OPS, going through my flight plans for the month, when I saw that Jeep of his zip by, heading out to the ramp. Must have been a half dozen or so 17s taxiing into position."

The thrush sang once more and launched himself out into the sunlight.

Carrington took a deep breath and turned toward Courtney, with a hollow stare. "You know how he was always parking that Jeep in the craziest places—never paid any attention to what was going on around him." Carrington stopped and looked at the ground, reaching down for a fallen limb as if he had to have something tangible to hold on to before he continued.

"He was heading out to one of the planes for something. I could see him waving at the pilot trying to—then he looked like he had forgotten something and he turned. With all that noise he couldn't have heard. He just kind of backed into it and disappeared. He just—*disappeared*."

Courtney tried not to picture what had happened, but his mind, like a movie projector, displayed it on an imaginary screen. The bright splash of color that had been G.W. Adams flashed in the propeller as the pilot's shout of warning was lost in the terrible scream of the engines.

Carrington's voice sounded soft and far away. "What a stupid way to go! With the whole German fighter corps waiting over there to kill him—to kill us all—he does the job for them. Twenty-five years in the army and he ends up like this. Never would listen to a thing anybody else said!"

Courtney didn't know whether to mourn Adams or hate him. During the past few months, they had gotten to be friends over a few drinks at the officers' club. Adams loved golf and Courtney had helped him with his short game. Now all the effort was wasted. New commanders always brought in their own Executive Officers. Courtney's sorrow vanished quickly in his growing anger at what Adams had cost him.

*   *   *

"There must be *something* you can do!" Courtney almost screamed into the receiver as he stood in the phone booth outside the base exchange.

"Sorry, my boy. Adams was the only real contact I had in the army. Now, if you'd joined the navy instead . . ." Tyson Demerie used this same tone of voice to explain to one of his constituents why it was inevitable that the man lose his farm. "You'll just have to make the best of it."

"What about the governor?"

"Sorry, I'm afraid I've already called in all my markers with the governor's office."

"Senator, the orders are being cut today! What about the deal we had?"

"Why that hasn't changed a bit, son. We'll have you elected in short order once you get back home." Demerie moved into his re-assuring grandfatherly tone. "This just means things may be a bit different for you in the service."

A bit different? The difference between dead and alive! That's more than a bit! Courtney's mind raced to concoct some kind of plan but he kept hitting brick walls.

"You still there, son?"

"Where else would I be?"

"Well, I have to ring off now. Can't keep a whole room full of businessmen waiting, can I? You just make the best of the situation. These things have a way of working themselves out. I'll give your best to Barbara."

Courtney held the receiver to his ear. The steady hum sounded like a perfectly tuned engine.

Across the quadrangle, a throng of flyers had gathered around the big bulletin board in front of Headquarters Squadron. Courtney watched an officer walk out the door of the building, a sheaf of papers in his hand. He pushed through the crowd of men and began to pin the separate sheets of paper to the big board. The men pressed in on him, jumping up to see over the ones in front of them, pushing toward the front.

Finally the officer shouted something and the men settled down. In a few seconds, he returned back into the building. Then the bedlam began. Some of the sheets were torn down from the board. Men snatched at them, ripping some of them to pieces. Fights almost broke out.

Courtney stood with his arms folded, watching the show. In a few minutes, he saw Carrington separate from the crowd and walk across the quadrangle toward him.

"Well, I saw our names. Right together like they've been all through training." Carrington tried to sound cheerful, but couldn't quite bring it off.

Courtney took a pack of Lucky Strikes out of his inside jacket pocket, tapped one out, and stuck it into his mouth. Then he put the pack away, letting the cigarette dangle from his lips.

"You're smoking?"

"Maybe. I haven't really decided yet."

Carrington looked at his friend with a puzzled frown. "You're a little crazier than usual today, I see."

"It's a crazy time we're livin' in, Harlan. Cabbages and kings. Unbirthday parties. Propeller deaths."

"Maybe I oughta wait awhile to give you the good news." Carrington forced a smile.

"Now's as good a time as any."

Carrington looked directly into Courtney's eyes, the trace of a smile still on his face. "There aren't any camels where we're going. That's good news, isn't it?"

Courtney took a kitchen match out of his left trouser pocket, flicking it with his thumbnail. The woosh of flame and smoke made him think of a puff of bursting flak. He lit the cigarette and inhaled deeply before breaking into a fit of coughing.

"You'll do all right," Carrington assured him. "Just need a little practice, that's all."

Squinting at him through the smoke, Courtney asked in a hoarse voice, "Well? Let's have the rest of it."

"Let's walk, shall we?" Carrington's voice took on a casual tone as they walked along the edge of the quadrangle toward their barracks. "You know, I always read a lot when I was growing up." He stared at Courtney. "How about you?"

Courtney knew what was coming, but he found himself drawn inexorably into the game. "Yeah. I used to read a lot."

They had entered a small grove of trees just outside the quadrangle. Carrington put his hands into his pockets, his voice pleasant in the sudden stillness. "You know what one of my very favorite books was?"

"I'm sure you're going to tell me."

"*Robin Hood*," Carrington smiled. "I hope it was one of your favorites too."

Part 3

8TH AIR FORCE

8

A GRANDLY SHINING PASSAGE

*I*t started as a faint distant noise, like a generator humming dully in the next room, then as it moved gradually overhead became almost deafening. Courtney slowly opened his eyes. A pale, smoky light filtered into the barracks. Most of the men were rolling out of their bunks, struggling into their uniforms. He sat up in the gloom, shivering slightly, and rubbed the sleep out of his eyes. "What's going on? Where's everybody heading?"

Carrington pulled his trousers up and threw his jacket on. "Hurry up! We don't want to miss this!"

Courtney dressed quickly, leaving his shoes untied and his jacket unbuttoned. He stepped into the flow of men pressing toward the faint glow of the barracks door.

They had arrived at Bovingdon, the orientation base outside London, the night before. Shortly after midnight, they had been officially inducted into the Eighth Air Force by a groggy colonel with a cup of coffee in his hand. Then the army's ubiquitous two and a half ton trucks, called deuce-and-a-halfs, had hauled them over to the barracks.

Outside, in the misty dawn, Courtney stood next to Carrington gazing up into the early English skies. Far up where sunlight was glinting like brass on a sweep of clouds, the Fortresses roared overhead in surgical precision. Their formations held tight and angular and were perfectly suited to bring the maximum amount of firepower to bear on the Focke Wulf 190s and the Messerschmitts 109s, the vanguard of Hermann Goering's air defenses.

"Go get 'em boys!" Courtney was surprised to hear this coming from Carrington.

Shouts of encouragement rang out from the travel-dazed men of the Eighth Air Force. In spite of himself, Courtney became caught up in the excitement—found himself cheering the American flyers on their way. And as wave after wave of the giant Fortresses thundered by, to his great astonishment, he discovered that he almost wanted to be up there with them.

"What a sight!" Carrington shouted above the cheering mob of half-dressed men, milling about in the chill dawn of their first day on English soil.

For the rest of that day—in every class room, in the mess hall, in the barracks area—wherever he happened to be, Courtney found himself thinking of the Forts and the men who flew in them. He wondered if the flak was heavy, how many fighters were thrown against them, how many had engine trouble—all the things that meant life or death for a flyer.

At 3 P.M., they heard the distant drone of the engines. In three minutes the classrooms were emptied, everyone standing outside gawking up at the skies. Faces drained of blood at the sight that greeted them from the skies. Gone was the grandeur of that early morning display of precision flying, that grandly shining passage across the heavens.

A very few of the Forts still flew in formation. Most were scattered like lost sheep among the sparse clouds. Engines were feathered; many trailed streams of smoke behind them, turning sections of the sky into giant writing tablets.

Courtney looked away from the crippled formations, devastated by what he had seen. Gone was the glory of morning, the thrill of bringing the enemy to his knees. He glanced at Carrington, who stood next to him.

Carrington's face reflected the horror that he must have felt in his soul. "There must be at least half of them missing. Half! How could they lose so many?"

But more came in. For the next hour, the men stood transfixed, watching the wounded Fortresses straggle in, many on three engines, some on only two. The next morning when the distant roar of the formations reached the barracks, none of the flyers moved to run outside and greet them. No one even got out of bed. Most merely grunted, turned over and slept, or tried to sleep as the bombers thundered overhead on their way to the continent.

* * *

Ten days later the newest members of the Eighth Air Force found themselves in still another deuce-and-a-half, jouncing along a wet road through the English countryside.

"Anything but the 100th group!" Carrington leaned close to Courtney's ear to be heard above the rumbling of the truck tires on the rough road.

"What's wrong with them?"

"Don't you ever pay attention to anything? They're the most hard luck outfit over here."

"High losses, huh?"

"The worst. Some of the other commands are bad, but not like the 100th."

Courtney turned his face directly toward his friend's, barely able to make him out in the darkness. "See if you can follow this logic. Wouldn't it figure that replacement crews like us would likely be sent to the outfits with the highest losses?"

Carrington made no response and didn't talk at all until they reached their base.

They arrived at the airdrome sometime past midnight. In the dim light that glowed from windows of several prefabricated metal buildings, Courtney noticed that the base, or parts of it, had been newly constructed. Raw dirt had been dozed and piled in no particular order about the scarred earth. Trails, rather than roads, led through the woods.

A gaunt man in his thirties, wearing the gold oak leaves of a major on his collar, walked slowly over from the closest building to where the men were piling out of the truck. "Evening, boys. I'm Major Hand. Hope y'all had a good trip."

"Another illiterate Southerner," the New England-born Carrington whispered in Courtney's ear.

"Welcome to the 271st Bombardment Group here at Stonewell Air Base."

A collective sigh of relief escaped the men. They congratulated each other for several moments.

"You boys disappointed at not making the 100th, I'll bet. Well, that's the way it goes sometimes."

Some of the men laughed nervously. Others merely basked in the glow of their good fortune.

"Come on in and we'll get things sorted out."

The men filed into the headquarters building, leaving their duffel bags piled outside. Inside, they took seats at three tables made of freshly milled lumber. The pine tar made the room smell like a lumber shed at a sawmill.

The major stood behind a smaller table at the front of the room, shuffling through their papers. "Looks like the 253rd Squadron gets the lot of you. A driver will be along in a little while to take y'all to the squadron headquarters. Best of luck on your new assignments."

Carrington raised his hand hesitantly. "Major, we've heard a lot of rumors about how rough things are over here. What's the real scoop on casualties?"

The major shook a Camel out of a pack on the table. Holding a silver lighter between his thumb and three fingertips, he made a flicking movement with his wrist and suddenly the lighter appeared open in his hand with the flame burning. He lit the cigarette, obviously enjoying the effect of his theatrics on the men assembled before him.

"I don't think I asked for a vaudeville show, did I?" Carrington mumbled.

"See this," the performing major declared in a slightly deeper voice, pointing with his cigarette to a large wall chart crowded with names. "It's our combat roster. We've been here ninety days now and we've lost a hundred and twenty-nine percent of our combat personnel."

The men shuffled nervously in their seats, waiting for the smile to appear; for the major to laugh and tell them the whole thing was just a joke that he played on all the new replacement crews. His face remained stony.

"You just had to ask, didn't you?" Courtney muttered to Carrington. "Can't leave well enough alone! I hope you sleep good, now that we all know."

Three hours later, they were seated in the back of a personnel truck on their way to Squadron Headquarters. Major Bradley Price, the squadron commander, awaited them outside a metal building smaller than the one at group. The men clambered wearily down from the truck in the first light of dawn, their faces pale and drawn after a hard day and a sleepless night.

Price looked like he had just stepped out of a shower into a freshly pressed uniform. With his white hair, he gave the impression of age although he was only twenty-nine. He was wiry and short and his brown eyes stared out from his thin face with a genuine concern for these young men who had been thrust suddenly into this battleground in the skies.

"Welcome to the 253rd, men," Price said warmly. "Glad to have you with us. We're three combat crews below our minimum strength."

"No questions for the major?" Courtney whispered to Carrington who stood close beside him.

Carrington grunted in reply, his bloodshot eyes now slits in his face as he struggled to keep his head up.

"I know you men are ready to get some shut-eye, so I'll have you taken out to your quarters." Price smiled benignly at the sleepy flyers. "Just wanted to welcome you aboard." He turned to leave, then reconsidered and faced them again. "Things probably aren't as bad as Major Hand painted them. He tends to—dramatize once in awhile."

They immediately got back into the truck and bumped along a rough-cut trail out to the combat site. Stumbling out of the truck for the last time, the men looked dejectedly at the small metal Quonset huts they would be living in.

The driver, a corporal in rumpled overalls, slouched against the front fender of the truck chewing a big wad of gum. "This is for the officers," he said in a flat Boston accent. "Over there is where the enlisted men stay. You can see that the huts are exactly the same. We ain't equipped for special privileges over here."

"This guy must be a relative of Stoddard's." Courtney stared with glazed eyes at the corporal.

"The huts are spread out to keep down the damage from German bombing raids," the corporal continued in his practiced speech. "Personnel trucks make regular rounds along the perimeter of the field during the day and real early in the morning when there's a mission."

The men were asleep on their feet by now, staring with long-ing at the squat little huts where they knew there would be some kind of beds.

The little corporal gave the men a final thin smile. "Combat personnel are quartered separately from *permanent* personnel. Have a good sleep."

*   *   *

The light flicked on overhead, shocking Courtney out of his first night's sleep at the base. The day before he had dozed fitfully along with the others, had gone to chow, met the sergeants in his crew briefly and groggily, and at last had dropped off into a deep sleep around 10 P.M.

"Briefing at six, men. I'll be waiting outside for you. You got five minutes or you can *walk* to OPS."

The disembodied voice had a strange effect on the men. It only added to the sense of unreality at being in a strange place and awakened in the middle of the night.

Courtney squinted at his watch—04:30 hours. "You awake, Harlan?"

Carrington pulled his head out from under his pillow. "Call me in sick, will you?" he mumbled.

Fumbling at the pile of clothes at the foot of his bunk, Courtney pulled on a pair of silk socks and wool ones over them. He then struggled into some long G.I.s and put on his light cover-alls over this. Next came the bulky flying boots.

Courtney glanced over at the other two officers who shared the hut with him and Carrington. Myron Selig, a small sharp-featured man from Akron, Ohio, was the navigator and Les Sharp, a flat-faced mining engineer from Montana, served as bombardier. Struggling into their new gear, they looked as lost and forlorn as he felt.

After a ten-minute ride in a weapons carrier, they pulled into the Admin Block, a collection of concrete buildings inherited from the RAF. They stumbled over to the latrine and two minutes later down to the officers' mess.

"I wonder what this is all about," Carrington asked anybody within the sound of his voice.

"Beats me," Sharp drawled. "Since we met the rest of the crew and drew our equipment yesterday, nobody's let us know anything. Never *saw* such a close-mouthed bunch!"

Crowding around with the other crews outside the officers' mess, they overheard snatches of conversation about the weather, flak reports, and fuel capacities.

"I'm getting a bad feeling about all this." Carrington's eyes were wide with apprehension. "The things these boys are saying sound a lot like mission talk."

A tall, lanky pilot just ahead of them turned around. His expression was as casual as if he had an early tee time on the golf course. "You think we're all up because we enjoy the early morning fog?" He surveyed the new men briefly. "Listen real good at the briefing. You just might make it back today."

A heady warmth greeted them inside the mess hall. Steam pipes ran around the walls near the ceiling. The smell of strong coffee and frying bacon made them feel a little better as they stared at the mounds of food piled in serving trays on a stainless steel counter. Four men in tee shirts and white aprons stood behind the counter.

A tall man with thin shoulders and a tube of fat circling his waist just above his belt plopped a big spoonful of yellow, waterlogged mush down on Carrington's plate.

"What's this?" Carrington asked, staring at his plate as if the man had dumped a dead rat on it.

The man was already digging his spoon back into the yellow, watery mound. "Scrambled eggs. The powdered kind. Purty, ain't they?"

The next cook, who had the shoulders of a hairless grizzly, served from a heaping pan of bacon. As it spattered onto the plates from his tongs, it looked like strips of greasy rags. Pancakes, toast, and chipped beef completed the morning fare.

"I thought you had *some* taste left even after these months in the army." Courtney sipped the dark, steaming coffee from a heavy white mug while he stared at Carrington and the other two officers in his crew wolfing down their oily breakfasts as though they had been prepared by a French chef. "How can you put that goop inside of you? You'll be sliding out of the cockpit all day."

Pausing with the watery eggs dripping down through the tines of his fork, Carrington mumbled around a mouthful of bacon and pancakes, "Gotta keep my strength up." Then he smiled to himself. "Dear old dad would puke though, if he saw what I've had to eat in the army."

"Hope somebody woke up our radio man and the gunners." Selig chewed mournfully, his eyes staring at the far wall. "I'd like to get to know them a little better as long as we're depending on each other to stay alive up there."

"Give it a break, will you, Selig? At least while I'm eating," Sharp growled behind his flying fork. "That's all you can talk about— staying alive."

After breakfast, Courtney moved toward the oversized Nissen hut where the briefing room was located. Jostling his way through the door and into the building, he found a seat down front near a low platform made of old timbers. A blackboard hung on the wall behind the narrow stage and another board with a black cloth over it hung next to it. Two hundred or so folding chairs stood on the bare concrete floor, arranged in rows facing the stage. A double line of naked hundred-watt bulbs hung from black cords along the length of the ceiling.

Courtney took an aisle seat. Carrington sat next to him with the other flight officers in the next two seats. As the briefing room began to fill up, he took note of the men ambling in and milling about. They looked nothing like the stateside soldiers he was used to seeing.

Officers and sergeants appeared to wear whatever happened to suit their fancy—coveralls or leather jackets. The officers wore either hard caps or leather flying helmets with the earflaps turned up. The gunners had on black wool skullcaps, fatigue caps, or their flying hats. They were altogether a rag-tag, sleepy, elbowing, ill-tempered, mumbling, shuffling mob.

"All right—let's settle down, men." The briefing room's silence was churchlike one second after Colonel Henry Bowman, the Old Man, spoke. He was thirty-five years old and looked fifty. Lean and leathery, his dark eyes sunk deep into his skull, he had the appearance of an off-duty ghoul.

Never one to drag things out, Bowman flicked the cloth off the map board with his pointer. The length of red twine ended just inside the North Sea coast, and turned around for the trip home. Muffled sighs of relief filled the room. It was not going to be a long haul over the interior—over countless anti-aircraft batteries and through droves of 190s and 109s.

Bowman began his explanation of why Emden had been selected as today's target—why it would bolster the Allied cause and crush the Axis powers. What he didn't say was that it had been chosen partially as a milk run because two days before, the strike on Bremen had cost the lives of 129 men. The flyers only cared that the length of red twine was short.

Next on deck was "Dead-Calm" Baker, (no one knew his real first name or if they did, had forgotten it) the weather officer. The name fit his dead-pan expression and calm demeanor. He dearly loved weather, any kind of weather, and his blue eyes grew intense in his chubby face when he spoke about it. "We've got four- to six-tenths stratocumulus at twenty-five hundred to three thousand, tops forty-five hundred, decreasing to nil just off the English coast; five- to seven-tenths altocumulus at eleven to twelve . . ."

The flak officer was up next. After he had expounded on the prospects with his meaningless meager-to-moderate at . . . , moderate at . . . , meager at . . . , regarding the fly-over areas, (everyone but the new crews knew by now that his information had no foundation in the realities they faced in the skies) the briefing ended.

The sergeants shuffled out the door for the armament shop to pick up their machine guns. Navigators, bombardiers, and radiomen clustered in small groups for their special briefings. As the flying control officer was on sick call, the Old Man himself gave the pilots and copilots their order of taxiing and told them where they would be flying in the formation.

Bowman fixed his eyes on Courtney. "Tight formations! That's the secret to long life over here! I know you new men have heard it all before, but you can't hear it too much. The Jerries can spot a new crew on their first circle around—and that's the Fort they'll go for every time."

"I've only got twenty hours high altitude formation flying," the other new pilot in the group explained, in a strained voice. With his fair skin and freckles, he looked about eighteen, even in the rugged overalls and heavy boots. "They told me in the States there wasn't time for any more."

"Normally takes sixty to eighty hours to be a pretty fair high altitude pilot, but nobody gets anywhere near that much training. You're about average." Seeing the fear in the man's eyes, Bowman spoke in the tone a scoutmaster might use. "You'll do fine. Just don't throttle back and forth much and stay in tight."

When Bowman dismissed them, Courtney left the briefing room thinking of the *ten* hours high altitude training he had gotten just before leaving for England.

* * *

The ground fog swirled in the light breeze as the ten-man crew rode in a weapons carrier around the perimeter track of the field. No one spoke. The growl of the engine seemed almost a sacrilege in the still morning, broken occasionally by the distant cry of a homebound owl.

In the hazy half-light Courtney spotted the great dark shape of the 17 he had yet to fly. Although fear twisted at his stomach, the first sight of their ship called up feelings that went to war with the fear—feelings that he had no name for. He knew it couldn't be courage. He had never been able to see any profit in that particular emotion.

"Well, what do you think of her?" Carrington waved his hand toward the 17 as he stepped out of the carrier.

Courtney stared at the ship, barely able to detect *Miss Behavin'* painted on her side beneath the cockpit.

The sergeants hefted their guns down and the crew walked across the hardstand toward their ship. They splashed softly through pools of oily water, their sheen breaking apart like shattered glass, then returning to placid, blue-gray curves on the surface of the pools.

Courtney found the underside hatch handle, opened it, and let the crew scramble in. With Carrington beside him and the sergeants positioning their guns, he went through the preflight. He threw the big ignition switch on the central control panel, checked each battery switch, and turned on the master battery switch. Then he flicked the hydraulic pump switch to automatic.

When the preflight was almost completed, Courtney turned the rest of it over to Carrington and crawled down to the nose of the ship, called the <u>greenhouse</u> by the aircrews, where Sharp sat backwards in his bombing seat in the nose so that he faced Selig at the navigator's table. He could never get used to the strange gray-green light that came through the Plexiglas above and around them. It made the men inside look like characters out of an H.G. Wells novel. "Everything ship-shape down here?" he asked, trying to sound confident.

Selig turned his ever-sad eyes on Courtney. "This is the real thing, isn't it?"

"Naw, Selig," Sharp growled, a tinge of disgust in his voice. "They're just making a movie this morning. John Wayne and Jimmy Stewart will be here any minute to take over for us so we can go on back to bed."

"Stewart really *is* over here!" Selig looked smug with his knowledge that had taken Sharp by surprise.

"Whadda you talking about?"

"He's a pilot just like Courtney here. Stationed on one of the bases around here somewhere."

"Git outta here!"

Courtney took the little man's side. "It's true. I read it in the *Stars and Stripes*. He's flying a Fort. It does seem kinda like a movie when you think about it that way."

"Life *is* a movie!" Selig's voice carried his usual sorrowful assurance. "I keep waiting for the director to yell 'Cut!'"

Courtney was starting to get depressed. He felt he had to get out of the greenhouse or be dragged into some kind of emotional tar pit. "Don't worry. We'll be fine," he smiled behind a wall of self-assurance fragile as a porcelain teacup.

"Sure." Selig mumbled, shuffling through his charts. "And Hitler's going to appoint Albert Einstein as the new commander of the Gestapo."

"I'm telling you the truth," Courtney lied. "I'll keep us in tight to the formation and we won't have a bit of trouble. Like flying a mail drop to Atlantic City."

Selig pored over his charts and Sharp checked the Norden bombsight for the fifth time to make sure it was properly mounted on its platform.

Courtney dropped through the lower hatch, noticing that the gunners had finished their jobs and were squatting at the edge of the hardstands having a smoke. He had been introduced briefly the day before and wanted to go over and give them a pep talk before the mission, but after his session with Sharp and Selig, he couldn't summon up the courage.

Carrington stood under a small elm on the opposite side of the 17, gazing out at the pearl-colored ground fog that hung over the field. "Well, Robin, how goes it with the Merry Men?" he smiled as Courtney walked up.

"Selig's got Sharp in stitches up in the greenhouse," Courtney grunted. "Just one joke after the other."

"The gunners over there look like they'd just as soon be someplace else."

Courtney glanced over at the group of sergeants, huddled together like Neanderthals at the cave mouth. "Can't blame them. They know it's my first mission."

"You're as good as anybody here," Carrington said flatly. "All you got to do is relax and let those magic fingers of yours do the flying for you."

Courtney grinned, pulling a pack of Luckies from his overalls. "Somebody told me they lost a dozen Forts last week—just from this base. Most of 'em new crews."

"I'm trying not to think about things like that right now." Carrington's face seemed to drop. "They say the worst thing we'll face is a bunch called Goering's Abbeville Kids. They're the toughest and most experienced flyers. You can spot 'em easy, because they paint the noses of their ME 109s red and yellow. They keep coming right at you no matter what you hit 'em with." He shivered involuntarily and rubbed his hands together briskly to try and hide it. "Brrrr! Chilly out here!"

Courtney suddenly thought about Arnold Cooper's funeral. He tried to force it from his mind, but the images held fast. *Dry leaves rattled against the tombstones in the little graveyard outside Centreville, Georgia. The dark-haired, pleasant-looking widow sat with her three children, tiny replicas of their father, on folding chairs at the edge of the grave. An American flag hung proudly over the coffin of the man who had served four terms in the Georgia House of Representatives.*

A drab-green pickup wheeled onto the hardstand, the round-faced driver, his ears poking out like tiny catchers' mitts beneath his fatigue cap, leaned out the window. "C'mon! C'mon! I ain't got all day."

"Sweet truck!" one of the sergeants called out as they began ambling over to the truck.

"Gimme a Hershey!"

"Sorry, nothing but O'Henrys today."

"Don't give me that! You're just keeping them all for yourself." The scowling gunner grabbed the edge of the truck window. "You've put on twenty pounds since you got this job!"

"Aw right! Aw right!" The driver reached down to the floorboard, came up with a fistful of Hershey bars, and passed them out the window. Then he handed out the K-rations. "Better come and git it!" he yelled over to Courtney and Carrington.

Courtney walked over to the pick-up. He took four Hersheys and the K rations. "Thanks."

The driver revved his engine, then leaned back out the window. "Oh, Lieutenant! I almost forgot. There's a ninety-minute delay." He sped off toward the next Fort.

Courtney went over and broke the news to Carrington and the men. Then he sat down on a stack of engine tarps at the edge of the hardstand. In spite of all he could do, the memory of Cooper's funeral embedded itself like a driven nail in the forefront of his mind. He kept seeing the three children in their dark little coats, chubby legs dangling over the edges of their chairs.

Thirty minutes later, a Jeep drove deliberately along the perimeter track, turning in at the mouth of the hardstand. As it stopped next to the aircraft, a leathery old sergeant from OPS shouted. "Hey, pilot! You hear me, pilot?"

Courtney stood up. "Yeah! What is it?"

"Mission's scrubbed! Got it? Mission's scrubbed!"

9

THESE PRECIOUS DAYS

*T*he mess hall had been transformed—gaudily. Red, white, and blue bunting hung in great looping curves along the walls and below the ceiling, fastened from steampipe to steampipe. A makeshift bar had been set up with white table cloths laid across the stainless steel serving counter. Stools had been procured from some restaurant or pub in the English countryside. A local band had set up on a hastily constructed platform over against the wall just outside the kitchen door.

"Maybe we should just go on back to the hut." Carrington surveyed the crowd of officers milling about or settling in at the tables. "I feel like an impostor."

Courtney felt alive for the first time in a long while. "Oh, yeah, what are you, a German agent? You're beginning to get strange on me again." He tried to put out of his mind the missions that lay ahead.

"These guys have made more strikes than I can count. Lost buddies right and left." Carrington looked at the flyers as they drank, laughed and smoked. "What have *we* done? One scrubbed mission. We're not even on the board."

"Give it a rest. The women are gonna be here in a minute or two." Courtney listened to the band, six locals in formal dress who looked like happy morticians or depressed comedians. "Smile, will you? Have some fun!"

From outside the building, Courtney heard the rumble of engines and the grinding of brakes above the cacophony of the band tuning their instruments. A fleet of RAF buses and vans from Cambridge began pulling into the parking area.

The first thing that caught Courtney's eye were the smooth legs of the women in their skirts as they thronged into the room. It was such an unusual sensation after weeks of nothing but khakis and overalls and heavy flight boots. There were a few WAAF uniforms among the crowd of young women from the homes of merchants and farmers and professional men. But even those female representatives of the Royal Air Force wore skirts. Skirts and dresses and lipstick—and the intoxicating smell of perfume and powder.

Carrington perked up immediately, the clouds vanishing from his face. "Look how many there are!"

It occurred to Courtney that many of the girls had dates with the 129 men who were lost to the strike on Bremen. He pushed the memory to the back of his mind as he surveyed the women with a practiced eye. "I'm sure you want to stay faithful to Renee of the many love letters, so I'll just keep these English lovelies away from you tonight. You'd only hate yourself in the morning."

Carrington thought briefly of his college sweetheart back home. "Renee? Do I know someone named Renee?"

Courtney stared at a willowy girl in a sea-colored dress with a mink coat draped about her arm. She went straight to the bar, ordered a vodka poured over ice, and drank it in three swallows. When she turned toward him, her blonde hair swirled about her shoulders like a shimmering cloud as it caught the amber lights of the bar.

The band began to play "Blue Moon" and the flyers moved among the women, leading them out onto the dance floor before they could find seats at the tables. Courtney found himself dancing with a short blonde whose fluffy ringlets and childlike voice made him think of Shirley Temple. Having almost forgotten anything but the world of men—a world of gruff voices, beards, and short bristly hair—he lost himself in woman softness and woman smell. This stranger had become for him all women as he held her close, moving smoothly to the music.

The song ended with a flourish. Courtney gazed down at the small, upturned face. "Hi. I'm Mark Courtney. How about something to drink?"

"Frances Patmore. You can call me Fran," she replied in her small voice. "A sherry, if you please."

"I please," Courtney smiled. He led her over to their table and seated her. Carrington was nowhere in sight. After pushing his way to the bar, he returned with a scotch and water and a wine glass of sherry.

"Lovely place you have here." Fran glanced about the officers' mess with its frumpy decorations.

"Well, it's not much, but it's home," Courtney said with the air of a down-home country boy.

"I love the way you Yanks talk," Fran confessed brightly. "Especially the Southern boys."

"Well, you're just gonna love the dickens out of me, Frannie." Courtney laid it on thick. "'Cause I'm as Southern as fried chicken for Sunday dinner."

Fran giggled and sipped her drink. The band broke into a controlled and sterile rendition of "Little Brown Jug." Across the sea of Army Air Corps green and swirling pastels, Courtney saw the willowy girl with shimmering blonde hair heading toward their table on Carrington's arm.

"Diana Marlowe, this is Mark Courtney and—friend." Carrington held Diana around the waist like a Saxon warrior holding a tavern wench.

He's really playing this red-blooded American soldier role to the hilt. "A pleasure," Courtney nodded, taking Diana's hand. It was slim and pale and soft, and it sent a tingling up his arm and down the back of his spine.

After the introductions were made, Courtney returned to the bar, managed to yell loud enough to get two more drinks, and shoved his way back to the table.

Diana felt a lingering warmth where Courtney's hand had held hers. She glanced at his slate-gray eyes and disarming smile as he placed the drinks on the table. Desire began inside her like soft music. It moved in a slow, enticing dance as she watched the way he moved, listened to the slow, smooth vowels of his speech. Surprised, she fought against it. She thought feelings like this had died when a solitary Spitfire had disappeared into the murky depths of the Channel. *Not again! Never, never again!* "Let's dance, Harlan." She grabbed his arm, pulling him onto the floor.

Courtney watched Carrington and Diana move about the crowded dance floor as the band played "Moonglow." *Not as good as Ellington or Goodman could play it, but not too bad.* He glanced at Fran who was moving in her chair in time with the music, then back at Diana. *I thought she kind of went for me at first. Must be slipping. Sure haven't had much practice with the ladies these last few months.*

"How about a dance, Yank?" Fran had a pouty expression on her face, making her look even more like Shirley Temple. "You losing interest in me already?"

"Never," Courtney beamed. "How could I lose interest in the prettiest girl here?" He took her hand and led her onto the floor, his eyes dazzled by the soft lights glistening in Diana's hair.

The hours passed to the increasingly languid sound of the band, the jostling and pressing together of bodies on the dance floor and three fist fights. Courtney and Diana sat together, watching Carrington and Fran jitterbug to the band's tired version of "In the Mood."

"I do so like to watch the young people having fun," Courtney quipped.

"How do they still have the energy to dance?" Diana's sleepy eyes turned toward Courtney. Through the fog caused by alcohol and weariness, she thought he looked almost like Dale, then the resemblance disappeared and he became himself with those soft-hard gray eyes and auburn hair that was just getting long enough on top to have a slight wave.

Courtney gazed back at Diana. *If she'd leave the booze alone, she could be a real looker. She's had some rough times, all right. You don't get circles under your eyes like that overnight. Still—she's got class. Probably comes from old money. Maybe even a touch of British nobility there somewhere.* "How'd you get here tonight? You don't look the type to hitch a ride on an RAF bus."

Diana suppressed a yawn. "Quite simple really. I drove into town after lunch. Just dilly-dallying about, shopping, one thing or the other. Happened to see the girls lined up for the buses. As a lark, I just climbed aboard—and here I am."

"Your folks have a house around here?"

"Yes."

Might be a chance here to make life a little easier. "I'm certainly glad you came." The band began to play "September Song" as the singer caressed the lyrics with a rich baritone. "This is the last number. May I have this dance?" Courtney stood up and held out his arms toward Diana.

"Yes, you may." Diana moved into his arms for the first time that night. Their eyes met for what seemed a long time. Then his arm circled her waist, guiding her smoothly about the floor. She felt his lean, hard body pressing against her, smelled the sharp scent of his aftershave, and the warmth of him seemed to burn inside her. Suddenly she saw Dale's face for just an instant—then she was lost in the warmth and the movement and the music.

One hasn't got time for the waiting game.

* * *

The Fort climbed in a slow, easy spiral as the fields below turned into a giant quilt and the houses and barns became a child's toys and then merely specks against the pattern of the quilt. Higher still, the earth, through the breaks in the rounded gray clouds, was a soft and hazy blue. Far above, other clouds were dazzling white against the hard blue sky and shot through with silver where the sun struck them.

"Oxygen check!" Courtney had a mild case of the shakes, but controlled his voice skillfully.

"Check in," Carrington sounded. "One."

"OK." Selig responded.

"Two."

"Yep," barked Sharp.

The check completed, Courtney spoke evenly into the intercom. "Pilot to crew—Pilot to crew. We're on our way to Emden, boys. Remember, it's not too far inland so we shouldn't get too much ack-ack."

The Fort leveled off and Courtney eased it into his slot in the formation. Soon they left England behind and headed out over the North Sea.

"Pilot to crew. Be ready for fighter attacks about half-way across the North Sea. This is your first mission so keep your eyes open. Don't let 'em surprise us. We'll be fine as long as they don't get in close on us."

Carrington looked all around him. As far as he could tell, Courtney was holding as tight in the formation as any of the other pilots. He looked over at him and gave the thumbs up sign. Courtney nodded back.

After going through another oxygen check, Carrington was able to relax a little. *He's flying as good as anybody—maybe better. A natural-born flyer.* He watched with more than casual interest as Courtney adjusted the trim through a button on the automatic pilot with a delicate touch that was in direct contrast to the tremendous strength of the cables and the mass of the airplane.

Carrington thought back to the dance at the officer's club, remembering Courtney and Diana on the dance floor as the band played the last bars of "September Song." As he watched Courtney flying the Fort, he thought, *He handles her like he handles a woman on the dance floor.*

Hour after hour, they droned on toward Germany. Courtney was staring down at the hammered pewter surface of the North Sea when it happened. The number three engine began to vibrate too much and then started slowing down. Thin gray smoke trailed from under the cowling.

"Pilot to Copilot."

"Go ahead."

"Looks like the fuel pump or magneto's out on number three. She's finished for today. Feather her."

"Roger."

The propeller slowed down, then ceased to spin altogether. Courtney tried to keep up, but gradually the formation pulled away from him. He knew it would be suicide to continue. The German pilots always picked out the stragglers because they were virtually defenseless without the security of the formation where a wall of machine gun fire could be thrown at any attackers.

"Pilot to crew. We're heading for home." Courtney pulled out of formation and began the long flight back across the North Sea. *If I can get enough aborts, maybe I can manage to get a staff job before I have to tackle any of the tough missions.*

Carrington felt relief that they were heading back, but frustration that they got no credit for the mission. *Still twenty-five to go!* "Copilot to crew. It's a long way back. Don't go to sleep on me. And watch out for enemy fighters!"

After hours of boredom and cold and the strain of being alone in an ocean of air filled with swastikaed birds of prey, the Fort slipped through a low ceiling of clouds above the hedgerows and farmhouses of East Anglica. For Courtney, the most beautiful sight was black streaks of burned rubber from the tires of other 17s who had set down at the end of the long concrete runway. He touched down gently and taxied along to the thumping of the tail wheel. A Jeep with *Follow Me* painted in big yellow letters on a high black board led them over to the dispersal point.

Courtney opened a hatch and climbed out into the chill damp air of England. A slow, heavy rain began to fall. The trees around the perimeter of the field glistened dully in the lead-colored light that barely filtered through the clouds. The crew stood under the wings of the Fort, waiting for a ride back to OPS.

The long flight back had been uneventful except for the battle taking place in Courtney's mind. When the smoke cleared, he had developed a plan.

I can always find a reason to abort. So many things can go wrong. Engine trouble, hydraulics, cables, oxygen system. But I can't do it every time. Only when that red twine stretches out a long way into the interior of the continent—only when the targets are critical and the flak and fighter defenses are the worst. I can fly the milk runs—manage to get a position somewhere inside the formation, fly tight, stay off the edges. Work on a position with headquarters staff while I'm still on flying status. Yes sir, Mark, ol' boy, you're gonna make it just fine.

Courtney decided to try out the preliminary phase of his plan at once. *If this goes well, everything else should fall into place.* "What did you think about our first mission?"

Carrington squatted on the tarmac, leaning back against one of the big tires of the Fort. "I think it was great! We didn't have to fly it."

"My sentiments exactly." Courtney squatted down next to Carrington, speaking in a hushed voice so that Selig and Sharp couldn't hear him. He could hear the bull session going on with gunners on the opposite side of the Fort. "Maybe if we're lucky, we'll have a *lot* of problems."

Carrington looked puzzled, then his eyebrows lifted slightly as the import of Courtney's words hit him. "What kind of problems are you talking about?"

Courtney's gray eyes glinted slatelike in the failing light. "Did you know that if you throw one of those Fortress's engines into an extra-rich carburetor position, it starts smoking like its about to catch on fire?"

Carrington looked out into the gray curtain of rain that was turning everything but concrete and tarmac into a sea of mud. His profile was clean and sharp against the dark treeline. When he looked back, the decision had been made. "You're the aircraft commander. What you say goes."

*   *   *

"Diana's told us a lot about you, my boy." James Marlowe sat in a tall wing-backed chair across from his wife, his long legs crossed, as he held a cup of tea in his thin hand.

"I hope it was all good, sir." Having found out that Diana's father was *Sir* James Marlowe, dubbed a knight of the realm, Courtney was dressed to the nines in his best uniform and gleaming shoes. Never one to miss an opportunity, he felt that Marlowe's connections could prove useful to him.

"What there was of it. Diana's not given to lengthy conversation these days. I understand you're a member of Georgia's parliament."

Courtney smiled. "Not exactly. I'm—I *was* a state representative. If things go well, I plan to return to public service after the war."

"Admirable of you. I had a go at it myself, but this blasted hip of mine put me out of commission in a fortnight's time. Couldn't take the rigors of all that travel." Marlowe gazed at the crackling flames in the fireplace. "Take some good advice, my boy. Make a place for yourself in this world before you get too old."

"I intend to, sir."

Marlowe abruptly changed the subject. "What do you think of our daughter?"

Courtney expected the question. "I think she's a splendid girl, actually." *How's that for a touch of the Brit, Marlowe?* "Well bred, obviously. And if you don't mind my saying so, sir, absolutely beautiful."

Marlowe watched the flames again, the muscles along his jaw line working under the slightly overlapping skin. "She's had a bit of a problem these last two years."

"I hadn't noticed," Courtney lied. *It's obvious she has a problem. Nobody drinks like that without something gnawing at their insides.*

"She's been staying in London a great deal lately—we keep a small apartment there. But her mother managed to persuade her to come visit with us for a few weeks." The firelight flickered in Marlowe's eyes as he stared at the dancing flames. "She looks much better now. Put some of her weight back on. Beginning to get her health back."

"Why—what's the matter?" Courtney liked Diana, but the question was purely academic.

Marlowe explained how his daughter had lost the only man she had ever loved. "Her mother and I were hoping she'd come out of it with time, but she just doesn't seem to care anymore." Marlowe turned his sorrowful eyes on Courtney.

Well, here it comes. "What a dreadful loss for her to have to endure!"

"Diana seems awfully—fond of you, my boy. You do seem rather a gentleman." Marlowe recrossed his legs, groaning slightly. "This bloody English weather! I need a year on the Mediterranean. We—that is, Doreen and I thought you might take an interest in her. You understand. Spend some time with her. Keep her from thinking so much about the past."

"Why, that would be a great pleasure for me, sir. Can't think of anything I'd rather do. But . . ." Courtney frowned, looking down at his feet."

"What's the problem?"

"Well, with all these missions, I just won't have much free time. It's not exactly an eight-to-five job."

Marlowe rubbed his left ear between his thumb and forefinger. "Quite so. Silly of me to miss the obvious. Comes with age, I suppose. I do have some friends in the RAF. And since they work closely with you chaps, perhaps we—all of us being Allies—could somehow arrange for you to have a few stand-downs now and again. Perhaps a bit of liaison duty between the bases. All proper and above board, of course."

Courtney's mouth smiled, but the mica glint in the eyes remained fixed. "Of course."

*　　*　　*

Diana stood in one of the few places that still seemed real to her, in a world turning more and more into a kind of misty, spectral realm of darkness and nightmares and blurry strangers. From the high balcony, she gazed down at the peaceful slow curve of the

Thames, glistening in the moonlight like a silver necklace laid down across the city.

"Penny for your thoughts." Courtney stepped out onto the balcony in his sock feet. He wore only his trousers and unbuttoned jacket. Sipping on a glass of ice and water, flavored with scotch, he lay his hand on Diana's shoulder.

"They aren't *worth* a penny."

Courtney squeezed her. "C'mon now, that's no way to act. What happened to the life of the party?"

Diana glanced over her shoulder at him. Her eyes were dull and puffy. "She's sobering up."

Maybe it's not worth it, putting up with this lush just to get out of a few missions. I might have to start working on another plan. "Want me to get you a drink?"

Taking the drink abruptly from his hand, Diana drank half of it down. "Ugh! How awful! This is nothing but *water*." A spark of anger flickered in her eyes. "Is that what you've been drinking all this time?"

"Anything wrong with that?"

"No wonder you always seemed so—in control of yourself." Diana was confused. Her thoughts were scattering like leaves before the wind. Something *was* wrong here, but it seemed so silly to fault someone for *not* drinking. Suddenly it hit her. "Control! That's it, isn't it? You always have to be in *control*! In control of yourself— *and* everyone around you."

Courtney looked at Diana with a condescending smile. "What's wrong with *that*?"

Diana trembled slightly and looked away. "Control and manipulation. That's why you've been so nice to me and my parents. I know Daddy's helped you out somehow through his friends in the RAF. You don't care about me at all. You only care about yourself and what you can get out of people."

Her brain isn't as soaked as I thought it was. As the thought formed in Courtney's mind, he felt behind it a pang of regret, of remorse—a slight flickering of something, long buried, he had forgotten was ever a part of him. It troubled him. *Maybe I do care for her. No—it's not worth it!* "How can anyone care about you? You won't let them get close enough. So you lost Dale! Thousands die every day in this war! You think everybody who loses someone close to them should crawl into a bottle?"

Diana turned back toward him. A tear glistened like a tiny clear pearl as it slipped down her face. "No."

Her voice was so soft Courtney barely heard her. He reached out and took her hand in his. The touch of it gave him that same warm tingling as the night he met her at the base dance—and it bothered him that this was something about himself that he *couldn't* control. "Maybe we could help each other get through these times. For a while, anyway."

Diana held onto his hand. She knew he was the kind of man who could love only himself. They had crossed her path before and she had always avoided them. Now it just didn't seem to matter anymore. "What a pair we make! You want everything in the world—and I don't want any part of it."

Courtney realized that for the first time in his life someone knew him for exactly what he was—maybe better than he knew himself. He put his arm around Diana's shoulder again and pulled her close. But this time he did it because he knew she needed someone to hold her and it was a strange sensation for him that he could still do such a thing.

10

THE OUTCAST

What's this all about?" As usual, Sharp knew absolutely nothing about what was going on. He always stumbled into the briefing room asking the same question.

Selig, the perpetual disseminator of news, answered in his emotionless tone. "We're getting a new group commander. Wing feels that Henry—"

"Henry?" Sharp interrupted. "Since when do you call Colonel Bowman 'Henry'?"

"Since he's not in the room," Selig said blandly. "Now, if you'll allow me to continue . . ."

"Go ahead," Sharp growled.

"As I was saying, Wing feels that," Selig nodded at Sharp, "*Colonel Bowman* isn't living up to their expectations. He's not producing the percentages that they feel are necessary to bring the war to a swift conclusion."

"What kind of percentages do they want?" Selig felt uncomfortable away from his Norden bombsight where the numbers always did what they were supposed to.

Selig glanced over at Bowman, who was talking to a tall, dark-haired lieutenant colonel. "I believe the figure they mentioned was one hundred percent casualties for each mission," he said offhandedly. "Not all dead, mind you. Wounded count too."

Sharp's eyes grew round as he tried to speak. "Wha—what do you mean, *one hundred percent casualties*? You've got to be kidding!"

"Yes, Sharp, I'm kidding," Selig said conversationally, after the mandatory pause to let his words take effect. "Better sit down. I think we're about to begin."

Courtney sat in his usual aisle seat with Carrington between him and Selig. He listened with amusement as Selig baited Sharp, who always took the hook. Since he had invented the little game of torturing Sharp with outlandish information, Selig had become the picture of contentment.

Sharp now stood above the little man, red-faced. "Are you crazy? Making up things like! If you weren't such a dried-up little shrimp—why I'd—"

"Sit down, Lieutenant!" Bowman had appeared on the platform, his dark eyes burning a hole into Sharp's face.

"Yes, sir!" Sharp muttered, slamming down into his seat.

"All right—let's get settled down, men!" Bowman began every briefing with exactly the same words. Several times the flyers had deliberately seated themselves in complete silence before his arrival. As he stepped before his men, all rigid and as quiet as statues in their folding chairs, he opened the briefing.

Bowman paused his usual five seconds before continuing. "Today my part of the briefing will be mercifully short for you. It will also be my last."

A murmuring ran through the crowded room as the flyers that hadn't heard the news expressed mild surprise.

Sharp turned to Selig. "Well, you got part of it right. Bowman's pulling out."

Selig smiled with satisfaction. He always injected some truth into the game to keep Sharp nibbling at the bait.

"I'm being kicked upstairs." Bowman tried to smile, but couldn't pull it off. Everyone in the room knew that it meant he couldn't handle the job the way Wing wanted it. He would be given a pointer, which he wouldn't use, and a desk to prop his feet on—which he *would* use a great deal. "It's my privilege to introduce your new group commander, Colonel Zack Kane." Bowman shook hands with Kane and stepped forever out of the lives of the men in the 271st Bombardment Group.

The man who stepped up onto the platform next to Bowman had a chiseled face and a slightly hawklike nose. His hair was black as a crow's wing and his bushy black brows shaded eyes so dark they looked as if they had no pupils. He stood well over six feet with wide shoulders and lean hips.

Selig cursed under his breath, whispering to Carrington out of the side of his mouth. "Not him!"

"Him who?" Carrington whispered back.

"'Killer' Kane! He's out to win this war all by himself—and he'll kill us all to do it!"

Carrington knew this was not a part of Selig's game. The little man's face was twisted with fear. Carrington turned and broke the news to Courtney.

Courtney smiled knowingly back at Carrington. "Aw, c'mon. He can't be *that* bad."

"The 271st has *two* things wrong with it," Kane began. "*Cowards* and *crybabies!*"

Carrington barely turned his head toward Courtney, whispering, "He *can* be that bad!"

Selig began to mumble a Jewish prayer for the dead. Sharp missed what was said and started asking everyone around him when he saw their faces drop. A black cloud settled over the men of the 271st.

"Not all of you," Kane continued, his eyes burning with an intense light. "Not all of you by a long shot!"

The flyers sat erect, hanging on every word Kane said, unlike their half-dozing postures during a Bowman briefing.

"Some of you have exemplary records. Good as any I've seen." Kane began pacing back and forth on the stage, never taking his eyes off his audience. "But it only takes a few slackers to ruin things for those of you who *are* doing the best you can at a job none of us finds particularly enjoyable."

Courtney felt an uneasy prickling sensation at the base of his neck. His PAD (Plan to Avert Death) had been working better than even *he* could have imagined. Not only had he become an expert at orchestrating aircraft problems, but Diana's father had proven invaluable in arranging stand-downs for him. And the "liaison" job meant *more* days off.

As he watched the dark, scowling Kane pacing back and forth, Courtney was reminded of a panther he had once seen in the zoo at Atlanta when he was a child. He remembered thinking then how the great cat so desperately wanted to get at him. Now, as he half-listened to the rumbling voice coming from the platform, the thought suddenly occurred to him that there were no bars between him and Kane.

"It's been my experience—and it's considerable, I can assure you—that the pilot sets the tone for the whole crew. If he's doing his job, then chances are the rest of the men are doing theirs." Kane stopped in the center of the stage, gazing out at his new flyers like a wolf at spring lambs. "I've got every pilot's personnel file on my desk right now."

Courtney began to squirm uneasily in his chair. His throat seemed constricted and he coughed to clear it. Carrington gave him a guilty look.

"However—I have yet to look at any of them!" Kane let his words sink in. "As far as I'm concerned, what you did under Colonel Bowman is history. What you do from now on is what counts with me! Do your jobs and the files will be opened only to put your commendations in them."

A few barely audible sighs of relief escaped several pilots scattered about the room.

"Let me refresh your memories on one thing. In order to get credit for a mission, the formation must do one of three things: fly the mission full course and drop on the target; drop on an alternate target; or engage the enemy in combat—and that doesn't include spotting a burst or two of flak. Briefing tomorrow at oh-five-hundred-hours."

Kane walked abruptly off the platform. The men of the 271st stared blankly at each other as if they had all just had the same hallucination.

Finally, Sharp said in his Montana drawl, "I think this Colonel Crane's gonna be all right." Sharp was greeted with a few catcalls, boos, and groans as the flyers got to their feet with chairs scraping on the concrete floor. They shuffled woodenly out of the briefing room, lighting cigarettes, rubbing their faces—most speaking in hushed tones about the fate of their group.

"Kane," Selig said flatly as he folded his notebook and stuffed it inside his coveralls.

Sharp frowned at him. "Cane? What's that supposed to mean?"

"It's the new commander's name." Selig threaded his way through the disordered chairs toward the door.

"I know that." Sharp tagged along behind Selig like Brer Bear after Brer Fox. "Why do you keep telling me things I already know? If it wasn't for me, that big gunner from the 504th would have busted your face at the . . . ," he trailed off as they crowded out the door.

"Well, what do you think about our new commander?" Carrington slouched along next to Courtney as they left the briefing room and headed down the walkway toward the kitchen.

Courtney stared at the rain running off the metal awning that covered the walkway. It spattered with a musical sound into the shallow pools of water, collecting along the edge of the concrete. "I think he makes Mussolini look like a cloistered nun." He glanced at Carrington. "How about you?"

"I think all the problems with the *Miss Behavin'* have already been repaired. I *don't* think we'll have to abort anymore. That's what *I* think." Carrington knew that the pliable Bowman philosophy of waging war had been supplanted with one as fixed and uncompromising as a burst of flak.

*   *   *

"Stuttgart! Another ball bearing plant. The only thing worse than that is Schweinfurt! I'd like to disembowel the man who invented the ball bearing!" Carrington sat next to Courtney in the *Daddy's Girl*, finishing the preflight check.

"You've told me that *four* times since the briefing." Courtney pored over his charts, still unable to comprehend the great distance they would have to fly over Germany's heartland. "While you're in a homicidal rage, direct some of it at Kane, will you? He's the one responsible for these impossible missions and—to make things worse, he put us in the low group today."

Two hours later they were droning over the English Channel toward France, where their course would take them across the country and into Germany.

"Navigator to crew—Navigator to crew! Enemy coast five minutes away."

"Pilot to crew! Watch out for enemy fighters!" Courtney had managed so far to abort or fly milk runs. He had never flown his crew on a mission like this before—one where they would face intense fighter opposition and heavy flak over the target. He remembered Kane's words from the briefing that morning, "Remember men, you're in the big leagues now. You're hitting 'em on their home ground—right in the heart of the Fatherland. Let's show 'em what American fighting men can do!"

As Courtney watched the French coast slip by beneath him, he felt fear grip his insides like an iron hand. His breathing became labored and he broke out in a sweat in spite of the subfreezing temperatures of the 20,000 foot altitude. He glanced to his left at the flight of P-47s escorting them. Soon they would be at the end of their fuel range.

"Bombardier to crew! Bombardier to crew! Fighters at twelve o'clock low." Sharp's voice was crackling over the radio. "Can't make out what they are, but they sure don't look like ours."

Courtney looked down through the thin traces of cloud. "109s! At least a dozen of them! And that's just the ones I can see from here. Give me a report on bogies. Tail!"

"Tail here. I see about twenty more eight o'clock low."

"Right waist!"

"Too many to count. Must be forty or fifty at twelve o'clock low."

"Turret!"

"Turret clear!"

The German pilots waited patiently for the Thunderbolts to turn back. In a few minutes, they reached their fuel limits, dipped their wings in farewell and banked off toward the north. The Messerschmitts immediately pulled up to the altitude of the formation of Forts and began circling, looking for the most vulnerable positions to attack.

"Pilot to crew! I want the air full of lead if those fighters come in!"

"Copilot to Turret."

"Go ahead."

"Three fighters at five o'clock high. Keep your eye on 'em. I'll watch high and forward.

"Pilot to Tail. Anything back there?"

"No. Clear below and behind now."

"Keep a close watch." Courtney barely had the words out when directly in front of him, a 109 appeared as if by magic. He bore straight in, lights flashing from his wings as he hurled a deadly barrage of 20mm cannon shells and 30 caliber machine gun bullets at the Fort. "Fighter twelve o'clock level! Get him—get him—get him!"

The crew, never before tested in battle, froze. The Fort quivered as the fighter's projectiles slammed into it. Turning his belly over as he reached the heavily armed bomber, the 109 slipped over into a perfect barrel roll and dived out of range of the formation. Neither Sharp, Selig, nor the turret gunner—the only three who could have defended their aircraft—had fired a single shot at the enemy fighter.

Immobilized by fear for a split second, Courtney exploded into the intercom, a stream of profanity pouring over the crew, especially the three who had the fighter in their sights without firing a shot. Drained by the near disaster and the outburst of emotion, Courtney tried to speak in a calm, controlled voice. "We were lucky . . . very lucky that we weren't blown out of the sky that time. I'd consider it a personal favor if all of you would point your guns at any enemy aircraft that come within range and press your triggers until those fighters are no longer in the air." Courtney had seen understatement work in the past when threats and curses fell on deaf ears. He hoped it would this time.

After a few more runs, the fighters pulled away. The formation droned on toward the target in tight formation, their lethal payloads sure to attract more resistance.

"Pilot to crew. Don't waste ammo. We've got a long way to go. When a fighter quits firing, leave him alone. Hit the ones that are coming in. They're the ones that do the damage. Hit the ones coming at us—ruin their aim!"

"Ball to crew—Ball to crew! Fighters at four o'clock low. A whole flock of 'em!"

They were close to Stuttgart now and the Germans fought with the desperation of men fighting to defend their homes. Rushing up to intercept the Forts, they swarmed over the low group like hornets. The German pilots had abandoned their usual cautious tactics and attacked from all directions. They gave no thought for personal safety in their burning drive to teach the Americans a lesson in disaster.

A bright glow caught Courtney's attention. He glanced down and to his left in horror. A 17 had burst into flames. Long streams of fire swept back past the tail. *Jump! Jump! Get out of there!* He kept waiting for even one chute to blossom, but none did. The great aircraft hurtled over and over, trailing smoke and fire on its way to the earth.

Wham! The *Daddy's Girl* shuddered as a burst of orange flame and roiling black smoke exploded next to it. Shrapnel spanged against the metal skin of the ship, some of it slicing through in jagged holes. Huge puffs of black smoke began bursting all around the formation, the hot shards of metal ripping at the Fort with every close burst, probing for flesh.

"Bombardier to Pilot."

"Go ahead."

"We're on the bomb run."

Courtney cringed in the knowledge of what that meant. He had to fly straight and level to provide a stable platform for the bombardier and his Norden bombsight. All around him, the 17s held to their courses.

An explosion ripped the right wing off a plane next to the *Daddy's Girl*. It tumbled over and over down miles of air toward the earth. Courtney held true to the course. On the right, another Fort took a blistering hail of machine gun and cannon fire from three fighters. It went into that shallow circling descent that was peculiar to a 17 when its controls are gone. The engines sent twisting columns of smoke spiraling upward from the doomed ship. Again, Courtney saw no chutes.

Suddenly, pieces of wings, tails, and fuselages rained down from one of the higher groups that was being torn apart by the fighters. Courtney glimpsed one ship going down. The fuselage had torn off next to the trailing edge of the wing. All four engines were still running as the ship turned round and round like a piece of paper falling in still air.

The black clouds thinned and disappeared altogether. Then the fighters hit them again! More than before, now that they were close to the target. An FW-190, the leading edge of its wings winking death, screamed past the left wing of the Fort, its heavy fifty-caliber slugs slamming into the fuselage to the right of the waist gunner's position. A burst of cannon fire from another 190 shattered part of the Plexiglas shield near Carrington. Wind howled through the cockpit.

That was when Courtney lost it!

The mission, the bomb run, Kane—everything was swept away as the blood-driven, bone-deep instinct for survival seized him. Taking control of the aircraft from the Bombardier, he launched into heavy evasive action. As more fighters roared in for the kill, he threw the ship up and down and from side to side in tremendous, buffeting lunges.

"Stay on the bomb run!" Sharp roared on the intercom. "Pilot—I need to control the aircraft!"

Courtney continued the evasive action as the 109s and 190s swarmed about them. Then they were gone. He released control back to the Bombardier.

"Too late! A wasted trip this time!" Sharp snapped into the intercom. "Might as well dump 'em. Bombs away!" The ship lurched upward as the bombs fell away two miles south of the target.

"Radio to Bombardier!

"Go ahead."

"One bomb's hung up in the bomb bay! I'm going back to release it."

"All that jumping and banging around!" Sharp took a verbal shot at Courtney for making the whole trip useless. "Hang on! You stay where you are. We need your covering fire up there. I'll get it loose."

"Roger, Bombardier."

Sharp grabbed his portable oxygen bottle and took a long screwdriver with him to trip the shackle that held the bomb in place. Struggling back through the narrow passage to the bomb bay, he found himself breathing heavily. The bottle was good for four minutes—with no exertion.

When Sharp reached the bomb bay, he studied the ten-inch wide catwalk that ran between the rear cockpit door and the radio room, and alongside the bomb racks. The sub-zero wind howled through the open bay doors, flattening Sharp's flight suit against his body. Five miles below him, somewhere on the other side of the white billowing clouds, lay German soil.

Sharp took a deep breath and moved four cautious steps out onto the open catwalk. His head spun slightly and his vision blurred. *Just cut it loose and get outta here!* He leaned over, tripped the shackle, and watched the bomb drop off into space, getting smaller and smaller until it disappeared into a cloud top.

What a beautiful view! I could watch this all day. Sharp realized there was something wrong with his just standing there, looking down at the sunlight turning the clouds into cotton and silver. As he turned to leave, the entire bomb bay suddenly rose up and away from him, becoming smaller and smaller until he saw, as if through a swirling fog, the entire underside of the huge aircraft leaving him behind, rising farther and farther above him until it disappeared into the white clouds.

They left me! Wait'll I get back to the base. That little shrimp, Selig! I'll bet he's behind this! Sharp felt the darkness closing in over him. He got one last glimpse of the billowing clouds. Then he saw an unbearably bright explosion of white light.

"Navigator to Pilot."

"Go ahead."

"Sharp's not back yet."

"Better go check on him."

"Will do."

The diminutive Selig had no trouble making his way back to the bomb bay. *That big lummox! I should have known better than to let him go back there by himself. How would he ever get along without me?*

*   *   *

Courtney stood nervously outside Kane's office. The pewter-colored light of yet another dreary English day filtered through the narrow window at the end of the long hall of the headquarters building.

"Come in!" The rumbling voice seemed to slam through the heavy door.

Courtney straightened the tie to his dress uniform, took a deep breath, and went in. Stopping exactly one pace in front of Kane's desk, he snapped to attention and saluted. "Lieutenant Courtney, reporting as ordered, sir!"

Kane ignored the traditional, *At ease*, command, continuing to initial a stack of forms on his desk. Courtney remained straight as a tin soldier while Kane read, initialed, and shuffled through the papers. Courtney's arm ached as he held it rigidly bent at the proper angle, the fingers of his right hand extended with the tip of his right forefinger touching the shiny bill of his hard cap.

In a few minutes, Kane glanced up from his work. "Well, don't you look spiffy?"

"Thank you, sir." Courtney felt rubbery in the knees as he faced Kane. It was the first time in his life that he had come against someone who was totally unaffected by his attempts to manipulate him.

After shoving the stack of papers aside, Kane picked up a file from his desk. "I've finally gotten to read a personnel file, Lieutenant. *Yours.* The first one." Kane paused and smiled coldly at Courtney. "Aren't you honored?"

Courtney remained fixed in the reporting position. "Yes, sir— I m-mean, no, sir!"

"This file is like a mirror of what I see standing before me right now." Kane's mouth still smiled, but his eyes held the threat of storm clouds.

Courtney started to speak, and for the first time since he could remember, he could think of absolutely nothing to say. Without words he was totally helpless. He felt his lower lip begin to quiver and clamped his mouth tightly to control it. *Get ahold of yourself! He's just another man!* But even as he forced the thoughts into his mind, Courtney knew that Kane was like no other man he had known before.

Kane held the file balanced on his right hand as if he were a waiter serving hors d'oeuvres. He pointed to it with the forefinger of his left hand. "Well—aren't you interested in the tale the mirror has to tell?"

"Yes, sir." Courtney tried to use his press conference voice, but it came out sounding like Andy Hardy asking his father for the car keys.

"On the surface, this looks good—*pretty* almost," Kane said icily, tapping the file with a hard finger. "But if you look a little closer—look behind the facade of pretty words—there's no substance. It's like one of those Hollywood movie sets. You think you're looking at a castle, but it's only paint and papier-mâché propped up with some wobbly two-by-fours."

Courtney felt hollow and cold—drained by a fear that latched onto him like a living thing. He felt sweat trickling from his armpits down along his rib cage. *He's got me! And there's not a thing in the world I can do about it!* Courtney felt utterly without hope. Suddenly, an image flashed unbidden into his mind. *Arnold Cooper's three children sat next to their mother, chubby legs dangling off their chairs, staring at their father's casket as it rested above the grave directly in front of them.*

Kane's face lost all expression as his eyes burned into Courtney. "I'm knocking the props out from under you, Lieutenant! No more stand downs. No more *special* duty. *And* no more of the joy of your young life—aborts. The next time you do abort, I'll judge whether it was warranted or not. If it isn't, I'll see you court-martialed—that is, if I can't have you *shot* for desertion under fire!

"You made it impossible for your bombardier to drop on target. That means you risked the lives of your whole crew on that mission for *nothing!*" Kane lowered his voice, but it remained hard as granite. "And—through your deliberate actions, you created the problem that cost a good man his life."

Courtney felt as though he was slipping into a bottomless black pit from which there was no return.

"I can see you're pleased about all this attention I'm giving you. No need to thank me though. You deserve it. You're a *special* man. And since you are, I've made some very *special* arrangements for you." Kane paused briefly, then his flat hard voice cut the heavy silence of the room. "You'll be getting some replacements in your crew—whenever I happen to come across a man who is as cowardly or as worthless as you are. Either one will qualify him for *your* crew. I don't expect there's anybody else but you in the whole *wing* with *both* those attributes."

Kane looked down at another stack of forms on his desk as though Courtney no longer existed. "Dismissed!"

Courtney saluted the top of Kane's head, did an about face, and walked to the door. Rubbing his numbed right arm, he opened the door to leave.

"Lieutenant! One more thing before you leave." Kane gave Courtney a hard thin smile as he turned around. "In recognition of your *special* new status, I decided to rename your aircraft as a small token of my respect. You'll find the name *Outcast* painted in big *yellow* letters on the nose of your aircraft!"

11

CRAZY AS A LOON

You're gonna get two new men today." Carrington sat across the table from Courtney, eating a pile of watery scrambled eggs and some chipped beef that looked like brown sawdust.

Courtney leaned forward over the table so he could hear above the clamor of the officers' mess. "I didn't expect Kane to do it this quick. How'd you find out? You must have connections I don't know about."

"One of 'em is replacing *me*. That's how I know. I'm being transferred to reserve until they get enough men to form a new crew—which with my luck will probably take them about thirteen minutes."

"Who knows? Maybe you'll get a break." Carrington had been with him since he began training. Courtney suddenly felt empty inside with the loss of his closest friend. "Maybe there won't be any new men for a while and you'll get some rest."

"Maybe *you'll* get Jimmy Stewart as your new copilot," Carrington grinned.

Courtney laughed for the first time in days. "You hear anything about the new men?"

"Yep," Carrington muttered through a mouthful of eggs.

"Well—?"

Carrington finished swallowing. "One's a lunatic. The other's merely a drunk."

Courtney's smile faded into oblivion. "Don't kid with me about something like this."

"I wish I were kidding—for your sake." Carrington averted his eyes, sipping the tar-colored coffee. "I found out over at Personnel. They all thought it was hilarious."

"Give me the worst." Courtney conjured up a mental picture of Kane standing against a high stone wall in the first pink glow of dawn. His hands were tied behind his back and a black cloth was wound around his eyes. A six-man firing squad dressed in black uniforms and armed with Thompson submachine guns held their weapons at port arms. He saw himself raise a sword in his right hand. *"Ready . . . aim . . ."*

"Well, the copilot is Lieutenant Rich Bong. He's from Amarillo, Texas. He's about the same size as a ten-year-old Jap, but acts like he's Joe Louis—always starting fights. Never won one yet that anybody can remember."

Courtney bit into a piece of cold toast. "Doesn't sound too bad. I can live with that."

"I'm not finished." Carrington tried to suppress a grin. "He wants to kill Hitler."

"Don't we all?"

"I mean personally, up-close. He actually wants to fly to Berlin and knock him off like a hired assassin." Carrington found himself beginning to enjoy the dialogue.

"I don't think I want to hear anymore about Bong." Courtney hated to continue the conversation, but felt compelled to do so. "What's the other one like—the drunk?"

"He's taking Sharp's place. Lieutenant A.C. Barnes. Everybody calls him Acie. Comes from a family of Tennessee bootleggers, but they threw him out for behavior unbecoming a member of their family."

Courtney kept seeing himself on a mission with these new men. "You mean he couldn't behave himself well enough to suit a bunch of bootleggers?"

"Yep. Legend has it he drank too much. Kept cutting too deep into their profits."

"I've got a drunk for a bombardier?" As liquor never was one of Courtney's weaknesses, he couldn't abide drunks. "How's he gonna find the target? He probably can't find his bed at night!"

"That's why you got him." Carrington drank the last of his coffee and stood up. "Well, I have to get on over to Admin. I'm sure they've found something totally irrelevant to the war effort for me to do. See you in the funny papers."

"I think I'm there already." Courtney felt as alone as if he were at the South Pole. He forced himself to stand up. *Might as well go face them. Sitting here won't make things any better.*

* * *

After Courtney had introduced himself to Bong and Barnes, he sat with them and Selig in the back of a personnel truck on the way to the *Outcast*. He had first seen the name at twilight the day before, glowing in two-foot-high letters on the nose of his aircraft as it sat among the trees.

Courtney noticed immediately the gleam of the fanatic in Bong's pale blue eyes, set close together beneath his hemp-colored hair. *Got to keep a close eye on this one.*

Glancing over at Barnes, dark and brooding in the dim light of the truck, Courtney thought he had never seen a more morose looking character. *You really fixed me good, Kane.* Barnes' eyes had the glazed look of a punch-drunk fighter.

"You really a Jew?" Bong asked Selig bluntly, staring at his thin, hooked nose. "I ain't never met a Jew before."

Selig turned his sad, brown eyes on Bong. "No. I'm a Bavarian Prince. Hitler wanted to use me as a breeder for his Aryan Master Race, but I escaped."

"Didn't believe in what he's doing, huh?" The gleam in Bong's eyes grew brighter. "Me neither. Did I ever tell you about this idea of mine how we can end the war?"

Selig glanced over at Courtney, a look of disbelief on his face. "No, I don't believe you've had the chance, since I only met you five minutes ago."

Courtney shrugged slightly. When most of the crew had given him the cold shoulder after the death of Sharp, Selig treated him the same as he always had. It was a lesson in tolerance that Courtney would not forget.

"Well, here's my plan to end the war. Since you're the navigator, I need you in on it." Bong glanced about in a conspiratorial manner. "I've done a lot of research on Hitler. His habits, where he likes to stay and all that. If we could just make a little detour on one of our missions, we could . . ."

Thirty minutes later the planes were lined up on the hardstands or the taxi strips. Dawn was an hour and a half away and the darkness was broken by the moving lights of the aircraft as they taxied out onto the runway. Sudden beams of brightness split the night as the pilots hit the landing lights to help them see their way around a particularly bad turn.

Finally all the aircraft had pulled up close together near the end of the runway. Courtney watched the glow of the instrument lights before him and for some reason it reminded him of Christmas. *I wish Santa Claus was flying this mission for me. That's a nutty thought! Keep it up Courtney—you'll end up like this guy sitting next to you.* He glanced over at Bong who had a self-satisfied smirk on his face like he was guarding some dark secret from the rest of the world.

The sound of the engines settled down to a steady rumble as the lead plane took its place on the runway. The pilot revved up the engines to a deafening roar as the whole plane shook. He released the brakes and the ship lurched down the runway. From Courtney's position, it looked like a series of speeding lights with an eerie blue-white glow under the wings from the overheated superchargers. Then it was airborne and the next aircraft was already roaring down the runway after it.

After lifting off into the darkness, Courtney kept his eyes on the distant lights ahead of him. With the coming of dawn, they linked up in mission formation and soon were cruising along over the North Sea. Courtney had slept little the past few nights and it had begun to tell on him. He found himself nodding off into the droning dimness of the cockpit. *Got to get some sleep or I'll be useless when the fighters hit us.*

Courtney glanced over at Bong. On the intercom he said in a tired voice, "Bong, you want to take it for a little while?"

Bong turned to him and his face had become placid, the eyes serene as a child's. "Sure thing."

Noticing the change in Bong's demeanor, Courtney felt comfortable in letting him handle the ship. As he drifted off into the soft darkness, he heard Bong mumbling something to Selig on the intercom. Courtney felt he had been asleep for hours when a loud voice awakened him.

"Are you crazy? Give me that pistol!"

Courtney, startled out of sleep by Selig's shouts, saw Bong holding the wheel of the aircraft with his left hand. In his right he had his .38 revolver trained on Selig. "What's going on here?" Courtney mumbled sleepily.

"He's taken over the aircraft." Selig had regained his composure. He strained to control his voice. "Says we're going to Berlin to end the war."

Realizing that no one was on oxygen, Courtney looked down and saw that the Fort was zipping along no more than five hundred feet above the ground. "That's enough, Bong. Give me that pistol or you'll be sent to the guardhouse." It was a hollow threat and he knew it as soon as he spoke.

"I don't think so." Bong's eyes were those of a cornered animal. "They don't send you to the guardhouse for winning the war. Now, everybody settle down and we'll have us a nice little ride."

Barnes suddenly appeared in the cramped door of the pilot's compartment. "Hey, Bong, you got the right idea, boy. I'm behind you all the way."

Bong smiled crazily at Barnes. "I'm glad there's at least one other sane man on this plane."

Leaning over quickly, Barnes whispered something in Selig's ear. The little man glanced at Bong, squeezed past Barnes, and disappeared.

Barnes leaned against the pilot's seat as if he were having a drink at the enlisted men's club. "Yes, sir. This is the best thing that's happened to this outfit."

Strapped into his cramped seat, Courtney felt helpless to do anything. *Well, if I live through this, Kane will have me shot for desertion.*

Suddenly, from directly below them in the greenhouse, the twin fifty-caliber machine guns opened up. Bong jerked his head down at the same instant that Barnes' fist hammered into the side of his jaw. He leaned over limply against the seatbelt as the .38 clanked onto the floor of the compartment.

Courtney immediately took control of the aircraft. "Pilot to Navigator. What's our position—what's our position?"

Barnes squatted down and picked up the pistol, jamming it in the pocket of his flight jacket. Then he unhooked Bong and lifted him from his seat.

"Where you taking him?"

"We'll settle him down under the turret. I'll find enough loose wire to wrap him up nice and tight." Barnes began dragging him through the door.

"Barnes . . . ?"

Barnes looked at Courtney with a half-smile. "It's only been a minute or two. We ought to be able to make it back to the formation all right."

Selig came over the intercom with a position report and a new course already plotted. Courtney pulled the Fort into a steep climb and banked toward the west.

* * *

"There's an old legend about the lions, you know." Diana held onto Courtney's arm with both hands as they walked along Trafalgar Square.

Courtney bumped against an Aussie infantryman as he pushed through the crowd of uniformed men and elegantly clothed women, bundled against the cold night air. "A legend! You mean like Sir Gawain and the Holy Grail?"

Diana smiled, blushing slightly. "I'm quite sure there's no holy origin to *this* legend."

Lifting his eyes toward the statue of Admiral Horatio Nelson, flanked by two huge lions, Courtney scolded Diana good-naturedly, "You do love to keep me in suspense, don't you?"

"Well, according to legend, started by some foreign soldier I would imagine," she squeezed Courtney's arm, "the lions roar frightfully whenever a virgin passes by."

Courtney laughed, putting his arm around Diana. "Want to take another turn around the square?"

"No," Diana smiled, although her eyes held a far away look completely removed from smiling and laughter. She spoke in a soft sad voice. "I heard the lions roaring each to each—I do not think that they will roar for me."

"What was that about?"

"With apologies to T.S. Eliot," she concluded. "It's a loose adaptation from one of his poems."

Courtney stopped and gazed into Diana's soft, sea-colored eyes. "You're a strange girl, Diana Marlowe. I'd like to see exactly what goes on inside that lovely head of yours."

Diana stared up into his face. "No, you wouldn't."

Courtney felt an unwelcomed tenderness as he gazed into the sad, inconsolable face of Diana Marlowe. *Distance* was the one word that had described his relationships with women. He truly believed that it was the best and most purposeful way for him to live his life. But now, this most self-destructive of all the women he had ever known was drawing him in close to her with absolutely no thought of doing so.

Feeling uneasy under his direct stare, Diana suggested, "Buy me a drink?"

In reply, Courtney brushed her silky hair back from her face and kissed her tenderly on both cheeks, letting his lips linger on her soft skin. He noticed the delicate dark circles beneath her eyes that had become a permanent part of her appearance. Still she had a bruised beauty about her that made her the most desirable woman of his short life. As he kissed her on the lips, he felt her stirring, then responding as her arms went around him. They stood like that, on the square in the chill of night with the boisterous crowd surging around them—and for those moments they both forgot about themselves as they became lost in each other.

Diana stepped back, breathless and flushed. "I—I didn't know I could still . . ."

Courtney felt embarrassed at the unexpected passion that had taken him. "It's not like we haven't done—things before." He regretted it the moment he said it, but the moment was lost. The words still rang coldly in the darkness of the square, almost tangible as, like a witness to a crime, they pointed at him.

"No—it's not like that at all, is it?"

"Diana, I'm—I didn't mean . . ."

Diana turned and began walking away. Over her shoulder, she called back, "Come with me—if you want to."

Catching up to her, Courtney asked uneasily, "Where are you going? The pubs are all closed."

"I'm not going to a pub."

"Well, where—"

"I'd just as soon not talk now, if you don't mind." Diana deliberately moved his arm from around her waist, walking briskly down the sidewalk in the blacked-out city.

Courtney followed along beside her for several blocks. They passed the Strand and came to an ancient building with stone steps leading up to a heavy wooden door with leaded glass. It was set into a tall archway flanked by Doric columns. No sign gave indication as to what kind of place it was.

Diana opened the door and walked into a dim, marble-floored foyer. Beyond it, a lighted room held a crowd of men who were mostly flyers.

"What is this place?"

"A private club." She walked on into the crowded, noisy, smoke-filled room toward a long mahogany and brass bar.

A short bartender with slicked-down dark hair walked over to her. He wore a striped shirt with a black bow tie and a huge handlebar mustache. "Can I 'elp you, Miss?"

"It's me, Harry."

The bartender's eyes flickered in recognition. "So it is! Miss Marlowe. You was Flying Officer Banning's sweetheart. What a fine pilot 'e was! A real loss when the Jerries got 'im, it was. It's been so long I almost didn't recognize you. And what'll it be for you tonight, Miss Marlowe?"

"Scotch, please."

"And for the gentleman?" Harry turned to Courtney.

"The same. Only could you put a bit of ice in the glass?"

"You Yanks!" Harry winked at Diana. "Never will civilize the colonials, will we?"

Courtney looked at the uniformed men at the tables and along the bar. They were mainly members of the Allied Air Forces—Australians, Canadians, South Africans, and a few from the Free French and Free Polish Air Forces. "Does this place have a name?"

"The Bazooka Club." She waved her hand toward the crowd. "The boys started it so they'd have a place to go when everything else closed."

Harry returned and sat the drinks on the bar. Smiling at Diana, he lifted a small glass of scotch in his left hand. "I looks across at you."

Diana picked up her glass, and touched it to Harry's. "I catches your eye."

Harry downed his drink and hurried off toward a loud group of flyers at the opposite end of the bar.

Courtney sipped from his drink. "What was that all about?"

Diana's eyes looked back into the past. "Just something we used to do in here."

"What does it mean?" Courtney wanted to ask who the *we* was but thought better of it.

"I haven't the foggiest. An old English toast. I imagine Dale probably . . ."

Courtney reached over and lay his hand on Diana's. "I didn't mean anything by what I said outside. I don't think of you that way at all. I just—"

"Doesn't matter!" She pulled her hand away and swallowed the rest of the scotch, then lifted the glass toward the bartender. "Oh, Harry . . ."

Courtney stared at Diana as her eyes grew bright from the straight liquor. He could almost feel the wall between them.

"What's it like bombing the Krauts at night?"

Courtney glanced at the man who had spoken. At first he thought it was Jimmy Stewart, then noticed the insignia that identified him as belonging to an American fighter squadron. He sat at a table with a British flyer who had a jutting chin and a mass of curly dark hair.

"Sometimes it's like a Sunday cruise on the Thames. Some nights it's a rough show!"

The American drank from a pint of bitters. "I'll take my chances in the daylight."

"Something to be said for that, I suppose. It's not for me though. The worst of the night bombing is the searchlights. Can't see a bloody thing when they hit you."

"You have any close calls?"

The Brit looked away, then decided to tough out the story. "One." He took a long pull at his glass. "We were in a Wellington bomber. Got hit by a burst of flak in midship. Banged us around a bit, it did. Pilot asked me to take a look around to see if the control cables had been damaged."

Courtney, listening intently, thought of the mission when they had lost Sharp.

"On the Wellington, the rear entry hatch cover becomes part of the walkway through the waist. Anyway, I picked up me torch and started back into the waist flicking the switch. Bloody thing wouldn't turn on. Then I dropped into space! Flak had knocked the hatch cover off! Managed to get a grip with one hand and hung on like blazes—no chute, you know!"

The American stared at him wide-eyed. "You were hanging out of the plane with one hand?"

"Blasted wind almost dragged me out—couldn't reach anything with my other hand. Thank God, I was on a long cord! So scared I couldn't talk though. The pilot heard these funny noises I was making and sent somebody back. Grabbed me just before I took off for good. Took two men to pull me back in, the way that wind had me. Bit of a show, you know."

Courtney kept seeing Sharp in the bomb bay of the Fort the whole time the British flyer was telling his story. Although the temperature inside the club was fifty degrees, beads of sweat broke out on Courtney's forehead. He shivered involuntarily and gulped down his scotch.

Diana lay her hand on his arm. "Something the matter? You don't look well."

Waving for the bartender, Courtney began to tell Diana about Kane and how he was transferring every misfit in the group to his crew. He hadn't intended to mention anything about the war, but the words came rolling out, seemingly beyond his control. The one thing he didn't mention was the new name Kane had chosen for his aircraft. When he finished speaking, he found himself almost as weak as when he returned from a mission.

"Why would he do such a thing to you?" Diana's nature could not sustain anger. She still felt the pain of Courtney's remark, but fear for his safety was stronger.

Courtney thought briefly about the question. "Sometimes a new commander gets it in for one guy. I just happened to hit Kane the wrong way for some reason."

"How will you ever fly a proper mission with a crew like that?" Diana felt the cold weight of fear against her breast. She wrestled against the thought of another death in the air.

"That's what I keep asking myself. I still have some of the old crew and one of the new ones—fellow named Barnes—seems to be all right. If it pours—he'll drink it, but he's kept it to off-duty hours so far." Courtney smiled, partly from the third scotch he was drinking and partly from the memory that came to him. "I watched them haul Bong off in a straight jacket, screaming the whole time that we were all crazy for keeping him from his sworn duty. That was a sight that warmed my heart."

"I don't want anything to happen to you." Diana spoke softly, trying to control the feelings that were so much stronger than the words she spoke.

Courtney forced a smile. "That makes two of us. I'll just have to make this bunch of misfits into the best crew in the air force if I want to survive."

"What if he gives you such intractable men that you can't do it?"

"Just have to kill the 'Killer,' I guess."

"Who?"

"'Killer.' That's his reputation and his name. 'Killer' Kane." Courtney felt himself being dragged toward despair in spite of his outward show of confidence. "Let's forget about the air force for a while."

Diana had pushed the incident on the square down into her cellar of painful memories. That's how she pictured the place where she put the things she couldn't face. She seldom looked down there, but when she did she saw that it was getting dreadfully cluttered with the beginnings of a cobweb or two. It bothered her in the small, cold hours of the morning when she thought about the memories she would have to face someday—someday, but not just yet. "Would you like to go back to the apartment?"

"You're a gypsy mind reader," Courtney smiled. He had thought the night was ruined. "You're not mad anymore? You know, about what I said."

"Oh, that!" Diana leaned forward, took his face in her hands and kissed him deeply on the lips. Tonight there would be someone warm to reach out and hold on to in those hard hours before the light comes. "It's in the cellar."

12

SURVIVAL

I told you they'd have me flying again before I got any rest." Carrington sat across from Courtney in the officers' mess. "One crummy stand-down and I'm back in the air."

Courtney felt a little more secure with his old copilot in the crew once again. "Yeah, but now you're back with the pilot and crew of the *Outcast*. If that doesn't make you happy, you're a hard man to please."

Carrington took a bite of his Spam sandwich, washing it down with hot chocolate. "Believe it or not, this crew is better than that other bunch I was with."

"They're coming around, all right." Courtney sipped his chocolate. "I think they're beginning to realize that if we don't all stick together and do our jobs, none of us is gonna make it. We still have a long way to go though."

"Today wasn't bad, especially the waist and turret gunners." Carrington swallowed the last of his sandwich. "I sure could have used 'em on that *other* ship I was with."

Courtney got up and walked with Carrington out of the officers' mess. "I'm not sure if *anybody* can fly or shoot or bomb good enough to suit Kane. He just keeps pouring it on. Not only the *Outcast*, but every aircraft in the whole group."

"Trying to live up to his reputation, I suppose." Carrington glanced at Courtney, then looked off into the distance. "He's dedicated to what he's doing though. Believes more lives will be saved in the long run by hitting them hard now than by taking the easy missions. Destroy the means of production and they won't have any more fighters to send up against us."

"He believes in saving at least one life that I know of," Courtney said bitterly. "His *own!*" I don't see him holding tight and steady on any bomb runs. Never have even seen him off the ground in *anybody's* Fort."

"You didn't know?" Carrington stopped and turned to Courtney with a surprised look.

"Know what?"

"He doesn't fly because Wing won't let him."

"Yeah, I'll bet!"

"It's true. He was one of the first pilots over here. Flew somewhere between forty-five and fifty missions. Finally they told him he was too valuable to risk so they put him on staff and grounded him."

"Fifty missions? That's *some* record!"

"He barely made it back from a few of them. I heard ol' Doc Kraft say he dug enough shrapnel out of Kane when he was on flying status to start a scrap metal business." Carrington stopped, gazing out at the ground fog that hung like damp gauze over the field and into the surrounding trees. "Whatever happened to the sun? You think it's still up there?"

Courtney glanced up at the bright spot in the haze. "I kind of hate to hear Kane's a bona fide hero. Makes what I gotta do that much harder."

"Why's that?"

"I finally let the crew badger me into asking Kane to slack off on us a little. Give us a break now and then—a little rest. Every other crew has had a three- or four-day leave in London except for the *Outcast*. The boys are beginning to think nothing they do will be good enough to earn some time off."

"Once you get on *his* list, it really takes something to get off." Carrington shook his head sadly. "Come on, let's get on over to interrogation and tell Intelligence a pack of lies so we can get some sleep."

* * *

"I'd rather bomb Washington, D.C. than Berlin! Hitler didn't do nothing to me." Sergeant Little Tenkiller sat with the rest of the crew in the group interrogation room after his third mission on the *Outcast*. Short and chunky, he had long, coal-black hair that he kept tucked up under a black wool cap. Born and raised on a wind-swept, barren Cherokee reservation in Oklahoma, he harbored a burning hatred for the white man's government—which to him was epitomized by the nation's capital city.

Dominic Ragusa, a hulking button-man for a New Jersey "family," rose to the defense of his country. As a naturalized citizen, he was grateful for the opportunities that America had given him to break as many bones as his job required, with a minimum amount of time behind bars. "You little half-breed! You'd bomb Franklin D. Roosevelt? He's in a wheelchair."

"You probably put him there you big Mafia kneebreaker!" Tenkiller shot back. "What happened? He didn't pay his loan back quick enough?"

"You can't call me a kneebreaker, you traitor!" Ragusa bolted upright, knocking over a chair. "You ain't even an American! I'll break you in half!"

"Any Indian is worth ten white men." Tenkiller was on his feet. "'Course, you ain't exactly white and you ain't even from this country!"

"I'm an American and I got the papers to prove it. Where's yours?" Ragusa sneered down in Tenkiller's face. "My *bulldog's* got a better pedigree than *you* do!"

"That's enough, men!" Courtney stepped between them. "We're all Americans here or we wouldn't be in this room together. Kane's gonna be here any minute, so just sit down and be quiet."

With much grumbling amid threats of head bashing and scalp taking, the two men took their seats.

Luke Hatfield stood to his feet, his mild voice and demeanor in sharp contrast to Tenkiller and Ragusa. With a boyish face and cornsilk hair, he looked like he'd just stepped off a *Boy's Life* magazine cover. "I just got some new tracts in the mail. Thought ya'll might be interested in taking a look at 'em."

Most of the men groaned and turned away, their chairs scraping on the concrete in harsh denial to Hatfield's offer. Some listened with interest. They admired Hatfield's coolness under fire and envied his ability to sleep like a baby on nights before even the roughest missions. They also didn't want to offend the best gunner in the entire group, because the *Outcast* had a much better chance for survival with Hatfield behind the twin-machine guns of the ball-turret. A few of the flyers raised their hands.

Hatfield had been transferred to the *Outcast* because of his staunch refusal to quit sharing his faith, which had alienated him from many of the men in other crews. He handed tracts to the four men who had their hands raised. "Jesus understands what we're all going through." He smiled with an assurance as strong and genuine as the faith that gave it birth. "He wants to help us. And the first step is salvation. 'If thou shalt confess with thy mouth the Lord Jesus, and shalt believe in thine heart that God hath raised him from the dead, thou shalt be saved.' It's that simple, boys."

After the first time, Courtney never tried to stop Hatfield from giving one of his brief sermons. Hatfield had turned those intense blue eyes on him and said in his quiet, gentle manner, "I'll never interfere with our duties, Sir, and I'll always keep it short, but this is something the Lord's called me to do." He had always been faithful to his calling and to that promise. Courtney listened as Hatfield finished his short message.

"We can all have a certain measure of peace, even with them Germans trying to blow us out of the air." Hatfield walked back to his chair, sat down, and closed his eyes. The words that he spoke, almost under his breath, were heard by everyone in the room—and lodged in the hearts of some of them. "'For whether we *live*, we live unto the Lord; and whether we *die*, we die unto the Lord: whether we live therefore, or die, we are the *Lord's.*'"

Courtney sat in an aisle seat near the back of the room and studied his less than desirable crew. After the first mission, he decided that Tenkiller and Ragusa, with their competitive natures would be perfect standing side by side in the two waist gunner positions. It had worked out better than he had expected as each man stepped behind his twin fifty-caliber machine guns determined to shoot down more German fighters than the other. In missions number two and three they had made almost as many kills as any other waist gunners in the group.

Barnes continued to be an accurate and dependable bombardier. He also drank himself into oblivion unless there was a mission the next day, but he always seemed to know which days would be stand-downs.

Selig remained with the *Outcast*, although his behavior had always been exemplary and his navigation skills were as good as anyone in the group. Courtney finally decided that it had to be because he was a Jew. When he mentioned it to him, the little man shrugged his shoulders and said in an unconcerned tone, "It's *always* been like that for us." To Courtney's continued amazement, he never once blamed him for Sharp's death.

All the crews from the mission were swapping stories about their particular adventures when Kane stormed into the room—as usual. Everyone snapped to attention.

"As you were. It'll be a little while before we begin." Kane walked among his men, encouraging them. He had already gotten some preliminary information on the mission. "Good formation, Lieutenant. Nice shooting, Sergeant."

Kane had yet to congratulate anyone on the *Outcast*, so all eyes turned on him as he approached Hatfield. "I heard you got three confirmed kills today. Is that right?"

Hatfield jumped to attention.

"At ease, Sergeant. Just answer the question."

"I believe that's right, sir."

Kane gazed down at the frail-looking man and rubbed his chin thoughtfully. "You know, Hatfield, if you'd quit driving the men crazy with this religion business, I just might transfer you out of the *Outcast* into a reputable aircraft."

"Sorry, sir, but I'd sooner stop breathing as to quit talking about Jesus." Hatfield held Kane's stare. "I don't mean no disrespect by it."

"I know you don't, Sergeant. Well, it's your funeral," Kane shrugged, walking away.

When the debriefing was over, Courtney approached Kane cautiously. He had never spoken to him one-to-one since that last excruciating encounter. "Colonel, do you have a minute? I'd like to talk to you."

Kane turned and looked at him with a blank stare. "Make it quick."

Courtney averted his eyes, unable to look at Kane while he talked to him. "Well, sir, it's just that the men—"

"The *men*, Lieutenant?" Kane interrupted. "You said *you* wanted to talk to me. Which is it—*you* or the *men*?"

"Me, I guess, sir."

"Let me know when you find out for sure then." Kane turned to leave.

"*Me*, sir."

Kane swung back around. "Let's have it then!"

"Well, sir, it's been awhile since we've had a pass into town. The other crews all have—"

"The other crews aren't your concern, Lieutenant. Do you think you've earned a pass?"

Courtney glanced at Kane. "Well, yes sir, I do."

"I don't happen to agree. Anything else?"

Courtney was stunned, unable to reply to the stonewall finality of Kane's answer. Kane had extended his sentence without even hearing the evidence.

Suddenly, Kane spun around and stepped back in front of Courtney. He waved his hand about the room. "You see all these men, Lieutenant?"

Still stunned by Kane's abrupt denial on his request, Courtney glanced about the room.

Kane continued without waiting for a reply. "They're just ordinary Americans. But they've been called to do extraordinary things for their country—and most of them are giving the best they have to give."

Courtney glanced at Kane, then back to the men milling about or filing out of the room.

"You ever read comic books, Lieutenant?"

Puzzled by the question, Courtney answered haltingly. "Uh—yeah, I guess so." *Uh! I haven't said that since I was thirteen years old.*

"You *guess*? Don't you know anything for *sure*, Lieutenant? Don't answer that!" Kane shook his head slowly. "If you've read any comics, you've seen the Charles Atlas advertisements on the back page."

Courtney remembered the muscular Atlas and how he transformed a ninety-pound weakling into a he-man. He almost smiled as he saw again the bully at the beach kick sand into the skinny man's face. Then, after using the *Dynamic Tension* program, the Atlas disciple came back, reversed the tables on the bully, and got the bathing beauty in the bargain.

"Well, I put all the ninety-pound weaklings in the *Outcast*." Kane let the words sink in. "And in order to get out—you gotta look like Charles Atlas to me!"

* * *

"Villacoublay—south of Paris." Kane held his pointer on the target. "It's an aircraft work shop factory. The Initial Point for the bomb run should be easy to spot—it's the Eiffel Tower."

Courtney sat in his usual seat in the briefing room, listening to each of the staff officers give their spiels. He had long since learned to discard all but the essential information. *Altitude—twenty-five thousand feet. Temperature—forty below zero. An escort of P-47s will take you halfway to the target. Flak—moderate. Jerry's got his best fighter groups protecting Paris, so you can expect to have your hands full over the target.*

Four hours later, the *Outcast* droned along in formation five miles above the French countryside north of Paris. The P-47s had reached their fuel limits and turned back.

"Bombardier to crew! Fighters at nine o'clock! More down low and coming up at us!"

Courtney had expected the best that Germany could throw against them. He was stunned at what he saw! Four fighters, flying so close together they looked almost like one huge four-engined aircraft, bore down on them. *Surely they'll split apart before the final attack. The greenest pilots know better than this! Must be a training flight.*

The four 109s rushed in at full throttle. Eight hundred yards out, the first bursts of cannon fire flashed along their wings. It was like inviting the grim reaper into the cockpits with them. The whole formation cut loose at the single target that the tight-flying 109s presented. Immediately the sky was ablaze with tracers. The enormous firepower of the Forts ripped the four fighters apart. Within seconds the devastating mass of fifty-caliber slugs left nothing but four puffs of black smoke and a sky full of debris. It was so easy! There were a few moments of complete silence on the intercom of the *Outcast*.

Finally Selig spoke in his solemn tone. "Hitler must be raiding the asylums for his pilots these days."

"It was a nutty thing to do," Barnes drawled. "Kinda like watching four German versions of Bong in action."

"Pilot to crew. We're getting close to the target." It bothered Courtney that fighter resistance had been so light. *Maybe they're concentrating on one of the other formations.* "Keep your eyes peeled now. They don't call this low formation 'purple heart corner' for nothing."

"Navigator to Pilot."

"Go ahead."

"Ten minutes to the I.P."

"Roger."

A few minutes later, Selig was back on the intercom. "I.P. at one o'clock."

"I see it, Navigator." Courtney gazed down at the huge steel tower rising up from the heart of Paris. "Hard to miss the Eiffel Tower."

"Navigator to Bombardier."

"Go ahead."

"On the bomb run in three minutes."

"Ball to Pilot."

"Go ahead."

"Flak—six o'clock low."

"Tail to crew. Flak—five o'clock level."

Wham! Courtney felt the *Outcast* shake violently. Wham! Wham! Wham! The ship rocked and pitched from the concussion. Shrapnel slammed into the aircraft.

"Copilot to waist. Anybody hurt back there?"

"A few good-sized holes. Nothing too bad yet."

Far below, out of his sight, Courtney knew a battery of four guns had them in their sights. Salvos were bursting all around them—and each one crept closer! This was always the worst part for Courtney—109s could be shot down. There was no way to fight back at shell bursts.

"Wham! The flak burst rocked the aircraft. The number three engine began to vibrate heavily.

"Copilot to Ball."

"Go ahead."

"Can you see any oil leaking from number three?"

"It's throwing oil real bad!"

"Pilot to Copilot—feather number three."

Ahead of him Courtney saw that the sky was a roiling mass of black smoke. *We'll never get through this. It's a solid wall of shrapnel!*

"Bombardier to Pilot. We're on the bomb run!"

The heavy "whoosh" of a shell burst sounded to the left and orange flame blossomed in the center of the explosion. Shrapnel clanged into the number two engine.

"Turret to Copilot."

"Go ahead."

"How do the instruments look on number two engine?"

"Instruments are normal."

"Let's hope there's no fire."

"What else do you see?"

"Both wings are full of holes."

"Turret to Ball. Any damage under the left wing? Look for fuel leaks."

"A lot of holes. No leaks yet."

"Bombs away!"

As the aircraft lurched upward, Courtney saw the sky suddenly explode into bright orange. Something slammed into his left hip, jolting him in his seat. The left side of his face felt hot and warm. At first he thought someone had kicked him. The sound of the engines sounded far away and a dark cloud seemed to have settled around him. Time seemed to have lost its meaning—to have no place in this strange world. Finally he realized once more that he was in the cramped cockpit of a B-17. He gazed slowly to his right and wished for the rest of his life that he hadn't.

Carrington sat upright in his seat, his wide eyes staring ahead into an infinite distance—his hands draped loosely over the wheel. Courtney contemplated the jagged piece of shrapnel. It vaguely reminded him of a particular piece of jigsaw puzzle he always had problems finding a place for when he was a child. The edges were sharper of course, but he thought if he could only see the part embedded out of sight in Carrington's left temple he would know for sure whether it was the right piece or not.

Clang! The noise brought Courtney rushing back. He tore his eyes away from Carrington.

"Ball to Copilot—Ball to Copilot."

Trying to shake off the drowsiness that pressed down on him, Courtney answered. "Pilot here. Go ahead."

"The ball got hit. My eyes are full of glass. I can't open 'em." Hatfield spoke as calmly as if he were making small talk over oily bacon and watery eggs.

Courtney shook his head again to clear it. The sky was empty of flak. "You hit anywhere else?"

"No. Just glass slivers in my eyes."

"Want us to get you out now or wait 'til we're over water?" Courtney had leveled the Fort off and begun to pull back into position.

"I can wait, all right. I'm as well off here as I would be in the radio room."

A huge chunk of flak tore through the open bomb bay with the sound of shrieking metal.

"Tail to Pilot. The Fort behind us exploded."

"Pilot to crew. The controls are damaged, but we've still got three engines. Keep a sharp watch for fighters 'til we're over the Channel."

Courtney had lost all sense of time. The left side of his head felt like it was on fire. His left hip and leg had almost no feeling. He glanced down once at the shredded flight suit, covered now with dark, frozen blood. As he surveyed the sky about him, he saw no other enemy aircraft. In the formation ahead, the empty slots of lost Forts beckoned to him. He eased the throttles forward to catch up and took his place within the safety of the remaining aircraft.

Sometime later after the group had reached a lower altitude, he glanced down and saw the shadow of the *Outcast* streak across the shoreline of France and out onto the whitecapping surface of the Channel.

"Turret to Pilot."

"Go ahead."

"We got trouble with the hydraulic system."

"How bad?"

"We won't have any brakes when we land."

"Can't you raise the pressure temporarily?"

"Nope. Fluid's all gone!"

"Pilot to crew. We'll have to land without brakes. I'll try to rev up number one and two engines when we touch down. Should ease us off into the muddy field at the right side of the runway. That ought to stop us."

On the final approach, Courtney brought the *Outcast* in as slow as he could without stalling. As he dropped through the haze he stared at the sight below him in shock. Both sides of the runway were lined with cheering men. His vision was becoming more and more cloudy. "Pilot to Turret. Can you see what's going on down there? I can't turn off the runway with all those idiots standing around like a gaggle of geese."

"Looks like a bunch of the Headquarters staff. Must be having a welcoming home party for us. All of 'em look like they're holding drinks."

When the wheels touched down, Courtney opened his side window, leaning out briefly to wave and shout for the men to get out of the way. They smiled and waved back at him, cheering the crew home. The attempt almost cost him control of the damaged aircraft, as it slipped off to the right. He straightened it back onto the runway, in a blind rage at the men who threatened to destroy his crew as surely as the German flak and fighters.

Then it was too late! The end of the landing strip was on them and they went bouncing off across a rough field, crashed through a wooden fence, and were speeding toward a country lane.

Courtney felt a slight impact, then the plane lurched crazily over as it careened off into a vine-covered ditch. The left wing struck a massive oak and ripped off with a terrible shrieking of metal. It was the last thing Courtney remembered as he slammed against the wheel and plummeted into a rushing darkness filled with swirling red lights.

Part 4

TENDERNESS AND FIRE

13

HELEN

*A*ll through the gray afternoon the sun had slipped along just above the overcast. Now as it fell in the western sky toward distant Land's End, it burst through. Light slanted in through the high window, lying like a pale yellow bar across the tiled floor. The room smelled slightly of decayed flesh with a heavy overlay of antiseptic.

Diana sat next to the bed in a hard straight-backed chair painted white. She wore a pale blue cotton dress trimmed in white lace. Her hair was freshly washed and toweled dry—shimmering like gossamer in the half-light of the room. A warm glow seemed to radiate from her scrubbed face, absent of makeup except for some hastily applied lipstick.

How pale he looks! Oh, Mark, why did I have to meet you? Why couldn't I just live day to day and not care about anybody until—until it's all over? Now they've started their killing. Just look at what they've done to you! They won't do it all at once like they did to Dale. They'll kill you a little at a time and then one day—you won't come back anymore. But then I can't really lose you, can I? You've never given me any reason to believe that I even have any part of you to lose.

Mark groaned quietly and stirred coming out of his sleep. His left hand raised slowly, touching the heavy bandage on the side of his head. Then he brushed the dark hair back from his face and slowly opened his eyes. He blinked, rubbing his eyes with his thumb and forefinger, then opened them wide. "Diana—" His voice was a hoarse whisper. "How did you know I was here?"

Diana took his right hand in hers, staring at the dark flaky skin on his fingertips where the forty-below temperature had done its icy work. "My fairy godmother told me. We British girls all have fairy godmothers." She rubbed his fingertips gently with her own, trembling slightly at the hard, dead texture about them. "Do they hurt?"

"What?" Courtney struggled to sit up in the bed.

"Here, let me help you." Diana took his arm, helping him to ease up in the bed. Then she plumped up two pillows and arranged them behind his back.

"Does *what* hurt?"

Diana held his hand up. "Your fingers."

Courtney brought his hand over in front of his face as though he had never seen it before. "Must be frostbite. Hadn't really noticed before. I think I left a few pieces of myself in the *Outcast*. Guess I was too preoccupied learning how to get along without 'em to worry about my fingers."

Diana took his hand again, holding it between both of hers. "How badly are you hurt?" She tried to conceal it, but the pain of asking the question crinkled her eyes and tightened the corners of her mouth.

"My head hurts like the dickens, but Doc says it's mostly superficial. Might have a couple of scars." Courtney touched his head and winced slightly. "Lost a little piece of ear too. That could be an improvement though."

"I don't understand."

"I always thought my left ear was bigger than the right one." Mark tugged at his right ear. "Maybe that shell burst evened them up. A little high-altitude surgery by the boys from Berlin."

Diana felt a heavy undefined sadness settle over her. She thought of how short life was—and how very fragile. A Bible verse that she had memorized as a child seemed to burst through the mist of the years. *For what is your life? It is even a vapour, that appeareth for a little time, and then vanisheth away.*

"Diana, are you all right?" Courtney touched her chin with his dark fingertips. "My jokes aren't that bad, are they?"

"No," she smiled sadly. "I'm fine."

"Well, anyway, the leg's the part that's gonna take a while to heal. Bone damage." Courtney shrugged. "Should be almost good as new from what they tell me though."

"I'm glad." The simple words paled into insignificance next to the glow in Diana's eyes. She felt relief wash over her at the good news, but the sadness lingered all the same.

Courtney noticed the bright beginning of tears in Diana's eyes. He fought to hold onto his distance. *I don't want this. There's no place for her in my plans—if the boys from Berlin let me live long enough to get back to the States. Hey, I like the sound of that phrase. "The boys from Berlin." That ought to fit right in with my war veteran speeches.*

The next question was even more difficult for Diana to ask. "Are they—will you have to go back?"

"No reason not to, soon as I get all healed up. That's what Doc says." Courtney tried to sound matter-of-fact, but the dread of returning to combat cracked in his voice.

The sun dropped behind a wall of heavy clouds beyond Land's End. Gray light filtered like smoke into the room, bringing with it the chill of approaching night.

"Even the hospitals don't have enough heat nowadays." Diana shivered slightly.

The door eased inward. A woman in her late-twenties with short, carrot-colored hair and eyes like a pale summer sky stepped into the room. She wore a threadbare gray uniform and carried a pail of water and a mop. "Oh! Sorry, love! Didn't know your lady friend was visiting."

"It's all right. Come on in, Helen. You won't bother us." Courtney eased his hand out of Diana's as if he considered it a weakness to show affection. "This is Diana Marlowe. Diana, Helen Southwell."

"Pleased to meet you, Ma'am."

"How do you do?" Diana noticed the red, almost raw looking skin of the woman's hands and the heavy weariness in her eyes. Even so, she felt that the room had brightened with Helen's presence, almost as though she had rescued a bit of the sunlight before the clouds took it.

"Oh, she's a pretty one, she is, Lieutenant—and a real lady too! You'd better watch your manners." Helen smiled brightly at Diana. "Not many like her about these days."

Only on every street corner, Diana thought bitterly. *Or in every pub.*

Courtney glanced at Diana. "I agree completely, Helen. I was a stranger in a strange land 'til I met the lovely and gracious Miss Marlowe."

"Well, I'd better be about me work. They don't pay me to stand about running me mouth." Helen began mopping the floor briskly.

Diana noticed how quickly she moved at her work, never wasting a motion, never missing a spot on the floor. It spoke of long years of drudgery. "Where *do* you get your energy, Helen? I'd be spent in five minutes at that."

Helen glanced over at Diana with a puzzled frown. "Never thought about it, I guess. With two little ones to support, there's precious little time for thinking."

"Oh, I see." Diana felt that somehow she had been given a valuable lesson, even though Helen had only meant to answer her question.

As Helen worked, she sang "Amazing Grace" under her breath, occasionally smiling brightly at Diana or Courtney. She soon finished and leaned briefly on her mop, glancing at the shining floor. "There—that should do it for another day."

"Another beautiful job, Helen," Courtney grinned.

"It ought to be. I done enough of 'em, I have." Helen picked up her mop and pail, nodding at Diana and Courtney. "Good day to you both."

"There goes an amazing woman," Courtney observed.

Diana looked at the door where Helen had just left. "She is? In what way?"

"When I first got here, she had just gotten out of the hospital herself."

"But she doesn't look ill," Diana said in a concerned tone. "Maybe a little weary."

"Doctor said she had a stroke," Courtney continued. "It was a mild one, but she probably should have taken more time off from work."

Diana sat with her hands folded in her lap, saddened by the news about Helen. As she glanced at Courtney, however, her own problems came back to her. She had been stung when Courtney had pulled his hand away from her. *I can't let myself get close to him. I just can't! I have to do something for these Americans who are risking their lives for us though.* "How long before you can leave the hospital?"

"A week or two. There's a metal rod and some pins holding the leg bone in place. I can probably get around on one crutch with a little practice." Courtney grinned at Diana. "Suppose you could get me a black patch for me eye and a parrot for me shoulder?"

Diana laughed softly. "Aye, matey. And we'll fly the skull and crossbones from your crutch."

Courtney's smile slowly faded as the feigned British accent reminded him of the language games he and Carrington always played. He saw again the staring eyes and the jagged hunk of shrapnel that had destroyed all those creative and beautiful thoughts of his best friend in the world.

Diana noticed that Courtney was staring moodily out the window. *Maybe he's just tired.* "I'll be leaving now. Maybe we'll go over to the apartment when you can get about. Have some tea or something."

"Sure." Courtney dreaded being alone in the room with his thoughts. "Maybe we'll go see Helen and her family one day. She's asked me over for a visit."

"Perhaps." Diana felt as awkward as a thirteen-year-old on her first date. She couldn't decide how to take her leave of Courtney. It seemed that being with him was always like the first time. She leaned over and kissed him on the forehead.

As she was leaving, Courtney stopped her. "Are you coming back to see me?"

Diana knew that she would, but putting it in words seemed such a chore. "Yes. In a day or two."

Then she was gone and Courtney was left with the ghosts of his dead friends. His mind played over and over scenes that he didn't want to see: Sharp trying to fathom what outrage Selig was drawing him into; Carrington puffing along beside him in training as they cursed Stoddard under their breath; all the faces of the men who left nothing behind but empty chairs in the briefing room after a mission to Stuttgart or Schweinfurt or Bremen.

Courtney watched the last of the light fade at the window. Because of the city's blackout, he was in almost total darkness. As he lay on the fresh linen, listening to the murmuring hospital noises, the soft voice of Helen Southwell seemed to linger in the room. *I once was lost, but now am found, Was blind, but now I see.*

* * *

"How're you feeling, Lieutenant?"

At the sound of the familiar voice, Courtney slowly came up from the drifting darkness. The face of Kane appeared above him like some malevolent apparition. He struggled to sit up in bed—or run away. In his half-sleep state, he couldn't figure out which. "I—I'm fine, sir."

"Good." Kane stood rigidly at the side of the bed, holding his flying cap with both hands. "Looks like the place is clean. They treating you all right here?"

"Yes, sir." Courtney was now fully awake. Kane was the last person in the world he expected to see at his bedside. Had it been Dwight Eisenhower, he wouldn't have been nearly as shaken. "Food's good too."

Kane glowered down at him, his expression never changing. "Better than the officers' mess?"

Courtney couldn't decide if Kane was kidding or serious. "Yes, sir."

Kane placed his hands behind his back, still holding his hat as he paced the length of the bed. "That was a good piece of flying you did on the Villacoublay mission. I've never known many that could make it back in a 17 that badly shot-up."

"Thank you, sir." Courtney waited for the kicker. *What's he up to now?*

Stopping at the foot of the bed, Kane turned his dark eyes on Courtney. "The doctors say you'll be back in a month or so. Almost good as new."

"So they tell me, Colonel."

Kane gazed out the window. The sun had lost heart against the heavy clouds that covered the south of England. "Have to go now. I'll just make it back for debriefing."

As Kane turned to leave, Courtney spoke to him for the first time without any pretense. "Colonel—thanks for coming by."

Glancing back at Courtney, his dark eyes almost placid, Kane merely nodded his head and left.

Courtney stared through the half-opened door as Kane walked away down the hall. At the nurses' station, he stopped and waved the duty nurse over to the counter. He spoke with her briefly as she glanced toward Courtney's door. Then he was gone.

The nurse left her station and walked directly down the hall to Courtney's room. A stately woman with gray eyes and brown hair, she reminded him of his mother's oldest sister. As she handed him two white pills and a paper cup of water, she proclaimed, "Well, I can see now that we've got to take better care of you."

Courtney gave her a puzzled frown. "I don't understand—?"

"Your Colonel says you're a *special* man and you deserve *special* treatment." She smiled, tucking his sheet and blanket in. "I think he may be right."

Again Kane had stunned him! Courtney had fought so long to gain even a grain of acceptance from Kane and now that he had given up, the simple words were, somehow, almost too much for him to bear. To his utter amazement, he felt a tear spill over from his left eye and onto his cheek.

Courtney cleared his throat, wiping the tear away with the back of his hand, and lay back in the bed. After the nurse had gone, he turned on his side and stared for a long time at the light growing brighter from the high window.

* * *

"What's this?" Courtney sat in an overstuffed chair in Diana's suite in the hotel, his bad leg propped on a hassock. He held up Diana's scrapbook as she walked into the room.

"Just some friends of mine. Classmates, people I grew up with." Diana sat on the edge of the hassock, facing him.

Courtney turned the pages slowly, gazing at the bright young faces that looked so eager to take life on. "What happened to all your female friends? I've only seen one or two in here."

Diana took the book carefully out of his hands and folded it across her breast with both hands. "Most of them are still alive. Women don't have to go into combat."

At first the words struck Courtney as deceptively simple. "You mean this is a book of dead people?" he asked with a disbelieving smile.

"Precisely." Diana got up and placed the book on a shelf next to the chair. "In fact, I call it my *Book of the Dead.*"

Courtney felt a chill run down his back. Something about her doing this filled him with dread. "Isn't that kind of morbid? Keeping a book full of nothing but dead people?"

"Drink?"

"No thanks."

Diana went into the tiny kitchen and returned with a heavy glass full of scotch. She took a swallow and rubbed the cool smooth surface of the glass against her cheek. "What would you know about it?"

"I've seen a lot of men killed."

"In somebody *else's* country." Diana took a long swallow of the scotch and coughed. "How many of them grew up with you? How many did you know since they were three or four years old? Did you see Liberty's city hall leveled by German bombs—see your churches and schools burn to the ground? Have you seen a child's twisted arm sticking like a discarded toy out of a pile of rubble?" Diana took a deep breath, her voice becoming almost a whisper. "I hardly think it's the same."

Courtney was caught off guard by the passion in Diana's voice as she spoke.

"I'm sorry. It's not your fault. You're risking your life for us and I blame you for this horrible mess the world's in. I'm truly sorry." Diana walked to the door that led onto the balcony and gazed out the glass insert at its top.

"Don't be sorry. It's my fault." Courtney struggled up from the chair, took his crutch, and made his way painfully over to her. "I just didn't understand."

Diana turned to him. "No. Maybe you're right. Maybe it *is* morbid. I started keeping the book as a way to—to honor them, I suppose. Then I found myself sitting for hours at a time, just staring at all those dead faces. Faces that are gone forever. I tried to remember them as they were when they were alive, but it got so I couldn't do it any longer. All I saw were corpses and coffins and graveyards."

Courtney put his good arm around Diana and pulled her to him. She lay her head on his shoulder as her arms went around his waist. Hot tears coursed down her cheeks onto his neck. He could almost feel the torment and the grief flowing out of her through the tears touching his skin. Her hair smelled as fragrant as spring flowers—her warm softness flowed against him, into him, and he knew at that moment that he no longer had the strength to leave her.

*   *   *

"I'm so glad you could come!" Helen Southwell stepped out into the tiny brick garden behind her row house. She wore a neatly ironed pale blue dress. Her eyes shone with hospitality. "We'll have tea out here, if you don't mind. It's precious little sunshine we've had in the last few weeks."

Courtney eased himself down onto a small stone bench against the rough concrete wall that ran the length of the miniature garden. He stretched his injured leg out along the cool smooth surface, leaning his crutch against the wall. "It's nice out here."

Diana sat in a white metal chair next to the bench. She noticed the flower pots stacked neatly against the opposite wall, then her eyes picked out a toy Spitfire on the damp brick next to the back door. A dull pain rose in her breast. Tearing her eyes away, she glanced around. "Yes, it is."

"It'll be a bit lovelier when I get me flowers planted." Helen nodded at the flower pots. "So busy at the hospital, I just haven't got to it yet."

Diana let her eyes wander toward the back of the garden and saw a boy and girl playing near the crumbled rear wall. They were so quiet, she hadn't noticed them at first.

"Children, come meet our guests," Helen waved to them. As they came running up, she put her hands on their shoulders. "This is my brave little soldier, Donny. And this is Kate. She's the mistress of the house when I'm at work. She does let our neighbor, Mrs. Fletcher, help out a bit though."

Kate, three years old and the image of her mother, smiled shyly. Five-year-old Donny, with dark brown hair and gray eyes a little lighter than Courtney's, stared at the American's stiff leg.

"Children, this is Miss Marlowe and Mr. Courtney. They're going to be our guests for tea. You can entertain them while I get things ready." Helen beamed at her children and returned to the kitchen.

"That's a lovely dress. Here, let me fix your bow." Diana turned Kate around and retied the bow at the back of her red dress. "It looks nice with your pretty blue eyes."

"Thank you. My mum made it for me." Kate took the hem of her dress in both hands and held it out. Then she held her arms up toward Diana.

Diana felt a warm sensation in her breast as she picked the child up and sat her on her lap. She smoothed Kate's bright hair down with her fingertips. "Your hair's so soft and shiny!"

"Mum made that too."

Donny was giving Courtney a close inspection. "Are you a soldier?"

"Kind of," Courtney smiled. "I fly airplanes."

Glancing over his shoulder at the kitchen door, he whispered, "Do you bomb the *bloody* Jerries?"

"Yes, I do that when they let me get close enough," Courtney laughed. "They don't much care for us bombing their factories though, so they send up fighters and try to shoot us down." He demonstrated the aerial combat with his hands.

"My daddy went to war."

"He did? Where is he now?"

"Mum said he got killed." Donny glanced over at Kate, playing patty cake with Diana. "Kate doesn't understand. She's just a child, you know."

Courtney was at a loss for words. *Seems like everywhere I turn, I never know what to say anymore. Whatever happened to the old Mark Courtney? He could turn a phrase with the best of 'em.* "Well, we men have to protect the women, don't we?"

"Yes, sir," Donny grinned, holding himself up straight. "I have to take care of me mum too, now that Dad's gone."

"Do you hate the Germans, Donny?" Courtney had been thinking of all the friends he had lost to German flak and fighters. He regretted his words to the boy at once.

"Oh, no sir. I'm a Christian. Mummy says we should never hate anyone. We pray for the Jerries just like we pray for our own people."

Helen backed through the kitchen door holding a tray laden with cups of tea, sugar cookies, and two glasses of punch for the children. She sat it down on a rickety metal table and began serving. "Sorry there's no cream, what with the rationing and all. Don't have a proper tray either. The cook gave me this one. Said they were only going to throw it out."

Diana noticed the mismatched, chipped cups and the serving tray which had come from the hospital cafeteria. Helen's dress had been mended several times and the children's clothes, although clean, were almost threadbare. *What kind of woman is this? How can she be so happy all the time? Left alone to raise two children. All that hard work at the hospital.*

"You get down now, Kate, and let Miss Marlowe have her tea." Helen began pouring the tea.

"Please, not now, Mum," Kate begged. "We're having ever so much fun."

"She's fine, Mrs. Southwell." Diana felt such comfort holding the child, she couldn't bear to put her down. *Must be the times. I've never cared that much for children before.*

After serving everyone, Helen sat on the very end of the stone bench sipping her tea, her face glowing with pleasure as she watched Diana playing with Kate. *She needs children of her own, she does. She has such a heart for them!*

"Mum, Lieutenant Courtney drops bombs on the bl—on the Jerries. He's a hero. He got wounded." Donny beamed up at his new friend.

"I'm not a hero, Donny. I just didn't get out of the way fast enough," Courtney laughed.

Donny glanced over at Helen. "Daddy was a hero, wasn't he, Mum? He got a medal."

Helen's eyes gazed into a far-off time. "Your daddy was always a hero to me, Donny." Then she brightened. "He did get a medal for valor though."

"Where was he stationed, Mrs. Southwell?" Courtney could see that she needed to talk about her husband.

"He was with General Montgomery at El Alamein. That was when they finally defeated Rommel." Helen sipped her tea thoughtfully. "The last letter I got from him, he said the Jerries were whipped and they were driving them along the coastal road toward the Americans in Tunisia. Told me he expected to be home on leave in a month or two. The next letter I got was from his commanding officer."

Diana gave Kate a hug. "I'm sorry you didn't get to see your husband again, Mrs. Southwell."

"Oh, I'll see him again all right, Miss Marlowe." Helen spoke with such assurance that Diana at first thought the woman had lost her grasp on reality, then she quickly realized that Helen referred to an entirely different kind of meeting. "No need to fret yourself about that."

Diana thought back to all the years she had known Dale. "How long were you married?"

"Seven years," Helen smiled. A gentle light glowed deep within her eyes. "But I had known him most of my life. You see, we were both orphans. Grew up together in the same orphanage. He's the only man I ever loved—ever will love for that matter. Jesus said we're not married in heaven like we are here on earth, but I know I'll be with my husband again one day and whatever it's like where our Lord Jesus is will be just fine with me."

Diana and Courtney glanced at each other. Neither had heard anyone speak with such confidence before about things unseen. Helen talked as though her husband had gone on a vacation rather than having been killed in the bloody fighting of North Africa.

The visit passed swiftly for Diana, and as the evening chill began to fall in the little garden they said their farewells. She had held Kate the entire time and could hardly bear to put her down when it was time to leave. It was as though Kate's absence had left an empty place inside her that was being filled by a coldness. Donny shook hands with Courtney and saluted him. Kate hugged Diana so hard that Helen had to help pry her loose.

As Diana and Courtney left Helen's front door, he stumbled. Diana steadied him and they continued along the sidewalk with Courtney's arm around her, leaning slightly on her for support.

It occurred to Diana that she had seen her mother and father walk in the same fashion after he had been injured.

14

OLD THINGS ARE PASSED AWAY

What a pretty dress, Mum!" Kate was walking along the aisle of the department store holding onto Diana's hand when she saw the dress hanging on a display stand.

Helen glanced at the pink party dress with the white satin ribbons along the bodice and hem. "Yes, darling, it is lovely. But we're just here to keep Miss Marlowe company."

"Would you please call me by my Christian name, Helen?" Diana chastised good-naturedly. "You make me sound like the mistress of a girl's boarding school."

"I guess maybe it does at that," Helen agreed. "Diana. There— that *does* sound better."

Diana ran her hand across the tiny ribbons that trimmed the bodice of the dress. Then she smiled down at Kate. "I think every young lady should have a pink party dress at least once in their life. What do you think, Kate?"

Kate stared up at her mother. "Did you hear, Mum? Do you think so too?"

Helen shook her head sadly. "I'm afraid it's far too expensive, dear."

Diana motioned to a short dumpy salesgirl with rosy cheeks and a round face. She hurried over to them, with a cheery greeting. "Why, Miss Marlowe, it's been ever so long since I've seen you in here."

"There don't seem to be many gala affairs to dress up for any more, Annie." Diana glanced down at Kate. "But here's a customer who needs some help."

Annie knelt down next to Kate. "Good morning, Madam. And how may I be of assistance to you?"

Kate looked up at her mother and giggled.

Helen stepped closer to Diana and whispered, "Mi—Diana, I can't let you do this. We're just here to keep you company."

"Where's the fun in money if one can't buy a few presents for one's friends?" Diana had no intention of buying anything for herself when she asked Helen and Kate to come along with her, but she expected that Helen wouldn't come if she knew the real reason for the invitation. "You're a Christian woman, Helen. You wouldn't want to hurt my feelings now, would you?"

Helen stared at the eager, upturned face of her daughter still admiring the dress. "I guess I don't," she relented. "Thank you ever so much." Helen knew she had been playfully deceived by Diana and she was torn between her need to be independent and the look of joy in Kate's eyes at the thought that she might get the dress. Somehow she knew that Diana felt the need to do this for them even more than they needed her.

After Annie had taken the dress from the display rack, Diana motioned for her to follow along with them. In half an hour's time, she had persuaded Helen to let her buy clothes for both the children. In another ten minutes, Helen had a new coat, dress, and shoes for herself.

Carrying their bundles and bags, Diana led them to the little Tea Shoppe on the second floor balcony overlooking the main floor of the store. They found a table next to the railing and placed their orders with a frail, mousy looking waitress in a red-and-white striped dress.

"I can never thank you enough for your kindness, Mi—Diana." Helen's face looked like that of a young girl as she beamed at her daughter. "Maybe it's selfish of me, but it's so good to see my children getting some things that I could never afford to buy for them. If Bill had only . . . Well, some things are best left alone I suppose."

The waitress returned, placing three bowls of ice cream on the table. Kate's eyes were wide with wonder as she reached out with a finger, scooping the chocolate syrup off the ice cream and putting it in her mouth.

"Use your spoon, Kate." Helen handed her a spoon, wiping the chocolate off her mouth with a napkin.

"I never had *this* on ice cream before, Mum." Kate scraped more chocolate off with her spoon. "What *is* it?"

"Just chocolate syrup, darling. Do you like it?"

"Oh, it's *ever* so good!"

Helen took a bite of ice cream, relishing the cool, smooth texture of it. "I worry about Donny and Kate sometimes," she commented almost absently. "If anything ever happened to me . . . Bill and I don't have any folk around that we know of except for a distant cousin or two." She shook her head slowly. "Listen to me, will you? Still talking like he was alive and strong and coming home from work at five o'clock."

Diana knew she would have given up long ago. "Is it very hard on you?"

"Oh, no." Helen brightened at once. "I wouldn't trade places with the Queen Mother herself." She took another bite of ice cream, letting it melt in her mouth as she swallowed it a little at a time, savoring the rich sweetness of it. "Sometimes the memories get a bit heavy, you know, but it always passes. It's strange how they can make me happy and a little bit sad all at the same time. Doesn't make sense—now does it?"

"I think it makes perfect sense." Diana reached across the table and patted Helen on the hand. She was coming to realize just how much Helen had loved her husband and how very special their marriage must have been. *I wish I could have seen the two of them together.*

"Donny gets along famously with your Lieutenant, he does." Helen seemed to lift out of her brief reverie. "Not many young men around anymore with the war and all."

"I think Mark was more excited about going to the zoo today than Donny was." Diana thought how different Mark seemed to be when he was with Donny. It was as though he could let down his guard and be himself. "We were certainly lucky to meet you and your children, Helen."

"Lucky for me, I'd say." Helen couldn't imagine why a lady with Diana's background would make such a statement about her. "You know—it's almost like we was family!" She ate her ice cream slowly, gazing at Kate's messy pleasures and enjoying the company of her new friend.

Diana stared at the shoppers below them on the main floor of the department store. She wondered how many of them had lost husbands or sons or brothers in the hard years since the British expeditionary force had left to defend Northern Europe against the seemingly invincible German blitzkrieg. Dunkirk had taken a terrible toll on the British forces as well as the morale of the people, but they had held fast.

As Diana watched Kate spooning the last of the ice cream from the bottom of her bowl, she thought of the circumstances that had brought them all together: Mark, from his little home town in the southern region of America; herself, meeting him by the merest chance of climbing on a bus for no reason whatsoever; and Kate and her children, who had somehow brought them closer together—given them a new way of looking at the world. *Maybe Helen's right. We do seem like a family.*

"Well, shall we go?" Diana saw that everyone had finished their ice cream. "We'd best stop at the grocers *and* the butchers *and* the bakery on our way home. After their day at the zoo, I'm sure the boys will both be famished."

"That Lieutenant of yours seems to have picked up an appetite lately." Helen cleaned the chocolate and ice cream from Kate's face, setting her down on the floor. "No wonder though, the way Donny has him running about whenever they're together."

"I've never known him to eat so much, Helen," Diana agreed. "Must be your marvelous cooking."

Helen blushed slightly at the compliment. "It *is* good to have a man about the house to cook for again."

* * *

Helen Southwell stood at her kitchen sink, washing dishes. Through the window she watched Diana and Kate playing dolls in the little garden area. Back near the crumbled wall, Donny was playing soldier, attacking Rommel's Afrika Korps with his broomstick Sten Gun.

Helen hummed "Amazing Grace" as she worked. She saw Diana hold a tiny teacup up to her doll's face. Diana had bought two new dolls for Kate, as her old one was almost in pieces. One had red hair to match Kate's and the other was blonde. *God's grace brought Diana into our lives. She's been such a blessing! All the good things to eat and clothes for the children. Poor creature, and she seems so sad!*

Smiling at her good fortune, Helen began drying the dishes and putting them away. *Miss Marlowe's in love with the Lieutenant. It was on her face that first day I saw her at the hospital. And he loves her too, although he may not know it yet. But there's something about the two of them— something that won't let them tell each other or show each other. People put themselves through such misery sometimes. Well, the children and I will pray especially hard that God will work things out for them. It's such a shame to see two people waste their lives when they could be so happy with each other. And Miss Marlowe needs a child to fill that emptiness I see in her eyes.*

Through the panes of glass, Kate seemed to waver slightly and sway before Helen's eyes. At first she thought the child was falling down, then Helen realized that she had grabbed onto the counter to steady herself. As she stared out the window, a circle of blackness seemed to be closing steadily in about the garden area. Then she heard a roar like a formation of German bombers flying over during the blitz. The circle of darkness closed to a bright pinpoint of light, so intense she couldn't look at it. The light winked out. Helen felt herself catapulted upward at great speed and swept away into the roaring darkness.

* * *

Diana walked into the dayroom, glancing about until she saw Courtney. He slouched in a battered leather lounge chair with his bad leg propped on a small table, seemingly lost in the book he was reading. Wearing a faded maroon hospital robe, blue pajamas, and cloth slippers, he could have been a patron of an old folks' home, but for the thick auburn hair combed straight back from his youthful profile. As she got closer, she saw that the book propped on his chest was *The Yearling*.

"Mark?"

He flinched slightly and glanced up at her. "Why didn't you tell me you were coming? I haven't even shaved." His face, thinner since his injury, broke into a bright smile. "Probably look like I stepped out of a bad dream."

Diana couldn't dredge the words up yet. "*The Yearling*—is it a good book?"

"Yeah. Strangely enough, it is—for a book where an animal plays a big part. Those things are usually maudlin." Courtney put a cigar wrapper in the book for a marker and closed it. "Takes place in the Florida Everglades. It's about a boy who adopts a white-tail deer as his pet."

"Are you feeling well today?" Diana shifted about uneasily on the tiled floor.

Courtney knew the unexpected visit wasn't without purpose. It suddenly occurred to him that Diana planned to tell him she no longer wanted to see him. He felt a weakness began to take him, almost as he had felt when he had lost so much blood from his injuries. "Why'd you come?" He stared into her soft blue-green eyes, looking for a glimmer of hope.

Diana glanced down, then looked across the room toward a middle aged man with thinning blond hair who guided his wheelchair over to a table stacked with magazines. "It's Helen. She's had another stroke."

At first Courtney thought he had misunderstood her. "Another stroke? That's not possible! She's done so well."

"She's in the emergency room now. They don't know how bad it is yet."

"What about Donny and Kate?"

"They're with Mrs. Fletcher, but they can't stay there. She's moving back to Hastings next week." Diana stared pleadingly at Courtney. "What's going to happen to them?"

"Let's go down and check on Helen." Courtney reached for his cane. Diana handed it to him, taking his hand and helping him to stand up.

When they reached the emergency room corridor, a big red-faced man with a white smock and stethoscope banged out of the swinging doors. He wore horn-rimmed glasses and a harried expression.

Diana stepped in front of him. "Doctor, may I speak to you a moment?"

"Yes, but make it quick. I'm in a bit of a hurry." He glanced down at the watch on his thick wrist.

"I'm here about Helen Southwell. She was brought in about five hours ago."

"Are you a relative?"

"A friend." Diana's face was drawn with concern. "She and her husband were both orphans. I don't think she has any family to speak of."

"I'm afraid she's having a rough go of it. There's been a great deal of cerebral hemorrhaging." The doctor glanced at Courtney, then his face softened as he spoke to Diana. "She actually died once, but we were able to bring her back around. The next forty-eight hours will be critical."

"Where is she now?"

"They're moving her into a private room. It would be best if she were in the critical care unit, but with the war, there are so many who need the beds more than she does." The doctor glanced down again at his watch.

Diana took Courtney by the arm, as if she needed his strength to remain on her feet. "Thank you so much, Doctor. You're very kind."

The doctor took her hand in both his massive ones and smiled. "There's some who may take issue with that, but thanks just the same. I hope she does well."

Courtney leaned on his cane, watching the doctor disappear down the corridor. "Well, I guess there's nothing for us to do now but wait."

"And pray."

*   *   *

Courtney stood in the hall outside Helen's room. He held a paper cup of strong black coffee as he stared through the partially opened door at Diana, sitting in the hard white chair next to Helen's bed. It was her second all night vigil. Just as he started to take the coffee into Diana, he saw Helen open her eyes. Diana immediately took her by the hand and leaned close to her.

In the pale yellow glow of the bedside lamp, Helen's face was as serene as a da Vinci portrait. She seemed dazed at first, but quickly recognized Diana and smiled as though she had just awakened on the morning of her wedding day instead of in a hospital bed after a stroke.

Diana began speaking to her. Courtney could hear the low undertone, but couldn't make out any of the words. With some effort, Helen took Diana's hand in both of hers and spoke to her in a murmuring tone that to Courtney had a musical quality to it. The smile never left her. Her face seemed to radiate a light that was brighter than the lamp.

Courtney watched the two women for twenty minutes as they spoke. Then Helen placed both her hands on Diana's head and closed her eyes, speaking so softly that Courtney could no longer hear her. Every few seconds she would fall silent and Diana would speak in the same silent eloquence, her head bowed and her eyes closed.

In a few minutes, both women opened their eyes and gazed at each other. Courtney thought he heard Diana laugh softly, although tears were streaming down her cheeks. She leaned over the bed and embraced Helen who patted and rubbed Diana's back, soothing and comforting her as she would a child.

Courtney started to enter the room, when something seemed to stop him. He felt nothing in a physical sense, but was unable or unwilling to go any farther. It was as though he had no right to be in the presence of the two women. He closed the door quietly and sat down in a chair near the nurses' station.

Ten minutes later Diana came out of the room. Her smile seemed to brighten the dim hallway.

Courtney rose from his chair, leaning on his cane. "I saw her wake up. How's she doing?"

Diana walked over to him and took his arm. Kissing him lightly on the cheek, she murmured, "Why don't you buy me a cup of tea and I'll tell you all about it?"

*　　*　　*

Diana stood in the tiny kitchen, thinking what a change had been wrought in her life since she had first come to the modest little bungalow. She could almost hear Helen's sweet clear voice as she sang the words of the old song, *How precious did that grace appear, The hour I first believed.* She busied herself cleaning out the cabinets and putting all the kitchen items in boxes and, just as Helen had done, she watched the children playing in the garden.

"Do you think there's any chance for her?" Courtney stood in the doorway that led to the back of the house.

"No." There was no sorrow in Diana's voice as she pronounced the verdict on Helen.

"But even the doctors said they don't know for sure." Courtney felt some irreplaceable good would vanish from the world if Helen Southwell died. Since her stroke, he had found there were so many questions he wanted to ask her. *Why did I wait*?

"Helen knows."

Courtney felt restless and uneasy. Things had changed. Diana had changed! She hadn't had a drink in two days, not since that night at the hospital. It seemed he no longer had control of his life. He pulled up a battered wooden chair and sat down. "Tell me again what happened that night."

Leaning back against the counter, Diana glanced out at Donny and Kate. "When Helen woke up, the first thing she did was ask about her children. She said she had to make sure they'd be taken care of because she knew she was going to die. I told her they were living at my parents' home." Diana stared out the window. "She wasn't afraid at all. It was almost as if she was going off on holiday or something."

Courtney felt a chill at the back of his neck. He trembled slightly, shifting in his chair to try and hide it.

"And then she seemed to have a kind of peace about her children, a certainty that they'd be all right. And she started to tell me how much Jesus loved me." Tears glistened in Diana's eyes as she spoke. "She said there was nothing I could ever do to stop Him from loving me."

Glancing at the back door, Courtney felt a strong urge to get up and run out of the house. He was drawn to Diana's words, but something seemed to be pulling him away from her—something that he almost recognized.

Diana touched her eyes with Helen's apron that she had put on to do the clean-up. "Then she prayed with me and I saw how simple and easy it was, this—this wonderful thing that God has done for us through His Son. Through His death and His resurrection and His blood. I felt so *sorry* for all the things I had done wrong in my life! Then I asked God to forgive me and I asked Jesus to come into my heart and life and make me whatever *He* wanted me to be."

Outside the children played at their games, making the noises that children everywhere make when they are happy. Courtney envied them.

"Did Helen say anything else?"

"Yes, she did." Diana remembered the last words Helen had spoken to her and she smiled. "She told me there weren't any orphans in Heaven."

"You mean she . . ."

"I don't know, Mark. I just know what she told me."

"Do you realize that you haven't had a drink since—since that night?"

Diana's eyes narrowed briefly in thought. "I guess you're right. Haven't really thought about it."

Mark shook his head slowly. "You're like a different person now. I don't understand it."

She knew he had made the decision before he spoke.

"Diana, do you think I could have the same thing that you've got?"

Diana walked over to his chair and took both his hands, her face aglow in the dim light of the kitchen. "I thought you'd never ask, Mark—I thought you'd never ask!"

* * *

"Are the children settling in?" Mark walked steadily along next to the concrete railing of the hospital terrace. It led off the second floor dayroom and was used as an exercise area for the convalescing patients.

Diana walked along beside him, pleased at how well he was able to walk now. "Oh, yes! Mother already speaks of them as *her* grandchildren. They miss their mother terribly, of course, especially little Kate, but children are so resilient. They'll do just fine. Donny thinks that Daddy's the greatest hero since Wellington defeated Napoleon."

"I'll bet he shows him all that old war memorabilia every day," Mark smiled.

"At least twice," Diana agreed, "but Donny never seems to grow tired of it. It's like he's got a grandfather now for the first time in his life."

Mark gazed out over the city. In the distance he could see the great dome of St. Paul's Cathedral, still intact after the best the Germans could throw at it. "It's strange how I keep thinking about Helen's rough life and now this stroke."

Diana's brow furrowed slightly.

"Oh, they're *good* thoughts," Mark added quickly. "It seemed more like a celebration there in the hospital that night after you told me what she said. It could have been very sad, you know, since neither Helen nor Bill had families—no one to come and visit her. But it almost made me feel good in a way after you told me how she handled it. It was kind of like celebrating the end of a mission when we know we've fought well that day. The only sad part was the children not being able to stay with their mother. She seemed to know they'd be taken care of though."

"Oh, yes! She seemed perfectly sure of that." Diana noticed that Mark seemed to be walking without pain now. I'm glad your leg's about well."

"Yep. I even ran on it some the last two or three days." Mark jumped up and down on his injured leg. "Yes, sir. I've got a new leg—and a new heart."

"Heart?" Then Diana quickly realized what he meant. "That's the best part, isn't it?"

"No doubt about it."

They came to a wooden bench just outside the dayroom door and sat down. Courtney leaned back and stared up at the fleecy white clouds floating overhead. He took Diana's hand, feeling the same tingling warmth as the first night he had met her. "It's almost like we've just met each other."

Diana squeezed his hand, leaning her head against his shoulder. "It is, isn't it? It's like everything that happened to us before we met Helen was some kind of dream."

"Nightmare's more like it!"

"Well put," Diana agreed. "But as Paul said, 'Forgetting those things which are behind, . . . I press toward the mark . . . '"

"You know, the more I read that Bible you gave me, the more I realize that it's the only thing in the world that really makes any sense to me." Mark put his arm around Diana and pulled her closer. "There's a fellow named Luke Hatfield in my crew. I used to think he was mad as a hatter, the way he was always talking about Jesus and the Bible. Most everybody else did too. But nobody said a whole lot to him about it, because when things really got tough, they knew he was one man they could all depend on. Maybe he was like that before he became a Christian, I don't know. But it's hard to believe he could stay as calm as he always does without a lot of help from *somewhere*."

Diana thought about all the changes that had taken place in their lives in the past several weeks. "When do you have to go back?"

"Ten days."

"Will you have the same crew?"

"Yep. I'm kinda used to 'em now." Mark thought of the motley assortment of men that awaited him back at the airfield. "I'd probably feel out of place with a sane bunch."

Diana took Mark's face in both hands, reveling in the soft new light that shone in his eyes. "I wish I could say that I won't worry about you, but I will."

"I might feel insulted if you didn't worry just a little." Mark's eyes looked beyond the terrace and toward the past. "Luke used to say something that I've thought a lot about lately. Most of the time before we'd go on a mission, he'd just close his eyes and say, *For whether we live, we live unto the Lord; and whether we die, we die unto the Lord: whether we live therefore, or die, we are the Lord's.*"

15

A WALK IN THE PARK

You know what I like about the war?" Diana clung to Mark's arm as they strolled through Hyde Park.

Mark was taken off guard by the question. It seemed Diana had a knack for that. "Have you gone daft, woman?" he asked in his best imitation of a Londoner. "What's to like about it? Since I have to go back to it tomorrow, maybe you should tell me."

"The stars."

Courtney frowned. "The stars? Oh, you mean Olivier, Vivian Leigh, some of the others that perform for free at the stations down in the Underground."

"No, silly." Diana pointed up into the night sky. "Those stars. Because of the blackout, we can see them now. When all the city lights are burning, the sky's invisible."

"Haven't given it any thought, I guess." He gazed up at the light-spangled heavens. "Sometimes we leave on a mission before daylight, but I'm usually a little preoccupied. Not much time for stargazing."

They came to a bench and sat down. The evening mist had begun to thicken along the streets and across the grassy areas of the park. Above them, all was clear and shining.

"Diana, you remember that day in Helen's kitchen when I—got saved." Mark took her hand, watching the mist drift slowly on the soft night breeze. "Got saved. It still sounds strange to me. I remember when I was a boy in Liberty and we'd have a revival at the

Baptist church. Afterwards, people would go around town telling how they 'got saved.'"

Diana had a picture in her mind of Mark kneeling with her on the floor of the little kitchen with the sounds of the children playing outside.

"Well, I never said anything, but I had no idea what they were talking about. I figured everybody knew but me, so I kept my mouth shut." Mark smiled at Diana without thinking why he was smiling or what good smiling at her would do him. He did it because he felt like it. "I remember you asked me that day after I accepted Jesus as my savior if I felt any different. I said that I didn't."

"I've just started back reading the Bible after a long absence, Mark, but I don't ever remember seeing where God demands that we *feel* a particular way."

Mark thought about that for a few moments. "I never have either, now that you mention it. Well, what happened to me is—it just seemed that somehow the world had changed. Well, maybe not the world, but the people—it's hard to explain, but things are just *different*."

Diana felt happiness welling up inside her breast. She couldn't explain it, but it just happened to her at the oddest times and in the oddest places.

"Let me see if I can explain." Mark clasped his hands together and placed them under his chin. "There's this fellow at the hospital. He fought with Montgomery in North Africa, like Helen's husband did. I guess he's a nice enough guy, but something about him—or maybe about me—made me take an instant dislike to him. It got so bad, I couldn't stand to be in the same room with him. Well, the next morning after I accepted Jesus, he sat down across from me at breakfast. I spoke and he spoke and we had the best conversation—about ordinary things—but I really *enjoyed it*. Later on back in my room, I suddenly realized that all the hatred I had felt for him was gone. I can't explain it—it was just gone!"

The happiness in Diana broke forth in soft laughter.

Mark looked at her with a puzzled expression. "You're a strange girl, Diana Marlowe. I'm glad that can't keep a person from becoming a Christian."

"Oh, don't mind me. This happens every once in a while." Diana kissed him on the cheek. "It had nothing to do with what you said. The Apostle Paul said something about what happened to you though—about all things becoming new in Christ."

"Well, maybe not *all* things," Mark teased. "You're still a strange girl."

"And wouldn't you be bored to tears if I were otherwise?" Diana smiled broadly again as her happiness became too great for her to contain.

Suddenly the chilling shrieks of the air raid sirens split the stillness of the night. The eerie, mournful wailing sent people scurrying to the shelters. On the other side of the common, an anti-aircraft battery stood in ominous silhouette, a bulky darkness in the dim light.

"Should we watch the show?" Diana gazed with intense fascination at the brilliant beams of the searchlights, cutting through the night skies.

"Strange girl!" Courtney mumbled under his breath. "Why not? It's only a world war."

The thunder of the anti-aircraft battery drowned out all other sound, shaking them on their bench. High above them the red-orange bursts of the shells looked like a gigantic Fourth-of-July fireworks display.

Courtney thought of the many times he had been on the receiving end of just such an awesome display of firepower from the German gunners. One of the Heinkels flew directly into the path of the search lights, gleaming against the darkness. He put himself in the pilot's place, trying to imagine his terror as his aircraft made a beautifully outlined target for the big guns and the RAF night fighters.

All at once, objects began raining down from the sky, thudding into the walkways and rustling down through the trees. Courtney immediately realized that they were hunks of cast iron shell fragments. He jumped to his feet, holding out his hand to Diana. "Have you seen enough?"

"*Quite* enough, thank you."

They ran hand in hand across the street, taking shelter in the deeply recessed doorway of an old building. The night skies, stabbed by exploding shells and riven by the bright sweeping searchlights, formed a fantastic and lethal backdrop as they stood together beneath the stone archway.

Mark took Diana into his arms and pulled her close. They stood like that for a long time, close and warm against each other while the sky and the city exploded around them. Then he pulled back and gazed down at Diana. Her face had softened, the years seeming to have fallen away in these last days. The dark circles had faded and vanished completely. He marveled at the childlike wonder he saw in her eyes, at the rapt and innocent beauty that had blossomed from the ruins of her life.

Diana stood on tiptoe as Mark bent to kiss her. It was as though she had never kissed another man before. She felt both tenderness and fire, born of the blood and of the spirit. Her arms circled his waist as she drew closer, feeling that she was already a part of him.

Drawing away slowly, Mark touched Diana's lips softly with the tips of his fingers. "I didn't think it was possible."

"What?" Diana breathed.

"To love you so."

Diana felt Mark brush away a tear that coursed slowly down her cheek. "I've loved you since that first awful night we met. Oh, I don't mean it that way—it's just that *I* was so awful and I'd had so much to drink and—"

"I know exactly what you mean."

"I did fight against it *frightfully* hard, you know." Diana brushed his hair back from his forehead. "I didn't want to love *you* or *anyone—ever* again."

"Captivated by my boyish charms!" Mark teased. "Swept away by my sparkling repartee! A victim of the Southern drawl."

"Oh, hush—and kiss me!"

* * *

"You men gonna let the *Outcast* outdo you? Kane leaned on the small wooden lectern of the group interrogation room. "That bunch of misfits and deadbeats are hitting the targets better and shooting down more fighters than anybody."

Groans and mumbled curses spread about the room as the other men glared at the crew of the *Outcast*.

Kane didn't smile, but his scowl wasn't as fierce as usual when he said, "We did all right today. Those Krauts will have a lot fewer submarines to prowl around the North Atlantic, thanks to this mission."

After the debriefing was over, Mark walked with Hatfield over to the long table set up at the end of the room. Roast beef sandwiches, coffee, and hot chocolate had been laid out for the men after their long hours in the air.

Filling a thick white mug with hot chocolate from the huge urn, Mark handed it to Hatfield. "You really saved us down in that ball turret today. Never saw a day when they hit us from below so many times. You saw those Jerries coming at us like you never had an eye injury! It's amazing!"

"Like we used to say back home," Hatfield smiled, "'jist another day choppin' cotton.'" He sipped the hot chocolate. "What we need is a purty girl to serve this to us during the mission. It would sho'ly taste good when the temperature gets down to about twenty below on that long flight back home."

Mark sipped his coffee thoughtfully, staring wearily at the ragtag group of men in their flight suits and heavy boots milling about in the room.

"Lieutenant, I'm proud of the way you've been handlin' yourself."

"Whadda you mean?"

"You know *exactly* what I mean." Hatfield glanced around at some of the crew of the *Outcast* crowded around the table. "They've been giving you a hard time since you got saved. Callin' you *Jesus Boy* and all them other names. But you stood your ground. That ain't easy to do. Always happens though when a man *really* means business with God. Funny how them kind of people never seem to bother the Sunday Morning Christians."

Courtney grinned at Hatfield and wondered how God could pack so much courage into such a little man. "I haven't done anything."

"Just don't never back down on your faith," Hatfield warned solemnly.

"I won't."

"You know, Lieutenant, that bunch of heathens and you and me are turning into a pretty fair crew." Hatfield waved his hand at the men wolfing down the sandwiches. "Even ol' Kane said so—as close as he'll get to saying it anyhow. Them boys'll make fun of you, but they got confidence in you now. They believe you can get them back home safe on even the roughest missions."

"What makes you say that?"

"Heard 'em talking over at the enlisted men's club the other night. Went in to listen to some Glenn Miller music. I'll be backslidin' next thing you know." Hatfield pointed to Ragusa. "You see that big

Mafia legbreaker. He was braggin' to everybody in the place how the *Outcast* had the best pilot in the whole Eighth Air Force."

"Ragusa said that about me!" Courtney responded in amazement. "He hasn't said two words to me since I got back to the group."

"Well, he was sayin' a lot of 'em *about* you. Remember on the way back from that last mission to Bremen how thick the fighters got right before we reached the North Sea? Well, Ragusa was tellin' everybody how you handled that big Fort like it was a fighter when you went into them evasive maneuvers."

Courtney remembered then how he had caught Ragusa staring at him several times since he got back as if trying to figure out what was wrong.

"That big waist gunner from the 544th, you know the one who won the arm wrestling championship—that was before Ragusa got here though. Well, anyhow he started tellin' everybody how you wasn't nothing but a coward and a goldbricker. Ragusa got up and walked over to where he was and—"

"You're really wound up tonight, aren't you, Sergeant?" Courtney interrupted the animated little man with a grin. "Where do you get the energy?"

"Sorry, Lieutenant." Hatfield finished his hot chocolate. "Well, anyway, I just wanted you to know the boys are all behind you, even if they do give you a hard time."

"That's good to know, Sergeant. Just wish I could get Kane on our side."

Hatfield gave him a sly smile. "Might be easier to get the Red Sea parted again."

Courtney shrugged wearily. "I expect you're right, but then we can't have everybody love us, can we?"

"That's a fact, Lieutenant. That's a natural-born fact." Hatfield turned and pushed his way toward the crowded table. "All right, you bunch of Nazi-killin' heathens, step aside and let a man of God get him a bite to eat!"

As Courtney watched Hatfield shove his way to the table, he thought of Paul, another small man who never backed down once he had put his hand to the plow.

*   *   *

Courtney awakened in the anemic gray light of what should have been sunrise, but had been only a gradual brightening of the eastern clouds for the past four mornings. The Quonset hut was silent except for an occasional cough or someone tossing in their sleep. He gazed out the window. The persistent English rain still fell on the airdrome, silencing even the raucous and arboreal arguments of the crows.

When he remembered he was to meet Diana in the village that morning, Courtney rubbed his eyes and rose from his bunk with renewed energy. The three-day stand-down had been as bad as the missions—almost. Kane had insisted that everyone be checked out on the new F model Forts that had been flown in from the States. Then there were the interminable hours in the briefing room with charts and maps for the anticipated new targets.

But today belonged to him and Diana! When he had dressed and stepped outside, the rain had become a heavy mist. He walked over to the latrine, showered, shaved and put his clothes back on. Then he hitched a ride over to Admin, getting there just in time to catch the liberty bus into the village.

The East Anglican farmlands passed by outside the windows of the bus like the gently rolling swells of the sea. They were blanketed as usual under the covering of soft white mist that they seemed to breathe upward into the damp air. The bus traveled alongside a train, its smoke white as the mist, as it clicked steadily along the tracks. The thatched roofs and stone walls of the farmhouses were darkened by the rain. Crossing over cobblestones and passing a pub, they rolled into the village.

As he walked along the main street of the village, Courtney noticed the shabbiness of the people. The women wore no stockings and only the younger ones wore lipstick, given to them by Americans. He smelled the fresh baked bread and the raw meat in the butcher shops. The clothes in the shop windows had ration-stamp notations on them and the bookstores stocked almost no new books.

This was the life of a people under siege, so much closer to the cauldron of war than America. They seemed spirited and cheerful, but looked a little weathered like the old brown buildings and the time-worn cobblestones, all under a heavy and seemingly eternal gray sky.

"Mark! Over here!"

He looked around and saw Diana standing next to her little green roadster. She wore a neat gray tweed jacket and slacks beneath her tan raincoat. Her hair was so shiny, it seemed to be collecting the pale light around her. "You certainly picked a good day for a picnic," he said in mock protest. "But then there are no good picnic days in England."

"Once upon a time we had one," Diana smiled. "I think it was shortly before the Battle of Hastings." She came into his arms and held him close.

Courtney shivered beneath his leather flight jacket. His hard cap was soaked from walking in the drizzle. "Let's go *inside* somewhere."

Diana kissed him soundly on the lips and stepped away from him, pointing toward the sky. "Look! The rain's almost stopped. We can't waste the day inside." She reached into the car for a wicker basket. Then she took an umbrella from the back seat. "We'll take this just in case."

"You still want to have a picnic?" Courtney glanced at the basket. "Why don't we go to your parents' house? Drink something hot and sit in front of the fire."

Diana smiled and kissed him again. "I want you all to myself today. Just follow me."

Mark tagged along with her, mumbling, "Yes, sir, a strange girl. A strange, strange girl."

Diana led the way down a narrow alleyway paved with smooth bricks that ran between a bookstore and a haberdashery. It came out onto a well-worn path down through an open meadow. The path led toward a river lined with ash and willow, their wet leaves gleaming silvery in the gray light.

Under a spreading ash, Diana directed Mark to rake away the top covering of leaves. She took a small blanket from the basket and spread it on the dryer layer of leaves. With a piece of string, Mark hung the opened umbrella from a low limb directly above them. Diana took their lunch of mutton sandwiches, pickles, pears, and hot tea in a thermos out of the basket and arranged it along with cups and napkins on the blanket.

"Now, isn't this lovely!" she beamed, admiring her handiwork. "We're snug and dry."

Mark turned from the river and stared at her with an incredulous expression on his face. "Snug and dry?"

"Well, almost," Diana corrected herself. "For the English, any-way."

After they had eaten the sandwiches and drunk the hot tea, Mark felt much better. "I hate to admit it, but it really isn't too bad down here by the river."

From out in the meadow, a cowbell clanged now and then as its owner searched for greener pastures. There was no other sound but an occasional errant breeze stirring in the leaves.

"My girlfriends tell me they like the American men better than ours," Diana informed Mark.

He had stretched out on the blanket, his head pillowed on Diana's thigh. "Is that so?"

"Yes, it is."

"And why is that, do you think?" Mark turned his head slightly, grinning up at her.

Diana replied almost shyly. "Well, for one thing, most of you seem so athletic, so—physical."

"Do go on."

"Then you don't have any problem saying what's on your mind. You're more direct and talkative."

"The English men sure talk a lot in the pubs." Courtney yawned and closed his eyes.

"Oh, they're perfectly sociable among themselves. That's where they feel at home." Diana ran her fingers through Mark's hair, letting them trail along his neck. "It just takes forever to get to know them and then you never know what they're thinking."

"When do you want to get married?"

Diana thought she had misunderstood him. "Pardon me?"

Mark opened his eyes, his expression as placid as the smooth surface of the river. "I merely asked when you wanted to join with me in holy matrimony. You know, tie the knot, unite in marriage, plight troths, and so on."

Diana quickly collected her wits. "I don't know what you *primitives* do over in the Colonies, but in polite society the aspirant bridegroom gets down on one knee and proposes to his intended bride. That is, *after* he asks permission from her father."

Mark gazed up at Diana with a wry smile. "You know, you're awfully independent for such a strange girl. Men don't stand in line to propose to girls as strange as you are."

"Those are my conditions." Diana crossed her arms over her breast and stared out across the river.

"A willful, haughty girl as well." Mark rolled over and knelt before her on one knee. He thought of the word games he had played with Carrington and how miraculous it was that he and Diana could do the same thing. It suddenly occurred to him that Diana would now be his best friend as well as his wife. Taking her hand, he implored, "Diana Marlowe, will—"

"Of course, I will, you foolish man. I thought you'd never ask!" Diana threw her arms around Mark's neck and kissed him soundly and well. She would forever recall that dreary gray day with the mist drifting across the river and the cowbell clanging out in the meadow.

* * *

Diana opened the front door and walked into the slate-floored foyer. Through the drawing room door, she saw her mother rise from her chair next to the fire and walk slowly toward her. The expression on her face was exactly the same as it had been that dreadful day when the flight officer had come to tell them about Dale. Her first thought was that something had happened to Mark. *No, that can't be! I've just left him!*

"The hospital rang." Doreen took Diana's coat and hung it on the halltree."

Even though Diana knew that the chance for good news was slight, she remained calm.

"Helen's vital signs seem to be weakening. If it continues, she may not last the night."

Somehow Diana had a sense of peace, even at the prospect of losing Helen, who had led her into the most important decision of her life. "Where are the children?"

"I put them down for their naps a half an hour ago." Doreen was terrified that Diana might react as she did to Dale's death. "Are you all right, child?"

"I'm fine, Mother."

And Doreen could tell that she meant it. "You go on to the hospital and be with her. We'll see to the children."

Diana hugged her mother, then smiled warmly into her eyes. "You've always been such a blessing to me. I guess I didn't always know how fortunate I was to have you, but I do now. Thank you for all the years of love."

"You were always an easy person to love, Diana. Well, *almost* always." Doreen smiled and kissed her daughter on the cheek. "You run along now."

16

ABOVE THE RHINE

*R*oger, Navigator. Be right down." The call from Selig came shortly after the drop on the second Schweinfurt mission. Mark tapped Doak Jennings, his new copilot on the shoulder and motioned downward with his thumb. Jennings nodded and took the controls. A dark, introspective lawyer from Flagstaff, Jennings had proven to be a capable flyer. No one knew why he had been exiled to the *Outcast* and he never told them.

After unplugging from the permanent oxygen system and hooking into his portable bottle, Mark crawled down into the greenhouse where he found Selig poring over his charts on the navigator's table. Once during every mission, after Sharp's death, Selig would call for Mark to come down and check his figures on plotting the course to or from the target. Selig had never made a mistake to anyone's knowledge, but had developed this harmless quirk that Mark always went along with.

Selig held up the clipboard to Mark who quickly tallied the figures and gave him the OK sign with thumb and forefinger. Taking the clipboard back, Selig glanced at Barnes and saw him busily scanning the sky for fighters through the Plexiglas nose of the plane. Selig scribbled something on the paper and handed it back to Mark.

Mark stared at the clipboard. *Thanks for being a friend.* He wrote, *You too!* and handed it back to Selig.

As Selig nodded his head slowly, Mark could tell that he was smiling under the oxygen mask. Mark patted him on the shoulder as he turned and bent over his maps and charts spread out on the navigator's table.

Before he turned to go back to the cockpit, Mark glanced out the right window of the greenhouse. In the hazy distance, almost a hundred miles behind him, he saw a gigantic column of black smoke rising a half mile or more up into the bright sky. Their bombs had nicked the jugular of the German war machine that day. He wondered how many civilian workers had been lost in the inferno caused by the raid.

As Mark turned to leave and stared ahead and downward to the north, down through the cottony clouds so much closer to the earth than he was, he saw the sparkling ribbon that was the Rhine River, somewhere between Bonn and Düsseldorf. He could barely make out the tiny specks on its shining surface that he imagined were German barges carrying their own cargoes of destruction. *What a beautiful day!*

In the passageway from the greenhouse to the cockpit, Mark crawled on his knees and one hand, his free hand holding the walk-around oxygen bottle. He climbed up through the trapdoor into the cockpit. As he was standing up to get back into the pilot's seat, he saw them roaring in toward the formation—three 109s at eleven o'clock! The *Outcast* was the lead ship. He knew all three fighters would hit them first.

Mark leaped for the pilot's seat and had just made it when something like a crashing freight train slammed into the Fort. Instantly a blast of icy air howled up the passageway from the greenhouse.

The ship lurched over onto one wingtip and into the initial stage of a flat spin. He felt it losing altitude rapidly as the turning motion began.

Grabbing the buffeting controls just in time, Mark gradually pulled the Fort out of the beginnings of its fatal spin. He glanced at Jennings. The copilot's face was smeared with blood from a cut above his right eye. He seemed to be more dazed than seriously hurt as he tried to wipe the blood away from his eyes with his heavy glove.

The powerful sub-zero wind shooting up the tunnel that ended at the little trapdoor between Mark's and Jenning's seats, quickly turned the cockpit into a miniature arctic region. The blown-out nose of the plane funneled it in at tremendous speed. Smaller streams of wind blew through holes in the instrument panel. As his ears recovered from the incredible noise of the explosion, Mark heard little but the shrieking wind.

Mark glanced to his left, his eye caught by the black smoke pouring out of the number two engine. He saw that the needle on the manifold pressure gauge was jumping rapidly. The engine itself began to shake violently. Afraid that it would rip itself out of the wing, Mark reached over and killed the engine. They would gradually fall behind in the formation, but at least they would keep flying.

Buckling into the seat and plugging back into the permanent oxygen supply, Mark yelled into the intercom. "Pilot to crew! Pilot to crew! Damage check!"

"Waist to Pilot! OK."

"Ball—I'm stuck in here. A shell knocked out the electric motor on the turret!"

"Pilot to Ball! Can you operate it manually?"

"No go! It sheared the handle of the crank off."

"We'll get you out, Luke."

"When somebody gets time, they might use that outside crank. I think it's still workin' all right." Hatfield's voice was almost drowned out by the wind whistling through the shattered Plexiglas of the ball. "This thing's shot-up and it's gettin' kinda windy down here."

Mark thought how casual Hatfield sounded trapped down in the ball turret, freezing and defenseless against another fighter attack."

"Radio, OK."

"Tail—fine back here!"

"Pilot to Turret! Come in, Turret!"

"Pilot to Navigator!" Mark knew there would be no answer, just as there hadn't been from the turret, but something forced him to make the check. "Pilot to Navigator! Damage check!" After waiting ten seconds for a reply, he didn't bother to check the bombardier.

"I'll go see what I can do."

Mark looked over at Jennings speaking over the intercom. He had taken his gloves off and managed to staunch the flow of blood from his forehead. With a cloth stuffed under his leather flight cap to hold it in place over the cut, he eased out of his seat, wincing as he felt the furious rush of wind up the narrow tunnel, knowing the nose of the plane had been blown out.

"Better let me go check it out. Think you can manage the ship?" Mark had been adjusting the trim-tab wheels and throttles to steady the line of flight of the yawing aircraft. So many of the instruments were dead, he had little idea of the condition of the remaining engines.

Jennings nodded and took the controls.

As Mark leaned over to get out of his seat, he looked down through the trapdoor and saw a hand reaching out along the floor of the tunnel. It groped ahead, then the arm and the head appeared. Selig! He was pulling himself along with his left arm, the right arm dragging limply at his side. As the little man struggled forward, Mark saw that his right leg was missing below the knee. He trailed the tattered remnants of his flying clothes along behind him. The stump of leg was still bleeding, but the blood was already beginning to coagulate in the numbing cold.

Selig rolled over on his back. The explosion had ripped off his helmet and oxygen mask. He writhed on the floor of the tunnel, his desperate eyes on Mark as they pleaded for oxygen. With his good hand, he slowly pointed toward his mouth.

For a moment, Mark was transfixed by the little man's agony. Then he grabbed his walk-around bottle and the spare mask from behind his seat, jumping through the trapdoor into the icy wind. Fitting the mask over Selig's face, Mark plugged it into the oxygen bottle. Selig immediately settled down. He relaxed as he held the mask close with his good hand, a look of contentment spreading over his tortured face. But the bottle only held four minutes of air. Selig would have to be moved to a permanent oxygen supply—quick!

Pointing toward the bombardier's station in the nose of the aircraft, Mark stared carefully at Selig. After taking a few more deep breaths, he shook his head slowly and pointed downward. Mark couldn't imagine Barnes tumbling through space, but instead had a vivid picture of him slamming his fist against Bong's jaw the day Bong had hijacked the Fort for his abbreviated attempt at reaching Berlin to assassinate Hitler.

Mark knew that he had to get Selig out of the wind or he would soon freeze to death. He lifted him beneath both arms, struggling to push him up through the trapdoor. He knew Jennings couldn't help, as he had all he could do to keep the damaged aircraft flying straight and level.

Finally he got Selig through, easing him toward the rear of the plane. Climbing up into the cockpit, Mark took his and Jennings' flak suits and spread them over Selig. Ripping pieces of the shredded flight suit, Mark wrapped them around the stump of the severed leg to stop the bleeding. Then he plugged Selig into the permanent oxygen system and took the walk-around bottle for himself.

Unclipping the first-aid kit from the wiring-diagram box on the back of the copilot's seat, Mark opened the lid, taking out a morphine ampule. He showed the ampule to Selig, pulled the leg of his flight suit up and plunged the needle into his thigh. In a few seconds the little man lay back like a baby in his cradle, his hand holding the oxygen mask against his face.

Mark noticed that the stump of the leg was still leaking blood in spite of the intense cold. He reached back into the kit, took out the cord provided with the tourniquet kit, and looped it around the leg. Then he made it fast and put the kit away. Having done all he could for Selig, Mark stood up to go to the rear of the aircraft.

A tap on his shoulder startled him. He turned around and saw Jennings pointing out the right window. Leaning over, he saw the number three engine beginning to smoke. It was still running smoothly. He pointed to the instrument panel for Jennings to watch the gauge closely. Jennings nodded as Mark went through the door of the cockpit.

One glance upward at the bloody, crumpled heap in the upper turret told Mark that it was hopeless. Nevertheless, he checked just to make sure. There was no pulse. The engineer and turret gunner had just come aboard that morning. Mark couldn't remember the man's name.

Mark navigated the narrow catwalk through the empty bomb bay cautiously, remembering Sharp's fatal plunge to the earth. He had a sudden horrible picture of him hurtling through space with some wide-eyed farmer leaning on his hoe, watching the American flyer dancing on German air.

At the end of the cat-walk, Mark hurried past the radio compartment to the ball turret. He quickly cranked it into line and opened the hatch. Hatfield climbed out as slowly and deliberately as he always did from his bunk each morning. Mark saw him smiling behind his oxygen mask as he nodded his head in thanks.

"Selig's still alive," Mark puffed over the intercom. "We'll have to get him back here to the radio room."

"I'm right behind you, Lieutenant." Hatfield, plugged into his portable bottle, followed Mark up to the cockpit and with surprisingly little difficulty managed to carry Selig back to the radio room. They hooked him into the oxygen system and covered him with flak suits.

Mark turned to Hatfield, pulling his mask off to talk to him briefly. "You'll have to man the upper turret."

Hatfield didn't have to ask why. He moved forward in the aircraft to the cockpit door. Then he climbed up into the upper turret to protect the ship from attacks from above and front, as it was the only gun left working that could do that.

As Hatfield was leaving the radio room, Mark felt a vibration that seemed to run all through the aircraft. Shortly afterwards their airspeed dropped suddenly. Jennings had cut the number three engine and feathered it. Mark plugged into the intercom. "Pilot to Copilot."

"Go ahead, Pilot."

"With two engines, it's gonna be touch-and-go whether we make it back or not."

"You wanna try the landing gear now?"

"That's the idea. I'm going into the ball."

"Roger."

Mark climbed down into the ball turret. He thought an earlier fighter attack had damaged the underside of the aircraft and now from underneath it, he could see that the area around the right landing gear was riddled with holes. "Go ahead, Copilot."

"Roger. Landing gear down."

Mark watched the left gear fold downward and lock in place. The right gear opened slightly, bucked and jerked for a few seconds and stopped. "Right landing gear's out."

"Roger, Pilot."

"I'll try the manual release." Hatfield had been listening on the intercom.

"Go ahead, Turret." Mark's mind was racing now. He could tell from the damage that there was little chance the gear would work at all. He knew Selig could never survive bailing out, and six other men were also depending on him.

In a few minutes, Hatfield came back on the intercom. "Turret to Pilot. She's dead. Couldn't get it to budge an inch."

"Roger that, Turret. Pilot to Copilot. I'm on my way forward." Mark took a last look at the right gear, ripped by the heavy slugs of the fighters, before he climbed out of the ball turret. The left gear rose back up into the wing and locked into place.

By the time Mark had settled back into the pilot's seat, he had made his decision. "Pilot to crew. When we get back to Stonewell, I'm going to make one pass before I set it down. *All*—I repeat *all* crew members will bail out. I won't have enough fuel to allow for any mistakes."

* * *

At the exact time that Barnes was blown out of the nose of the *Outcast* by the attacking 109s, Diana sat in the hospital cafeteria, watching the big red-faced doctor with the horn-rimmed glasses walk toward her.

When he reached her table, Diana set her cup down, holding his eyes with a steady gaze. "She's dead, isn't she?"

The doctor nodded. "Ten minutes ago. I'm sorry. There was nothing else we could do for her."

"I know that," Diana nodded solemnly.

"Is there anything I can do for *you*?" The doctor lay his big hand gently on Diana's shoulder.

"Nothing, thanks."

"You sure you're all right?"

"Yes." Diana rose from the table, taking the doctor's hand in both of hers. "Just have to make some arrangements." She took a deep breath, yearning for sleep. "I'd better be on my way."

Three hours later Diana leaned out the window of her roadster at the front gate of Stonewell Airdrome. "I have to see Lieutenant Mark Courtney."

The young airman, his dress tans neatly pressed and his face scrubbed and shiny, stepped over to the car. "I'm sorry, Ma'am, the base is a secure area. You'll have to have special permission to enter."

"But—there's been a death in the family," Diana pleaded wearily. The extended wait at the hospital had taken its toll on her and she longed to see Mark—to release in his arms the burden and the strain of the long hours.

The young guard noticed Diana's disheveled appearance and the almost desperate need in her eyes. He sensed absolutely no threat in this soft spoken and cultured woman. "Are you a relative of the Lieutenant's?"

"Fiancée."

205

"Well—I guess it'll be OK." He noted something on a clipboard and handed her a placard to put in her window. "You'll have to take this to Admin. Stay on this road, take the first left, and you're almost there."

"Thank you very much." Diana placed the placard on her dash. "Anybody in particular I'm to ask for?"

"Colonel Kane—although he's usually busy. Somebody there'll help you though." The airman saluted smartly and stepped back into the tiny guard shack.

Diana found the Admin building with no trouble, entering a door marked Commanding Officer. Several wooden desks stood on the bare concrete floor of the room. Two straight-backed chairs collected dust against the near wall.

A man in his late forties with a bulbous red nose and a big mangled cigar between his teeth stared up from a cluttered desk in the far corner of the room. "I'm Sergeant Overland," he said brusquely. "I don't know how you got on this base, but somebody's made a big mistake."

"But—he gave me a pass." Diana felt uneasy in this world of men. Everything she had seen since entering the airdrome was so bland, solid, and utilitarian. There was no color or softness at all in this alien environment. *How do they live like this*? "I'm Diana Marlowe and I'm looking for Lieutenant Mark Courtney. It's very important that I see him!"

At that moment, Zack Kane stepped quietly out of his office door behind Diana.

The burly sergeant got up and walked over to her. "It's very important that you leave this base right now! We're trying to fight a war here, lady!"

"That's enough, Sergeant!"

Diana whirled around at the sound of Kane's voice. The sergeant nodded, swaggering back to his desk.

At first Diana felt a pang of fear at the sight of the tall lean man with the growling voice and the hawklike face. Then she saw his dark eyes soften.

"I'm Colonel Zack Kane, Lieutenant Courtney's commanding officer. Are you the young lady he's going to marry?" Even after the toll her long vigil at the hospital had exacted from her, Kane was taken by Diana's fragile beauty.

"Yes, sir, I am."

"What's so important that you have to see him now?"

"There's been a death in the family—well, she's not actually a blood relative, but Mark and I are the closest thing she has to a family." Diana felt weak, but braced herself at the prospect of seeing Mark shortly. "Anyway, she's been sick for awhile and we're caring for her two children—my parents and I are . . ."

Kane had spent long years weighing the strengths and weaknesses of his men. He reasoned now that Diana Marlowe could face the truth better than being left alone to agonize about what she didn't know. "We just got word on Lieutenant Courtney. He's about thirty minutes behind the rest of the formation. Should put him about forty-five minutes out."

"Is he all right?"

"His plane's in pretty bad shape," Kane muttered, turning toward the door. "Some of his men are injured, but as far as I know, he's not." He looked back at Diana, bewildered and vulnerable in this world of fighting men. "I'm going over to the tower in a little while. Would you like to come along?"

"Oh, yes! Thank you so much!"

* * *

Diana followed Kane outside and climbed into the drab, army-green staff car. Heading along the makeshift road to the airstrip, Kane thought he could see another side of Mark Courtney. He had heard of Diana through the base grapevine, but she wasn't at all what he had expected. Not flashy or loud, but a woman of breeding—of grace and quiet beauty.

Diana stared at the clouds scudding across the sky. *A storm blowing in! Oh, God! Please let Mark make it in safely before it hits!* She glanced over at Kane, whose jaw muscles were working under the tight skin. "Awfully decent of you to let me come along. My father's retired from the army. I know you must be breaking some sort of regulation."

"That's one of the few good things about being the boss," Kane growled softly. "Who's going to report me?"

"Is Mark a good pilot?" Diana regretted it the minute she said it. "Oh, I'm sorry! I shouldn't have asked that."

"It's all right." Kane almost smiled at her. "Yes, he's an excellent pilot."

"I don't mean to be a nuisance, it's just . . ."

"This friend of yours who died must have been a very special person."

Diana brightened. "Oh, she was. I could go on about her forever. I guess to most people she would be as ordinary as kidney pie, but she made such a change in out lives and now we have her children."

Kane pulled up to the base of the rickety looking wooden control tower. *Yes sir, I've certainly learned something about Mark Courtney today!* "Would you like to come up into the tower with me?"

Diana merely nodded, followed Kane over to the stairs and climbed after him to the landing that led into the glassed-in room where the controller sat at his table. In his early twenties, he held a heavy microphone in front of his pale, chubby face.

Dispensing with introductions, Kane picked up a pair of binoculars. "How many still flying, Sergeant?"

"Just one, sir. The *Outcast.*"

"What's her status?"

"She's lost another engine, sir. Courtney's bringing her in on two." The sergeant pressed the send button. "Tower to *Outcast.* What's your position?"

"*Outcast* to Tower. We're two minutes out."

Diana could barely recognize Mark's voice in the garbled static of the radio. She tried to imagine him fighting to hold the damaged aircraft on course, peering ahead in the failing light as he sought the runway—she could not.

A few drops of rain spattered against the plate glass of the tower, then stopped. Kane's eyes narrowed as he glanced at them. "Is he still going to try to belly-land it after the others bail out?"

The sergeant at the mike looked back over his shoulder. "That's what he said. The fire crew's standing by."

"What do you mean, Colonel?" Intent on trying to spot the plane in the deepening gloom, Diana had only heard part of the brief exchange.

"His landing gear's been damaged." Kane's dark eyes mirrored his concern as he turned them on Diana. "He's ordered the rest of the crew to bail out."

"But why doesn't Mark bail out with them?"

Kane looked back toward the distant end of the runway. "He's got a man too badly injured to bail out with the rest of them. The man may die anyway, but Courtney won't leave him."

"Couldn't—couldn't you just order him to bail out? I mean, if there's little chance for the other man anyway?"

Kane thought of the change he had seen in Mark since he had come back from his injuries. "He'd never do that." He looked into Diana's pleading eyes, knowing that she had almost lost Mark once. "I don't want him to—to go down disobeying an order. Can you understand that?"

"Yes."

The muted drone of engines drew their eyes back to the window. Above the treeline at the far end of the long concrete strip, Diana saw the *Outcast* glinting dully in the pewter-colored twilight. As it grew steadily larger, she saw that it was wavering, listing slowly to the right and then back to the left. One by one, six chutes blossomed whitely against the darkening sky. As the Fort passed close by them, she could clearly see that the nose section had been blown apart. Two engines, the wings, and the fuselage had been ripped and torn by machine gun blasts.

The Fort banked slowly back toward the east, its landing gear still stubbornly locked. Receding into the distance, it banked again, lining up for the final approach.

"Tower to *Outcast*. Runway is clear. Emergency team standing by. Over."

"Roger that, Tower. These engines are about to shut down on me. This one's gonna be a keeper."

The Fort dipped dangerously close to the runway, nose steeply down, then pulled up. Slowly it leveled off, closer and closer to the concrete strip. It touched down with a shrieking of metal that Diana heard in the tower. She saw sparks flying outward all around the aircraft as it careened down the runway. The last Diana saw of the *Outcast*, it slid past the tower, disappearing in a shower of sparks behind the stand of trees that lined the end of the runway.

The fire engine and two crew trucks were already rushing past them on the way to the crippled aircraft. The terrible screeching of metal on concrete faded away, followed by a loud crash. The silence that followed was almost worse than the noise. Kane was already on his way down the stairs, followed closely by Diana. They ran across the tarmac. Just before they reached the tree line, an orange glow suddenly brightened the deepening twilight with a loud *Whoomp!* that rattled the glass in the control tower.

Kane stopped at the edge of the trees, turning around to look at Diana, an expression of regret on his face. As she stared at him, a feeling a numbness crept over her. The acrid smell of oil and aviation fuel from the hardstand filled her nostrils. She felt unreal, as if the months she had known Mark had never happened. Trembling, she fought the desire to give in to weeping and anguish with a strength she didn't know she possessed.

Relying on her new found strength, Diana ran along next to Kane through the darkling woods and out onto the end of the runway. In the flickering light from the burning aircraft, a lone figure staggered toward them, carrying what looked to be a crumpled bundle of rags. Beyond him, the fire crew was spraying the plane with white foam.

Diana could see flames licking at the back of the flight suit. "Mark! Mark!" As she tried to reach him, she felt Kane grab her by the shoulders, holding her back.

"It's all right! He's going to be all right!"

Even as Kane spoke the words, Diana saw two men rushing toward Mark. The first threw a blanket over his back, extinguishing the flames. As the second man took the bundle that Mark was carrying, she saw it was a small man who was missing one leg. He was limp and helpless.

Diana broke free of Kane's grip, running toward Mark who had fallen to his knees on edge of the runway. "Mark!—Mark!" Diana shouted breathlessly as she ran.

Mark looked up, a twisted smile beginning on his sooty face. He struggled to stand up but got only as far as one knee.

Throwing her arms around Mark, Diana finally broke into great gasping sobs. Unable to speak, she held tightly to him, feeling all the pain of the last terrible hours flow out of her, feeling his arms around her—knowing that he was alive.

Gradually the sobbing ceased. Mark pushed her back gently, gazing into her eyes. Her face was smudged from rubbing against him. "I know I must be in heaven," he said hoarsely. "Only an angel could have a face like that."

Diana took his dirty, smoke-blackened face in both hands, kissing his forehead, eyes, cheeks, and finally his lips with a passionate desperation. Then she threw her arms around him, clinging tightly as though she couldn't get close enough.

In the flickering shadows cast by the burning aircraft, the crew chief walked over to Kane. "Colonel, looks like we've got the fire under control."

"Good work, Sergeant."

The sergeant glanced over at Diana and Mark, as they knelt together almost as one person in the gathering darkness of the airdrome. "Looks like Courtney's got a way with the ladies, don't it, Colonel?"

Kane scowled at the burley, gray-haired crew chief. "You'd better show a little respect for your new commanding officer, Sergeant!"

"Sir?"

"You heard me!" As Kane spoke, Mark and Diana rose and walked toward them, arm in arm. "My job here's finished. *Captain* Courtney's your new Group Commander."

EPILOGUE

*D*iana sat on the tender spring grass at the edge of the glade, watching Donny and Kate at their play. She wore a pale green dress that her mother had made for her and was barefoot, the grass cool against her feet and legs.

Down by the brook, Donny brandished his wooden sword, his battlecry ringing among the trees as he rescued Kate from the Black Knight. Diana had told them this game of her childhood and they had immediately adopted it as their own.

Mark, in his wrinkled khaki trousers and green army tee shirt, lay asleep, his head pillowed on Diana's lap. As she listened to the sounds of the children, she slipped back through the years, seeing Dale again kneeling before her after *his* victory over the Black Knight—saw again the little girl that she had been, taking the colors that Dale lay at her feet. With a placid smile, she realized that the pain of the memories had vanished like a leaf on the water, drifting away into the quiet woodlands.

As Diana ran her fingers through Mark's hair, he stirred from his sleep, then slowly opened his eyes. "I must have dropped off to sleep." He sat up slowly and stretched.

"If you didn't, it was an awfully good imitation," Diana smiled. "The fake snoring was excellent."

"I don't snore," Mark said defensively.

"And how would you know? Do you stay awake and listen to yourself sleep?"

Mark rubbed his eyes, shaking his head slowly. "What a strange girl you are!"

"No, I'm not, but some of my family are." Diana had found that she loved to tell Mark stories about her family.

"Oh, yeah. Like who?" Mark asked groggily.

"Like my uncle Reginald. He got himself elected to Parliament." Diana noticed the skeptical expression on Mark's face. "Oh, he truly did!"

"I'll bet." Mark never knew when to take Diana seriously, but as always was drawn into the game. "Could I persuade you to tell me something about this uncle of yours?"

"Since you put it so nicely—yes. Well, on his first day in Parliament, Uncle Reginald took the floor in the House of Commons and told the whole assembly every scorching detail of his wife's affair with one of London's rising young actors."

"You're serious, aren't you? He did the whole thing to get back at his wife?"

"Oh, yes," Diana yawned. "His political backers were somewhat miffed at him, of course, but he said it was a matter of honor. Wanted *everyone* to know what kind of woman she was—and they did. The tabloids went *absolutely* wild!"

"A matter of honor? That doesn't make any sense."

"And well it shouldn't. He was quite mad at the time." Diana shrugged and yawned again, covering her mouth with her hand. "Excuse me. I've grown awfully tired all of a sudden. Well, anyway, Uncle Reginald seems to have gotten over it now though. There's even some talk of his running for his old seat again."

"Well, I for one have risen above such mundane pursuits." Looking at her with a dead-pan expression, Mark assumed an air of formality. "War hero that I am—you've seen the medal that validates this fact—I henceforth cannot be seen in the company of a silly girl with such strange relatives."

Diana leaned toward him, let her hand caress the back of his neck, and kissed him soundly.

When she pulled back, Mark let his breath out with a *whoosh*! "Unless of course she's the kissing champion of the western hemisphere." He reached for her. "More—I want more!"

Pushing him away with her hand on his chest, Diana said smugly, "What a beast you are! You simply *must* learn some self-control!"

Mark growled and threw Diana down on her back, biting her noisily on the neck. Diana tried to hold him off, laughing until she was breathless. Then they sat up together, holding hands and smiling into each other's eyes.

"We are *frightfully* silly, aren't we?" Diana glanced toward the brook where Donny and Kate were lost in their fantasies. "I think we should grow up a *little* for the children's sake. After all, we'll be their parents when the adoption papers are finalized."

"We'll grow up together—the four of us." Mark kissed her quickly on the cheek. He lay back on the grass, staring up at the white billowing clouds moving slowly across the April sky. "Right now, I just want to be a boy again—before I go back."

Diana lay beside him, resting on one elbow. "Is it so very awful for you?" She felt so relaxed and secure near Mark—and sleep felt like an old friend now.

Mark glanced over at her. "No. Not anymore, it isn't. I've learned to deal with the flying, but facing all those crews at that first briefing—sending them out on that first mission. I'd rather just be a pilot." The words sounded strange to Mark as he spoke them. He thought back to the time when he would have given anything to get off flying status. *Old things are passed away.* The Scripture gave him a great comfort. "It's just a job that has to be done before 'Mere anarchy is loosed upon the world.'"

Diana raised her eyebrows in surprise. "Yeats? You know *The Second Coming* by William Butler Yeats?"

"Some of us in *The Colonies* have actually read *The Bard* himself, old girl."

"A civilized Yank! Now I've seen everything!" Diana smiled, resting her head on Mark's shoulder as he put his arm around her. It seemed since his near-fatal crash, she could never get enough of being close to him. "Where will we live after we get married, my love?"

"London—Liberty—Shangri La. What does it matter, my fairest of the fair, as long as we're together?"

"And how will you support me?" Diana's voice was trailing off as she approached sleep.

"Tinker, carpenter, or perhaps a sword swallower—but I don't think I'll ever be a politician. Mark turned to Diana and kissed her softly on her forehead. *There is a widow with three children that I have to try to make amends to somehow though . . . and there's Gatewood . . . and then I'll be free of every hold politics has on me.*

Mark felt Diana's soft breath against his neck as he listened to the sounds of the children at play. Diana dreamed of a shining place where there were no orphans. And the war was very far away from them.

GILBERT MORRIS AND
BOBBY FUNDERBURK

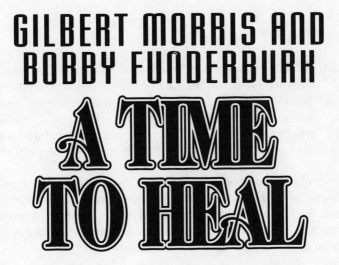

A TIME
TO HEAL

WORD PUBLISHING
Dallas · London · Vancouver · Melbourne

Library of Congress Cataloging-in-Publication Data

Morris, Gilbert.
  A time to heal / Gilbert Morris and Bobby Funderburk.
    p. cm. — (Price of liberty series: #6)
  ISBN 0–8499–3512–1
    1. World War, 1939–1945—Fiction. I. Funderburk, Bobby, 1942– . II. Title. III. Series: Morris, Gilbert. Price of liberty ; 6.
  PS3563.08742T565   1994
  813'.54—dc20
                                     94–27309
                                        CIP

Printed in the United States of America

456789 LB 987654321

To Jeannette Troescher, my sister-in-law,
Whose gentle spirit puts me in mind of a passage
from Paul's second letter to Timothy: "And the
servant of the Lord must not strive;
but be gentle unto all men."

Bobby

CONTENTS

Part 1

THE GOOD AND
GENTLE NIGHTS

1

THE CRACK OF THE BAT

Clayton McCain would never forget that day in early April 1942 when Ted Williams came to Liberty, Georgia. It was a time when sunlight, as gold as freshly churned butter, poured down warmly on the tender spring grass of the outfield and on the dusty pitcher's mound as Clay walked toward it from the bullpen where he had rocked the second-string catcher back on his heels with his fastball; a time when Diane Jackson, whose soft auburn hair and green eyes he loved even more than baseball, couldn't bear to be apart from him. It was a time when he woke each morning full of life and slept untroubled through the good and gentle nights, as yet untouched by the random butchery of war.

Breathing deeply the heady perfume of the sweet olive trees planted in precise rows along the fences, Clay glanced toward the stands, and there he was! Ted Williams, the man who had become the premier player in baseball at the age of twenty-four, actually sat behind home plate in the ballpark at Liberty High School. He had hit .406 for the Red Sox in '41, and everyone in the sporting world felt that he would probably be the last man to have a four-hundred season.

Oh, Lord! How am I ever gonna pitch this game with Ted Williams watching me? Clay brushed a lock of light
face, leaned his rangy six-foot-three-inch t__
the rosin bag. Taking a deep breath, he closed his eyes. Letting his breath out slowly, he thought, *Well, big league baseball's all about how a man can handle pressure. I reckon this is as good a time as any to see if I can pitch when I'm under the gun. Just throw 'em like I was practicing with that old tire in the back yard and let the hair go with the hide.*

In the bleachers, J.T. Dickerson, sipping from a bottle of Coke liberally laced with moonshine, sat next to his longtime friend,

Benny Risemer, a scout for the Red Sox. J.T. had dressed to the nines for the occasion, which meant he had put on his cleanest dirty shirt and most unwrinkled sport coat, and had scraped most of the dried mud from the soles of his shoes.

J.T. had also shaved and had almost washed his thick brown hair, but he decided that slicking it down with a few drops of Wildroot Hair Tonic would suffice. "How about it, Mr. Williams? You think we've got another Bob Feller out there on the mound?"

Williams, in his brown sport coat and open-collar shirt a taller, cleaner, younger version of J.T., sat on the other side of Risemer. "There's only *one* Bob Feller, J.T. Let's wait and see how he handles this game. He knows we're up here watching him now. And I wish you'd stop calling me *Mister* Williams. I'm young enough to be your son."

J.T. took a pull from his Coke bottle. "Anybody that swings a bat the way you do is *Mister* to me. One day a quarter of a century from now I'll be telling the boys in the War Veterans' home how I sat on the bleachers one beautiful spring day with the great Ted Williams."

Smiling, Williams shook his head and gazed out at Clay who was throwing the last of his warmup pitches. He took note of the young pitcher's smooth, effortless motion that was either a part of a man or not—it could not be learned.

J.T. glanced down at the growing pile of peanut shells at Risemer's feet. "What do you think, Benny?"

"I think the best thing that ever happened to me was not letting you talk me into staying in law school when we were at Harvard. I got to play ten years at shortstop and then landed this scouting job, which is almost as much fun as playing. That's what I think." Risemer brushed his hands on the pants of his gray suit, slick with wear from his dozens of train trips to high schools around the country scouting prospects for the Red Sox.

"You just can't help some people, I guess," J.T. retorted. "Here you are bumming around the country when you could be a prosperous and respected counselor like me."

Remembering the promising future J.T. had during their years at Harvard, Risemer smiled almost sadly at his old friend. "I think the second best thing that ever happened to me was letting you talk me into coming down here to see this kid, McCain. He'll go down in the record books if he can hold it together up here." Risemer tapped his right temple with a stubby forefinger.

"He can," J.T. offered with conviction. "He's had a lot of practice at getting mentally tough. Comes from good solid stock, but his folks don't have much money, so he's had to help pay his own way. He's worked at the *Liberty Herald* the whole time he's been in high school."

"Maybe he's got guts enough to make it in the pro's then," Risemer agreed. "Talent doesn't mean a thing without a whole lot of tenacity to go along with it."

"That was a great idea—calling Williams in on the deal." J.T. turned the Coke bottle up again. "How did you talk him into coming down here?"

"Fishing."

"Fishing?"

"Sure, he loves it. I just told him some of those fish stories you've been boring me to death with for years—you know, about those fifteen-pound bass in the lake outside of town—and he decided he could spare two days away from spring training if he could get a crack at one that size."

"Biggest one I ever heard of weighed eleven pounds, Benny. I told you that."

Risemer gave him a wry smile. "What's four pounds among friends?"

J.T. chuckled softly and took another quick swallow from his bottle.

Risemer took off his gray fedora and wiped his bald head with a red handkerchief, glancing at J.T.'s bottle. "You ought to ease off on that stuff. Your liver's probably the size of that catcher's mitt down there."

J.T. held the bottle up in front of him; the sunlight gleamed faintly through the dark liquid. "Closest thing I've got to a wife, Benny. Got to be faithful to her."

"What you need is a divorce. You're a lawyer—or so you tell me. Handle it yourself." Risemer frowned. "Have the Yankees been back in touch with your boy yet?"

"Not as far as I know." J.T. pictured himself in a courtroom arguing for a divorce from his whiskey bottle. "Your Honor, the defendant and I have irreconcilable differences," he would say, pointing to the bottle in the witness chair.

"Good. I think Ted can swing the deal for us," Risemer mumbled, popping peanuts into his mouth. "What kid could turn down the greatest hitter in baseball?"

J.T. glanced over at Williams. "Let's just hope they don't bring DiMaggio down here before we get Clay signed up. I'd hate to see him playing with the Yankees."

"Don't even think about it," Risemer grimaced. "DiMaggio at the plate and McCain on the mound for the Yankees. They'd have the Series wrapped up for the next decade."

"You really think he's that good?"

"I think he's that good," Risemer nodded sagely. "What do you think, Ted?"

"With two years experience he could be the hottest pitcher in the game." Williams leaned forward and watched Clay blaze a fastball past the batter for strike three. "If I'm any judge at all, that fastball's already better than ninety miles an hour. All he needs now is a little more control and a couple of years to fill out and build up some more strength and stamina."

Settling back with his arms resting on the seat behind him, J.T. breathed the mild, flower-scented air deeply into his lungs. The liquor coursed darkly through his brain as it always did when he took his first drinks of the day, giving him a sense of warmth and well-being.

The first baseman caught a high pop fly to put out the third batter. J.T. gazed down at Liberty's rising star as he walked back to the dugout from the pitcher's mound. Thinking back over the years that he had known Clay, he felt a private sense of accomplishment. After all, he *had* been the first one to show the boy, eight years old at the time, how to pitch a baseball and had given him pointers on his game until he made the high school varsity squad at the age of fourteen. *I threw away my shot at pro football. Maybe I'll get to watch Clay make it big in baseball. Wouldn't that be great?*

For the rest of the game, J.T. let himself slide into reveries of the past, talking little with Risemer and Williams as he sipped from his Coke bottle, refilling it from time to time from a silver flask he carried in his jacket pocket. He remembered the years when Clay had done yard work at his office and his house, until he had sold it and started living at the office as his law practice began dissolving in alcohol.

Dobe Jackson had given Clay a job at his newspaper, the *Liberty Herald*, at J.T.'s request. This had not only helped Clay and his family financially but had also put him in close proximity to Dobe's daughter, Diane, and the two of them had been virtually inseparable for the last two years.

J.T. had seldom missed one of Clay's games, even the ones out of town. He thought of himself as a kind of father by proxy since Hartley Lambert, who owned the lumber mill where Clay's father worked, never let his employees off before six o'clock unless someone in the family died.

Lost in these and many more memories, J.T. snapped back to the present when a cheer went up from the crowd at the end of the game.

* * *

"Oh, Clay, you're the best baseball player in the country." Diane Jackson leaned over the dugout as Clay slipped into his blue Liberty Rebels letter jacket trimmed in gray.

Clay felt his knees grow slightly weak as he gazed at Diane's sea-green eyes in her heart-shaped face. The smooth skin across the bridge of her small nose was lightly freckled and her lips were full and pink-tinged and moist. "There's a fellow in the stands who might give you an argument about that," Clay smiled, glancing at the three men who were headed his way.

Several stragglers were following along after Williams, holding out papers and pens for autographs, but the majority of the Liberty fans had gotten theirs before the game.

Diane turned around to face the bleachers. "Why, it's just J.T. and some bald-headed man and—my goodness, it's Ted Williams! I recognize him from *Life* magazine."

As the crowd was dispersing, noisily reliving the most exciting plays of the game, several students and a few parents stopped by to congratulate Clay. He reddened slightly, uncomfortable with the adulation of his growing army of fans, not quite ready to accept his celebrity status.

Risemer leaned on the four-foot tall chain-link fence as Clay stepped out of the dugout. "Great game, son. I'm Benny Risemer, J.T.'s old buddy from Harvard."

"Y-yes sir," Clay stuttered, feeling awkward in the shadow of the game's greatest living player.

"Let me introduce you to Ted Williams," Risemer grinned. "You might have heard of him. He plays a little baseball from time to time."

Williams held out his hand. "How are you, Clay? I haven't seen pitching like that since I went down swinging at Bobby Feller's fastball."

"Thank, you sir." Clay shook Williams's hand, glancing at him, then over at Diane.

Clay introduced Diane while J.T. stood by beaming like a new daddy outside a maternity ward. He felt like handing out cigars.

"How'd you like to throw a few by me, Clay?" Williams asked in a level voice.

Clay merely smiled, kicking at the dirt with his cleats. When he looked up he saw that Williams was dead serious.

"C'mon, Mr. Williams," J.T. interrupted. "He just pitched nine innings."

"He'll have to pitch to twice as many batters as he did today if he makes it to the pro's."

"How do you feel, kid?" Risemer mopped his head, squinting in Clay's direction.

Clay glanced over at Diane, as if for assurance. "Fine. Let's do it."

* * *

Diane and J.T. went over to the bleachers, and Williams hopped the fence, stepping down into the dugout where he rummaged through a heavy canvas bag stacked with bats. Selecting one and grabbing an ancient catcher's mitt off the bench, he stepped back out.

"You expect me to catch this kid?" Risemer held his hands out pleadingly. "Look at these things. They're soft as Ebbits Field cotton candy."

Williams grinned mischievously, tossed the mitt to Risemer, and walked off toward home plate. Taking off his jacket along the way, he dropped it on top of the dugout.

"There's no disgrace in getting hit out of the park by Ted Williams," J.T. assured Clay nervously. "Just stay on your toes after you throw the pitch."

Glancing over at Diane again, Clay took off his jacket and headed out to the mound.

"The things I do for the Red Sox," Risemer grumbling under his breath wearily as he walked around to the gate following after Williams.

Most of the crowd had left, but a few, seeing what was happening on the field, took seats in the bleachers.

Clay thought he had been nervous with Ted Williams in the stands, but now he faced him in the batter's box. Sixty feet away, the man looked ten feet tall as he set his feet firmly in place and took a few practice swings.

"You want a few warmup pitches?" Williams called out, standing relaxed, resting the bat on his shoulder.

"I'm OK."

Williams took one more swing, then held his bat high, his hips shifting slightly as he dug in for the pitch.

Rubbing the ball briefly in both hands, Clay slipped his glove back on, went through his windup, and whipped his best fastball waist high down the center of the plate. The crack of the bat ended his brief dream of getting one past the Red Sox slugger.

With an effortless swing, Williams had connected dead center, sending the ball sailing over the center-field wall.

Clay watched the ball climb higher and higher against the blue curve of the sky. It had just begun to drop when it disappeared beyond a stand of tall pines.

Picking up the rosin bag, Clay fidgeted with it for a few seconds. He threw the next ball three feet over Risemer's outstretched mitt.

A few chuckles ran through the crowd.

"Let's see you do any better," Diane said angrily to Keith Demerie, whose father, Senator Tyson Demerie had gotten him classified 4-F.

Demerie, a burly, blond twenty-year-old, home from his job as a page at the state capitol, smirked back at her. "Your boyfriend ain't ready for the big leagues *yet*."

Williams took the ball from Risemer and walked out to the mound with an encouraging smile on his face.

Clay glanced up at him, then began kicking the hard-packed dirt with his cleats.

Handing the ball to Clay, Williams shrugged. "Don't let it bother you. You're going to get heckled by the best when you make the majors."

"Yes sir." Clay squinted in the late sunlight, trying to smile, but he couldn't quite pull it off.

Williams thumped the bat on the pitching rubber. "Everybody has to deal with nerves. You just settle down, and I'll tell you a story about somebody who helped me in a tough situation when we're finished out here."

"Thanks, Mr. Williams." Clay felt a little better as he watched him walk away.

Stopping, Williams turned and squinted back at Clay. "You've got a good compact windup—except on the fastball. You stretch it out a little—not much, but enough that any sharp-eyed hitter can see it coming."

Clay thought about what he had just heard. Trying to picture his windups in his mind, he realized that Williams was right. He could almost feel the slight difference when he threw the fastball. *He'll be expecting a curve after what he did to my fastball.*

Williams now stood in the batter's box, swinging his bat smoothly across the plate.

As Clay prepared to throw, he deliberately used his ordinary windup, but his mind was intent on the fastball. He threw it as hard as he had ever thrown a ball in his life, catching the inside corner of the plate just above knee level.

Surprised, Williams tried to adjust his swing to the unexpected speed at the last moment, but his bat whiffed by slightly late and an inch above the ball. He grinned broadly at the lanky young pitcher, nodding his head in approval.

Applause broke out in the stands, punctuated by cheers from Diane and J.T.

Williams motioned for Clay to follow him back to the dugout. *Might as well let him finish on a good note. I've seen all I need to anyway.*

* * *

Clay caught up to Williams as he picked his jacket up from the roof of the dugout and slipped it back on. "Thanks for letting me get that one past you. But you didn't have to do that—no one would have blamed me for not getting a strike on you."

"I've never deliberately missed a ball in my life, son," Williams scowled. "You better learn this is serious business if you plan to stay with it."

Caught off guard by the abruptness of his response, Clay stammered, "I-I'm sorry, sir. I just thought . . ."

Williams replaced the scowl with a boyish grin, not at all unusual for his mercurial personality. "Forget it. It'll make a good story for the news hounds when we play together in our first World Series game."

Clay felt like he had when he had gotten his first bike that Christmas morning years ago; he remembered that J.T. had bought it for him. "You said you had a story for me?"

Giving him a thoughtful glance, Williams walked into the dugout. "Come on down. I like the smell in here—just like every other one I've ever been in. No matter where you go in the country, dugouts all smell the same."

Clay glanced over at the fence where J.T. and Diane waited with Risemer, then went inside, sitting next to Williams on the scarred bench. In the open space between them, *J.T.—1917* was carved into the rough oak.

Williams stuffed his bat back into the heavy bag at the end of the bench, gazing thoughtfully out toward home plate where the team manager, a pie-faced boy of fifteen was heading out to collect the bases. "You know, I was just as nervous as you before I played my final game last year."

Clay stared at him with a look of amazement. He thought of how confident Williams always looked at the plate, even in the tightest situations.

"Yes sir, I was awake half the night in that hotel room in Philadelphia. September 27, 1941. It was cold and rainy, and I thought the games might be canceled. It's a night I'll never forget."

"You played a doubleheader the next day against the Athletics," Clay volunteered.

"That's right. I had my .400 average." Williams opened and closed his left hand, the muscles in his forearms rippling like small cables beneath the skin. "Ready to go into the record books. They even told me I didn't have to play."

"You mean so you wouldn't take a chance on losing your .400? That must have been some decision to make."

"It was pure agony until a friend of mine laid it on the line for me."

Clay remained silent, feeling like he was being let in on a little bit of history from the man who had made it.

"Hugh Duffey hit .438 for the Sox in 1894. He was coaching me a little at the time."

"You know Hugh Duffey?" Clay thought he had been out of the game for years. "My grandpa used to talk about him when I was a little boy."

"Well, ol' Hugh didn't believe in coddling us young players—wouldn't allow any prima donnas to come close to him." Williams smiled. "He told me, 'Look, kid, go up there and take your cuts. If you miss, you just don't deserve it.'"

Clay thought it was good advice and decided to remember it for the future.

"And he was right," Williams continued. "I went on out there and took my cuts."

"And hit four for five in the first game, including your thirty-seventh home run."

"How about the second game?" Williams glanced about the dugout, taking pleasure in the cleat marks, carvings, and other leavings of the hundreds who had found their way here giving to and taking from the game.

"Two for three," Clay replied quickly, "and you told the reporters that you didn't want anyone to say you 'walked in through the back door.'"

"I did say that, didn't I?" Williams grinned and stood up. "Maybe that's good advice too—like Duffey gave me. Don't ever go down with your bat on your shoulder, kid."

"Are you going in the service, Mr. Williams?" Clay wasn't sure if he should ask, but it seemed the natural thing to do.

"Sure. Isn't everybody?"

"I am," Clay agreed. "Just haven't decided which branch I'm going to join yet."

"They're making noises like they want me to go in Special Services," Williams said with a frown. "Fighter pilot—that sounds much better, don't you think?"

"Yes sir," Clay grinned. "Special Services would be kinda like getting in through the back door wouldn't it?"

Clapping Clay on the shoulder, Williams laughed, "It sure would, kid. You're gonna do just fine when you get to Boston. What do you say we both join up in the fall and have this thing over with by Christmas?"

"Fine with me."

Clay walked with Williams toward the fence where Diane waited for him with J.T. and Risemer. He had felt a sense of unreality at actually sitting in his home dugout talking with Ted Williams. His mind reeled with images of the majors—the thunderous roar of the huge crowds packed tightly into the stadium, the clipped grass and freshly striped and raked infield, his own name blaring over the loudspeakers when the lineup was announced, the headlines leaping at him from the morning newspapers, and that feeling that was like no other when the last batter went down swinging.

Farewells were said and the three men walked off together, J.T. listing slightly like a sloop in a gentle swell. Clay stood at the fence next to Diane watching them until they disappeared around the corner of the concession stand.

"Want to go to the picture show tonight?" Clay placed his arm across Diane's shoulders, pulling her gently to him.

"Sure." She lay her head against his shoulder. *For Whom the Bell Tolls* is playing. Gary Cooper and that Swedish girl, Ingrid Bergman, are in it."

"I read the book." Clay began walking toward the gym where a few stragglers from the team were filing into the locker room. He took his arm from Diane's shoulders and held her hand. "Hemingway's one of my favorites."

"Oh, you read everything," Diane said with mild admiration. "The story's kind of sad, isn't it?"

"Well, it takes place in Spain during their civil war." Clay thought of the war his own country was now fighting, which had started so suddenly and viciously that quiet Sunday morning last December with the bombing of Pearl Harbor. "I don't think there *are* any happy wars, Diane."

2

IT TOLLS FOR THEE

"Well, I guess you really liked that movie, didn't you?" Clay took the damp handkerchief Diane handed back to him as they walked out under the marquee of the Liberty Theater. "This one was a two-handkerchief tear-jerker. You finished yours off, and now mine's sopping wet, too."

Diane pushed Clay lightly on the shoulder. "Oh, hush! Women like to cry sometimes."

"I thought I'd cry myself for a while there," Clay remarked in mock sincerity.

"You did? When?"

"When I saw the price of the tickets." Clay smiled. "Twenty-five cents apiece. They must think this is some kind of Broadway opening night."

Ignoring his attempt at humor, Diane took Clay's arm with both hands as they walked among the thinning crowd of movie-goers and spoke to several of their friends. She wore a lavender sweater against the chill night air but still shivered slightly as an errant breeze swept past, sending leftover winter leaves scraping dryly along the sidewalk.

Without asking, Clay took off his letter jacket and draped it around her shoulders. Little acts of thoughtfulness like this always made him feel chivalrous, as though he were Sir Walter Scott laying his cloak across a puddle for the queen. "I don't think I've ever known you to wear warm enough clothes. You always manage to underdress."

Squeezing Clay's arm, Diane stood on tiptoe and whispered, "If you think I'm underdressed now, just wait till we get married." She turned her head away and blushed slightly even as she spoke the words.

23

Clay stared down at her, open-mouthed.

"Besides," Diane continued with mock arrogance in an attempt to cover up her embarrassment, "that's what I've got *you* for. To look out for me."

Clay felt his throat constricting at the thought of what Diane had said. Images of filmy nightgowns and silk stockings floated around at the back of his mind. He pushed them aside mentally and tried to control his voice, but it cracked slightly as he spoke. "Well, you sure *need* some looking out for all right."

Clay's reaction was not lost on Diane, and she felt an undefined sense of satisfaction at the effect she had on him. Suddenly, the last scene of the movie they had just seen came back to her. "Oh, Clay, I wish you didn't have to go in the army!"

"We've gotta whip the Japs before they start landing on the beaches in California," Clay responded, trying to sound like Brian Donlevy in *Wake Island*. "Everybody's joining up."

"Not everyone."

"Everybody that's healthy and not too old. It's every man's duty as an American." Clay felt suddenly as though his words had a hollow ring to them, as though he were playing a role that would eventually catch up to him.

"Keith Demerie isn't going. He's twenty years old and healthy as a horse."

Clay frowned down at Diane. "His daddy's a senator. Politicians always manage to pull off stunts like that for themselves or people they know."

"Daddy's got a lot of connections with the newspaper, Clay." Diane felt uneasy as she broached the subject but plunged ahead anyway. "I bet he could get you a job where you'd be excused from the draft."

They had come to the Liberty High campus. Pale light from the streetlamps fell across the grounds, casting murky shadows beneath the huge oaks. Clay led the way to one that stood close by, tilting the sidewalk with its roots, and sat on a stone bench beneath it. Diane sat next to him, afraid that she had offended him by what she had said about the job.

The schoolyard held a breathless silence as though resting from the activities and incessant noises of the day. With June approaching, the school bell would soon forfeit its clamorous authority, giving way to the long, indolent days and soft nights of summer.

Memories of all the years he had spent on these grounds flooded over Clay. He saw himself as a first grader, carrying his lunch in a brown paper sack; as a junior high student, when Bonner Ridgeway, the gravelly voiced coach first recognized his remarkable ability to throw a baseball. He remembered the first time he kissed Diane on this very bench when they both had to stay after school for passing notes in class.

It seemed to Clay that the night was wearing down to a kind of sadness. It weighed him down. He was experiencing the end of things before their rightful end; his childhood lay behind him, and he longed for and feared what lay ahead for him as a man. He could never admit to, nor even articulate, the emotions that raged through him at the most absurd times and for no apparent reason.

"Clay, I-I'm sorry if I said anything wrong," Diane said hesitantly. "I just can't bear the thought of you going off to war. What if . . ."

It took Clay a few seconds to realize who was talking to him. Diane's words seemed to be coming from a time years before. "Don't let it bother you. I know you're just worried about me—but I'd *never* do anything like that." He took her face in his hands, kissing her gently on the mouth. Her lips were parted and moist, and he was surprised at the eagerness of her response. He put his arms around her and lost himself in the warmth and wonder of this unexpected passion.

In a few seconds Diane pulled gently away. "There has to be something we can do."

Clay took her hand, squeezed it, and stared down the street at the series of streetlamps that led to the next block, disappearing from sight where the street curved around the base of a low hill.

"Are you OK, Clay?"

Laying his other hand on top of hers, he patted it gently. "I'm just fine."

"You're awfully quiet."

Clay took a deep breath. "I was just thinking about Lyle Oliver."

"I didn't know you were friends with him."

"I wasn't really. I knew him and Billy and Marcell Duke.

25

Marcell whipped the dog out of me in a fistfight in the locker room once." Clay gave Diane a half smile. "That's about as close as *we* ever came to being friends."

"Well, he was a lot older than you." Diane leaped to Clay's defense.

"Wouldn't have mattered. Marcell could knock a steam engine off the tracks with that right of his." Clay stared up at the star-filled sky. "It's funny to think of Lyle dead now and Billy and Marcell off in the Marine Corps. I think they're in boot camp at Parris Island. Seems like it was just last week we were all in school together right here."

Diane lay her head on Clay's shoulder, taking his hand in both of hers.

"I guess Lyle came to mind because he got killed at New Caledonia—wherever that is. Somewhere out in the Pacific is all I know about it. Billy Christmas told me that before he joined up." Clay felt himself tremble slightly and hoped that it was only in his mind—that Diane felt nothing. "A Jap mortar got him, and Billy said that his buddies carried him all the way back through the jungles to the ship—but he died anyway. He's buried out there on that island ten thousand miles away."

The distant lonesome whine of a heavy truck out on the highway gave voice to Clay's feelings.

"Billy told me about how Lyle's mother said that he got saved right before he joined the Marines. I didn't know what to say." Clay turned to Diane as though expecting a parable of explanation like he had heard about in the Bible.

"Saved from what?" She shrugged, trying to avoid any further discussion of the subject.

"Well, you and your family go to *church* every Sunday. What does it really mean?"

Diane fidgeted on the bench. "Daddy says it's expected of us—with him owning the newspaper and everything. He says religion is the 'opiate of the masses.'"

"What's *that* supposed to mean?" Clay responded with some irritation. "Makes about as much sense as saying, 'work is the curse of the drinking class.' I think it's gonna take more than a lot of fancy sayings to get us through this war."

"Let's not talk about things like that anymore." Diane climbed into Clay's lap. "Why don't we just pretend that there's no old war at all?"

"Fine with me." Clay shook off the memories, brightening with the feel of Diane, warm and soft against him.

"I know!" Diane slid off his lap, pulling him up from the bench. "Let's go to Ollie's for a malt."

Clay was concerned about Diane's wanting to get him out of the draft by using her father's influence—knew that it hinted at some deeper trait in her—but in the fashion of youth, somber thoughts proved too heavy to carry for more than a few moments. "Now you're talking some sense. A chocolate malt can take care of a whole lot of worries."

* * *

"Look over there! Ben's back!" Clay entered the neon glare of Ollie's Drugstore with Diane, walking across the black-and-white tiled floor to the marble-topped counter. "Hey, Ben. How's Liberty's only Medal-of-Honor winner doing these days?"

Ben Logan, wearing his simple Navy dungarees and light blue shirt, stood at the far end of the marble-topped counter. Just under six feet tall, he was lean and hard with black hair, piercing gray eyes, and finely chiseled features. Even after two months, the attention his decoration attracted still made him uneasy. "Real good, Clay. How 'bout you? Hi, Diane."

Clay shook his hand, clapping him on the back. "Them big shots in Washington still got you traveling all around the country selling war bonds?"

"Yep. Sometimes I think it's worse than boot camp." Ben shifted the subject away from himself. "Speaking of big shots, I thought I saw Ted Williams sittin' in the stands out at the ball game today."

"You sure did!" Diane chimed in, taking Clay's hand. "He came down here to get Clay to sign a contract with the Boston Red Sox."

"I always figured you'd make it to the majors someday, Clay." Ben grinned at Diane. "Even when we were kids, he could throw a rock over the tops of the trees on the other side of the swimmin' hole."

"How's Rachel, Ben?" Diane saw the "good ol' boy" stories coming and tried to head them off. "I hardly ever see her around town anymore."

"She's workin' down at Hightower's in the office after she gets out of school. She's going to night school at the college this summer to take some business courses—thinks it'll help her get a promotion."

"Y'all getting married?" The hottest news in town was what was happening in the life of the man who had been to the White House to meet the president, and Diane wanted to be the first to hear any juicy news about Ben.

"Not unless Tojo and Hitler both surrender on the same day," Ben laughed. "I think we'll wait till the war's over."

"Here's the medicine for your mama, Ben." Ollie Caston walked behind the counter from the door that led to the pharmacy and storage areas. His scalp gleamed through the short brown crew cut, and his black bow tie provided a neat punctuation mark for his white shirt and apron. "Hope she gets to feeling better."

"Thanks, Mr. Caston," Ben replied, taking the white paper bag. "I'll tell her you were asking about her."

Turning to Clay and Diane, Caston spoke with obvious pride. "And what can I get for the next strikeout king of the American League? And his lovely lady, of course."

"Two chocolate malts, Mr. Caston," Diane answered for them, "and make them thick."

"You ever get one here that wasn't thick?" Caston grinned. "How 'bout you, Ben? It's not often I get two big celebrities in here at one time."

"No thanks. I better get on home."

"It's on the house," Ollie offered. "It's not often you get *anything* for free in this world."

"Aw, c'mon, Ben," Clay complained. "It might be another year or two before we see each other again."

Sensing that Clay needed to talk to him, Ben quickly relented. "OK. I never could resist one of Ollie's malts."

"Y'all go sit down. I'll bring 'em over to you in just a minute." Ollie began scooping ice cream from a cardboard tub in the freezer beneath the counter, flinging it with practiced efficiency into a tall silver cup.

Clay glanced at the five marble-topped tables at the front of the drugstore near the plate-glass window. They were all filled, mostly by sailors and soldiers whose girls appeared duly impressed by their uniforms. "There's a place." He pointed to the last booth in a row of three against the far wall.

"I know you boys want to talk about old times," Diane admitted. "I see Angela Spain over there. I think I'll go try to find out what's happening with her."

As Ben watched Diane walk toward the first booth, Angela noticed him and waved. She brushed her long dark-brown hair back from her face with an enticing gesture that seemed as natural and unaffected as if she had been sitting alone at her dressing table. Her violet eyes were shaded by incredibly long lashes, and they closed slightly as she smiled at him.

Ben remembered that cold, rainy night four years earlier when he had followed Angela down a dimly lit hallway with gleaming hardwood floors and oil paintings in heavy gilt frames on the walls. He saw again the small alcove overlooking the backyard of the mansion; felt the softness of the wine-colored velvet cushions on the window seat. As he followed Clay to their seats, he nodded to Angela, forcing the memory from his mind.

Sliding into the booth, Clay remarked knowingly, "I'd sure like to hear what Angela tells Diane. I bet it'd make a drunk sailor blush."

Ben ignored the remark, gazing at a skinny, pasty-faced private in army green who was dropping nickels into the jukebox. As he returned to his table, "Praise the Lord and Pass the Ammunition" blared from the speaker.

"It's no wonder you never see her with her husband." Clay, like most other young men in Liberty, was fascinated by Angela Spain. "She can't be more than twenty-two, and he's thirty years older than that if he's a day. Guess Morton's just too old to keep up with her."

"Maybe he works a lot, Clay," Ben said flatly, trying to put an end to the discussion of Angela Spain. "How're your folks getting along?"

"Same as always," Clay shrugged. "Mama hardly ever goes anywhere and Daddy works all the time. I think Hartley Lambert would lay down and die if he had to give his men a day off, except for Christmas and Thanksgiving. I hated working at that place on Saturdays before I got on at the *Herald*—never even had a chance for a break."

Ben nodded and glanced up at Caston who set their malts on the table and rushed off to wait on four Marines who had just taken seats at the counter. They were gawky, in their late teens, and fresh out of boot camp.

"Mm, that's good." Ben drank directly from the tall glass, leaving a brown mustache across his lip. "I used to dream about Ollie's malts when I was at sea."

Clay sipped his malt thoughtfully through the straw. "Ben, what's it like? Being in battle, I mean?"

Taking another long swallow of the malt, Ben leaned back in the booth. "Hard to explain. For me it happened so fast it's all still kind of a blur."

"Yeah, I hear that the waiting around part before the fight is the worst thing about it." Clay wanted to hear some tried-and-true plan from Ben that he could use to take the chill of fear out of his thoughts about the war.

"I don't know about that. When those Jap planes hit us, the first thing I remember is looking down the barrel of that 20 mm cannon." Ben could see the uncertainty in Clay's face and knew that he was experiencing what all young men did as they left their school years for the prospect of facing an enemy who seemed invincible, or at the very least vicious and without principle. "You going to join up?"

"Yeah. Everybody I know is—just about."

"Decided what branch yet?"

Clay shook his head and took a sip of his malt.

"Navy's all right if you don't mind looking at a whole lot of water every day."

Clay smiled at Ben. Pushing the glass aside, he leaned both elbows on the table. "Maybe the Marines. If Billy and Marcell can do it, so can I. What do you think about that?"

"If you wanna fight that's the place to be all right." Ben had heard rumors about the island-hopping campaigns that were being planned in the South Pacific and knew the Marines would be the first ones on the beaches. *No sense in worrying Clay. Men are going to get killed everywhere in this war. Look how many went down with the*

Arizona. *I was almost one of them.* "They probably have the best training in the world."

"Don't Sit under the Apple Tree" by the Andrew Sisters began to play from the jukebox. One of the Marines, a short, stocky man who looked older than his three friends, slid off his stool at the counter. He had black hair and a swarthy face. Walking over to a table, he asked the skinny private's chubby girlfriend to dance.

The private was on his feet and in the Marine's face before he could finish his invitation. "She ain't got no truck with Jarheads—and neither do I."

The stocky man smirked at the skinny army private—then without warning, swung his big fist at the boy's pale face. The boy seemed to vanish as the blow expended itself on air. A fraction of a second later, the Marine's eyes bulged with surprise and pain as the young private buried his fist almost up to the wrist in the heavy man's stomach.

Hearing the commotion, Ben slipped out of his booth and grabbed the soldier from behind before he could straighten the Marine up with a smash to the chin.

"Let me go! I'll kill him!" The boy struggled against Ben, his arms pinned to his sides.

"Turn him loose!" the big Marine gasped. "He hit me from behind!" Then he gazed up at Clay, who had stepped in front of him. At six foot three and 190 pounds, Clay got the man's attention. Noticing Clay's arms and shoulders, corded with muscle from helping his dad at the lumberyard and years of sports, he decided that this was not a one-man job. Glancing at his three buddies, he saw that Caston already had them under control.

"C'mon, boys," Ollie grinned, a Louisville Slugger balanced lightly in one hand. "We're all on the same side in this war. Sit back down and have some ice cream on the house."

With some grumbling, the two men returned to their separate seats, scowling at each other as they parted. Ben and Clay walked back to their booth.

"I like the way you handled that, Sailor," Angela spoke under her breath as Ben passed her booth.

Ben glanced at her, his face reddening slightly, but didn't respond.

Diane joined them as they sat back down. "Well you two sure earned your malts tonight."

"How's Angela? She have any good stories for you?" Clay's smile was almost a leer.

"No, she didn't," Diane shot back. "And if she did, I certainly wouldn't tell you."

"You must have talked about something."

"Angela always looks so sad. I thought she could use some company."

"She doesn't look sad to me, and she has a whole lot of company from what I hear."

"You just wouldn't understand, Clay. Men never do about these things," Diane explained as though she were talking to a first grader. "She did tell me she saw poor ol' J.T. stumbling down the street on her way over here."

Clay's eyes narrowed in concern. "Maybe I better go look for him, help him get home all right."

"Want me to come with you?" Ben asked. "I've got Daddy's truck outside."

"Nah. I'll probably find him quicker on foot." Clay stood up and gave Diane a hand out of the booth. "I know where he usually winds up when he gets a snootfull. He'll head back down memory lane."

Ben swallowed the last of his malt, grabbed his paper bag, and joined Clay and Diane. "Guess I better get this medicine on back to Mama. Nice seeing y'all."

"Would you mind taking Diane home? I'll ride with you and then you can drop me off at the school. Sometimes J.T. ends up down there."

"Sure thing," Ben nodded. "You really like ol' J.T. don't you, Clay?"

Clay's eyes looked at something in the past. "He spent a lot of time with me when I was growing up. Daddy only had Sundays off, and he was always give out then."

As they were leaving, the skinny private dropped another nickel in the jukebox and leaned back against it, staring at the swarthy man who still sat at the counter with his buddies. When "This Is the Army, Mr. Jones" began playing, he returned to his girlfriend, scowling fiercely at the Marines.

"You gotta give him credit," Clay laughed. "The little guy's got courage."

Ben's face clouded over. "I hope so. He's gonna need a lot of it where he's going."

* * *

Clay walked across the parking lot toward the football stadium, his shoes crunching in the loose gravel. As he climbed the wooden steps and walked along the rail that followed the sideline, he glanced about looking for J.T. The fragrance of night-blooming jasmine hung in the cool air. Anemic light from streetlamps and nearby houses transformed the structure into the perfect refuge for dark shadows and darker thoughts.

In the first two or three months after the attack on Pearl Harbor, the people of Liberty imposed a blackout on their town. Now, after four months of parades and posters and political speeches, it was still in effect but few adhered to it, believing their country invincible.

Watching strips of wispy black clouds float across a quarter-moon, Clay caught a slight movement out of the corner of his eye. J.T., cast into silhouette at the very top of the stadium, lifted his silver flask to his lips. Feeling the need to shake off the unease that had settled over him since his talk with Ben, Clay sprinted up the steps, taking them two at a time.

"Clay, my boy." J.T. attempted to get up, but immediately lost his balance and thumped back down on the wooden bench. "Pardon me if I don't rise for the occasion. I seemed to have dropped my equilibrium back in the gravel."

Clay didn't smile as he gazed at J.T.'s swollen face. He affected the insidious grin of a court jester, but in the pale light his rheumy eyes seemed suffused with an unfathomable melancholy. "Why do you do this to yourself, J.T.?"

Sipping again from the flask, J.T. held it aloft and spoke in Shakespearian intonation, "'Twas for love I flung myself on Dionysus' altar.'"

"What?"

"For true love, my boy—mine, not hers." J.T. stood shakily to his feet, railing at the thin blade of a moon:

"How like a winter hath my absence been
From thee, the pleasure of the fleeting year!

33

What freezings have I felt what dark days seen!
What old December's bareness everywhere!"

Clay took him by the shoulders, easing him back down to his seat. "You're not making a lick of sense. Why don't you let me take you on home?"

"Don't care for the vaunted Bard, eh?" J.T., his eyes shining with alcohol, turned toward Clay. "Well, let me put it in the idiom of this cultural desert I find myself in. It was a woman that drove me to drink—and I never did write and thank her."

Nodding his head, Clay murmured, "I heard those stories about you and Ellie—before she married Hartley Lambert. You were the star quarterback on his way to Harvard Law School and she was queen of everything at Liberty High."

J.T. leaned back against the railing, his face slack with defeat as he stared listlessly down onto the field. "Ellie was my whole life—and she couldn't even wait for me to finish school."

"Maybe breaking hearts runs in her family," Clay mused.

A puzzled frown crossed J.T.'s face.

"Her daughter," Clay explained. "Look what Debbie did to Ben Logan when they were in school together."

"I remember that."

"Well, it looks like Ben got over it fine," Clay continued. "You can too."

"Ben got some help."

"Help?"

"Spiritual help, my boy," J.T. muttered. "He got religion sometime after he went in the Navy."

"Why don't you try it then?"

"I don't know. Maybe I'm too old to change—too set in my ways."

"Let's get on home now." Clay stood up, shivering slightly. He had forgotten to get his jacket back from Diane again. "You'll catch pneumonia out here."

"Religion," J.T., his face turned toward the heavens, mumbled to himself as though he were alone in the empty stadium. "'For we wrestle not against flesh and blood, but against principalities, against powers, against the rulers of the darkness of this world, against spiritual wickedness in high places.' Maybe that war is worse than the one we're fighting with Germany and Japan—or maybe they're the same war."

"You sure do know a lot about the Bible for somebody that don't care about religion."

J.T. turned to Clay as if just noticing him for the first time. "I read all the great literature. I've had plenty of time for it since I've . . . neglected my law practice."

Clay took J.T.'s hand and pulled him to his feet. The two of them walked slowly down the steps: a young man who would soon rush headlong into battle—an older one who engaged the enemy each morning when he rose to face another day.

3

LILA

Gazing at the paintless frame building whose windows had mostly fallen victim to that deadly amalgam of boys and rocks, Lila Creel felt her spirits sink. *Maybe I should have stayed in Chicago. At least I could count on a paycheck from the* Tribune *every week. No! I wouldn't live through another one of those winters no matter what!*

Lila pushed a few strands of her gray-blond hair that had worked free of her French roll back from her high forehead. Her strong chin and slightly upturned nose sometimes gave a false impression of arrogance rather than the determination that was a truer portrayal of her nature. Her intelligent gray eyes gazed disdainfully at the former home of the *Journal* that she had purchased with her life savings and her husband's insurance money.

Goldenrod, dandelions, and assorted other weeds and flowers grew in rampant disorder about the long-neglected lawn of the building. Spilling in a purple cascade from a broken-down trellis, wisteria lent an air of springtime gaiety to one end of the small front porch.

The yard had one redeeming feature: a magnificent oak. Its branches spread over the roof, sheltered most of the front lawn, and extended almost to the other side of the narrow, quiet street. The morning sunlight softly patterned the ground beneath the tree with shadow and drifted like green-gold smoke in its crown.

As she reluctantly followed the sidewalk to the porch and summoned her courage to face whatever awaited her inside the building—hoping that the press was in better shape than the yard—Lila noticed a man shambling down the sidewalk. He was about six feet tall, slim, and wore an expensive brown sport coat with khakis and scuffed work shoes.

Looks like he's down on his luck. Maybe he could use a few dollars. "Excuse me, but would you like to do some yard work for me?"

J.T. stopped at the end of the walk, taking in Lila's trim figure in her cream-colored silk blouse and tailored gray slacks. He started to walk on but something in her no-nonsense, straightforward approach struck a chord somewhere deep inside him. "You don't waste words, do you?"

"Usually not."

"You're not from around here," J.T. continued, his appetite now whetted for some conversation. "I'd certainly remember you if you were."

Lila looked closer at J.T. as he walked down the sidewalk toward her. He was decades older than when she had gone to school with him, of course, but even with the week-old growth of brown and gray beard and the disheveled appearance, she recognized him. "J.T. Dickerson. You played quarterback for Liberty High!"

Stunned, J.T. stopped in his tracks, trying to remember where he had met this confident and seemingly guileless female. He had seldom met a woman who appeared so self-assured. "I'm afraid you have me at a disadvantage."

"We went to school together."

"Are you certain? I think I would remember someone as striking as you."

Lila raised her delicate-looking hand to her throat in a graceful motion, then put it quickly back down as though she had violated some kind of self-imposed rule. "No you wouldn't. I was a rather *unobtrusive* freshman, and you were a senior football star. That's like two people living on different planets."

J.T. tried to picture Lila as a fourteen-year-old but couldn't get the image in focus.

"My name was Lila Kronen. I'm planning to use my maiden name again now that I've come home."

J.T. remembered the family but not Lila. "Your daddy was a conductor on the railroad."

"Yes, he was," Lila smiled. "We moved to Chicago at the end of my freshman year when Daddy got a promotion. It's a bit different from the South."

"So I've heard."

Lila stepped up onto the porch, seeing in J.T.'s eyes that, even with her prompting, he remembered only her daddy. It was as though she were in the ninth grade again. She glanced around at the screen door hanging from one hinge and the leaves and scraps of paper collected against the wall. Turning back toward J.T. she made an obvious study of his rumpled appearance. "As I remember, you had been accepted by Harvard Law School."

"Yep." J.T. walked over to the porch and sat down, leaning back against a once-white column. "Course you don't want to be too hard on them. Even men who run revered institutions like Harvard occasionally succumb to human frailties. Not only did they admit me, they let me graduate."

"Oh, I didn't mean . . ." Lila began.

"Yes, you most assuredly did," J.T. interrupted her. Then he gave her a warm smile. "And I probably deserve it—for some reason or other."

Lila felt the color rise in her face. "No, you don't."

"You mean I didn't offend you somehow when we were in school together? I didn't miss many." J.T. watched her walk the few steps to a porch swing, test it for stability, and sit carefully down. "I was pretty full of myself back then."

"No, you didn't even know I was alive," Lila confessed, swinging gently back and forth. "I guess maybe that's it. You had everything—including the prettiest girl in school. 'And he glittered when he walked.'"

J.T. thought of the ending of the poem by E. A. Robinson that Lila was quoting from. "Let's hope I don't end up like Richard Cory did."

Lila stared into J.T.'s deep brown eyes, sensing something that caused her to look quickly away. "Oh, you won't! Don't even think such a thing!"

Seeing that he had made her uncomfortable, J.T. changed the subject. "You buy this place?"

"Yes. I'm beginning to think I made a mistake." Lila frowned at the wrecked screen door.

"Calvin sell it to you?" J.T. asked, referring to the mayor who also owned Sinclair Real Estate.

"Why, yes. How did *you* know that?"

"Ol' Calvin has a tendency to—*romanticize* the properties he has listed on occasion." J.T. grinned, looking at the old building. "This place is solid though. Made out of heart-pine timbers a termite would break his teeth on."

Lila gave J.T. a half smile, still trying to figure out whether she liked him or not. "I'm sorry I asked you to do the yard work. I didn't know you were a lawyer."

"Forget it." J.T. shrugged. "I'll be over here first thing in the morning."

"Oh, no, I couldn't let you do that!" Lila waved her hand as if dismissing the suggestion that a Harvard graduate should do yard work. "Forget I asked."

"It was a valid offer and I accept." J.T. grinned. "Besides, I could use the exercise—and the money."

Lila found J.T.'s willingness to do manual labor a refreshing change from the attitudes of the professional men she had known in Chicago. "Well—all right."

"You really going try to publish the *Journal* again?"

"That's what I had in mind. I hope the machinery inside is in good shape."

"You have any experience in the newspaper business?" J.T. gave her a skeptical glance.

"Twenty years at the *Tribune*."

"That oughta help some." J.T. nodded as he glanced at a squirrel scampering up the massive trunk of the oak. With his face turned away from Lila he asked, "Is your husband in the newspaper business, too?"

"No." Lila's voice took on a somber tone. "Howard was an invalid for the last fifteen years of his life. He died on Christmas Eve."

"I'm sorry." J.T. got up and walked across the porch, pushing the screen door carefully aside and testing the brass knob on the heavy oak door. It swung smoothly inward. "Let's see if it looks any better inside."

Lila eased out of the swing and followed J.T. into the front reception area. The counter was cluttered with old folders, and a five-year-old Hightower's Department Store calender hung on one wall. Offices on either side of the reception area were furnished with heavy antique desks and wooden swivel chairs. Dust coated everything, including the hardwood floors that nonetheless still retained some of their gloss.

"I've seen worse," J.T. said matter-of-factly, walking into the long, cement-floored room in back. Banks of windows ran along the high ceiling on both side walls all the way to the back of the building where an overhead door led out onto a loading dock. A few rolls of newsprint lay scattered about. Like the front offices, dust lay like a blanket on everything. "I'm no expert, but it looks like the press is in pretty good shape."

Lila walked about, inspecting everything carefully. "It's much better than I had expected after seeing the outside. Looks like cleaning is all it really needs."

J.T. continued on to the back, walking out onto the loading dock. Flipping a wooden spool on end with his foot, he sat down. "I'd like to see the *Journal* coming off the presses again."

Walking over to the edge of the loading dock, Lila gazed at the weeds growing along its base and out of the cracks in the concrete ramp below. "You have an interest in the publishing business, Mr. Dickerson?"

"J.T.—please! You make me sound so respectable." He stood up and walked over to where she stood. "I have an interest in seeing that Dobe Jackson doesn't have so much influence over public opinion in this town."

"He owns the *Liberty Herald*, doesn't he?"

"That's right. And Dobe could stand a little competition. Might make him a little less grandiose in those pontifications he calls editorials."

With J.T. so close to her, Lila could smell the alcohol that seemed to be seeping out of his pores. "Sounds like you don't particularly care for him."

J.T. merely grunted. "You got a typesetter?"

"The best. Typesetter and layout man. He's got real printer's ink flowing in his veins and all the other old clichés of the newspaper game." Lila's expression turned inward as she thought of her longtime friend. "His name's Henry Steinberg, and he's retired from the *Tribune*."

"Well, you've got a good start." Without further discussion, J.T. walked down the concrete steps at the side of the loading ramp and headed down the driveway at the side of the building.

Caught by surprise at the abruptness of his departure, Lila stammered, "B-but, I thought . . ."

"See you tomorrow." J.T. waved over his shoulder.

* * *

Henry Steinberg waved to Lila as she entered the restaurant of the Liberty Hotel. He stood to his full five-foot-six inches, two inches taller than Lila, as she weaved her way through the early morning crowd over to his table next to the window.

Henry's neat white mustache twitched beneath his stub of a nose when he became nervous, and he was very nervous now on this, his first trip to the deep South. His eyebrows, bristly imitations of the mustache, perched like fuzzy caterpillars above the deep-set dark eyes. Parted in the middle, his thin white hair lay close to his head. He smelled mildly of witch hazel.

"Morning, Henry." Lila smiled, taking the chair he had pulled out for her.

"Good morning," Henry replied, slipping quickly back into his seat.

"My, you certainly look dapper this morning," Lila observed, noticing his neat dark suit and bow tie. "But then you always were a stylish dresser."

Even at the age of sixty-seven, or perhaps *especially* at the age of sixty-seven, Henry, like most men, was susceptible to flattery. It seemed to give him a sense of confidence. "Thank you, Lila. You just made an old man's day."

Lila glanced over her shoulder, motioning to the waitress. "You may be the youngest man I know, Henry."

After the waitress brought coffee and they had ordered breakfast, Lila spooned sugar into her cup, adding a dollop of thick, pale yellow cream. "Umm, that's so good! I'd forgotten what real coffee tastes like."

"It's strong, but it does have a certain body to it, doesn't it?" Henry mused, preferring to sip his black, having developed the habit at work when the pressures of the job made it more efficient to grab a cup and run.

"What time did your train get in?" Lila felt comfortable having an old friend like Henry in town as most of the people she had known—the ones who were still alive—were now little more than strangers to her.

"Midnight or thereabouts. I walked here from the station. Got to see some of the town." He glanced around the room. "It's a nice place."

Lila breathed in the heady and distinct smells of Southern breakfasts being served at the tables near them. "Then you won't mind living here for a month or two until we see how things are going to work out at the paper?"

"Not at all."

The waitress returned, setting the steaming plates of food in front of them. She had short blond hair. "I know ya'll ain't from around here. I hope you like the food."

"It looks wonderful," Lila assured her.

After refilling their coffee cups, she waddled off toward the double swinging doors that led into the kitchen.

"What's this?" Henry pointed to a pile of grits that dripped with butter.

"Grits," Lila informed him, slicing off a portion of patty sausage and chewing it with relish. "I told you about them. Go ahead—you might be surprised by how good they are."

"I don't think I want to rush headlong into this Southern culture."

"Where's your spirit of adventure, Henry?"

"Now that looks respectable," Henry ventured, pointing to the sausage Lila was eating. He cut off a piece of his own and held it in front of his mouth with his fork. "Is it good?"

"It is if you like possum."

Henry dropped his fork as if it had suddenly grown hot and it clattered to the plate. "Oh, Lord! Possum?"

Lila tried to keep a straight face but couldn't hold it. "No, Henry, it's just plain old pork sausage like we have in Chicago," she laughed. "Maybe a little spicier."

As they ate, Lila noticed that Henry devoured the sausage, eggs, and the homemade biscuits with their brown, flaky crusts and soft chewy insides. But he never let his fork touch the grits. When he had finished, all that remained was a white congealed mound standing like a culinary wallflower at the edge of his plate.

"What's your new business look like?" Henry asked over a fresh cup of coffee.

Lila glanced at Henry, then stared out the window. The street lay in heavy shade from the ancient elms that lined it. People walked at their leisure along the sidewalks on their way to work or to shop or simply to be out on such a bright May morning. She noticed the decidedly older and female composition of the people, as most of the able-bodied men were at the war or traveling to it or training for it. "I think you'd better make that determination for yourself."

"It's not that bad, is it?"

"The press looks OK, but the building isn't what you'd call palatial."

"Utility is what I'm used to anyway." Henry placed the tips of his forefingers together and rested his chin on them. "Give me a decent press and a place to work, and I'll be happy. After two years, I can't wait to get my hands stained again."

Lila felt comforted by Henry's solid, reassuring dedication to work and his competence in his trade. "You'll be the heart of the business, old friend."

"And you'll be the spirit—and the soul." Henry grinned. "Let's go see it."

* * *

J.T. had taken his shirt off and the waistband of his khakis was stained dark with sweat. Over the years, during his ever-decreasing periods of sobriety, he had always gone back to an exercise routine—a holdover from his years of participating in sports in high school and college. Now, although out of shape, his muscles still rippled smoothly under his white skin as he swung the swingblade, sending tall weeds flying before it in a storm of green. He had finished most of the front yard by the time Lila drove up in her green Plymouth coupe with Henry.

After Lila had introduced them, she surveyed J.T.'s work. "What time did you start?"

"Sunup." J.T. leaned on the swingblade. "This is the most fun I've had since my last root canal."

"I'll bet you didn't learn how to do this at Harvard," Lila smiled, surveying his work.

"Nope. I never had a course that made this much sense up there."

"I'm going to show Henry around," Lila said, motioning for

him to follow her. "I think you'd better take a break before you get heatstroke."

J.T. stretched the muscles of his arms and back. "Not just yet. It's become a personal grudge match between me and the weeds—who'll give in first."

Lila smiled and dodged a flying swatch of weeds as J.T. went back to work.

Inside the building, Henry walked briefly about the front offices before going into the back area where the real work was to take place. He walked slowly around the printing press, poking into narrow openings with a trained finger, bending, kneeling, stooping, and covering every inch of it with his practiced eye. Then he completed another circuit, stopping occasionally to make adjustments with an assortment of spotlessly maintained tools he took from a small, brown leather satchel.

"What do you think, Henry?" Lila had stood by silently, knowing that Henry took to his work with a tireless devotion and surgical precision.

Henry put the final instrument back in his case, closing it with a flick of his wrist. "I think this is going to be a lot of fun—that's what I think."

Lila breathed a sigh of relief. "You think the machine's all right then?"

"It's a beauty," Henry beamed, turning back to look lovingly at the dusty press.

"Thank the Lord. I was so afraid there might be something major wrong with it." Lila gazed at the dust particles dancing slowly in the sunlight that streamed in through the high windows. "My budget wouldn't handle expensive repairs."

"Where do we start?"

"I guess we help J.T. outside." Lila began walking toward the front with Henry close by her side. "Then these offices," she said, stepping into the reception area. "And finally we'll tackle this back area. It'll take a while I'm afraid."

Henry nodded toward the window. Outside, J.T. was still flailing away at his green enemy. "How does he fit into the scheme of things?"

Lila leaned against the counter. "I haven't quite figured it out myself yet."

"Do you know him, or is he just someone you flagged down on the street to help?"

Lila thought about the question for a moment. "Both I guess." Then she explained who J.T. was.

"Why would a Harvard lawyer want to work like a hired hand?"

"I have an idea his practice isn't exactly booming," Lila explained "His breath smelled like a miniature distillery when he stopped by yesterday."

Henry frowned at her. "I don't care if he is a part of your glorious Southern past, Lila, we don't need to involve some winehead in this little enterprise."

"I think there's a gentleman somewhere beneath all that crusty exterior, Henry," Lila mused, staring out the window. "Besides I'm only hiring someone to help us get this place in shape—not marrying him you know."

* * *

Lila sat at the same table in the Liberty Hotel's restaurant where she had had breakfast that morning, only now J.T. sat across from her instead of Henry. It was eight-thirty, late for a weeknight in Liberty, and only a few customers remained. Two waitresses plodded among the tables after their long day's work, cleaning up the last few dishes. Another stood near the cash register; a cigarette dangled from the side of her mouth as she added up her receipts for the day.

J.T. took a final bite of banana pudding, leaned back with a long sigh, and folded his hands across his lean stomach. "Boy, that was good. I'd forgotten what an appetite a hard day's work can give a man."

"You certainly put in a day's work all right," Lila agreed, sipping her coffee.

They had both gone home, J.T. to his office and Lila to the hotel, and cleaned up before meeting in the restaurant. Lila wore a simple pale blue dress with tiny yellow-and-white flowers on it. J.T. had put on his last clean white shirt, which he had picked up at the cleaners the month before, and had pressed most of the wrinkles out of his cleanest khakis.

"I feel better than I have in a long time—bone tired but good." J.T. gazed into Lila's eyes, causing her to glance out the window. "Reminds me of when I used to saw logs with Earl Logan during the summers. His daddy was a logger and a pulpwood man, and we'd work for him to make a little spending money."

"I saw a picture of a sailor named Logan on the cover of *Life* magazine. He stuck in my mind because he was from here." Lila looked back at J.T., noticing the flush of sunburn on his face. "The president decorated him with the Medal of Honor."

"That's Earl's boy. He sure turned out better than anybody in this town thought he would—including his daddy."

"I'm finding the old hometown is more interesting than I'd remembered." Lila reflected briefly on the past. Boring was the word that came to mind. As she let her gaze wander around the restaurant, she noticed a young dark-haired girl seated at a table in the far corner with a sailor who sported a thin mustache and a boyish smile on his tanned face. "For instance, that looks like an interesting pair over there. I'll bet they're high school sweethearts out for a final evening before he goes overseas."

J.T. glanced over his shoulder. "You'd lose."

Lila gave him a quizzical look.

"I never saw the boy before, so chances are he's just passing through."

"And the girl?"

"That's Angela Spain, she's only twenty-two and she's married to Morton Spain. He's a lawyer who's twice her age—at least."

"Well, she certainly is lovely."

"That's about the only thing that girl has going for her." J.T.'s voice carried a weariness in it that went deeper than just a hard day's work.

Lila had become intrigued by the prospect of finding out more about Angela, and her expression suggested it to J.T.

"She grew up in a shack outside of town—poor as Job's turkey." J.T. took a final swallow of his coffee. "Her daddy ran off and left her mama and her and her month-old brother. The boy died of pneumonia that winter."

Lila's eyes glistened with interest.

"Like I said, looks was all Angela had. When Morton's wife

was killed in a car wreck, she managed to—get his attention you might say, and in six months they got married. She couldn't have been more'n seventeen at the time."

"He must know this kind of thing is going on in a town this small." Lila glanced over her shoulder at Angela who was holding the sailor's hand across the table.

J.T. stared out the window at an old Negro man, shambling down the street in threadbare overalls and brogans. "I think he knew it would happen when he married her. But there ain't a whole lot of men who use good sense when it comes to picking the right woman."

"It's kind of sad for both of them, isn't it?" Lila stared at Angela, feeling her own loss and all the years that she now struggled to believe weren't wasted.

"Yeah, well I guess most of our wounds are self-inflicted—including Angela's."

Lila felt a twinge of anger stirring in her breast. "That's a rather callous attitude, isn't it?"

Noticing the slight flush in Lila's cheeks, J.T. realized that his remark probably came from his not having had a drink all day. He thought of the half-full bottle in the drawer of his desk. "Well, sometimes it's more callous in the long run when people *ignore* the truth."

"I'm not talking about *ignoring* anything. I'm talking about having a little understanding for human frailty." Lila felt the evening drifting into ruin and decided to stave it off. "I think I'll go on up to bed. It's been a long day."

"Yes, it has." J.T. grabbed the check from the table, stood up, and headed across the almost deserted restaurant toward the cashier, leaving Lila still seated.

"Are you coming back tomorrow?" She called to him, turning around in her chair.

J.T. stopped and gazed back at her. "I don't know yet. Expect me when you see me."

Part 2

THE ROSE-COLORED
AFTERGLOW

4

ANGELA

*T*he narrow, rutted gravel road ran across the rolling pine barrens to the west, leading toward Liberty. Where it dropped out of sight behind a low ridge, the red sun burned against a hard winter sky.

At the bottom of the long, slow climb of the road, woods began with an overgrown path that led beneath huge oaks and beeches to a clapboard shack. Kudzu had climbed halfway up its walls and had reached long tentacles through the bare windows and along the rotted front porch. Now, in mid-December, the leafless vines looked like the gray skeleton of some amorphous and primordial beast that had been locked in a death grip with the ramshackle building.

In the rose-colored afterglow, Angela Spain stood next to her black LaSalle, parked on the bare ground at the side of the road where the path began. Her face held a pale and remote beauty, the porcelain sheen of her skin a marked contrast to her deep violet eyes and long dark lashes. She pulled her mink coat closer about her as the wind rustled through a few dry leaves that clung stubbornly to the oak limbs above the road.

Angela was eighteen, had been married six months and, one hour and twenty-five minutes earlier, had been unfaithful to her husband for the first time. Afterward, she had felt inexorably drawn back to this place where she was born and had lived the first seventeen years of her life.

She could almost see herself as a little girl in her printed floursack dress trudging up from the little stream that ran behind the house. Her syrup bucket full of water spilled over its shiny sides as she stumbled over a root, falling headlong onto the hard-packed dirt of the path. Dusting herself off, she set her jaw, picked up the bucket, and headed back through the dusty gloom of the late afternoon woods.

Angela walked slowly toward the little building as the twilight settled like gray-green smoke through the trees. She remembered the day her father had left them. She had been about eleven. Her mother had stood on the front porch holding Angela's infant brother as her father carried his cardboard suitcase out to the road, squinted into the rising sun to his left, and disappeared behind the trees and underbrush as he headed west down the gravel road.

At fifteen Angela had blossomed, and at seventeen her mother had managed to have her meet Morton Spain, who had been a widower for less than a year. A few months later, they were married amid howls of protest from Spain's son, Taylor, who was not much younger than Angela.

Angela's mother had dreamed of living in the apartment above the garage behind Spain's mansion and got her wish. But she was to enjoy the fruits of her less-than-honorable labor only until the following Thanksgiving when, like her infant son, she too died of pneumonia.

Sitting down on the ruined porch, Angela took a half-pint bottle of scotch from inside her coat, and, unscrewing the top, took another quick swallow. Frowning with distaste, she took two more swallows and put the bottle away. A placid look came over her face as the alcohol burned her throat and stomach, flowing warmly through her veins until the sharp-edged uncertainties of her life seemed dulled and blunted and bearable.

* * *

"Where in the world have you been all day?" Morton Spain, clad in soft leather slippers and a burgundy bathrobe, stood at the top of the concrete steps that led from his portico to the back door of his huge home on Peachtree Boulevard. His red-rimmed eyes, the pouches beneath them purple tinted and permanent, glared at Angela through the window of her LaSalle as he continued his tirade. "You're hardly ever here anymore when I get home from work!"

Angela took a deep breath, slid out of the car, and walked around it toward her husband. Leaning against one of the columns that was a miniature of the huge white ones on the front of the house, she took off one of her high-heeled shoes and rapped it against the base to loosen a bit of mud stuck to the sole.

Spain ran his hand nervously over the few strands of graying black hair that covered his shiny head. "Well, aren't you going to give an account of yourself?"

Angela glanced up at her husband. The wrinkled skin under his neck hung loosely above his paunch, dwarfing his thin shoulders and chest. She thought briefly of the man she had been with only a few hours earlier and of how she had sat at the window after he had gone, watching a convoy of olive drab army trucks roar by on the highway in a seemingly endless line as they headed east. "I went out to the old shack."

"You mean that place where you grew up?" Spain had found Angela's behavior for the past month increasingly more difficult to deal with. He was used to conformity and dependability, qualities that she seemed to abhor with a vengeance. "Whatever for?"

"I don't really know." Angela shrugged, slipping her shoe back on.

Spain watched her climb the steps toward him. The flickering light from the wrought-iron gas lamps danced in the sheen of her long dark hair, and he felt his chest constrict as he tried to control his anger. "I'm worried about you, darling. Are you feeling well?"

"I'm all right."

Following her into the house, through the rear foyer, and into the kitchen, Spain watched her walk to the stove and pour herself a cup of strong black coffee. "I'd like one myself if you don't mind, sweetheart."

"Fine with me." Angela sat down, still wrapped in her mink coat, at the formica-topped table and spooned sugar into the steaming coffee.

Spain poured himself a cup of coffee and sat down with her. "Angela, I know your mother's death has been a terrible blow to you, but you're going to have to get yourself together. We can have a good life here."

Angela gazed into her husband's sad, dark eyes, feeling little more than pity for him—and disgust with herself. He had done everything he could to make her happy, refusing to accept what everyone else in town knew—that she had married him at her mother's insistence to escape the short slide into the poorhouse that was their obvious fate. "I know we can, Morton," Angela lied, taking his hand across the table.

"That's my girl." Spain's face brightened. "Why don't we fly to Atlanta this weekend: take in a show, eat at some disgustingly expensive restaurants? You know how you love the shopping there."

Forcing herself to smile, Angela nodded. "You're a good husband, Morton. I don't deserve you."

"Don't say such silly things, darling. After the terrible time you had growing up, you deserve *some* happiness in this life, and I'm just the one who can give it to you." Spain felt like a fifteen-year-old again just being in Angela's presence.

"But what can I give you in return?" Angela held his gaze over the rim of her coffee cup.

"Well, why don't you go and have your bath and slip into something comfortable, and I'll bring some chilled champagne and iced shrimp to your room." Spain's expression was that of a four-year-old waking on Christmas morning.

Angela sighed deeply. "I'm really bushed tonight, Morton. Maybe tomorrow."

Spain's face dropped, but he quickly regained control. "You do look a little weary."

Angela got up and kissed him on the top of his head. "Good night," she crooned as she left the kitchen.

"Good night, sweetheart," Spain muttered wearily. "See you in the morning."

Angela's heels clicked on the gleaming hardwood floors of the dimly lit hallway. Oil paintings in heavy gilt frames hung along the walls. The faces of generations of Spain's family seemed to glare down on Angela as though she had no right to enjoy the comfort and muted splendor of the house.

As the first note sounded from the piano, Angela stopped, listening to the music that drifted through the quiet and scented air. "Stardust"—her favorite. Removing her shoes, she quietly entered the drawing room. The heavy jade green curtains had been closed against the streetlights, and a brass floor lamp cast an amber glow about the room.

Taylor Spain sat at the piano, his eyes closed as his slim fingers moved skillfully across the dull-yellow ivory keys. He had dark hair and fine features and would have been handsome except for the acne that marked his face like a cruel joke.

Angela dropped her coat on the arm of a divan and sat down, curling her legs beneath her as she leaned back, savoring the lovely, delicate, bittersweet melody of the song.

The song finished, Taylor opened his eyes and glared at Angela. "What do you want?"

Angela smoothed her black wool skirt across her knees. "I want us to be friends."

Taylor merely grunted and began flipping through the sheet music on the piano.

"I mean it, Taylor." Angela's voice was soft and clear, inviting as a soft bed at the end of a long day.

"I like to pick my own friends," Taylor mumbled, glancing through the music.

Angela stood up and moved slowly across the room, her stockinged feet whispering on the plush wool rug.

Taylor forced himself not to look at her, and willed his mind free of fantasies.

Stopping at the edge of the baby grand, Angela leaned on it with one elbow. "Taylor . . . my only brother died when he was just a baby. I hoped we could be . . . kind of like a brother and sister, a real family."

"You married my father. Why don't you try being a *wife* to him for a change?"

"I respect your father very much." Angela felt the words sticking in her throat. "He's a kind and gentle man, and he takes good care of me."

"You haven't answered my question."

Angela put her hand to her mouth, chewing at the flaking polish of a fingernail.

"You've made our family a laughingstock. I'm ashamed to be a part of this family." Taylor lifted a piece of sheet music out of the stack and placed it in front of him.

Angela flinched as he played the first few bars of the song with a new energy. Without speaking, she turned and left the room. Walking down the long hall toward her bedroom, she felt the notes of "The Lady Is a Tramp" strike her back like thrown stones. The heavy bedroom door gave her a sense of comfort as she closed it and locked it.

Muted light from a streetlamp shone through the long diaphanous curtains, giving the darkened room an underwater quality. Angela lay across her bed, staring at the ceiling. She tried to put all thoughts from her mind, but memories clicked on and off like moths flickering in and out of a beam of light.

After a long while, Angela rose wearily from the bed and went into her bathroom to soak in a tub of hot water. After slipping into her nightgown, she turned down her covers and stood at the side of her bed. With effort, she flicked on the bedside lamp and opened the drawer of her nightstand. She dug to the bottom of the drawer and retrieved a brown paper bag, flattened and worn.

Angela lay back on the pillow, stared at the bag for a few seconds then opened it and took out a faded black-and-white print. As was her nightly habit, she smoothed its crinkled surface and held it under the amber glow of the lamp. It was the only picture she had left of her father. He stood in front of the little shack next to her mother, pregnant with her second child. Smiling wistfully, she held onto her husband's arm as she leaned against him.

As always, Angela was drawn to her father's eyes as they stared at something outside the frame of the picture. She had wondered for years what he had been looking at in that long-ago and lost moment of time when the camera's shutter snapped. Then she let her eyes wander behind her mother and father to the porch where she saw herself as a thin, almost hollow-eyed ten-year-old, staring at her father as though he were more apparition than flesh and blood.

After putting the photograph away, Angela turned out the lamp and lay staring at the long curtains. They seemed to be collecting the weak light from outside, trying to store it inside their wispy translucent folds. She tried to think of where her life was taking her, but the future seemed remote as a fable.

*   *   *

"We'll have those little yellow savages whipped in six month's time with men like Ben Logan fighting for this country." Morton Spain aligned himself with the heroes, although he knew full well there would be no fighting for *him* in this war just as there hadn't been in the last.

Angela walked along the station platform next to her husband, observing the huge turnout for Ben's homecoming. Red, white, and blue bunting had been strung from all the buildings, poles, and trees in the vicinity of the railroad station. Streamers of crepe paper and American flags fluttered in the breeze. "Welcome Home Ben" signs abounded in the hands of the people and were tacked to virtually any stationary and upright object. "This is quite a turnout for someone who was run out of town."

Spain cleared his throat. "Well, he—ah, wasn't actually run out of town as I recall."

"Oh, c'mon, Morton," Angela objected, knowing that her husband had always refused to discuss the subject. "Ben beat up Keith Demerie in Ollie's Drugstore—a public place. You think anyone believes the good Senator would let that happen to his son without getting his pound of flesh—one way or another?"

Spain gazed down the platform where the high school band was assembling in preparation for their customary off-key rendition of "Stars and Stripes Forever."

"Here we are, like everyone else in town, waiting to welcome home Liberty's biggest hero as if we had all been right there with him on the deck of the *Arizona* shooting down those Jap planes." In spite of their surroundings, Angela felt compelled to press the issue of what had happened to Ben Logan. "But where were we when he needed somebody to stand up for him?"

"Whatever happened, it turned out for the best, Angela," Spain snorted. "Let it be, will you?"

"Someone told me you sat in as ad hoc judge the day Ben came to court." Angela let her words sink in as she watched the back of her husband's neck redden slightly.

Spain pointed down the tracks. "Here it comes, right on time," he said, as if dismissing Angela's words. "Too bad everyone's not as reliable as that train."

"You forced him somehow to join the Navy just to get him out of town, didn't you, Morton?"

Glancing down at his wife, Spain set his jaw when he spoke. "It was for the boy's own good. He was just throwing his life away here selling moonshine."

"Well goodness knows we can't have that kind of thing going on, can we?" Angela knew that Moon Mullins' still had been an institution in the town for years.

"We can't have him committing assault and battery." The day had started well, but Spain felt it beginning to slip away. "Something had to be done."

"It was a fight between two seventeen-year-old boys, Morton—and Keith outweighed him by forty pounds." Angela felt herself deriving a perverse pleasure out of this exchange with her husband. "If you locked up people every time we had a fistfight in this town, the streets would be deserted."

Spain felt anger burning deep in his chest. Glancing around at the crowd, he struggled to restrain himself. "I think it's time we dropped this subject."

Angela remembered how suspicious her husband had been years before when Ben had made deliveries from Ollie's Drugstore to their home; she had seen the yellow gleam of jealousy in his eyes. "No reason to get angry, Morton. After all, he was only a boy. But he certainly changed after he went into the Navy."

Spain's dark eyes burned with the onset of rage as he turned them on Angela. "I won't have you speaking like this in public, Angela."

Taking his arm, Angela reached up and straightened his tie. "Why, Morton, whatever has upset you so? You know you don't have a thing to worry about with me."

Angela walked along next to her husband, sensing that he was cooling down as she spoke brightly about the events of the day. Her attitude had changed to that of the loving, devoted wife. She didn't understand this need to torment her husband but knew that it came from some dark place inside her—a place she was afraid to shine the light on. It was as though she were punishing him for sins someone else had committed.

"Hello, Mayor," Spain greeted the little mayor with a slightly amused smile as he always did. "Everything going to suit you with the homecoming?" Bored, Angela wandered away while they talked.

Calvin Sinclair wriggled his tiny black mustache as he spoke. He looked like a slightly overweight Charlie Chaplin, reminding people of the Little Tramp character in silent films. "If I can find room for about a thousand people on that twenty-by-twenty foot speaker's platform, everything will be just fine. Everybody in town claims to be Ben's close kin or his lifelong buddy."

"Well I, for one, am content to stand down here among the masses," Spain replied magnanimously.

Sinclair squinted up at Spain. "I should hope so, Morton. I imagine you're the *last* person Ben Logan wants to see when he gets back home."

"I was only seeing that justice was done," Spain snapped at Sinclair. "You didn't know Logan was alive till you saw his picture on the cover of *Life* magazine—now you act like you're the father welcoming home the prodigal son."

Sinclair scowled at Spain. He was a crusty sort, tenacious and virtually impervious to insults. "Speaking of prodigals, Morton, you'd better keep an eye on your wife."

"What do you mean?" Spain jerked his head around in the direction Sinclair had nodded.

Angela stood beneath a red-white-and-blue sign proclaiming, "Ben Logan for State Senator—He's One of Us!" She gazed up into the face of Clay McCain with rapt fascination as she engaged him in animated conversation.

"Why she's just talking to Clayton," Spain proclaimed as though he had explained a riddle to Sinclair. "What in the world is wrong with that?"

Sinclair glanced at the young couple, then gave Spain a knowing smile. "I didn't say anything was wrong, did I?" he called over his shoulder as he turned and walked toward the speaker's platform.

Spain hurried over to his wife. "I wish you'd let me know before you take off like that, Angela. I feel like I'm trying to keep up with a child."

"Oh, don't be so bothersome, Morton," Angela shot back. "You expect me to stand there and let Mayor Sinclair bore me to death? I'm finding out all about Clay's big contract with the Boston Red Sox."

"When did this happen?"

Clay stuffed his hands into his blue letter jacket, smiling self-consciously. "It hasn't happened, Mr. Spain. I was just telling Ang—uh, Mrs. Spain that one of the Boston scouts had come down last year to look at me."

"Yes, well, I'm sure that's all very interesting, Clayton," Spain muttered. "C'mon, dear, let's find a good spot before they're all taken."

"This one's just fine with me." Angela smiled brightly, stepping a shade closer to Clay.

Spain took her firmly by the arm, leading her away. "C'mon, I think I see a better place."

"There goes trouble just trying to find the right place to happen."

Clay turned around to see J.T. Dickerson walking up behind him. He had shaved and combed his hair and wore a pinstriped suit coat over his gray Harvard sweat shirt.

"Hey, J.T. Glad you could make it."

J.T. stared at Spain as he led his wife hurriedly away. "You better watch that one."

"Angela?"

"It's just a matter of time before ol' Morton gets his belly full of her running around."

"Maybe she's just being friendly. Probably gets tired of hanging around that big house all the time." Clay felt a need to defend Angela in spite of all the gossip.

"I'm afraid she's going to get friendly one time too many," J.T. spoke in a somber tone. "Just hope you aren't around when it happens, son."

"Don't worry about that," Clay answered not quite sincerely. "She's too old for me."

J.T. shook his head slowly. "Yep, I expect she's nearly senile by now. Must be twenty-one at least—maybe even twenty-two."

5

THE CLEAR LIGHT OF OCTOBER

*I*t was the first autumn after the war began and 42 percent of American households had telephones. Inflation and unemployment registered exactly the same figure: 4.7 percent. A Harris tweed coat cost $26.95, and you could go into almost any department store and buy a washable rayon dress for $3.95.

Nine hundred and twenty-five AM radio stations around the country broadcast General Douglas MacArthur proclaiming: "The President of the United States ordered me to break through the Japanese lines and proceed from Corregidor to Australia for the purpose of organizing the American offense against Japan. . . . I came through and I shall return."

Americans also listened to programs like "People Are Funny" with Art Linkletter and "Fibber McGee and Molly" and heard Walter Winchell bring them the latest news. "Don't Sit Under the Apple Tree" by the Andrew Sisters, "Paper Doll" by the Mills Brothers, and "I've Got a Gal in Kalamazoo" by Glenn Miller, who also received the first gold record for "Chattanooga Choo Choo," were among the most popular tunes.

Liberty's young men departed with alarming regularity now for cities, countries and islands they had never heard of before at the beckon of their Uncle Sam. The railway station bustled with families bidding farewell to their sons and daughters, some of whom they would never see again.

The battle still raged for Guadalcanal at places like Ironbottom Sound, the Tenaru River, and "Bloody Ridge." Montgomery was about to launch his attack against Rommel's force at El Alamein. In the North Atlantic, the Allied shipping losses to the wolf packs reached a half-million tons per month.

* * *

Morton Spain knotted his red-and-gray-striped tie in a perfect four-in-hand and brushed his thin hair across his head for the final time before he walked down the hall to the kitchen. Taylor, still sleep-rumpled and drowsy, stood at the stove frying bacon. He wore jeans and a T-shirt and his acne showed as dull red blotches in the glare of the fluorescent lighting.

"Morning, son," Spain greeted him, painfully aware of the skin condition that even the best specialists in Atlanta were unable to treat. "You sure got things smelling good in here. I didn't know you could cook."

"A little something I picked up at college," Taylor grinned, brushing his dark hair back from his face.

Spain poured coffee and sat down at the table, opening the morning paper. "Says here that Gene Autry enlisted in the service. With him and Jimmy Stewart both in there, this war oughta be over in six months' time."

"I hear all four of the president's sons are in the armed forces." Taylor forked the bacon onto a small platter and reached for the eggs that sat in a white bowl on the counter. "You still eat your eggs straight up?"

"Yep."

Taylor broke two eggs into the grease that hissed and popped in the skillet. Turning down the burner, he moved them gently around with the spatula, splashing grease over their tops. "Dad . . ."

Spain stopped reading and stared over it at his son. "What is it, son?"

"I think I'm going to leave college and join up."

"Nonsense. You've only got two years left." Spain's voice held the courtroom authority he had practiced for years to perfect. "When you graduate, you can go in as an officer."

Taylor shoveled the eggs onto a plate and set it on the table. Staring down at his father, he spoke with hesitation, "Dad, I-I can't take it around here anymore."

Spain looked up from his eggs, the salt shaker held out in one hand. "What are you talking about? This is your home. I know it hasn't been easy on you and Rae since your mother died, but Angela—"

"That's exactly it—Angela." Taylor went back to the stove and broke two more eggs into the skillet.

"What has she done to you?"

Taylor turned around, shaking his head slowly. "Nothing. It's what she's done—is doing to you."

Spain had tried to bury his doubts about Angela—about their marriage, but there were times such as now when was forced to confront them. He picked up the newspaper and tried to concentrate on an editorial, then slapped it back on the table.

"You must have wondered why Rae married so quickly?" Taylor turned back to the stove, speaking in a more subdued voice now. "She'd only known Bill for a month. It was to get away from this house—this town."

Spain sighed, his shoulders slumping. "The two of you think I'm just an old fool."

Taylor turned off the burner and pulled a chair up next to his father. "No, Dad. I could never think that about you. I think you were lonely after Mama died. You just happened to run into the wrong woman."

"She's just so *young*, Taylor." Spain turned his anguished eyes on his son. "Give her some time. She'll settle down and things will be just fine."

"It's been four years, Dad."

Spain thought of the terrible grief he suffered after his wife's death and of how his whole world had changed after he had met Angela. He remembered those months when he had courted her and the envious looks he got from the men when he would take her to church or to a town picnic or simply for a stroll along the streets on a warm summer evening.

Lately, he found himself thinking more and more about those days and about the first few months of his marriage, which were the happiest of his life since he had been a young man. He dwelt on those fleeting times because for more than three years now there had been precious few times when he had had any joy or even peace of mind in his marriage.

"I know how long it's been, but there's still time for things to get better," Spain pleaded for understanding from his son. "They just *have* to."

Taylor saw that there was no sense in pursuing the matter any further. His father was hopelessly and senselessly in love with Angela. "Maybe you're right, Dad."

Spain brightened. "Certainly I'm right. Now you forget about this joining the Army business and get your mind back on your studies."

"Sure, Dad." Taylor knew that he would be coming back home very little now, if at all, and he still hadn't ruled out the idea of joining the service. One thing he was certain of—he had had all he could take of the crude remarks about his stepmother from the men in town.

Taylor took his plate and a cup of coffee and sat down at the table. "I never see you go to breakfast anymore down at the Liberty Hotel. You used to love going there to get the day started off with all your buddies."

Spain cleared his throat. "Well, I guess anything gets old after a while, and that was a habit for years and years." Spain could almost hear the chuckles from his friends as he would enter the restaurant each morning. Only twice did he actually hear any gossip about Angela, but it eventually reached the point when any time someone would laugh, he thought it was at his expense. Finally the day came when he could face it no longer, and the "habit of years" that he had dearly loved was over.

After Taylor had dressed and left to drive back to school, Spain sat in a metal glider on the flagstone terrace behind his house and enjoyed the warmth of Indian summer. The morning breeze moved through the willow limbs at the end of the terrace, creating a shifting pattern of sunlight and shade on the stones below. Gazing over the expanse of lawn, he stared at the rainbow haze hovering in the mist of the water sprinklers.

At the back of the property, Spain noticed Amos, his sixty-year-old Negro groundskeeper as he trimmed the hedge that surrounded the grounds. He wore his usual khakis and brogans and worked with his usual calm and deliberate pace that he would keep up all day long. Although he had employed Amos for almost twenty years, Spain suddenly realized that he knew virtually nothing about the man.

He's got a wife and three children—I think. I don't even know where he lives. Spain was so used to seeing his property perfectly manicured that the grounds might have been a painting that someone replaced with the changing of the seasons. *I'll have to make it a point to talk to him some day. But now I'll be late for court if I don't hurry.*

* * *

"Don't forget to take the package to the depot. Taylor needs that book as a reference for his pre-law exams." Morton Spain spoke to Angela from the driver's seat of his idling black Cadillac.

Angela stood under the back portico of their home, pulling her quilted housecoat about her against the morning chill. "I'll drop it off on my way to Hightower's. I want to buy some Halloween decorations for the house."

"That's for children, Angela. There's only the two of us here now."

"I don't care, Morton," Angela pouted. "I never had any as a child. Taylor and Rae would have made fun of me, but they're gone now."

Spain never ceased to be amazed at Angela's chronic and erratic metamorphoses from woman to child and back to woman again. "If it makes you happy."

Angela smiled at her tiny victory. "What time will you be back from Atlanta?"

"Probably not until two or three in the morning. You never know how long a hearing like this will last." Spain noticed with a gnawing sense of unease how his wife tried to conceal her delight at the prospect of his being away for so long. "I may just spend the night."

Angela walked over to the car and kissed him lightly on the cheek. "Poor dear! Don't work too hard."

"What do you do to occupy your time while I'm away on these trips, Angela?" Morton seemed unable to stop himself from asking the same tired question, the one that seemed to have become more riddle than question judging by Angela's inability to give him a sensible answer.

"Oh, you know. Polish my nails, listen to the radio, read a magazine."

"You need to develop some interests, hobbies—something. You must be bored to death."

"No, I'm not." Angela frowned.

"I'm only thinking of you, Angela," Spain reassured her. "I don't want you wasting your life."

Angela's face brightened. "How could you say I'm wasting my life when I'm married to you?"

Spain stared into Angela's violet eyes, disturbed at the peculiar cast he saw in them. Then without even attempting to return her smile, he drove away.

* * *

Angela drove to the depot along the quiet midmorning streets. Huge oaks and elms grew in front of the nineteenth-century houses, tall and gabled and white with gray wraparound porches. Painted with autumn colors of red and rust and copper, the ancient trees blazed brilliantly in the clear light of October. She loved this time of year with its crisp, dry air and the scent of smoke from chimneys and wood-burning stoves that many people, even in town, still cooked on.

Pulling into the depot parking lot, Angela saw people scattered along the platform near the train. Young men in uniform seemed to be at the center of each group. Old women and young women, some with tears glistening in their eyes, clung to their men-at-arms. There was an occasional handshake or slap on the back from fathers or brothers who, for the most part, hung back on the edges of the little groups.

Angela hurried up the front steps of the station, entered through the front glass doors, and took her package over to the counter.

Stanley Adams, the stationmaster, a short plump man with wire spectacles, waddled over to Angela from his desk. "What can I do for you, Mrs. Spain?"

Since the first time she had seen him, Angela had thought Adams looked like Santa Claus without a beard, even wearing his black uniform with its flat-crowned and shiny-billed hat. "I need to send this to Taylor—something important for his studies. His daddy will kill me if it isn't on today's train."

"Oh, I doubt that, Mrs. Spain." Adams peered at Angela over the rims of his spectacles. "I'll bet your husband never even gets mad at you."

Angela smiled and gave Adams a five-dollar bill. She waited for her change while he stamped the package and placed it on the cart with the other mail.

"Hello, Angela. My, don't you look lovely today." Lila Kronen, wearing a tan jacket over her brown sweater and slacks, stood next to the counter. Her smile radiated warmth as surely as the huge pot-bellied stove standing in the center of the station waiting room.

Angela turned to look at the older woman she had met at a luncheon at the country club. She had since seen her at several other functions and had become fond of her. "Why, thank you, Lila," she replied, glancing down at her burnt-orange dress. "Just something from last year."

"How's Morton?"

"He's fine. Over in Atlanta today on business."

"Here you are." Adams handed Angela her change.

"Thank you. Are you sure it'll go out today?"

"Guaranteed."

"How are things going with your newspaper, Lila?" Angela had heard that Dobe Jackson, who owned the *Liberty Herald*, was not pleased at all at the prospect of competition.

"Slowly I'm afraid," Lila admitted. "I'm here to pick up a part for the press. Henry says that sitting idle all that time was the worst thing that could have happened to it."

Angela glanced over at the three tables Adams had placed near the windows that looked over the station platform. With all the wartime traffic, he had decided to make a little extra money for himself by selling coffee. "If you're not in a hurry, we could have some coffee."

"They haven't unloaded the mail yet, Mrs. Kronen," Adams volunteered.

"Fine, " Lila smiled.

They seated themselves while Mr. Adams brought two steaming white mugs of coffee and placed them on the table. Lila handed him a dollar.

"I'll be right back with your change."

"You keep it, Mr. Adams," Angela said with a flick of her painted nails. "This looks like great coffee."

"A dollar for two dime cups? It ain't that great." Adams stared at the dollar bill as he went back to his counter.

"When do you think you'll get your first newspaper out, Lila?" Angela asked as she poured cream into her coffee.

"You sound like Henry." Lila glanced out at the people milling about on the platform. "It's been almost six months and I haven't been able to sell one ad yet. Maybe a handful of people have said they'd take subscriptions. Old habits die hard and everyone here is so used to the *Herald* that they're skeptical of anything else. I'll probably have to finance the first few issues with my own money until the good citizens of Liberty can see what they're going to get for their dimes."

"Well, you can put the Spain household down for a subscription," Angela beamed. "Morton says he's getting tired of Dobe Jackson's editorials condemning every German and Japanese on the face of the earth."

"I've noticed he seems to have some kind of fixation on the subject."

Angela had enjoyed the few conversations she had had with Lila and this one was no exception. Somehow, and she was unable to comprehend why, Lila made her feel like she was somebody special. "It's not like everybody in the whole country doesn't already know why we're fighting this war—he has to continually remind us like he's the only true-blue American and it's his duty to convert the rest of us. And even worse, the Japanese- and German-Americans had nothing at all to do with starting it."

"I should hope not," Lila agreed readily. "I was born in Germany, and I consider myself as loyal an American as there is in this country."

"I didn't know you were German."

"Oh, I don't remember anything about the country. I was only six months old when our family came here."

Angela chinked her teaspoon lightly on the side of her mug, her face thoughtful, then as if no one had ever thought of it before she proclaimed, "We all came over here from somewhere else, didn't we? I mean our families did even if we didn't."

Lila smiled at Angela's revelation. "That's right. And it's

thinking like Dobe Jackson's that allowed a man like Adolph Hitler to come to power."

"What do you mean?"

"I mean blaming a whole class or race of people—like the Jews—for a country's problems. It unites people against an alleged common enemy, plays on their fears like Jackson's trying to do with the Japanese and Germans who are as American as anyone else. And in his case, it sells newspapers for him."

"I think you might have some problems with Mr. Jackson before this war's over, Lila."

"I expect you're right, but I've had problems before." Lila sipped her coffee and stared at Angela, her brow furrowed in concentration. "We can't let that kind of thinking go unchecked in this country. It'll be the end of us if we do."

"You mean treating the Japanese here the same as the Japanese who started the war?"

"I guess I mean condemning any group of people for injustices they had nothing to do with." Lila felt like Angela was sometimes more her student than her friend and found herself enjoying the role of teacher. "For instance, slavery was a terrible blight on this country. But would you condemn every white person alive for its existence? It was abolished eighty years ago. No one alive now ever owned slaves, and only a small percentage did before its death.

"The sane thing to do is to right the injustices that still exist with the Negroes today. Give them the same freedoms and opportunities that everyone else has. What purpose would it serve to judge people now for the wrongs that happened before they were even born?

"I for one refuse to accept blame for what my forebears did generations before I came into existence." Lila noticed the puzzled expression on Angela's face. "I do tend to ramble on, don't I? Just tell me to hush when that happens."

"Oh, no." Angela smiled. "I don't have conversations like this with anyone else but you, Lila. It's certainly interesting for me and—different."

Lila shook her head slowly. "I guess I'm just frustrated that a mean-spirited man like Adolph Hitler can cause so much heartache and suffering in the world. I believe that every little petty tyrant like him that thrives on an agenda of bigotry and fear is nothing but a coward—inside they're just frightened little boys who have no abilities, nothing to offer the world, so they tap in somehow to hatred and jealousy, the absolute worst qualities of people, and manipulate them for their own despicable ends. Why do we even listen to them?" Lila stopped suddenly, placing her hand over her mouth. "I did it again, didn't I? Guess I'd better get my newspaper going so I can put all this in print. Maybe then I'll stop boring people to death."

Angela found herself staring in rapt fascination at Lila as she spoke so fervently. "I don't think you're boring. I do think you probably wouldn't be welcomed back to Germany though—not for a while anyway."

"You're probably right." Lila laughed.

Angela glanced out the window. "Look! We started all this speaking about Dobe Jackson, and there comes his daughter, Diane, with Clay McCain."

"J.T. told me Clay had joined the Marines."

"Poor Diane. Her daddy's been against her seeing Clay, and now he's off to fight with the Marines. I guess there are stories like that all over the country."

Lila had become intrigued. "What's Jackson got against Clay? I hear he's a fine boy."

"Fine, but poor," Angela said matter-of-factly. "It's a quality Dobe finds—distasteful. See, hanging around with you is helping my vocabulary."

"But he's going to sign with Boston, isn't he? He'll have plenty of money then."

"That's not sure enough for ol' Dobe, especially with the war on," Angela explained, staring at Clay's broad shoulders and slim hips as he stood talking with Diane and his parents. "If I weren't married . . ."

Lila gave Angela a knowing frown. "What's Dobe's idea of the ideal mate for his daughter?"

"Probably somebody like Keith Demerie." Angela made a face when she said it. "He's a decent looking-boy, but he won't do a thing without asking his daddy first. I think all Dobe cares about is the fact that Tyson Demerie is a senator and could help him out politically."

"You're giving me quite an education on the town, Angela.

Maybe it'll come in handy if I ever get this newspaper going. It helps to know the competition." Lila watched Clay kiss his mother and shake hands with his father. Then she saw Diane follow him over to the edge of the platform where he took her in his arms and kissed her then hopped aboard the train just as the engine's steam whistle gave a loud blast.

"I sure hope Clay makes it back all right," Angela said softly, staring at the line of green Pullman cars lurching out of the station. "He's such a nice boy."

Lila gazed out the window. Clay's mother had buried her face against her husband's shoulder. "They're all nice boys, Angela."

"I'd hate to be a man," Angela remarked, as though realizing for the first time the terrible uncertainty of war and the even more terrible finality of death. "I don't think I'd have the courage to fight."

"Most of us find the courage to do what we have to do—one way or the other. It's either that or give up on life," Lila observed. "Well, I guess I'll get back to work. I see Mr. Adams has the mail unloaded. You coming?"

Angela had noticed a sailor crossing the platform in his dress blues, carrying a duffel bag on his shoulders. He was slim and well built with short dark hair and a clean profile. Something about him made Angela think that her long-dead brother would have grown up to look something like he did. It never occurred to her that the young man bore a marked resemblance to the picture of her father that she kept next to her bed.

"Are you leaving, Angela?"

"What? Oh, sorry I didn't hear you." Angela glanced again at the sailor who was walking toward the door leading into the station with that overconfident tread common to young healthy men. "Not just now. I think I'll have another cup of coffee, maybe talk to Mr. Adams a few minutes." Lila watched as the sailor entered the station and walked over to speak with the stationmaster. He glanced back over his shoulder toward Angela.

"We'll have to do this again soon, Angela." Lila stood up to leave.

"I'd love to." Angela forced her gaze back to Lila. "I really enjoy being with you, Lila. I hope we can remain friends. There aren't many people I can talk to."

Lila picked up her package, waved goodbye to Angela, and left the station by the front door. As she walked across to her car, she glanced back into the station through the tall windows. Smiling down at Angela, the young sailor stood next to the chair Lila had just left.

6

CASUALTY OF WAR

"Wayne Perez," the young sailor volunteered, flashing a mouthful of white teeth in his deeply tanned face. "Mind if I join you?"

Angela knew he would be joining her as soon as she had glanced at him over her shoulder and saw his eyebrows raise slightly. She hesitated now, just enough to make him shift about uneasily, twirling his white cap on the forefinger of his left hand. "Well, I don't usually talk to strangers, but since you're in uniform I guess it won't hurt to have a cup of coffee with you."

"You're sure I won't be disturbing you?" Perez asked in an excess of politeness.

Angela merely pointed a red fingernail at her empty coffee mug.

"Sure thing," Perez said quickly and dropped his duffel bag against the wall next to his chair. Placing his own mug on the table, he hurried over to the counter with Angela's.

When he returned with the coffee, Perez took his seat, gazing in silence at the almost luminous glow of Angela's skin as the pale light through the window touched it. He dumped four spoonfuls of sugar into his mug, spilling a large portion of it on the table.

Angela loved to play the game. She stared disinterestedly out the window at the station platform, empty now except for a porter wearing overalls, a battered felt hat, and a red plaid shirt, who wheeled a cart back to its place near the loading dock.

Perez couldn't believe his good fortune, but he felt pressured to say something before this elegantly dressed and obviously well-off woman became bored with him and walked forever out of his life. "I'm from El Paso."

Angela turned her head slowly in his direction. "Sounds Spanish. Are you Spanish, Mr. Perez?"

"Mr. Perez? I haven't heard that three times in my whole life. Call me Wayne." Perez couldn't decide whether she was putting him on or not.

"Well, are you?"

"Am I what? Oh, sure! I don't speak the language often though. Papa said if we want to be good Americans we should speak English."

"He's probably right."

"By the way, I didn't get your name."

"English."

"English?"

"Angela English."

"Oh." Perez sipped his coffee, making a slurping sound in his nervousness.

Angela smiled into her white mug.

"Excuse me. This is my first time away from home—I guess I'm a little nervous."

"How old are you?" Angela stared straight into Perez's dark eyes.

Perez set his mug on the table, glancing over at the counter as though Adams could somehow give him more confidence. "Almost eighteen."

"Really? You look *much* older." Angela had decided to end the "make them uncomfortable first" stage of this destined-to-be-brief relationship.

"Papa said there's nothing like going into the service to turn a boy into a man." Perez sat up a little straighter in the wire-backed chair. "He still calls me his boy, though. You know how papas are about their children."

Angela thought of her own father, holding his little cardboard suitcase and squinting into the sun the morning he disappeared forever from her life. She remembered that he walked away without even a glance in her direction. For three years or more she had looked time and again at that same spot in the road, hope slowly fading that he would someday reappear where she had seen him last. "Yes. They're all the same, aren't they?"

"You still live with your family?" Perez glanced down at Angela's ring finger.

His glance wasn't wasted on Angela. She thought of her wedding ring and the three carat engagement ring resting in the bottom of her purse. "Yes. I think my daddy would just die if I tried to move out of the house. He doesn't want me to leave home even for a few days. We live over in Atlanta. I'm just visiting my aunt here in Liberty."

"I'm on my way to New Jersey now. I just finished boot camp in San Diego." Perez still couldn't figure out why Angela had any interest in him, but he was starting to relax and enjoy himself. "They gave me a month's liberty first. My mother sure didn't want me to leave when it was up."

"Why did you pick the Navy?"

"Oh, that was my uncle's idea—my papa's oldest brother. He's a drill instructor at boot camp in San Diego." Perez thought of his uncle sitting at their family's kitchen table in the little three-room apartment in El Paso and of how as a ten-year-old boy he wanted more than anything else to be like him—to wear a real Navy uniform and sail around the world to places he could only read about in books.

He thought as well of how he had dreaded the prospect of ending up like his own father, old beyond his years, with a sun-burned and craggy face and hands like gnarled brown wood from twelve-hour days in the elements, mixing and carrying mortar for the bricklayers on construction jobs. "What does your papa do for a living?" he asked Angela.

"Oh, he's a lawyer." As always, Angela was beginning to feel more like the person she had begun to create with her words than the person she actually was. "He gets so busy sometimes we hardly ever see him. But then he'll just shut everything down, cancel all his appointments—won't even take calls from judges—and we have barbecues in the back yard, go to movies, and sometimes stay at our cabin out on the lake."

Perez was becoming more and more confused about why Angela would want to spend any time with him. "I never even saw a lake till I joined the Navy."

"How long have you got?" Angela had decided that she would be safe with Perez and now wanted to spend as little time as possible in the public eye.

"Excuse me?"

"When do you have to leave?" Angela asked, a hint of irritation in her voice.

Perez glanced at the big schoolhouse clock above Adams' desk. Things were moving so fast he found himself in a kind of daze. "My train leaves at five-thirty. That gives me six-and-a-half hours."

"Why don't we go somewhere and have a drink—maybe listen to some music?"

Perez couldn't believe his good fortune. He felt like a kid on his way to the circus. "I'd really like that!" Pushing his chair back, he noticed the frown on Angela's face.

Angela leaned over the table, whispering, "Wait till I'm gone. My aunt wouldn't understand my meeting you like this—she's kind of old fashioned. She doesn't understand that we have to keep up the morale of our fighting men."

"Oh." Perez looked around the empty station waiting room, then gave Adams a glance. "You think he'd tell her about us?"

"They're good friends," Angela nodded, "and this isn't a very big town."

Perez picked up his empty coffee mug, turning it up as though he were drinking.

Angela slung the strap of her brown leather purse around her shoulder. "Wait ten minutes after I'm gone, then walk four blocks west. Wait for me on the corner where the gravel road intersects this street."

Perez, trying painfully to look nonchalant, nodded his head to each of Angela's instructions.

"You can leave your bag with Mr. Adams. Tell him you just want to walk around and see a little of the town." Standing up, Angela spoke a little too loudly, "Nice meeting you. You take care of yourself now."

"You too," Perez replied, grinning broadly at Angela then over at Adams. "Tell your papa I said he raised a fine daughter. Maybe I'll see you sometime after the war's over."

* * *

He wouldn't have noticed it at all as he drove past Slick Willie's Tavern except that it looked so out of place. Three muddy log trucks, their cabs bashed and dented from years of rough service in the woods, a handful of Model T's, and thirties vintage Chevrolets decorated the rutted gravel parking lot. Several horses, still harnessed to their wood-sided wagons, stood tied to trees at the edge of the woods.

Angela's black LaSalle had been backed carefully behind the tavern, but its shiny grill glinted in the sunlight, catching Spain's eye as he headed eagerly back toward home, grateful for the opportunity to spend the rest of the day with his wife.

Spain's Cadillac had broken down fifty miles outside of Liberty. Calling the courthouse in Atlanta from a service station while his car was being repaired to inform them of his delay, he had learned that the hearing had been postponed; the judge had suffered a heart attack on the way to the courthouse.

With the glimpse of Angela's car parked at that infamous tavern, the years of suspicion and doubt seemed to weigh down on Spain so heavily and so suddenly that he felt himself in danger of also having a heart attack. After driving five miles, his eyes clouded with the pain that seemed to sweep over him from deep in his chest, he pulled into a gravel drive with a leaning mailbox, backed onto the highway, and drove back the way he had come.

* * *

The muted ticking of the clock on the dashboard of Spain's Cadillac had been the only companion for his solitary vigil. When he glanced at it, it told him he had been sitting in the parking lot at the edge of the woods for an hour and twenty-five minutes. Several men, one or two in the company of heavily rouged and lightly dressed women, had stared at him as they left the tavern, clinging roughly to each other.

At one point a young sailor had walked from the front door to Angela's car and taken an overnight bag out of the trunk. He had then climbed the wooden steps up to the five rooms located on a bluff behind the tavern. He went into room number four, came back out without the bag, and returned to the tavern.

After he had seen the sailor, Spain's eyes became glazed and vacant, almost as though an opaque film had been slowly drawn over them. The pain in his chest intensified as unbearable pictures flickered at the back of his mind like worn-out copies of ancient silent films. His head seemed filled with the suppressed laughter of his friends when he passed their tables in the restaurant or encountered them on the street.

Spain recalled the day his son was born. He had gazed down at him in his mother's arms in the white bed of the white hospital room. He remembered that his wife had been the same age as Angela on that long ago day.

A man in greasy overalls, his eyes red and puffy from drink, staggered over to the car window, startling Spain from his reverie. He stood wobbly and glassy-eyed, motioning for Spain to roll his window down. "Name's Grogan. You need some hep?" he asked, slurring his words.

Spain stared up at the man, shook his head, and rolled the window back up.

Grogan took four steps sideways, reached for an imaginary object in front of him and fell backward against the base of a pine tree. Struggling to his knees, he vomited onto the carpet of pine needles, his whole body retching with the effort. With a deep sigh, he fell onto his back and lay there, barely breathing, his eyes rolled back in his head.

Spain glanced out the window at Grogan, then looked away into his past. Startled by a sudden peal of thunder, he watched as the first few raindrops splashed on the hood of his car. He felt he had been sitting there all his life.

Leaning over on the seat, he reached into the glove compartment and took out a nickel-plated revolver. He cradled the pistol in both hands as though it might try to escape. A smile came slowly to his face as though some revelation that had eluded him all his life had finally come into focus. While he stared out into the rain, the light in his eyes went out as suddenly as if someone had thrown a switch inside his head.

The rain began to fall in earnest, becoming a gray curtain between Spain and the tavern with its flickering pale blue neon sign. It drummed steadily on the roof of the car, rustling and hissing high above in the leaves of the trees.

Grogan lay undisturbed underneath the pine tree, his cheek pressed against the carpet of needles, his lips making a soft plopping sound as he expelled air.

* * *

Smoke hung in the stale air close to the ceiling and drifted in wispy clouds across the room. Most of the stools along the bar were occupied by men, the few tables scattered near the opposite side were filled with couples. Pabst Blue Ribbon, Chesterfield, and Lucky Strike signs hung in random patterns on the walls. A jukebox glowed softly at the back of the room.

In the center of the bare concrete floor, a short, stocky man in cowboy boots and a Western shirt danced with a thin woman in a flowered dress and high-heeled patent-leather shoes. A cigarette dangled between the fingers of her bony hand hanging across his shoulder.

As she watched the dancers, Angela felt as light and insubstantial as the smoke after her four whiskey sours. "You know what?" she asked.

"Whaa?" Perez, his eyelids drooping sleepily, tried to bring Angela into focus as he gazed across the table at her.

"You remind me a little of Tyrone Power."

Perez sat up, blinked slowly, and took a sip from his water-beaded bottle of Pabst. He started to speak, but his tongue refused to form the words.

"You drink much?" Angela was amused at the effect the beer was having on Perez. He reminded her more of a child pilfering from the cookie jar than a sailor out on the town.

Perez took a deep breath and spoke haltingly. "One time before. W-we had a leave . . . boot camp and they—they took me out to . . ."

"You know something else?" Angela felt like an older sister to Perez. She wished now that she hadn't rented a room for the two of them. "You look like you're about ten years old. Have you ever had a girlfriend before, Wayne?"

Perez gazed at Angela with a sleepy smile on his face. "S°—I mean, yes. I guess you could say that. Juanita. She lived next door." He pushed the bottle of beer away from him and propped his elbows on the table, supporting his face in both hands. "We went to the movies a couple of times. I don't know if that made her my girlfriend or not."

"That's sweet."

Perez nodded and sat back in his chair, still smiling dreamily at Angela.

Angela realized now that the whole thing was a big mistake on her part. She thought of how much she would have liked to have had a brother. "Maybe I should take you on back to the depot now. You don't want to miss your train."

The jukebox began to play Tommy Dorsey's smoothly sentimental version of "I'll Never Smile Again" with Frank Sinatra's vocals backed up by the Pied Pipers.

"Let's dance." Perez placed both hands on the table and tried to stand up. He immediately plopped back down into his chair. "Let's don't dance," he giggled.

Angela smiled affectionately at him. "C'mon, I've got to get you back to the station."

Perez leaned toward Angela, his face as placid as that of a sleeping child. "You know something—this may not be such a bad war after all."

"What do you mean?"

"If it wasn't for the war, I never would have met you." Perez took Angela's hand in both of his, patting it gently. "This is the nicest time of my life."

They were the last words he ever spoke.

Angela saw a hole open suddenly in Perez's face just above his left eyebrow—the muzzle blast almost deafened her. Perez's head jerked back as his body slowly slid down in the chair. A single drop like a crimson tear rolled slowly down his face, followed by a rush of blood.

Angela heard herself screaming and thought at first that it was someone else from some other place in the room. Putting her hand over her mouth, she watched Perez collapse onto the floor with that rubbery, insentient motion that only death can produce in the human body.

Scraping her chair back on the rough floor, Angela turned to stand up, stopping in horror. Morton Spain stood ten feet away from her. His dark suit and silk tie, ruined by the rain, clung to his bony frame. The top of his bald head shone in the dim light. The few strands of hair that normally covered it had become plastered to the side of his face.

Angela thought she could see her own death reflected in the

dark, bottomless depths of his eyes. *Oh, God! Don't let this happen now! I'm not ready to die!*

With his face twisted in anguish and rage, Spain pointed the revolver directly at Angela's breast. She watched a tiny curl of smoke wisp upward from the barrel, then it exploded with yellow flame as a searing pain shot through the outside of her right shoulder.

Angela felt the warm flow from her shoulder with her left hand as she stared again into her husband's eyes, absent now of all light. Spain took one step toward her and leveled the pistol. Then he hurtled sideways, his upper torso ripped and torn by the shotgun blast.

Standing shakily, Angela saw the bartender standing a few feet away, a sawed-off twelve gauge gripped tightly in his thick, hairy hands. Her vision began to go fuzzy as the tavern became a spinning blur of light and color and noise. Vague forms of men and women moved as though in slow motion toward the door, escaping the carnage.

Forcing her head downward, Angela stared at her husband's shattered body crumpled amid the cigarette butts and mud and his own blood. Near him lay Perez, his right arm twisted beneath his body, his visible left eye holding that long vacant stare into eternity.

The bartender wiped his right hand on his stained apron, walked over to Angela and took her by the arm. "You all right? Looks like he grazed your shoulder."

Angela stared into the man's tiny brown eyes, set deep into his fleshy face. She opened her mouth to speak, then the darkness bore down on her with a smothering pressure and she fell down, down into a bottomless well where the wind howled about her in the choking blackness.

* * *

The cold October light created a patchwork of sunshine and shade as it cast shadows from the tall and ancient tombstones across the leaf-strewn ground of the cemetery. In the top of a scarlet sweet gum tree, a mockingbird sang to celebrate the last good days before the onset of winter.

Angela didn't hear the bird's song or see the bright plumage of the tree as she sat in one the twelve velvet-covered chairs next to her husband's grave. None of the other eleven had been occupied during the service. Taylor and Rae refused to sit with their father's widow, and the other family members had taken their cue from them.

When the service ended, the crowd, most clad in black, dispersed into small family groups, walking across the cemetery toward their cars. Occasionally one or two would stop at a gravesite and speak in low voices. Engines roared or sputtered to life, tires crunched across the gravel drive, and conversations resumed their normal levels as the speakers reached the accepted distance from the deceased.

Still Angela sat with her head bowed, the black hat and veil covering her red and swollen eyes. Her right arm hung across her breast in a sling. She stared at her left shoe, its high heel and thin black sole caked with red mud where she had walked too close to the open grave.

Thad Majors bade farewell to the last of the funeral crowd, most of whom belonged to his congregation, and walked back to the gravesite. He had a crinkly smile that reminded most people of Roy Rogers, and he had pastored the First Baptist Church of Liberty, Georgia, for thirty-two years. Placing his hand gently on Angela's shoulder, he spoke with genuine tenderness. "Is there anything I can do for you, Mrs. Spain?"

Angela merely shook her head.

"Are you sure?" Majors continued, knowing that she had no family left in town. "You're more than welcome to come and stay at our house for a while."

Angela gazed up into Majors's open and honest face. "No, thank you. You're very kind."

"Well, I'll be going then." Majors glanced down the hill at the chauffeured limousine, idling in the driveway. "I'll be by to check on you. You call if you need anything."

Angela nodded and shook his hand.

"I'll be praying for you, Mrs. Spain." Majors turned and followed his shadow down to his car.

Angela heard someone sit down in the chair next to her and felt a soft hand press gently on her gloved one. Turning, she saw Lila Kronen and her presence seemed to Angela to make the day almost bearable.

"You mustn't sit here any longer. There's nothing left to do." Lila took her hand, urging her to her feet.

The two women walked together to the waiting limousine where the driver opened the door for Angela.

"Take her directly home. I'll follow in my car."

When they reached the house, Angela walked woodenly up the back steps from the portico and down the long hall to the huge living room with its heavy antique furniture and tapestry rugs. She sat down on a plush sofa, staring out through the tall windows at the long expanse of front yard.

Lila knew that any words of comfort would be useless at this time. She took off Angela's hat and shoes, lifting her legs up on the sofa. Then she went into the kitchen, made a pot of tea, and brought it to the living room. With some effort, she was able to get Angela to drink most of a cup.

A bright rectangle of sunlight moved slowly across the gleaming hardwood floor as Lila sat with Angela through the afternoon. Finally, as the pale gold light faded to gray, Angela leaned over and fell into a deathlike sleep with her head in Lila's lap. Lila hummed softly to her, stroking her hair and watching the stars through the windows as they winked on one by one in the vast purple dome of the sky.

7

AFTERMATH

*A*ngela thought the music was lovely when she first heard it, but the recording of "I'll Never Smile Again" on the jukebox continued to play over and over, louder and louder. She put her hands to her ears, but it didn't help. Glancing around, she found herself back in the tavern. The smoke, thick as heavy fog, burned her lungs. She found herself coughing, gasping for breath. Now the music had become nothing more than a high-pitched wailing sound laced with deep, horrible groans.

Struggling to stand up, Angela found that her arms and legs felt like they were made of lead, nothing but dead weight that she had no control over. She tried to scream, but no sound came from her open mouth.

With horror, she saw Perez sitting in his chair across the table from her. The gaping hole above his left eye was crusty with dried blood. It had streamed down the side of his face, pooling in the small hollow of his collar bone.

"I'm so sorry, Wayne." Angela's voice sounded cracked and dry, like that of a very old woman.

"You should have told me, Angela." Perez stared at her, his soft, dark eyes unbearably sad. "I didn't know. You should have told me."

Suddenly the concrete floor opened into a cavernous hole beneath her. She hurtled downward in a swirling maelstrom of wind and darkness and screams of unimaginable torment. Miles below, she could see light flickering in red and yellow waves across the bottom of a stony pit—smoke rose toward her in a black, malevolent cloud.

"Oh, God! Help me!" Angela sprang up from the dream, her body soaked in a cold sweat. Her breath came in ragged gasps as she struggled up from the twisted sheets. She ran into her bathroom and stripped off the soaked nightgown. Adjusting the water temperature to as hot as she could stand it, she stood under the shower until she stopped shivering.

After toweling her hair dry, she dressed in jeans with a red flannel shirt and penny loafers then went into the kitchen and made tea. As she sat at the table sipping the hot liquid, the huge rooms and expensive furnishings around her seemed more like a vast tomb than a home. She felt almost like an ancient Egyptian queen she had read about in one of the reference books in her husband's library. She had been buried alive with pomp and ceremony and all her earthly treasures.

No longer able to stand the emptiness of the house—the dolor of familiar surroundings had become her enemy—Angela grabbed her black leather jacket from the clothes tree and ran down the back steps of the portico to her car. She drove through the deserted streets while the dashboard clock ticked off the fleeting minutes of her life.

* * *

Angela found herself pulling into the parking lot of an all-night cafe on the highway outside of town. A hand-lettered sign above the door proclaimed: Smitty's—The Best Homemade Biscuits in the World. Paint flaked off the walls, and dust and grime caked a row of windows across the front. A yellow cur, his hide splotchy with mange, loped around from the deep shadows on the side of the building at the sound of the automobile invading his domain. A heavy chain jerked him up short before he had gone twenty feet.

After waiting a few seconds to make sure the dog was securely bound, Angela walked up the front steps and into the neon glare inside, taking a seat at the end of the counter on a stool covered in red vinyl.

Glancing around the nearly deserted cafe, she noticed a young couple sitting close together in a booth across from her. Eating hamburgers and greasy hash browns, they appeared as happy as if they had been dining in the most elegant and expensive restaurant in Atlanta.

The groom had unkempt brown hair and pimples. He wore a suit that had probably set him back five dollars. His bride, holding out her left hand every few minutes to admire her tiny gold band, wore a blue cotton dress and a heavy brown work coat. Freshly washed, her straight blond hair gleamed in the bright light.

"Hep you?"

Angela turned around quickly at the sound of the coarse voice. The man standing behind the counter wore a grease-stained apron over his ponderous belly. He sported several days' growth of dark stubble and his rheumy eyes squinted out from under bushy brows. A purple cobra, tattooed on his left bicep, entwined itself around a human skull.

She almost asked for tea, then glancing at her surroundings replied in a dry voice, "Coffee, please."

"It ain't fresh."

"That's OK."

The man waddled over to the coffee urn, drew a thick mug full and pushed it across the counter with coffee sloshing over the side. "Ten cents."

Angela fished a dime out of her purse, placing it in the man's pudgy hand.

"Holler loud if you want something else. I might be asleep." He disappeared into the back behind a curtain hanging over an open doorway.

"Oh, it's so purty. Where did you get the money to buy it?" The bride, still admiring her ring, spoke in a voice that was as much child as woman.

"Been saving fer a long, long time," the groom replied with obvious pride. "Nothing's too good fer my wife. You're jest as purty as a speckled puppy under a red wagon."

Angela heard giggling and a soft smacking sound as the bride expressed her appreciation for the compliment with a kiss. Then the sounds of eating resumed.

They can't be more than fifteen or sixteen. What chance do they have? Angela sipped her coffee, finding the cook to be a master of understatement with his choice of words, "It ain't fresh." *This stuff wasn't fresh yesterday.*

"This is a *good* hamburger." The bride seemed more than satisfied with her wedding supper.

"Best in this part of the country," the groom agreed readily. "We can come here after church on Sunday when the cotton crop's in and other times during the year when we got a little extra change in our pockets."

The bride smacked her lips and plopped ketchup onto her plate.

"Yessir. We gonna have us a real fine life. I ain't gonna haul pulpwood with Daddy for the rest of my life. No siree Bob. My cousin's got a body and fender shop in a little town just outside Atlanta."

"Atlanta? No kidding!" The bride's voice trilled with excitement.

"Yep. Course I gotta learn a little somethin' about the business first."

"You goin' to school?"

"Naw," the groom replied. "I got a mail-order book over to the house. It's got pitchers and everthang else you need to learn."

"Oh, I jes' can't wait!" The bride held her hamburger in midair, mayonnaise and beef fat dripped onto her plate as she spoke with youthful excitement of being newly married and moving to Atlanta. "I can see it all now. You and me living in one of them big ol' houses with a white picket fence and a brick sidewalk right up to the front porch—and maybe a young'un or two playing in the yard. I want a boy first. One jes' like his daddy."

The groom rubbed a particularly bothersome pimple on his cheek. "Now don't go puttin' the wagon in front of the mule. I gotta git my education first."

"You smart thang, you. You'll learn them books easy as pie," she assured him.

Looking back on her life, Angela wondered if she were ever that young and eager and full of wonder at what the future held, but could never recall such a time. She knew without a doubt that she had never shared such open and honest affection with anyone—not even her mother. She tried one more sip of coffee as the newlyweds finished their meal.

"I reckon we better git on back home," the groom said with a sly wink.

Taking her husband's hand and sliding out of the booth, the bride asked as she stared at the cluttered table. "Ain't you gonna leave him something?"

"Done paid him."

She glanced toward the door that led to the back of the cafe and raised up on tiptoe, almost whispering in his ear, "I mean something for a tip."

"Oh." The groom reached into his right front pocket and brought out two nickels and four pennies, holding them out in the flat of his hand. He thought of his next payday, which was almost two weeks away. *Well, I 'spect we won't need no money for a while anyhow.*

She smiled up at him, radiant as any other bride on her wedding night. "We only get married once, and besides he's a real nice feller."

"I reckon," the groom agreed. "Probably don't make much money either." Taking each coin in turn between his thumb and forefinger, he placed the two nickels and three pennies on the table. Glancing down at the remaining penny, he stuffed it back in his pocket. "I'll keep this 'un for luck."

The cook waddled out behind the counter and over to the jukebox at the end of the cafe. Dropping a nickel in, he punched two buttons and waved to the young couple. "How'd y'all like them burgers?"

"Jes' fine," they answered in unison, then laughed self-consciously.

"Y'all come back now."

They both nodded.

The cook walked back behind the counter and through the curtain.

Taking her husband's arm with both hands, the young bride sighed deeply and leaned on his shoulder as they walked together out into the night.

As Angela watched them leave, her eyes clouded with a longing she had felt all her life—for something unnamed and elusive. "I'll Never Smile Again" sounded from the jukebox, causing her to shudder involuntarily. Fishing some change from her purse, she dropped it on the counter and followed the young couple out the door. The chain clanked as the yellow dog reached the perimeter of his abbreviated world. This time he didn't bark.

Angela stood next to her car for a moment, watching the bride and groom as they walked across the parking lot onto the shoulder of the highway. Hearing a low rumbling growl, she glanced over at the dog. His yellow eyes gleamed in the wasted face.

In the dim light that filtered through the grimy windows of the cafe, Angela fumbled in her purse for the keys. She felt suddenly faint as she slumped onto the seat of the car. Taking a few deep breaths, she started the engine and jounced through a hole half full of water from last week's rain.

Angela passed the young couple as they turned onto a dirt lane that intersected the highway. As she glanced at them, the groom with his arm protectively around his bride, she found herself a victim of envy for what the young couple shared. A desperate need rose within her, an overpowering desire to lose herself somehow in that same shelter of affection.

Maybe someday I'll be a fine lady just like her. The young bride gazed at Angela with her own private longing as she drove past them.

The young man ruminated. *If I learn this body work stuff real good, I jes' might git to work on a car like that one day when we git to Atlanta. Wouldn't that be something?*

* * *

"Good morning, Lila." Angela walked into the reception room of the *Journal*, finding Lila sitting behind a desk banging away at a bulky black Royal typewriter. She wore a white blouse with ruffles at the throat.

Lila glanced up from her work, a yellow pencil clamped between her teeth. "Oh, hi, Angela. It's so good to see you! Where've you been keeping yourself?"

"At home mostly." Angela glanced around the room. It was freshly painted a pale green color. A wallpaper border in a dark green print ran beneath the walnut crown molding. Framed newspaper headlines hung on the walls, and in the far corner a coffee urn rested on a metal table with a white ceramic top. Several spoons stood upright in a tan mug of water next to a clear pint jar containing sugar.

Lila could see that Angela had lost weight by the way her wine-colored blouse and navy blue slacks hung on her small-boned frame. The black leather jacket looked a size too large. Her eyes were puffy and the skin beneath them had a bruised-looking cast from lack of sleep. "You need to get out of the house more, child. You're as pale as a lily."

"Maybe not *that* pale," Angela smiled.

Lila remembered the day of the funeral when she had spent the night with Angela, taking care of her almost as one would a small child. She had gone back to see her every day for a week afterward then gradually, as Angela appeared to be handling the tragedy better, Lila had thrown herself into the work at the *Journal*, which had lately occupied her time almost completely. "Are you doing all right now, Angela?"

"Oh, sure," Angela lied, thinking of the nights she spent driving around or simply walking the streets of Liberty, unable to bear the loneliness of her home.

"Why don't you come to church with me sometime?" Lila had asked her once before and had been promptly cut off. This time Angela showed some interest or at least wasn't inclined to hurt Lila's feelings. "It's nothing fancy, just a little wood-frame building out in the woods, but Pastor Shaw is a kind and godly man. You might even make some new friends."

"I-I don't know," Angela hesitated. "I haven't cared about being around people much lately."

Lila knew that the whole town was now aware of the circumstances of Morton Spain's death. As far as Angela's relationship with his family was concerned, this was dealt a death blow by the fact that his will had made her the beneficiary of the house and most of the money. For these reasons Spain's children and the remainder of the family had completely cut off contact with Angela. "Well, I guess I can understand that. You might find, though, that the people in our church are a little different from the crowd you've been around since your marriage."

"I don't know. Maybe later."

"No hurry."

"Anyway, I didn't come here to talk about me," Angela continued, happy to change the subject. "I wanted to see how you're doing with the newspaper."

"Well, Henry's been working like a miner getting the press ready and ..."

"I don't mean that part of it," Angela interrupted, sitting down in a heavy wood chair. "I mean the nasty editorials Dobe Jackson's been writing."

"About his favorite subject you mean." Lila glanced furtively around the room as though expecting an intruder at any moment. "Every German and Japanese in the country is an enemy agent—a spy behind every bush."

"Well, since you came to town, he's just about quit blasting the Japanese. And the fact is, I've heard rumors about your being pro-German."

"So he's stooped to that level, has he? I guess he's more worried about competition than I had thought." Lila leaned back from her typewriter. "I guess I've been buried in this place so deeply I haven't paid much attention to the real world. Maybe it's time to fight back." Lila thought of the murmuring behind her back whenever she went grocery shopping or to the service station.

"I haven't seen many people myself lately, but Liberty's a small town and word gets around quickly. There's no way to prove that he started all this of course, but if he's thrown the name *Kronen* around in the right places, he can cause you some problems."

Lila stared out the window, tapping on the arm of her chair, a pensive look on her face. She eagerly awaited the chance to put her own views before the public.

"Have you sold many subscriptions yet?"

"Precious few," Lila replied, shaking her head. "And I don't even want to talk about the advertising. That's the real financial backbone of the newspaper business. Change doesn't come easily here in Liberty."

Angela felt Lila would just as soon not discuss her business. "Does J.T. still come around?"

"Pardon? Oh, yes he does occasionally. When the notion strikes him." Lila shook her head slowly, a half-smile lighting her face. "What a strange man. Maybe *unusual* would be a better word. He works like there's no tomorrow when he decides to—then disappears for weeks at a time."

Angela stared at Lila as if to speak, then looked away toward one of the framed headlines hanging behind her.

"Oh, I know about his drinking, Angela," Lila admitted,

thinking as she always did of the destruction it had wrought in J.T.'s life. "But there's more to it than that. It's like he's deathly afraid that he might get too close to someone."

"I've heard good and bad about J.T. Depends on who you talk to." Crossing her legs, Angela twisted her wedding ring around on her finger. She thought it ironic that she couldn't seem to bear having it off now that her husband was dead. "There was an old lady named Annie Sims—everybody called her Butcher Knife Annie— who lived in a dilapidated mansion just outside of town. She barely managed a living by collecting junk in a little red wagon she pulled around with her."

"I've heard about her. That was the family that was so rich at one time."

Angela nodded. "Annie had to raise her niece, Jordan. Her daddy just dropped the little girl off one night on his way to prison. I think she was about five years old at the time. They never heard from him again."

"I don't see what you're getting at."

"Well, if it hadn't been for J.T. helping them, they would never have made it. According to what I heard, he bought practically all of Jordan's clothes for the first few years after she started school." Angela's eyes seemed to darken briefly as though a fleeting shadow had passed by. "I guess he was the closest thing she had to a daddy when she was growing up."

"I hadn't heard that story yet," Lila replied, still amazed at the human capacity to spread negative gossip, forgetting about the good qualities a person might have. "I have heard all about J.T.'s wild escapades. Guess I haven't been here long enough for people to say anything good about him."

Angela slung the strap of her purse across her shoulder. "I won't keep you from your work any longer." She gazed directly into Lila's eyes. "I want to thank you again for all you did for me after Morton . . . I never would have made it if you hadn't been there to help me. I'll never be able to repay you for what you did for me when there was nobody else."

"I was more than happy to do it, Angela." Lila thought of the twenty-one childless years of her own marriage. "I never had any children of my own. I guess maybe I just considered you my little girl for a week or so."

Angela's eyes grew bright with tears. Standing up, she quickly brushed them away. "Well I'll never forget it."

Lila could only vaguely imagine the torment that followed Angela around like a scavenger waiting for her to be robbed of her last strength, her final vestige of a will to survive. Although she had spent her life with words, she couldn't seem to think of any that would fit the moment.

Angela had never let herself show emotion and was uncomfortable with the strong affection and gratitude she now felt. "I have to go," she called over her shoulder as she opened the door. "Come by when you have time."

"I will." Walking over to the half-glass door, Lila watched Angela hurry down the sidewalk to her car. "Poor child! There's only one way she'll ever have peace in her life again."

Lila returned to her typewriter, but the flow of words now seemed as solidly frozen as a Chicago puddle in February. She had long felt there was a purpose in the unexpected daily events of her life. Falling to her knees on the hard wooden floor, she bowed her head, groaning in her spirit for Angela Spain.

Outside, the December wind suddenly moaned through the eaves of the old building as though it were angry at the woman kneeling beyond its reach.

After a long while, Lila rose and seated herself at the typewriter. The words flowed again with the steady rhythmic tapping of the keys.

* * *

Angela drove for hours along the back roads outside of Liberty. Beyond the barbwire fences, the trees stood stark and leafless in the rolling pasture land. Their limbs in black and precise silhouette against the gray sky appeared to have been cut with tin snips. Cattle bunched close together, their backs against the wind, waiting for dusk and the call that would come ringing across the fields, summoning them to food and a warm barn.

Stopping on the shoulder of the road next to a bridge, Angela walked down to the bank of a small creek, sat on the trunk of a fallen sycamore, and unwrapped the ham sandwich she had brought with her from home that morning. She took a bite, chewing slowly. It tasted like sawdust, but she forced herself to swallow.

She stood up and walked to the edge of the six-foot bank, gazing down at the clear water that flowed slowly over a rocky bottom in the shallows. Bit by bit she pinched pieces of the sandwich off, tossing them into the creek. Red-ear bream, hand-sized and smaller, rose from the depths, striking viciously at the bits of food in flashes of color.

Angela sat down on the bank, watching the fish at their unexpected meal. When they had vanished into their fishy hiding places, she stared out across the brown pasture. The sun settled behind the distant hills, streaking the sky with shades of pink and violet and magenta.

When the light had faded and the sky moved toward a midnight shade, Angela suddenly felt the December cold seeping into her body. Rising from the damp grass, she went back to her car to resume her journey to nowhere until the gravel or blacktop surfaces in front of her became blurred by a weariness that would allow her to go home and drop off into a few hours of troubled sleep.

8

DRAWN TO THE LIGHT

Angela noticed that the lights were still on in Ollie's Drug-store as she drove past. She glanced at the soft amber glow of the dashboard clock. *It's almost nine-thirty. I wonder why he's still open on Christmas Eve.*

The day had dawned mild and clear, but gradually a cold front had moved in from the northwest. By late afternoon, the sky was sealed with low gray clouds and the wind, tempered with an ironlike cold from the frozen wilds of Manitoba, drove the citizens of Liberty toward their fireplaces and woodburning stoves. A light rain began to fall at five o'clock and by seven the streets were deserted except for Moon Mullins making a few last minute deliveries of his bottled Christmas spirit.

Families gathered around their trees to celebrate the season with eggnog and fruitcake and presents. It was the one night of the year when children had gone to bed without threats of bodily harm. They tossed and turned and whispered in their beds, listening for the sound of sleigh bells. Although no one in memory had ever heard one, they all knew the sound would be so much nicer than that of church bells or those around the necks of cows. Morning seemed an eternity away.

* * *

For some reason unknown to her, Angela was drawn to the light inside Ollie's. Sleet ticked on her windshield as she pulled over to the curb beneath an ancient white oak. Its bare limbs wore a thin covering of ice, glittering in the pale amber light from the street lamps.

The cold cut through Angela's leather jacket and lavender

97

sweater as she left her car and walked the half-block to Ollie's. Entering to the sound of the bell on the glass-paneled door, she saw a solitary figure at the far end of the counter. He wore a jacket that was as dark as his hair. The man's head had been turned away from Angela as he looked toward the door that led to the back of the drugstore. The jukebox played Bing Crosby's biggest hit, "White Christmas."

Glancing around at the sound of the bell, Ben Logan smiled uneasily when he saw her step into the glare of the drugstore. "Merry Christmas, Angela."

As she walked slowly along the counter, Angela noticed that Ben wore his heavy wool uniform under his Navy pea jacket. His white cap lay on the stool next to him. "Merry Christmas, Ben. I should think you'd be home with your family."

"I had to pick up some more medicine for Mama. Seems like she just can't get well."

"Maybe your father's death is part of the reason," Angela suggested.

"I think you're right," Ben agreed. "She's always known that logging is dangerous business, but I guess you can never really be prepared for something like that to happen to your own family."

Wishing that she hadn't brought the subject up, Angela tried to lighten the mood. "Ollie didn't mind opening up on Christmas Eve? He should be considered for sainthood."

Ben smiled again, his teeth white against his face, which still held its tan from the hot Pacific sun and his days of cutting pulpwood with his father. "There are so many sick people calling him at home, he didn't have much choice about it if he wanted any peace on Christmas Day. He's filling the last prescriptions now. Said he's going to drop them off on his way home."

"I like that idea about sainthood, Angela." Ollie Caston leaned around the doorframe, his bow tie and neat brown crew cut giving the appearance of a much younger man. "Ben, I'm gonna be a little while finishing up back here. Why don't you fix you and Angela some hot chocolate?"

"Good idea." Ben walked around behind the counter, drew two mugs from the big urn, and nodded toward a booth. "Let's sit over there where it's comfortable."

Angela led the way to the last booth by the jukebox. She felt a sense of guilt and shame at being with Ben, but she preferred anything to the emptiness of her house, with its creakings and groanings in the night and the memories that seemed to come alive and prowl its many rooms. "Ben, Rachel won't mind if you and I—I mean . . ."

"No. I don't think so." Ben avoided the obvious question of why Angela was alone on such a special night. Like most everyone else in town, he had heard of the circumstances of her husband's death. But unlike most of them, he had absolutely no inclination to treat her as the town pariah.

"How do you like married life?"

Ben nodded his head slowly, a tender light coming to his clear gray eyes. "Best thing that ever happened to me."

Angela sipped her chocolate. "I just heard about your wedding a couple of months ago."

"Well, Rachel's daddy married us at his house. I don't think it made the society page."

Angela suddenly felt at ease with Ben. She couldn't explain it, but he now seemed like a brother to her. "When do you have to go back to your ship?"

Ben thought of the friends he had lost at Pearl Harbor. "I've been asking for sea duty since they first told me I'd be traveling around the country selling war bonds."

"What do they say?"

"That I'm worth more to the country here than if I went back into combat." Ben pictured the air above Pearl Harbor alive with Japanese fighters, heard the high, hard hammering precision of the Mitsubishi engine as the Zero roared in, strafing the men of the *Arizona* as they tried to flee their sinking ship. He could almost feel himself leaning hard into the shoulder rests of the 20 mm cannon, staring down the long clean length of its barrel—saw again the heavy slugs raking the aircraft from the propeller across the cockpit to the rudder—watched it tumble downward like a shot mallard, sending up a geyser of water from the oil-slicked surface of the sea.

"Ben—are you all right?"

"Huh? Oh, sure." Ben sipped his hot chocolate. "I just don't agree with the Navy brass. I think we need every able-bodied man where the fighting is."

Angela could see that talk of the war made Ben restless. "How's Rachel? I never see her around anymore."

Ben's mind leaped back to the present. "Fine. She spends a lot of time making baby clothes."

"Oh, that's wonderful! I didn't know," Angela declared, happy for the two of them. "When's the baby due?"

"April."

Noticing the gentle light that had come to Ben's eyes when he spoke of his wife and unborn child, Angela suddenly felt a heavy sadness settle over her, as cold and icy as the sleet she had left outside. She desperately needed to be loved, and the love that Ben so obviously shared with Rachel seemed to her so pure, so full of tenderness, that it caused her to weep in spite of all she could do to stop it. She bowed her head, both hands covering her eyes as unrelenting tears rolled down her cheeks.

Ben reached across the table taking her hand in his. "Angela, what's wrong? Are you sick?"

Weeping silently, Angela stared at Ben's blurry image, shaking her head slowly.

Taking a handkerchief from his coat pocket, Ben brushed her tears away, speaking in a hushed tone. "There, there. It can't be as bad as all that."

Angela took the handkerchief and finished wiping her eyes, dabbing at the wet trails of makeup that stained her cheeks. She had confided in no one since the death of her husband, not even Lila, but she felt strangely safe talking with Ben. "I'm sorry, Ben. It's just that I'm so lonely."

Ben knew the answer to Angela's loneliness and the terrible sorrow that was apparent in her eyes. He prayed that she would listen to him with an open heart. "Jesus loves you, Angela."

She paused in cleaning the makeup from her face, holding the handkerchief in both hands. "What? What did you say?"

"I said, 'Jesus loves you.'"

The sound of the name caused something to stir within the wounded heart of Angela Spain.

"Jesus is the answer to all your trouble," Ben continued, his voice strengthened by the conviction of his spirit. "I can't explain it. All I can do is to give you the message and tell you what he's done for me."

Angela sat perfectly still, her eyes full of wonder. She never expected something like this from Ben Logan.

"It was on the fantail of a ship in Sydney harbor when I first believed that Jesus is who he said he was." Ben stared past Angela and beyond the glare of the neon lit drugstore. "I was the most miserable man in the world. The girl I loved—or thought I loved—had dropped me flat, I got run out of my hometown, and I was just back to duty after my little brother's funeral."

"Pastor Shaw, Rachel's daddy, preached something at Pete's graveside service from the Book of John. Well, I started reading in the third chapter where the pastor's text had come from and by the time I got to chapter fifteen I had accepted Jesus as my Savior and Lord."

Angela glanced at Ben, then lowered her head. "But—but you don't know all the—things I've done."

"That's right. I don't." Ben touched her on the hand and she looked up into his eyes. "But Jesus does—and he loves you more than you could ever know. Nothing you could ever do would make him stop loving you."

"You think so?"

"I know so," Ben smiled and his face seemed to shine with the knowledge of what he said. He had never grown tired of telling the story of what Jesus had done for him; he found that the thrill and joy of it never diminished. "I know because he's my friend, and I can't explain that either, but he is. In the Book of John he told his disciples, 'I have called you friends.' And he'll be your friend, too, Angela, if you just let him."

Angela felt a struggle going on inside her. She wanted to get up and run from the drugstore, get in her car and drive forever out into the night. Gripping the table with all her might, she forced herself to speak. "I want Jesus. I want him to help me and take away this awful pain and loneliness. Could he do that for me, Ben? Could he?"

Ben squeezed her hand. "Oh, yes, Angela! That and so much more."

"But I don't know anything about religion."

"Doesn't matter. All you have to know is what God's word says and believe it."

"But there's no preacher."

"No, but Jesus is here. He said that he would never leave us or forsake us and that the Kingdom of God is within *you*." Ben took a small black New Testament from his jacket pocket. Without opening it he gazed directly into Angela's eyes and said, "'For God so loved the world, that he gave his only begotten Son, that whosoever believeth in him should not perish, but have everlasting life.'"

Ben had seen people come to Jesus before, and he knew that it was always accomplished by the power of the gospel, not by persuasive argument. He thumbed through a few pages of his New Testament until he came to the Book of Romans.

Angela could see that the pages of Ben's Bible had been marked and lined and dog-eared.

With no further preliminaries, Ben began to read in a clear tone, "'If thou shalt confess with thy mouth the Lord Jesus, and shalt believe in thine heart that God hath raised him from the dead, thou shalt be saved.'"

Looking up, Ben continued in his steady voice, "There's nothing we can do to earn salvation, Angela. Jesus did it all for us on the cross. Paul said, 'By grace are ye saved through faith . . . not of works, lest any man should boast.' It's a gift from God. All you have to do is accept it."

"But what do I do?"

"Just ask Jesus to save you."

Angela tried desperately to remember what she had learned about the Bible as a small child in Sunday school, but when she spoke, the prayer came directly from her heart. Closing her eyes, she bowed her head, still clinging to Ben's hand. "Jesus, I believe that you're God's son and that you died on the cross for me. I know I don't deserve it, but I ask you now to forgive me for all the wrong things I've done and make me the person that you would have me be."

Pausing, Angela glanced up at Ben, then lowered her head again. "I haven't read the Bible in years, and I don't know much about you, but if you'll just help me, Jesus, I'll live for you the rest of my life."

Ben found himself wiping tears from his eyes with the back of his hand. "Welcome to the family of God, Angela."

"I don't think I feel any different." Angela didn't know what to expect. She thought there might be some wondrous revelation from above, that the heavens would open or choirs of angels would sing some glorious song.

"That's all right. The Bible never says you have to *feel* a certain way to be a Christian. It's by faith, not feelings." Ben squeezed her hand again. "There's something I'm absolutely certain of though."

Angela stared at him wide-eyed, unaware of the tears that were spilling down her cheeks. "What's that?"

"The angels in heaven are rejoicing right now because you came to Jesus."

"How do you know that?" Angela gazed raptly into Ben's eyes as though he might be an Old Testament prophet come back to earth.

"Because God's word says it—that's how." Ben's face seemed to almost radiate light from the joy he felt. "Can you just imagine that? The angels of God up there singing and shouting praises because of what you just did. Can't you just hear them shouting, 'Glory to God, Angela's going to make heaven her home! Hallelujah, she came to Jesus!'"

Angela sat there smiling at Ben. She felt like she had never felt before although she didn't realize it then because she was so caught up in Ben's rejoicing for her. "I don't want to do anything wrong now, Ben, but I don't know what to do next."

Ben came back to himself, taking a deep breath before he spoke. "Excuse me. Sometimes I get a little carried away. Well, to start with you're going to make mistakes as long as you're in this world, Angela, so don't expect to be perfect. There *are* two things you need to do to start with though."

"What?" Angela was eager to do everything right.

"Take this and read it until you get your own Bible. I think the Book of John would be a good place to start." Holding out his New Testament toward her, Ben continued, "It's *so* important to stay in the Word, Angela. And remember no matter what *anyone* tells you, I don't care who it is—preacher, priest, the best person you know— if it contradicts this book, don't believe it."

Angela took the little Testament, holding it close to her breast. "What else?"

"Find yourself a good church."

"Where do I go?"

"Well, I think Rock Hill's a good church. That's where Rachel's daddy pastors," Ben said with some hesitation, not wanting to keep

Angela from finding her own way. "But God may have another place for you. Pray about it."

"I'm not sure I know how."

"Sure you do. You prayed a beautiful prayer tonight when you accepted Jesus. Start off by asking God to give you a good church to go to."

"All ready, Ben." Ollie stood behind the counter holding a white paper bag out toward the booth.

Ben stood up, taking Angela's hand to help her out of the booth. "Thanks, Mr. Caston. I know Mama really appreciates this. She hated to mess up your Christmas."

Ollie shook his head. "It's nothing. If it wasn't for folks like her, I couldn't afford that big turkey I got at home. Tell her and your whole family Merry Christmas for me."

Angela set both cups on the counter. "Thanks for the hot chocolate, Mr. Caston."

"You're quite welcome, Angela. Anything else I can do for you tonight?"

"No thanks. I'll be getting on home now. Merry Christmas to you."

"Same to you," Ollie smiled. "Watch yourself on the way home. It's getting nasty out there."

* * *

"Can I give you a ride home?" Angela walked along the sidewalk next to Ben.

"No thanks." Ben pointed down the street. "I'm in Daddy's log truck. Sure hope I don't have to drive Rachel to the hospital in that thing."

They stopped a half-block from Ollie's, standing beneath a streetlamp next to Angela's car. The sleet ticked rhythmically on the windshield and lay on the black surface of the car like beads of glass, glimmering in the pale light.

Ben gazed down at Angela's upturned face. It looked so much softer, almost like that of a child, as though years had fallen away in the last few minutes. "I'm so happy for you, Angela. I can't wait to tell my family."

Tears glistened in Angela's eyes. "Thank you, Ben. I owe you so much."

Laughing softly with the joy that seemed to overflow in him for Angela's new life, Ben shook his head slowly. "You don't owe me anything. It's just the way we Christians use the love that God pours out on his children. We give it away to others, and it just gets bigger and bigger."

Ben embraced Angela tenderly, and she pressed her soft cheek against his face. Beyond words now, Angela gave Ben a final smile and wiped the new tears from her eyes as she got into her car and drove toward home.

* * *

On the way, Angela heard the sound of the sleet on her car diminish, then stop completely. Snow began to fall; tiny flakes at first, and then larger, falling thick and heavy and soft through the beams of her headlights. She had never seen snow like this before. It was a dreamlike world she drove through now as though Liberty, Georgia, had been lifted up and set back down somewhere in Vermont.

Several times, feeling a presence in the car, she glanced at the passenger seat, but no one was there. It was a pleasant sensation, this snowfall dream of Liberty through the windshield and the comfort of an unseen Someone with her in the car.

Pulling underneath the portico, Angela turned off the headlights and sat for a few minutes watching the snowflakes drift and swirl in a silent soft whiteness across the flagstone patio and the lawn that receded into the darkness beyond the reach of the overhead light.

Angela got out of her car and ran up the concrete stairs with a lightness to her step she hadn't known since she chased fireflies in the star-spangled summer evenings of her childhood.

Taking the New Testament Ben had given her out of her pocket, she hung her jacket on the clothes tree and went into the kitchen. After making a pot of tea, she took Ben's gift over to the table, sat down and opened it to the Book of John.

"'In the beginning was the Word, and the Word was with God,

and the Word was God,'" she read out loud. "No wonder Ben thought it was so important to check out anything people tell me with what the Bible says."

Sipping her tea, Angela continued to read, and when something struck her as particularly important she would read it out loud, sometimes more than once.

"'And the light shineth in darkness; and the darkness comprehended it not.'" Angela pondered on this, thinking of the times she had sat in church not having the faintest idea what the pastor was talking about.

"'He was in the world, and the world was made by him, and the world knew him not.' Now isn't that something? Jesus made the world, and the world doesn't even know him. What a mixed-up bunch we human beings are."

Angela read the twelfth and thirteenth verses out loud and the words, underlined in Ben's book, seemed to ring through her soul like sweet music. "'But as many as received him, to them gave he power to become the sons of God, even to them that believe on his name: which were born, not of blood, nor of the will of the flesh, nor of the will of man, but of God.'"

"Oh, my Jesus! My Jesus. I truly believe in you. You seem like such a good friend already."

Angela read until she could no longer keep her eyes open. Then she showered, put on a freshly washed flannel nightgown, and took her little Testament to bed with her. After praying, it occurred to her that she had forgotten to be afraid and lonely in the vast and empty darkness of the house. In less than a minute she fell into a deep sleep, untroubled by the dreams that had tormented her.

* * *

Christmas morning dawned clear and cold with sunshine sparkling on the new-fallen snow. Angela dressed hurriedly in jeans and a white pullover sweater and rushed upstairs to the attic where she found a Nativity set and a hand-painted ceramic Christmas tree. Then she ran back downstairs into the spacious kitchen and set them up on one end of the long table.

"There, that looks all right, " she said, admiring her handiwork. "I guess it's kind of silly putting my Christmas decorations in the kitchen, but there's no tree in the living room anyway and these little things would be lost in that big room."

Angela made a pot of coffee and sat at the table drinking it from a bone-china cup while she stared wistfully at the manger with the tiny baby in it. "What a way to come into this world—in a dirty old stable. Well, I guess I might as well get used to it from the beginning. I'll never be able to understand why God does things the way he does."

Drinking the last of her coffee, Angela poured herself another cup and walked to the opposite end of the table. She leaned closer to the tiny child in the manger, staring at him and at his mother and father, wondering what must have gone through their minds to be part of God's eternal and wondrous gift to mankind. Suddenly her eyes grew bright with realization. "Today's his *birthday*. Happy birthday, Jesus!"

Angela hurried to the big walk-in pantry off the kitchen, returning with flour, baking soda, a bottle of vanilla extract, and a large can of Hershey's cocoa. Adding eggs and butter from the refrigerator as well as sugar from the canister that sat on the counter, she began blending it all together. Soon the warm, appetizing aroma of a cake baking began to fill the kitchen.

Unable to find any birthday candles, Angela returned to the attic where she located a foot-long red candle in a holder from last year's decorations. *Well, I guess this is better than nothing. Nobody'll see it but me anyway.*

Back in the kitchen, she mixed the chocolate icing in a bowl. When she took the cake out of the oven, she immediately began spreading the icing on it before it cooled. Pieces of cake began breaking off, falling to the table or sticking to her knife as she did her best to spread the icing evenly.

Standing back from the table, Angela observed her handiwork. "Well, let's hope it tastes better than it looks."

A sudden rapping on her back door, sounding almost as loud as gunfire in the stillness of the house, startled Angela. She looked down the hall through the dim foyer and saw Hartley Lambert's big blond face framed in the half-glass of the door.

Hartley, along with a few other pillars of the Liberty community, had begun to come skulking around Angela's back door at odd hours, starting a few days after her husband's funeral. She had always ignored them, refusing to even acknowledge that they were there.

Today she walked briskly across the foyer and jerked the door open. "Why, Mr. Lambert, whatever are you doing out here on Christmas morning?"

Bearlike in his heavy wool coat, Lambert's hard blue eyes lit up at the possibility of actually getting inside the house. "Just wanted to wish you a Merry Christmas, Angela. And I sure wish you'd call me Hartley."

Angela leaned to the side, looking behind him. "Where's Ellie and Debbie? I think a man should celebrate Christmas with his family. Don't you?"

Lambert gave her a sheepish grin. "Debbie's off somewhere and, well, you know how Ellie sometimes has a little too much— Christmas cheer. She probably won't get up till noon at least. Everybody's coming to the house at three o'clock for our annual get-together."

Gazing beyond Lambert, Angela found herself fascinated by the glittering whiteness of the morning. The world was covered with a soft blanket of snow, and the dark, leafless limbs of the trees shone with ice. The evergreens stood in bright fluffy rows. She felt that all this was another gift she had been given.

Lambert shivered, rubbing his hands together.

"Oh, I'm sorry! Come in, won't you?"

Lambert, grinning like a possum, followed Angela down the hall to the kitchen. *I knew she'd get lonesome for a man's company sooner or later, and ol' Hartley's got just the cure for a young widow left alone in this cruel world.*

"Coffee?"

"Yes, ma'am." Lambert sat down at the table without being asked.

Angela poured the coffee and sat it in front of him. He managed to brush against her hand as he reached for the sugar and spooned some into his coffee.

As Lambert sipped his drink, his eyes roamed the kitchen, falling on the opposite end of the table. "Funny place for Christmas decorations, ain't it?

"I don't think so," Angela smiled back brightly.

"Hm." Lambert noticed the cake on the counter. "That thing looks like somebody frosted it with a claw hammer. What's the cake for?"

"It's a birthday cake."

"Yours?"

"No." Angela picked up the cake, placing it on the table next to Lambert. "Want some?"

Lambert looked as though she had offered him a plate of worms. "No thanks. I'm not very hungry. Why did you use such a big candle?"

"It's all I could find."

Never saw a candle like that on a cake before. Lambert's curiosity finally got the best of him. "Whose birthday is it anyway?"

"Why, Mr. Lambert, you mean you don't know?"

"Hartley, please! Call me Hartley. You make me feel like an old man." He began to shift about in his chair. This was not at all what he had expected. "No I don't know whose birthday it is."

"Jesus."

"Jesus?" Hartley glanced over his shoulder as though looking for the nearest exit. "What about him?"

"It's his birthday."

"But he's . . ."

"He's here with *me*, Mr. Lambert," Angela replied sweetly, feeling almost ashamed at what she was doing. "He said that he'd never leave me or forsake me."

Nutty women—why do I always have to get hooked up with nutty women? It's not enough that I've got to live with one. "That's nice." Lambert took a last swallow of coffee and pushed his chair back from the table.

"You sure you don't want a piece of cake? I think it tastes better than it looks."

Lambert glanced over at the ragged cake. A piece of the chocolate icing oozed down the side, dropping off on the plate. "No—really. I need to lose a few pounds."

"Can't blame you, I guess. It does look kind of like I left it out in a thunderstorm."

"Well, thanks for the coffee." Lambert got out of his chair, walking quickly out of the kitchen.

Angela followed him down the hall to the back door. As he stepped out onto the landing at the top of the stairs, she called to him, "Mr. Lambert."

He twisted his head around as he held on to the rail on his way down. "What?"

"I just wanted to wish you a Merry Christmas. Be sure to give Ellie my best."

Lambert grunted as he reached the back drive, then he got into his big black Packard and gunned the engine. As he drove away, Angela saw him talking to himself.

Part 3

THE SIDEWALKS
OF LIBERTY

9

HOME

J.T. Dickerson had been sober for a solid month. Having grown weary of his erratic behavior and hours, Lila had told him that the next time he didn't show when he was supposed to he would be barred from the premises of the *Journal*.

"I'm proud of you, J.T." Lila shuffled through several sheets of copy she was proofing as she talked. Wearing a tan blouse and a brown gathered skirt with pockets at the hips, she looked the picture of businesslike efficiency.

Wondering why he found the *Journal* and its sometimes fractious owner so attractive, J.T. felt like a sixteen-year-old on his first date although he had never broached the subject of actually going out with Lila. "Don't get carried away with yourself, editor. It's just a trial separation. The bottle and I shared a lot of years together."

Giving him a stern glance over her gold-rimmed reading glasses, Lila continued her work. "I'm not trying to rehabilitate you, J.T., and I'm through preaching."

"Well, that's certainly a relief." J.T. hopped up on a desktop across from Lila, letting his legs dangle loosely over the side. "I'm afraid it may be a little late though. I think you've quoted most of the Bible to me already."

Lila finished her work and shoved the stack of paper aside, noticing the sly smile on J.T.'s lean face. She thought he looked quite presentable in his ironed khakis and wine-colored Harvard sweatshirt. He had freshly shaved and his thick brown hair was combed, although it was shaggy around the ears and neck. "You truly have been a lifesaver, J.T. If you hadn't gotten places like Hightower's and Three Corners' Grocery to handle the *Journal* we probably would have gone out of business. People pick up a lot of papers in those stores."

J.T. waved Lila's gratitude away with a flick of his hand. "You're not doing bad for a weekly tabloid, but I've been studying on this situation some. I've got some ideas that could help the *Journal* become a strong daily."

Lila knew J.T. was pausing for effect. She got up from her swivel chair, walked over to the coffee service, and poured a cup, holding it out in his direction.

Shaking his head, J.T. continued as Lila took her seat. "You know what you're doing wrong?"

"I know," Lila sighed. "I'm only a helpless little woman in a man's world and that just isn't done down here in the 'Land of Cotton.'"

"Wrong, Mrs. William Randolph Hearst," J.T. replied calmly. "You think because you spent a few years up in Chicago, you got all the answers."

Lila, playing an imaginary banjo, hummed the last few notes of "Dixie." Finishing with a flourish, she sang, "Look away, Dixieland."

J.T. gave her a smattering of applause. "Now if you're finished with your minstrel show, let's get down to business."

"Sorry. I think these months back in the South may have loosened me up a tad too much. Or maybe I'm having trouble believing that you're not putting me on. You've been known to do that before."

"I guess I deserve the doubts, but this time I'm serious. You're trying to compete with Dobe Jackson on his own ground and you can't win." J.T. hopped off the desk and began pacing back and forth. "It's like strapping claws on your fingers to go bear hunting. The bear would always win."

"Elucidate." Lila leaned back in her chair, holding her cup in both hands. "I'm afraid your parables are a little more complex than the ones I'm used to."

J.T. stopped, stared at Lila with mock ferocity, and resumed his pacing. "Well, Dobe's got the latest teletype and every other advantage that money can buy. He runs all the top syndicated columnists, gets the war news first. He's got all the technical advantages. You've got to simplify."

"And just where do I begin?"

"Picture journalism."

"How do you know about the newspaper business?" Lila was becoming intrigued with J.T.'s monologue now that she saw he meant business.

"I have a library card," J.T. smirked, reaching for his wallet. "Want to see it?"

"I'll take your word for it."

J.T. sat back down on the desk. The morning light streaming in the windows behind him threw his face into shadow, forming a border of diffused light around it. "More pictures. Preferably of Liberty and places close by. The folks around here would just eat it up."

Lila stared thoughtfully at the bright windows. "I think you're on to something. All I've been giving them is the boring facts about people they'll never see."

"Yep. And I'm not through yet." J.T. ran his fingers through his thick brown hair, brushing it back from his eyes. "A profile every week on one of our local boys in the armed forces. Not just hit or miss, but until the war's over. Talk to his family, teachers, friends—anybody that's close to him. Call the column something patriotic like," J.T. made a flourish with his hand as he created each title, "'Proudly They Serve' or 'Our Boys in Uniform'—even better, 'Liberty Goes to War.'"

Lila was out of her chair now, taking over for J.T. by pacing back and forth excitedly. "By george, I think you've done it, J.T. It's just the kind of thing that's so simple no one in the business has thought of it. Obviously Dobe Jackson and that bunch over at the *Herald* haven't."

"There's more."

Lila stopped, rubbing the back of her neck with her left hand as she gazed at J.T. "More?"

"I've even got your first story for you." J.T. felt good about being able to help Lila out, especially since the odds were stacked against her. He considered the waste in his life and thought maybe he was trying to make up for some of it.

"Pray do go on, Mr. Dickerson," Lila smiled with mock formality. "You're really on a roll."

"Clay McCain."

"With so many boys overseas, why choose him?"

"Because you can get pictures and a personal interview. He's coming home Friday."

"But he's only been gone . . ." Lila thought back to that day the previous October when she and Angela had seen Clay bidding his farewells to his family and Diane Jackson, "six months. Why's he coming home so soon?"

"He got wounded in the fighting at Tarawa." J.T. remembered Clay as a rambunctious little boy and thought of the times they had played ball together in the little courtyard behind his office. "From what I hear it was one of the bloodiest battles of the war. The Marines won't forget about Tarawa for a long time."

Lila thought about what a fine strapping young man she had seen on the station platform that October morning when Clay had left for the Marines. Shaking her head sadly, she spoke in a somber voice. "It's so sad! All these fine young men losing their lives or coming home with terrible wounds."

J.T. remembered his war, "The Great War—The War to End All Wars." He could almost hear the screams of men having legs amputated when the anesthesia was gone; could almost see the pale fear-ravaged faces of his men as they went "over the top," charging headlong across the cratered, blackened landscape of France into the hail of machine-gun bullets and shrapnel. "It's more than *sad*. There's *no* word for what it is."

Lila had known for some time that J.T. had fought in World War I, but he had never spoken of it. She decided to press ahead with the subject at hand. "Loads of pictures and news that's close to the hearts of the people. I think you've found the formula for the *Journal*'s success, J.T."

The lines in J.T.'s forehead slowly faded. "Yep. Don't forget me when you make your first million."

"What do you mean forget you?" Lila smiled. "You're going to be right here to help me make it—aren't you?"

"I don't think I follow you."

Lila went back behind her desk and sat down. "You mean to tell me you're going to come in here, drop this marvelous idea on me—and then just walk out the door? Why that's absolutely ludicrous."

"I've been known to be ludicrous in my time. In fact I've all but elevated it to an art form." J.T. shrugged. "But I usually know why."

"Because I've got no way to put your ideas into motion without you."

J.T. had a feeling he was going to regret his enthusiastic research into the newspaper business. "I'm not a newspaper man, Lila."

"Maybe not, but in about two days I can sure remedy that." Lila felt sure she had him trapped. "As a lawyer you already know how to investigate—gather pertinent information and organize it into a comprehensive written document."

"But . . ."

"Just give me two minutes," Lila interrupted. "All you have to do is forget the legal mumbo jumbo and write it in everyday language."

"Are you kidding?" J.T. gave her an incredulous stare. "I'm a lawyer. The whole legal profession is based on making things as obscure as possible."

Lila put her hands on her hips, tilting her head slightly to the side. "I'm trying to be serious here, J.T. This could be a whole new career for you."

"You think I'm kidding about this? You ever hear a lawyer make any sense when he's talking about anything to do with his work?"

Her brow knitted in thought, Lila replied slowly, "Hm—I guess I haven't."

"That's why we make such good politicians. Nobody ever has the slightest idea what we're talking about," J.T. continued, "and you can never get a straight answer to any question—unless maybe you're asking for the correct time."

Lila turned a level stare on J.T. "You gonna help me out or not?"

J.T. felt like something was caught in his throat when he tried to speak.

Seeing an opening, Lila rushed ahead. "You know *everybody* in town. All you have to do is stick to the bedrock of journalism— Who? What? Where? Why? When? and How?—and Presto! You're my star reporter."

"I think all those Chicago winters froze a good part of your brain cells, Lila." It had been a long time since J.T. had taken on a job where he would have to show up every week, and the proximity to this one had already begun to give him the willies. "You'll have to do it yourself."

"Can't."

"What do you mean—*can't*? It's your newspaper. You can do what you want to."

"First of all I don't have the time to take on anything new. I'm doing a half-dozen jobs already. Second, you know as well as I do that this little project would be perfect for you. I'm still just a Yankee outsider."

"You're a hard woman to say no to, Lila." J.T. turned, putting his hand on the doorknob. "I'll give it a try. But I dictate the column—somebody else is doing the typing."

"Deal." Lila walked over to the door and shook J.T.'s hand before he could leave.

J.T. cleared his throat. "I should have had better sense than to cut your grass when you first got here. One little favor and suddenly I'm your indentured servant."

Lila laughed softly. "Oh, it's not that bad! You'll love it—just wait and see."

J.T. grunted and stepped through the door.

* * *

The American offensive in the fall of 1943 called for a strike at the biggest of the Gilbert Islands on the morning of November 20. No one expected any tough resistance from the Japanese. Tarawa had been bombed for a full week and was pounded by the huge fourteen-inch guns from battleships for hours before the attack took place. In spite of this, almost all the 4,500 Japanese, sheltered inside their sand-covered concrete bunkers, survived.

Admiral Kelly Turner had been warned about the tricky waters around the island as there was a chance that the tides would be low then. He decided to take the risk—and lost.

The first waves of Marines assaulted the beaches in amphibious tractors called Amtracks. They made it. But the next waves in the flat-bottomed Higgins boats began crashing onto the coral reefs that were covered by only three feet of water. With the boats unable to cross the reefs, the Marines had to wade hundreds of yards to the beaches under murderous fire from the Japanese. Only about half of them made it.

Admiral Keiji Shibasaki, the Japanese commander had

boasted, "A million men cannot take Tarawa in a hundred years." He was wrong. Fifty-six hundred Marines took it in three days, but at a terrible cost: 991 dead, 2,311 wounded; 17 Japanese survived.

On the morning of November 20, 1943, Clayton McCain was a strong, confident nineteen-year-old hardened combat veteran with three campaigns to his credit. At sunrise on November 23, after surviving the last desperate banzai attack, he looked as though he had aged twenty years when two stretcher-bearers carried him, filthy, smoke-blackened, and hollow-eyed, down to the beach.

* * *

By the spring of 1944, the high school band no longer welcomed the sons of Liberty home on the station platform when they returned wounded or on leave. No crowds gathered waving flags and singing "God Bless America" for their returning heroes. Too many coffins had been unloaded and wheeled across to the depot since that Sunday morning attack on Pearl Harbor. Too many sons and husbands and brothers now lay beneath the shadow of the tilting old tombstones in the cemeteries of Liberty.

The railway station was still an exciting place for children and the dwindling few who were as yet exempt from personal tragedy as a result of the war. But for the majority of Liberty's citizens, the homecoming celebrations had worn thin. The bright and gaudy decorations and the patriotic songs had been undermined by the lingering memories of flower-scented funeral parlors and the sound of muffled weeping.

* * *

Clay couldn't imagine that he had actually lived in the town he viewed through the window as the train began slowing down to pull into the station at Liberty. From the height of the trestle, he gazed down on the green and shimmering water of the river where he had gone swimming and fishing; he saw the knotted rope hanging from the same lofty oak limb where he and his childhood friends had swung out from the bank high over the swimming hole and plunged with a stomach-churning dive into the water.

He viewed the high school and the baseball diamond in the

shimmering distance and watched his neighbors working in their April-bright flowerbeds or walking along shady sidewalks beneath the ancient elms and oaks and cedars. Downtown, people shopped and visited and did all the dozens of other things that made up their safe and comfortable days as though death had no road map to Liberty, Georgia.

Clay knew that this was his hometown, the place where he was born and raised; he knew that these all-too-familiar people were his own family and friends and neighbors. But he knew it in the same way a man knows he has a fatal wound—with knowledge and pain, but with no true acceptance of the reality of it, as though he could never be touched by the immutable hand of mortality.

The train stopped alongside the station platform with a hissing of steam and the successive jolting of the railroad cars. Clay sat perfectly still behind the protective glass. He felt that if he could carry the window off the train with him, he would be protected from whatever awaited him in this familiar and foreign place where the Marines had sent him at last.

He longed for a friend and knew that none awaited him on the other side of the glass, knew that they had all disappeared in blossoms of fire and thunder when shells had found their Amtracks or Higgins boats, or died screaming as they clutched the cold Japanese steel in their bellies, or simply dropped without a sound plunging through the surf toward the beach. No one in this strange and clean and vexingly quiet place that lay beyond the window could ever replace them.

Still, he longed desperately for a friend.

* * *

"Clay, I didn't think you were due home until tomorrow." J.T. walked briskly across the depot waiting room toward Clay who sat at a table gazing through one of the tall windows that looked out onto the station platform. His Marine uniform, complete with red chevrons on the shoulders and three rows of campaign ribbons across the left side of his chest, hung loosely on his tall frame. The toes of his side-buckled combat boots gleamed like mirrors in the slanting sunlight.

Clay had deliberately taken an earlier train so no one would be at the station to greet him. He was grateful though that if someone had to find him this soon after his arrival, it was J.T. instead of Diane or his parents.

With some misgivings Clay tried to sound happy to see him. "Hey there, J.T. Who taught you how to shave?" The words sounded as though they had been spoken by someone he used to know a long time ago.

"Well, when I finally hit puberty, I just had to learn," J.T. shot back. Then with a sheepish grin he continued. "Actually it kinda goes with the job."

"Ironed khakis and a clean shirt. You look pretty good cleaned up. Sit down and I'll buy you a cup of coffee." Clay heard himself speaking as normally as he always had with J.T., but he still felt like an impostor.

"Sure thing, but I'll go get it." J.T. walked across the polished plank floor and dropped two dimes on the counter, returning with two thick white mugs of coffee. As he came up behind Clay to set his coffee on the table, he surveyed him quickly from head to toe but could see no sign of a wound. He decided not to ask him about his injuries for now.

"I believe my hearing's going bad on me." Clay leaned his head to one side, tapping on his ear with the flat of his hand. "I thought I heard you say something about a job."

"Well, it's *almost* like a job," J.T. nodded, noticing how thin Clay was. It was as though the months he had spent in the Marine Corps had pared him down to bone and muscle. "Part-time reporter for Lila Kronen."

Clay's eyes narrowed in thought. "Lila Kronen . . . Oh, yeah. She's that Yankee from Chicago who was trying to start the *Journal* up again."

J.T. stared directly at Clay's eyes. They looked hollow and dull and seemed to be focused on something in midair halfway across the room. "She did start it up again. It's been a hard road, but the lady's got gumption."

"I expect Mr. Jackson was a big help to her, wasn't he? I know he must love the idea of another newspaper opening up in town," Clay remarked, thinking of Diane and how much he didn't want to have to face her—at least for a while.

J.T. grunted and sipped his coffee. "Dobe's had things his own sweet way for a lot of years. Maybe it's time somebody came along with some new ideas."

"New ideas? In Liberty?"

"That is asking a lot, isn't it?" J.T. smiled. "Maybe she'll just rework the old ones for the time being. Then go for a hot new issue like women's suffrage."

Clay caught J.T. watching him with a curious expression on his face. *What am I doing wrong? I wonder if I look all right.* He quickly picked up his mug and took a swallow of coffee to hide the self-conscious feeling.

J.T. noticed Clay's motion when he reached for the mug. He had leaned his right shoulder forward a bit to compensate for the arm that stayed slightly bent at the elbow. It kept that exact same angle as he sat the mug back down. He was afraid that he had embarrassed Clay and felt ashamed that he was holding him under a microscope. *I wonder if it's serious enough to end his baseball career?* "Want to hear something funny?"

"Yeah. I could use a laugh."

"It's about my job."

"That's pretty funny by itself—you and the word *job* spoken in the same breath." Clay tried to grin, feeling that his mouth had forgotten how. "Far back as I can remember, you took just enough cases in your law practice to keep from having to live in a cardboard box in the alley behind Ollie's Drugstore."

"Me with a job. I guess it is kinda funny at that." J.T. glanced again at Clay's eyes, being careful not to make him uneasy. He remembered that same vacant stare in the eyes of men who had spent too many months in the muddy fields and trenches of the Ardennes and Belleau Wood.

Clay merely nodded as though the conversation was taxing his reserves.

J.T. tried to lighten the dialogue. "You still haven't asked what's unusual about my job. Your lack of interest makes me feel kinda like it may not have the profound consequences I expect it to for the future of our country."

Clay almost laughed. "Tell me quick, before I bust a gut trying to figure it out."

"It's you."

"Me?"

"Yeah. You're my first assignment."

Clay shrugged, waiting for an explanation.

"Stories for the *Journal* about our boys in the armed forces. Not just the MacArthur's and Patton's and Eisenhower's that Dobe runs in the *Herald*." J.T. rubbed his chin with his forefinger. "I guess it'll be kind of like Ernie Pyle's columns—you know, stories about the ordinary soldiers."

"Everybody likes Ernie's stuff."

"Well, there'll be some notable exceptions in my work," J.T. explained.

"Like what?"

"First of all the quality of the writing won't be the same—Ernie can't hope to compete with me," J.T. grinned. "And second I'm not about to go traipsing all over the world like he does. Seeing one war up close is enough."

Clay hunched his shoulders slightly and seemed to shrink inside himself. He could almost hear the pop of the mortar tubes and the heavy crunching sound as they hit, sending hot shrapnel whining overhead. Laying his left hand on the right, he rubbed it back and forth across his knuckles.

"You OK, son?"

Clay took a deep breath. "I don't think I'm in the mood to talk right now."

"Don't blame you," J.T. agreed quickly, remembering how little he had spoken of his own war in the past quarter of a century since he had returned from it.

Realizing he was slumping in his chair, Clay sat up straight, but continued to rub his knuckles.

"Guess you'll take it easy for a while, huh?"

"I guess so."

"Maybe do a little fishing."

"Maybe."

J.T. hated to leave Clay alone; he wished he had the words to make things easier for him but could see that he had tolerated about all the company he could for the time being. "Guess I'd better get moving. Got to pick up a package for the *Journal*."

Clay tried to smile, but again his lips felt unable to fit themselves around one. "Good seeing you, J.T."

"You too, Clay." J.T. stood up and shoved his chair under the table. "See you again soon."

"You bet."

10

SHADOWS

"*A*ren't you having a good time, Clay?" Diane Jackson had worn her best party dress for the occasion. Cornflower blue with thin straps and a full skirt, it was designed to show her figure to its best advantage. "After all, Mother and I went to a lot of trouble to plan this affair for your homecoming."

Seated next to Diane on a stone bench in a shadowed alcove of myrtle trees, Clay stared across the long expanse of lawn toward the lighted terrace of the Jackson home. At Diane's insistence, he had worn his Marine dress uniform complete with campaign ribbons and his Silver Star. He hated wearing it now that he had been discharged from the Corps, but she had said that she wanted to show off her hero to everybody.

Couples danced to "I'll Walk Alone," played by a tuxedoed band of locals in a yellow gazebo. White-jacketed Negro waiters with trays laden with champagne walked among the elegantly dressed guests. A huge "Welcome Home Clay" banner hung from the eaves of the house. "I appreciate all the work you and your mother did, Diane. I guess I'm just not very good company right now."

Diane had been listening to the same excuse for two weeks and was running out of patience. "Well, you'll just have to *make* yourself good company then."

Clay, his elbows resting on his knees, glanced sideways at her without speaking.

Taking his hand, Diane spoke in a softer tone. "You're going to have to pull yourself out of this, Clay. All you have to do is be like you used to be."

"Is that all?" Clay stood up, pulling his hand free of Diane's. "Why didn't I think of that?"

125

"Won't you even try?" Diane rose and took his arm just above the elbow.

Clay flinched, drawing his arm away, his lips drawn thin from the pain.

"Oh, I'm so sorry! I forgot." Diane clasped her hands at her breast.

"Forget it."

Taking his hand gently, Diane guided him back to the bench. "Clay . . ."

Clay stared between his knees.

"You've just got to try and help yourself. For my sake," Diane pleaded. "And your mother's worried to death about you. You come and go at all hours, sleep all day, and ramble around who knows where all night . . ."

Clay tried to shut out the noise of Diane's rambling speech, finding it a bothersome and unnecessary drone in the forefront of the party noise.

" . . . even thought about going to work and . . ."

Clay found himself inexplicably drifting toward rage. Diane's voice somehow became entangled in his mind with the high-pitched taunts of the Japanese soldiers from the shell-blasted darkness of Tarawa. Just prior to a banzai charge, they had screamed the atrocities that they would commit on the Americans.

" . . . and even Daddy said that . . ."

Squeezing his hands together, Clay shut his eyes tightly as though it would block out the sound.

"Clay, what's wrong?"

Clay turned to Diane and saw her face grow suddenly pale as he looked at her. Her eyes widened and her mouth formed an O with an intake of breath.

Shaking his head, Clay fought off the anger and fear that had driven him for months in the Pacific. He reached out and took Diane's hand. "It's OK now. Really. I'm all right."

Diane relaxed, squeezing his hand. "Clay, you had the strangest look in your eyes. Almost like you . . ." she looked away ". . . wanted to hurt me."

"Don't even think such a thing!" Clay could see the fear in her eyes and feel the trembling of her hand. He knew he had to make things better quickly before she had time to think about the glimpse she had had inside him.

"I almost felt . . . afraid of you."

From the gazebo near the house, the band began to play "Rum and Coca-Cola."

Forcing a lightness to his voice, Clay pulled her up from the bench. "C'mon. Let's cut a rug."

Diane's voice cracked slightly as she answered. "That's all right. We don't have to."

"No. C'mon. I really want to."

Diane smiled, stepped around him, and took his left arm as they walked across the damp grass.

*　*　*

"Whew! That last one just about did me in." Sipping a glass of champagne, Clay leaned against the stone railing that bordered the terrace.

Diane stood next to him, gazing up into his face with an expression of adoration mixed with wonder at the abrupt change that had come over him. "I'm so glad you're having a good time. I thought you might have forgotten how."

Clay grinned the way he had before he left for the South Pacific. "How could I not have a good time with the prettiest girl in Georgia next to me?"

"Oh, Clay, I'm so glad you're happy!" Diane leaned against him, circling his lean waist with her arms. She lifted herself up on tiptoe to kiss him on the cheek.

"Want some more champagne?" Clay held his empty glass out in front of him.

"No thanks," Diane smiled sleepily. "I'm kind of lightheaded already."

"Be right back."

Clay walked across the flagstone terrace toward a bar set up outside the French doors that led to the dining room. Decorated with red, white, and blue bunting, it was manned by a Negro with skin so dark it had an almost purple hue to it in the light from inside the house. His starched white jacket looked as stiff as cardboard on his bony frame.

"Hey, I 'member you. Cletus Felder, right?" Clay greeted him with a big smile, clapping him on the shoulder. "We worked together at the lumbermill one summer."

Hearing Clay's too-loud greeting, Dobe Jackson glanced over his shoulder, frowning at the familiarity that Clay was sharing with his bartender.

"Yas, suh. Sho' did." Felder replied. "I still works there. Mr. Dobe he let me bartend sometimes to make a little extra change. I got nine head of young'uns."

"Doggone it's good to see you." Clay felt more at ease than he had since his return to Liberty. "Ol' Hartley's a tough man to work for, ain't he?"

Felder glanced around him. "No suh. Hit ain't so bad when you gets used to it."

"Ain't so bad! Who you kidding?" With his champagne-muddled thinking, Clay hadn't noticed that he was making Felder extremely uncomfortable. "We used to talk so bad about him I bet his ears were burning."

"Kin I git you something, suh?"

"Oh, yeah." Clay glanced at the assortment of bottles lining the shelf behind Felder. "I think I'll have a taste of that sour mash over there with a Coke on the side."

"Yes, suh."

Clay watched Felder pour three fingers of amber liquid into a shot glass, open a bottle of Coke from a galvanized tub of ice, and set it down next to the bourbon. Turning the shot glass up, he emptied it, shuddering as the fiery liquid burned down his throat. Grabbing the bottle of Coke, he gulped at it greedily until it was empty.

Felder watched in amazement, shaking his head slightly and making a small clucking sound under his breath.

"Whoa! That'll clear out your sinuses in a hurry," Clay gasped, slamming the bottle down on the bar.

"Could I speak with you a moment, Clay?" Dobe Jackson, wearing an elegantly tailored black tuxedo and ruffled white shirt, stood behind him. Jackson despised the thought of his daughter dating someone from a working-class background like Clay.

Considering it a personal affront to his standing in the community, he looked for every opportunity to chastise him about his lack of social graces.

Clay turned around, his eyes shining from the alcohol. "Why, certainly."

Jackson motioned for Clay to follow him. He walked down the side steps of the terrace and over to a shadowed area near an inside corner of the house. "I don't think it's a good idea—this fraternizing with the hired help."

"The hired help," Clay frowned, his brain fuzzy from the rush of alcohol. "Oh, you mean Cletus! He's a real good fellow—hard worker."

"You miss my point."

Clay shrugged.

"Hard work isn't the issue here," Jackson explained with exasperation. "It gives our other guests a bad impression of you. If you're going to see my daughter, you must remember at all times that image is important. You can't go around acting like white trash in front of our friends and family."

Clay stared at the haughty, condescending expression on Jackson's fleshy face. He suddenly lost the false sense of tranquility that the liquor had given him and felt a familiar rage build inside his gut, rising through his chest and up into his temples. For reasons he no longer tried to fathom, nothing was funny anymore. A red glow seemed to spread across his field of vision as the warmth reached his face.

The change in Clay was not lost on Jackson. He saw the dull, somewhat foolish expression dissipate from Clay's face, saw the dark granite gleam come into his eyes. Taking an involuntary step backward, Jackson stumbled over an empty champagne bottle. Arms flailing in the air, he leaned against the side of the house, regaining his balance just before he fell down.

Clay's face smiled, but his eyes remained cold and remote as though untouched by what was happening around him. "Are you all right, sir?"

"What?" Jackson pushed away from the house, straightening his bow tie. "Oh, yes. I'm fine."

"You sure?"

"Quite. If you'll excuse me, I must see to our guests." Jackson turned, walking briskly away with a single quick glance over his shoulder.

Clay took a deep breath, walked up the low flight of steps to the terrace, and over to the bar. "I believe I'll have a little more of that whiskey, Cletus."

"Yas, suh." He reached for a shot glass, set it on the table, and grabbed the square, black-labeled bottle.

Clay shoved the glass aside with the back of his hand. "Don't need this, Cletus."

"Yas, suh."

Popping the cork, Clay turned the bottle up and took a long swallow. A slow smile spread over his face. "Mighty good for what ails you, Cletus."

Glancing around, Cletus spoke in a low tone. "You gonna git sick, Mr. Clay."

"I am sick, Cletus." He waved his hand at the crowd around him. "Sick of all this."

"Come on now, Mr. Clay," Cletus pleaded. "Don't act like that. Dis whole thing for you."

"You're a good man, Cletus." Clay clapped him on the shoulder. "Better'n any of us."

"Don't mess up," Cletus warned, walking down the bar to serve a lady with golden hair and a silver dress.

Clay gazed over at Diane who was talking with Keith Demerie. He wore a replica of Dobe Jackson's tuxedo and looked very much like a bigger, younger version of Diane's father. Catching Clay's eye, Diane waved at him. Clay nodded, waited until she turned back to Demerie, then tucked the bottle under his jacket and walked down the terrace steps and out into the darkness.

*　*　*

Clay loved the sidewalks of Liberty. Taking an occasional swallow from his bottle, he followed them past the white two-story houses with their high wraparound porches and slate roofs. Shaded by ancient oaks, they had the air of gentle and satisfied old ladies who had lived their lives well. The mild April air carried the scent of roses, jasmine, and wisteria from the flowerbeds on their well-tended lawns.

But the scent of the sweet olive trees brought a sharp pain to Clay's chest. It all came back to him in a headlong rush of memory: the golden sunlight pouring down on the baseball diamond, the sticky feel of the rosin bag in his hand, and the sound of his fastball slapping against the catcher's mitt as he fanned another batter, and the sight of Ted Williams sitting in the bleachers—the greatest hitter in the game come all the way from Boston to watch him throw his fastball. He remembered the warm pride that flowed through him—and the cold prospect of failure.

Only two years had passed and to Clay it seemed as though it had happened in another lifetime to someone else. He found it more and more difficult to live with the man he was now, this man who was only a few months old—born on a blackened and torn coral island in the South Pacific amid the thunder of artillery shells and the screams of the dying, born with an arm no better than anyone else's.

Clay sat down on a wide concrete banister at the bottom of some steps that led up to a sloping lawn. He drew the bittersweet fragrance of the sweet olive deeply into his lungs and along with it the pain of remembrance. Pulling the cork from the bottle, he lifted it to his mouth. Then he held it at arm's length and turned it upside down over the sidewalk, listening to it gurgle empty.

Staring at the spreading stain of whiskey on the sidewalk, Clay lost himself in images of the major leagues as he had done countless times on the cramped Liberty ships or in a sandy foxhole. He could almost hear the roar of the crowd from the tiers of the cavernous stadium as he walked onto the manicured grass of the freshly striped infield; he could almost see headlines the next morning announcing another victory.

From an open window the sound of the Inkspots singing "A Lovely Way to Spend an Evening" drifted on the scented air.

Clay laughed bitterly and spoke out loud. "This certainly is a lovely way to spend an evening."

"I agree."

Startled, Clay leaped to his feet. He saw his high school English teacher, Leslie Gifford, walking slowly toward him. "Oh, hello, Mr. Gifford."

Crippled from polio, Gifford walked with a loosely swinging left arm and a right foot that slapped softly against the rough concrete sidewalk. He wore a tweed jacket from long habit, even though the evening was mild. He hardly realized anymore that it was to make his disability less noticeable. "I didn't mean to sneak up on you like that."

I must be losing my touch. No one would have gotten that close with-out me hearing them—not before . . . "Guess I was daydreaming." Clay glanced around him as though he just realized where he was. "Can you daydream at night? I never thought about that before."

"I suppose so," Gifford quipped, easing the weight of his stiletto-slim body onto his left leg. The stance gave a barely notice-able "S" curve to his body. "As long as you don't go to sleep. Then it doesn't count."

Clay smiled, remembering Gifford's unusual sense of humor from the classroom.

"So—what's the local hero doing out here all by himself?" Gifford continued, brushing his light-brown hair back out of his eyes. Unfashionably long, it touched his ears as well as his shirt collar. His eyes, the color of old pecan shells, held a strange sad light as he spoke. "I didn't think the lovely Diane Jackson ever let you out of her sight."

"I think her daddy would just as soon she never laid eyes on me again."

"Somehow that doesn't surprise me."

"Why?" Clay was puzzled. He thought Gifford had always been fond of him, even to the point of helping him with special writ-ing projects on the weekends. "Is there something wrong with me?"

"Most assuredly."

"What is it?"

"You have a deficiency that is patently obscene and virtually unforgivable in the mind of Dobe Jackson." Gifford spoke in a grave and level voice; the light from the street lamp cast a soft lumi-nescent glow over his face. With his small nose, full lips, and softly rounded chin women found him attractive in spite of the ravages of polio.

Clay let Gifford ramble on, thinking the solitary life he had chosen to lead with only his books for company most of the time caused him to be a little strange and unpredictable.

"Aren't you going to ask me what it is?" Gifford thought Clay was losing interest in the game.

"I did."

"Impecuniousness."

"Impecu—that sounds like one of those South Pacific diseases. What in the world does it mean?"

"You ain't got no money," Gifford explained in his best Georgia twang. "That's what it means, and that's why ol' Dobe will never be your bosom buddy."

"I'm not exactly choked up that he isn't." Clay always enjoyed Gifford's company and felt better after talking with him for only a few minutes. He thought it might be because Gifford hadn't asked him what he planned to do with his life. "Why don't you sit down a minute?"

"Don't mind if I do." Gifford stepped over and leaned against the concrete banister across from Clay's. "I certainly don't have anything pressing at the moment."

"Mr. Gifford, if you don't mind my asking, why do you always do everything alone?" Clay would never have asked a question so personal of anyone before he went to the South Pacific for fear that he would insult them or be rebuked, but now that possibility didn't seem to matter one way or the other. He was beginning to learn that fears he had before he went into the corps were no longer a part of his makeup.

Gifford reflected on the question a few moments. "Never thought of it much—maybe because no one ever asked me before. I guess it's just my way."

"That girl's PE coach wasn't too happy about it being just your way if I remember right," Clay ventured, considering himself a man of the world and perfectly qualified to discuss women with an educated man like Gifford.

Gifford glanced at him with a wry smile. "You knew about that, did you?"

"I think the whole school knew," Clay replied, enjoying this welcome respite from eyes that he considered more accusing than caring.

"An innocent diversion."

Clay tapped the whiskey bottle gently between his knees. It clinked against the concrete banister, reminding him that Gifford had said nothing about his drinking. "More like a romance according to the school gossip."

133

"A couple of movies and a fountain Coke at Ollie's hardly qualifies as romance."

"What was her name? I must be getting old." Clay remembered the pretty blonde teacher who had spent only one year at Liberty High, ostensibly leaving (and it was the prime topic of conversation in the girls' bathroom for weeks) because of the pain of her unrequited love for Leslie Gifford.

"Tennerman," Gifford offered solemnly, his eyes staring at the street lamps filing off into the distance. "Her name is Janet Tennerman."

"Yeah, that's it. Every boy in my class had a big crush on that lady." Clay stared across at Gifford. "She sure was crazy about you. At least that's what everybody thought."

"The cripple and the PE teacher," Gifford muttered almost bitterly. "Sounds like something Edgar Allen Poe would write if he were alive today."

"I didn't mean to bring up any bad memories for you, Mr. Gifford."

Gifford went on as though he hadn't heard Clay. "We live with the choices we make, Clay. Robert Frost wrote a poem about it, "The Road Not Taken.""

"You read it to us."

"And it does no good to blame our failures on," Gifford grabbed a handful of trousers, lifted his bad leg, and let it drop loosely to the concrete, "the bad breaks we get in this life."

Clay unconsciously rubbed his right elbow, feeling the tenderness where the bones were still mending.

"I have my work of course—and my books," Gifford continued, "and my one great success."

"What's that?"

"You mean *who* don't you?"

Clay rubbed his chin with his left forefinger. "Oh yeah! Leah Daniel."

Gifford smiled, a melancholy pleasure in his eyes. "Yes—Leah. The one big success in all my years of teaching. Scribner's shining new literary star."

"I read her first book. Short stories all about Liberty," Clay added. "I recognized a lot of the people, even if she did give them different names."

"Her second novel's going to be released in the fall." Gifford glanced over at Clay, the hint of a smile on his face. "Did I tell you she dedicated it to me?"

"That's great," Clay responded, seeing how proud Gifford felt that he had had a part in Leah's success. "You sure spent a lot of time with her."

"I gave her the basics, that's all," Gifford admitted. "Dave Stone deserves credit for getting her published."

As though someone had whispered in his ear, Clay felt the evening dwindling down to a kind of sadness. He dreaded the thought of going home and facing his father. "Well, I think I'll go find something to get into. Daddy's gonna chew me out anyway. Might as well make it worthwhile."

"What did you do?"

"Left my welcome-home party that Diane and her mother planned for me." Clay gave Gifford a sheepish grin. "I know Diane's called my house by now."

Gifford felt a twinge of pleasure that someone would snub Dobe Jackson's hospitality. "Why'd you leave?"

Clay remembered listening disinterestedly to the talk of stocks and bonds and annuities as he stood drinking with a small group of men who had satisfied their patriotic fervor by congratulating each other on the sacrifices they were all making for the war effort. "I don't know."

"Well, if you don't want to go home, you can sleep in my living room. I'll throw a quilt and pillow on the couch for you," Gifford offered, putting himself in Clay's position. "Call home first so your mother won't worry herself sick about you. Tell them you're staying over with a friend."

"You sure I wouldn't be putting you out?" Clay brightened at the prospect of a night without a detailed description of how he was ruining his future.

"Not at all." Gifford yawned and glanced at his watch. "I'm sure the night is just beginning for a young man like you, but it's past my bedtime."

"I wouldn't want to disturb you if I get in kinda late," Clay ventured. "I might walk around for a while. I've been kind of—restless lately."

"You won't bother me a bit. Of course neither would a strafing attack by the Japanese once I get to sleep." Gifford pushed off the banister with his good arm. "You'll find a quilt and pillow waiting for you on the living room couch."

"See you in the morning then."

Gifford massaged his bad leg briefly, then walked away, his right foot softly slapping against the concrete. "I'll leave the front door open," he called back over his shoulder.

Clay watched him go, a tragic figure shambling off down the sidewalk. He moved in and out of the amber pools of light from the streetlamps like an actor making his exit at the end of the final act of a play.

Clay knew, however, that Gifford never acted any part, never played to the sympathy of his audience. Just before he turned the corner and disappeared behind a well-trimmed hedge, Clay sensed a nobility about him that he had never seen in any other man.

11

SHORTY'S

Clay left the sidewalks of Liberty behind and strolled along the shoulder of a road that led to the highway, listening to the thick gravel crunch beneath the soles of his shoes. The soft spring air touched his face like a woman's fingertips. A sharp scent of pine filled his nostrils as he gazed upward at the pale moon, gliding through a star-crowded sky. As round and bright as a silver dollar, it bathed the world in a gossamer light.

Reaching the end of the gravel road, Clay turned right and saw Shorty's saloon across the highway from him. Set hard against a kudzu-covered bluff, it had once been a storage shed for hay. Two rough benches sat on either side of the front door along with a Pabst Blue Ribbon sign on the left and a green metal Lucky Strike circle with white lettering on the right.

Crossing the highway, Clay saw a battered and rusty Model T pickup back through a water-filled pothole in the parking lot. Straightening out with a grinding of gears, it clattered off into the night.

As he was about to enter the building, he noticed something glinting in the pale light. Leaning closer, he saw that a knife blade had been driven directly through the center of the Pabst Blue Ribbon sign and broken off. As though it were the natural thing to do, he grasped it with both hands, pulling with all his might. The blade didn't budge. He tried once more, shrugged, and stepped through the door.

"Hey there, Clay. Always glad to have our boys in uniform drop by for a visit." Shorty, who stood over six feet tall, wore his usual overalls and T-shirt. He had the large pale eyes of a fish who spent its life in an underground lake. The anemic light of the barroom gave the place the appearance that it had been submerged in murky water.

137

Clay walked across the sawdust-covered dirt floor to the bar as Jimmie Rogers wailed "My Carolina Sunshine Girl" from the jukebox. "Good to see you, Shorty. I see you had an interior decorator come in since I was here last."

Always a little slow on the uptake, Shorty protested, "Didn't do no such thing. It's looks too good *already* for the bunch that comes in here."

"You may be right at that."

Lifting a water-beaded bottle of Pabst from a galvanized tub, Shorty popped the cap off in an opener mounted on the side of the bar. "Here you go," he said, handing the bottle to Clay. "Have one on the house."

"Thanks." Clay took the bottle, sitting down on one of the wooden stools. "You about to close up?"

"I was, but take your time. I got nothing waitin' at home but dust and a sink full of dirty dishes."

"Sounds like Edna left you again."

"Yep," Shorty nodded. "That woman don't know how good she's got it."

Clay drank a swallow from the wet bottle rather than responding to Shorty's remark, thinking of the times he had seen Edna downtown with bruises or black eyes. He stared at the jukebox glowing in the dusky room on its platform of scrap lumber. Another Jimmie Rogers record began to play.

"How come you ain't at that homecoming party?" Shorty asked, filling the tub with bottles from a case on the shelf behind him. "Can't be over this early."

"How'd you know about that?"

"Society page," Shorty grinned. "You don't think ol' Dobe would let his precious little daughter as much as sneeze without puttin' it in that newspaper of his, do you?"

"Shorty—you read the society page?"

"Naw—I jest—"

"Yes you do too," Clay interrupted. "It's all over your face. I bet you know all the best gossip from the afternoon teas and bridge parties, too."

Shorty opened his mouth to respond. It stayed open, but no sound came out as he stared at something near the door directly behind Clay.

Turning casually around on his stool, Clay saw two men standing close together just inside the door. The one holding the long-barreled revolver was tall and angular and wore greasy khakis and a striped cap with a short bill. His nervous partner, dressed in a tattered black raincoat and brown fedora, had the shoulders of a lumberjack and the legs of a jockey. Both wore red bandanas tied across their faces in the manner of all good outlaws in the Hoppy and Roy and Gene westerns.

A big smile spread across Clay's face. He immediately thought of the man holding the gun as Roy and his partner as Hoppy. He couldn't have been happier if the two men had been dispatched to deliver him a chest of pirate's gold.

"Wha-whadda you want?" Shorty stood poised with a bottle of beer halfway to the tub.

"We from the First National Bank," the tall man cackled. "We gon' let you make a night deposit. Now ain't that the best service you ever had?"

Shorty, his mouth still open, remained motionless and silent behind the bar.

Hoppy walked around behind the bar. "You deef? Where's the cashbox?"

Before Shorty could answer, Roy screamed at Clay, "Whut you grinning at, soldier boy?"

"Marine." Clay grinned wider. He had wanted to vent the rage building in him since he had returned home, and now the two thieves were like manna from heaven. A thought brushed through the back of his mind that he could get killed, but it seemed trivial in the rush of adrenaline he felt.

"Whut?"

"I'm a Marine, not a soldier," Clay explained calmly. "A man in the *Army* is called a soldier."

Edging around to the end of the bar, Roy squinted his eyes as he tried to figure out why the tall Marine didn't seem at all frightened. He had never seen anyone react this way in any of his other armed robberies and felt that something had gone terribly wrong. "Shut up!"

"Anything you say," Clay replied even more calmly, his smile almost a laugh now.

"Quit *yakking* with that Jarhead and keep that *gun* on him!"

Hoppy growled from behind the bar. "You think this is some kind of *social* hour?"

Shorty had squatted down and taken the cigar box he kept the day's take in from under the bar behind the beer tub. "Here. It's all I got."

Hoppy snatched the box out of Shorty's hand and began rifling through it as though the whole thing were too heavy for him to carry along with him.

Clay yawned and made a stretching motion with both arms, extending the right one holding the beer bottle by its neck as far around as he could reach to give him maximum leverage. His left foot rested solidly on the dirt floor, and his left hand gripped the edge of the bar. He had decided that with his bad elbow, he could get more power with a sidearm throw, whipping his wrist through at the last moment.

Roy glanced at his partner, stuffing dollar bills from the cashbox into his coat pocket. He never saw Clay's arm whip around, sending the beer bottle hurtling through the air toward a spot three inches above the scab on the bridge of his nose.

The heavy bottle thudded with a sickening sound against Roy's forehead. He dropped to the dirt floor like a sack of feed, his revolver landing a foot from his outstretched hand.

Clay turned calmly around on his stool, gazing directly into Hoppy's eyes. "Looks like your friend's sleeping on the job. Reckon the bank'll dock his pay?"

Hoppy glanced at the front door, his eyes wide in disbelief at this sudden turn of events. He thought of the pistol, laying somewhere on the other side of the bar out of sight. Then he glanced back at Clay and put all thoughts of getting to the pistol out of his mind.

Shorty stood up and snatched the box away. "Give me back my money!"

"Why don't you empty your coat pockets, too?" Clay added in a level voice. "And take that silly handkerchief off your face."

The little man reached slowly behind his head to undo his mask, then suddenly bolted toward the end of the bar, making a break for the front door. As he rounded the corner, he stepped quickly over his fallen accomplice and sighted in on the open door to freedom.

As soon as the man broke for the door, Clay slipped off his stool and picked it up in both hands like a baseball bat. Waiting for just the right moment, he hurled it across the room. It caught the little man just above his ankles. Screaming in pain, he tumbled across the dirt floor. He came to rest doubled up, holding onto his damaged legs.

Clay was already standing above him when he scrambled up. He swung a roundhouse right at Clay's head, but missed. As his momentum carried him around, Clay clipped him on the chin with an uppercut.

Standing over the little man's crumpled form, Clay grinned broadly as he turned and glanced over his shoulder at the gunman lying at the end of the bar.

Shorty still clutched his cashbox. "I bet that's the last time them birds mess with us boys from Liberty."

"*Hot dog*, that was fun!" Clay walked over and picked up the heavy revolver from the floor. "Best time I've had since I got back from the Marines."

"You call a holdup fun?"

"It was for *me*," he shrugged, then glanced at the two men on the floor. "They probably wouldn't think so."

"I think they musta put something strange in your head in that Marine Corps, Clay."

Clay laid the pistol on the bar. The rust-pocked blue steel barrel glinted in the dim light. "Nah. They just polished up what I already had."

Shorty walked around the bar, stepped gingerly over the tall man, and squatted down next to the short one. As he retrieved his money from the man's pockets, he glanced over at Clay. "Ain't we gonna get the town marshall out here?"

Clay had a dazed look on his face. "Huh? Oh, yeah—sure. Gimme your truck keys. I'll go down to the jail and fetch him back here."

"What about them?" Shorty asked, glancing at the two unconscious men.

"Let 'em nap."

"They might wake up."

"You got any rope?"

Shorty, having fished all his money from the black raincoat, stood up and walked back behind the bar. Bending down, he fumbled behind some cartons and came up with two lengths of plowline. "That's all I got."

"It'll do."

Clay held out his hand for the keys. Shorty dug deep into his front overalls pocket and handed them to Clay who headed for the front door, tossing the keys into the air and whistling the Marine Corps hymn.

"You really gonna leave me with these two?" Shorty nodded toward the men again.

"Tie 'em up."

"You don't let your shirttail touch you till you get back—you hear?" Shorty hurried over to the tall man, rolled him over on his stomach, and began tying his hands behind his back.

* * *

"Yes, ma'am, I think they fit just fine." Sitting on the low stool next to Ora Peabody, Clay leaned back slightly and admired the chestnut-colored high heels he had just helped her stuff her pudgy feet into.

"Are you *sure* they're not too big?" Ora squinted down at her feet. She resembled Santa Claus's wife from the Coca Cola advertisements, but her husband, bitter from a logging accident that left him crippled, had none of Santa's disposition.

"Oh, no ma'am!" Clay responded quickly, fearing that he would have to prune her toes to get her feet into anything smaller. "They're just right."

"Maybe a seven-and-a-half?"

"They're perfect," Clay shrugged.

"Well—if you say so."

Clay tugged the shoes off and placed them back into the box. "You can pay at the register up front."

Ora pointed to the cash register positioned at the entrance to the shoe department. "What's wrong with that one?"

Clay stared across the bustling aisles of Hightower's Department Store, watching Diane enter through the revolving glass doors.

"Did you hear me, Clayton?"

"Oh, yes, ma'am." Clay handed her the black-and-white box. "I don't know how to work the register."

Ora gave him a puzzled expression.

"I just started this morning." Clay shrugged.

Ora placed the box on her ample lap. "Clayton, you were always a good student. Maybe it's none of my business, but . . ."

Here it comes. The first one.

"Don't you think you should consider your future more?" Ora continued. "Surely you can get into college or a least get a better job until you do."

"Well, this is just temporary, Mrs. Peabody. I'll probably enroll in the fall."

"Good. I'd hate to see you waste your talent, especially since . . ." she glanced at the right arm that hung down the side of his body at a slightly different angle from the left one. "Well, don't let it get you down, Clayton."

"No, ma'am." *You're such a joy to be around. No wonder Euliss always looks like he just swallowed a mouthful of spiders.* "Thanks, and you come back."

Ora tucked the box under her arm and waddled toward the front of the store.

Clay began to clear away the mess in front of Ora's chair where she had tried on sixteen pairs of shoes. As he carried the last boxes back toward the stockroom, he caught Diane's eye. Browsing through a rack of dresses across the wide main aisle from the shoe department, she stared in surprise at Clay.

Disappearing behind the curtains that covered the stockroom door, Clay began reshelving the boxes of shoes. *Maybe she'll go away. . . . No, not Diane.*

Thirty seconds later, Diane's face appeared between the curtains. "Clay, I *thought* that was you back here. What in the world are you doing?"

"Research."

Diane stepped into the long, narrow room. Her black-and-white-checked cotton dress was tailored perfectly for her trim figure, and her blond hair flowed as smoothly as water down to her shoulders. "What?"

"Research," Clay repeated, shoving the boxes back into their slots. "I'm writing a mystery novel about a shoe salesman. It's a murder mystery."

"Since when did you have any interest in books—especially writing them?"

"You know I used to always talk about Leah Daniel and how I'd like to get something published."

"Always? Maybe twice."

"More than that."

Diane put her hands on her hips, tilting her head sideways. "You're not making any sense at all."

"Sure I am," Clay insisted, shoving the last box home. "This is the perfect job for a great plot."

Diane held her position, giving him a skeptical look. "This better be good."

"You see this shoe salesman is really insane." Pulling up a rolling ladder, Clay sat on the third rung. "He hates women because his mama always wanted a little girl and made him wear dresses till he was thirty-four."

"What?"

"Well, maybe twenty-seven or -eight would be better," Clay admitted. "Anyhow—"

"Clay," Diane interrupted. "I've had just about enough of your nonsense!"

"Hold on—it gets better," Clay insisted. "Where was I? Oh yeah, this guy gets it in his head to bump somebody off—so what does he do?"

"I'm leaving right now if you don't stop!"

Clay felt he had to continue his story no matter what happened, knowing that this in itself was as insane as the tale he found himself spinning.

"Clayton? Are you back there?"

Hearing the sound of Ora Peabody's voice, Clay sighed deeply. "Be with you in a minute, Mrs. Peabody."

Diane's eyes glistened with tears. She quickly wiped them away. "Clay—stop this!"

"I'm almost finished," he insisted. "So—our man, having decided on his victim, sells her a pair of shoes—several pairs would be better—that are too tight for her. Like a lot of women, she would never admit they're too small, so she walks around with this excruciating pain until—"

"Stop!" Diane screamed.

"What? You don't like the idea?"

Ora Peabody's plump face appeared between the curtains. "Clayton will you please get out here? I need a smaller size in these shoes you just sold me."

"See what I mean?" Clay whispered to Diane as he stood up. His eyes had taken on a conspiratorial, almost paranoid gleam. "One second, Mrs. Peabody."

"Don't take all day now." Ora's face disappeared.

Clay took a box from the shelf. "The woman with the tight shoes complains so much that it drives her husband nuts, and he murders her."

Diane plopped down on a stepladder, leaning over with her face in her hands.

Clay left through the curtains and returned in five minutes with the same pair of shoes. "You all right, sweetheart?"

Diane looked up, her eyes red and swollen. "Clay, what's wrong with you?"

Slamming the box against the wall, Clay responded, "I don't know."

"Why did you leave your job at the lumberyard?"

"Hartley fired me."

Diane stood up and walked over to him. "You've just got to go to work at Daddy's newspaper. I can't understand why you're so set against it."

Clay stared down at the linoleum floor.

"You worked there in high school."

"I didn't have any choice then." He glanced up at her. "Your daddy despises me, Diane. The only reason he tolerates me at all is because of you."

"Don't be silly. Daddy's gruff with everybody—just about." Feeling the hollowness of her words, Diane tried to smile as though that would give them credibility. "If you'd just show him a little respect, I'm sure things would work out between the two of you. Won't you at least try?"

Clay shrugged and continued to stare at the floor, rubbing the top of his right hand with his left palm.

Diane glanced about the cluttered stockroom. "Clay, you've got to get out of here."

Looking up at her with a puzzled frown he asked, "What do you mean—quit my job?"

"Exactly."

"It's honest work."

Diane stood up, giving Clay's workplace another disdainful look as she walked toward the curtained doorframe.

"Well—what's wrong with selling shoes?"

"It *is* honest work," Diane agreed, "but it's *not* what I want for my husband."

"It's not exactly *my* dream job either, Diane." Clay clasped his right elbow with his left hand. "But people don't always get what they want in this life."

"Some don't. But then again some do." Diane leaned against the wall next to the door, giving Clay a coy smile.

"What's that supposed to mean?"

"You *do* want to marry me—don't you?"

Clay felt himself being lured into something that would change his life completely, like an animal toward the trapper's springed steel.

"Don't you?"

"Sure."

"Well then, you'll just have to leave all this," Diane flicked her hand at the room, "and go to work for Daddy."

Clay gazed stonily at her. "You think blackmail is a sound foundation for a marriage?"

"Oh, hush! That's a *dreadful* thing to say," Diane shot back huffily.

"What is it then?"

Diane stood up straight, her arms folded across her breast. "It's a wife wanting her husband to have a respectable job."

"Work for your father, huh?"

"You make it sound like I'm asking you to go to work picking cotton."

Clay felt he would be much happier dragging a cotton sack behind him in the broiling sun than being under Dobe Jackson's thumb all day.

"Well, what's your answer?" Diane had balled her hands into fists, placing them on her hips.

"Sydney or the Bush, huh?"

"What are you babbling about now?" Diane asked, irritation at the forefront of her voice. "I declare, sometimes I think you lost your brain somewhere out in that Pacific Ocean."

"Just an expression I picked up down in Australia," Clay explained, thinking that perhaps Diane wasn't far wrong about his mental state.

Diane continued to stare at him, her face becoming slowly flushed with anger.

"Absolutely, my precious." Clay felt he was betraying some long-forgotten ideal with his words. "Maybe ol' Dobe and me will be best buddies before it's all over."

"Oh, Clay, that's wonderful!" Diane rushed into his arms, kissing him on both cheeks and the mouth.

12

A CHEAP PIECE OF JUNK

"Do you think it's going all right so far?" Diane sat on the satin coverlet of her antique four-poster among a dozen or so stuffed animals.

Her older sister Peggy sat next to her, brushing her shiny red hair. "Good as any other engagement party I've ever been to. They all simply bore me to death."

"Oh, you think you're so sophisticated now that you've worked up in Washington for a year," Diane pouted. "It's just *got* to turn out OK after what happened at his homecoming party. I'll just *die* if he messes up this time."

Peggy lay the brush down and straightened the straps of her jade green dress. "I'll say one thing for Clay, he always was a handsome devil: tall as a silo and those shoulders are simply dreamy."

"I asked you about the *party*, Peggy!" Diane snapped. "I already know what Clay *looks* like!"

Peggy dismissed her sister's complaint. "Oh, don't be so jealous! He's *much* too young for me."

"It looks like almost everybody I invited showed up," Diane offered.

"And some that you *didn't* invite."

"Like who?"

"Like Angela Spain for one."

"I could just shoot Daddy for that!" Diane slapped the bedspread with the flat of her hand.

"*He* invited her?"

"No, but . . ."

"I didn't think Mama would let him get away with that," Peggy interrupted.

"As I was saying, he invited Lila Kronen as a gesture of

friendship to his opposition and told her she could bring a friend. So who does she bring?"

"None other than the infamous Angela Spain."

"Right."

"I don't think she's any worse than some others in this town who shall remain nameless."

"You're probably right." Diane grinned mischievously. "But she was always so—indiscreet. Everybody and his brother knew she was running around on poor ol' Morton."

"That's certainly true. I suppose guile is something that takes a lot of practice to really get right." Peggy stared thoughtfully at a huge white Teddy bear propped against the headboard. "Angela never was much good at it, was she?"

"Maybe she just didn't care." Diane slipped off the bed and straightened her skirt. "Anyway, I hear she's got religion now. Isn't that the cat's meow?"

"Angela got religion? *That'll* be the day." Peggy stood up and gave herself a final once-over in the dresser mirror. "We better be getting back. You don't want to leave Clay alone too long in the same house with Angela Spain."

"Oh, you!" Diane picked the brush up from the bed and tossed it at her sister.

* * *

"You better take it easy on that stuff, Mr. Clay." Cletus reluctantly poured another double shot of bourbon into Clay's heavy glass.

"I'm sober as a judge, Cletus," Clay replied, leaning both elbows on the bar as he surveyed the same crowd that attended his homecoming party milling about wearing silks and satins and summer tuxedos. At Diane's insistence, he had worn his Marine dress uniform again. "Judge Roy Bean that is."

"You 'member what happened last time," Cletus reminded him, shoving the glass across the bar. "Mr. Dobe won't stand for nothin' like that agin."

Clay downed the whiskey in one gulp. Letting his breath out with a hissing sound, he felt the liquid burn all the way down to his stomach. But he thought there wasn't enough liquor in the whole town to rid him of an image from the past month that kept playing over and over in his mind like a record stuck in the same spot.

Clay had given in to Diane's badgering and gone to her father's office at the *Liberty Herald* to ask for a job. After a two-hour wait, he had been ushered into the plush office where Jackson made him wait another ten minutes while he handled a phone call and sorted through some paperwork.

Gazing at Clay with a smug and condescending smile on his face, Jackson had spoken in his best "paternal benevolence" voice. "It's about time you came to your senses, Clayton. Now that baseball's no longer an option, you have to get on with your life."

"Yes, sir."

"I'm not cutting you any slack just because my daughter's infatuated with you."

Our engagement party's coming up, Clay thought. *You call that infatuation?* "I don't expect any."

"Good, we understand each other then."

Clay had nodded.

"Be at the loading ramp at three o'clock Monday morning," Jackson had said in a voice fraught with sarcasm. "You'll drive the delivery truck for the commercial accounts. The first time you're late will be your last."

Clay knew that the job he had been given was usually filled by men with limited abilities and was known to be a dead-end street as far as advancement with the newspaper went. "I'll be there."

Jackson had returned to his paperwork without a word as though Clay no longer existed.

Along with the whiskey, Clay felt the anger burning with a hotter flame in the pit of his stomach. The past weeks had been torture for him with Jackson or one of his toadies constantly badgering him on the job. He finished his drink and turned toward Cletus for another.

"Hello, Clay. Lovely party." Angela Spain, wearing a lavender blouse with a lace collar and a long white skirt, walked over next to him.

Clay glanced at her. "Yeah."

"You don't seem particularly pleased for someone who's getting engaged to such a lovely girl."

Scowling at her now, Clay inexplicably felt the anger rising again in his chest. It seemed to glow inside his brain, causing thoughts that he couldn't seem to shackle. "What do you know about how I feel? You don't know anything about me."

Puzzled and a little hurt at Clay's reaction, Angela turned away. "May I have a Coke please?"

"Yes ma'am," Cletus grinned, his teeth dazzling against his dark skin. "You look nice, Miss Angela."

"Thank you." Angela took a swallow of her Coke and turned to leave.

"It's her job to look nice—isn't it, Angela?" Clay sneered down at her.

"I'm afraid I don't understand."

"Oh, she understands all right," Clay grinned maliciously toward Cletus.

"You've had too much to drink, Clay," Angela offered in a soft voice. "Maybe you should lie down for a while."

"Now that's something you know all about, isn't it, *Mrs. Spain?*" Angela had never offended Clay in any way, but he couldn't seem to control the rage that had begun to spill out of him. "Lying down, that is—even if it's only for one-hour intervals."

Angela knew that people had talked about her behind her back for years, but no one had ever confronted her with her transgressions face to face. Even though it hurt terribly, somehow this was better. To her surprise, she felt no desire to strike back at her accuser.

Clay expected something other than this calm exterior presented to him by Angela. Directionless, his rage seemed to intensify as it sought a target.

Angela turned to leave the bar, but was stopped by Clay's next volley.

"Ol' Morton didn't know what he was gettin' himself into when he married this one," Clay glanced over at Cletus, then leered at Angela. "Did he now?"

"No," she replied quietly, "he didn't."

Clay had lost control now, his thoughts following no course of logic whatsoever. "I'll bet that little sailor boy wished he had never left El Paso."

Angela's eyes grew suddenly glassy with tears. "Excuse me,

please." She hurried off across the terrace toward the bright squares of the French doors.

"That was awful ugly, Mr. Clay."

Clay watched Angela enter into the brightly lit drawing room. "Some people just got no sense of humor, Cletus."

"Nothin' funny a'tall in what you said."

"Oh, come on, Cletus. Take it easy." Clay shoved his glass across the bar. "Hit me again."

"You wouldn't like what I'd hit you with." Cletus turned and walked to the other end of the bar.

* * *

"And don't you ever set foot in this house again, you ungrateful low-life drunk!" Dobe Jackson stood at his front door, rubbing his bruised jaw as he watched Keith Demerie, Taylor Spain and Hartley Lambert drag Clay down the circular driveway and across the freshly clipped lawn.

The three men heaved Clay down the steep slope. He tumbled sideways until he hit the street gutter at the bottom, groaned, and lay still.

"That'll teach you to talk to decent people that way," Hartley Lambert called out. "You oughta take some lessons from your daddy. At least he knows his place in this town."

Clay watched the three men turn and walk out of sight beyond the edge of the slope. With some effort, he managed to sit up, turn around, and lean back on the damp grass with one elbow. Taking his handkerchief from his back pocket, he gingerly wiped the blood away from the cut above his left eyebrow and his battered lips. One tooth felt loose when he touched it.

His head fuzzy with drink as well as the beating he had taken at the hands of the four men, Clay found that he was unable to reconstruct the events of the night. He vaguely remembered talking with Angela Spain and that he had hurt her feelings. After that— only a blur of motion, the sounds of men shouting at him, and the pain of fists pounding his face and hard shoes slamming into his ribs after he was down.

Clay lay back on the slope of the lawn, closing his eyes to fight off the nausea that was beginning to sweep over him. He felt revulsion at himself for what he had said to Angela and for the way he had behaved toward the others even though he could remember most of it only in bits and pieces.

"Clay . . ."

Pushing himself upright, Clay opened his eyes and glanced around.

"Over here."

Clay rubbed is eyes with both hands. As his vision cleared, he saw Diane standing only a few feet away next to a huge pine, almost lost in its deep shadow. Putting his hands at his sides, he leaned forward to get up.

"No—stay where you are!"

"I can barely see you," Clay muttered painfully through his swollen lips.

"Doesn't matter," Diane replied coldly. "This will only take a moment."

Clay ran his hands through his hair, pushing it back out of his eyes. "I really messed up good this time, didn't I? Well, I learned my lesson for sure and—"

"No!" Diane cut him off sharply. "I don't care if you learned anything or not."

"What are you talking about?"

"It's over."

"Oh, come on now, baby," Clay tried to sound as though he had merely used the wrong fork at dinner. "Don't make such a big deal out of this."

"I'm not making a big deal out of anything. You've done it all yourself."

With his head still spinning slowly and his vision blurry, Clay felt as though he were talking with a disembodied voice from the shadows. "Will you please come on over here so we can talk, Diane? This is stupid."

"I agree—and you've brought it all on yourself."

Clay's voice had a raspy sound from the harsh whiskey. The blood on his lips was becoming crusty, making it hard for him to form the words. "Diane, I'm sorry for whatever it was I did. I just don't remember much."

"You called my father a pompous . . . I can't even repeat what you called him. And you insulted Keith Demerie because he didn't go in the service."

Sounds like I was just telling the truth. "Well, whatever I did, I apologize."

"It's much too late for that. My family and I have run out of patience with you."

"But—what about our engagement—all the plans we made?" Clay pleaded, feeling that he was losing his last hope for straightening out his life.

"Here's what I think of our engagement!"

Clay saw a quick brightness as the ring arced through the air and hit him in the chest.

"I never should have accepted such a cheap piece of junk anyway!" Diane whirled around, her dress a brief flash against the shadows, and disappeared.

Lying back against the cool grass, Clay felt his head gradually beginning to clear, but as he returned to full consciousness the pain intensified. *Serves me right. I should have been blown to bits on Tarawa. So many good men were lost—men that had wives and children and jobs, good reasons to go on living.*

Clay listened to the sounds of music and laughter drifting out from the party behind him. From beyond the house, the band began to play "I'll Never Smile Again"; the sentimental melody sounded like the dream of a song in the distance.

The song took Clay back to the day he had left for the Marine Corps. Waving at him from the station platform, Diane had just disappeared from sight as he continued to gaze out the window at the last fleeting sights of Liberty. Four soldiers on their way to a replacement depot on the East Coast had formed an impromptu quartet in his car and had sung the Sinatra hit. The whole car had applauded at the end, making one request after the other until the men finally had to beg off with hoarse voices.

As Clay listened to the song, immersed in the tormenting memories, he could see nothing left that was worth living for. He struggled painfully to his knees, then stood up and waited until his head cleared. Brushing himself off, he straightened his tie, and walked off toward town, following his shadow from one streetlight to another.

* * *

"You shore saved *my* hide, boy!" Shorty opened a wet bottle of Pabst, and set it on the bar in front of Clay. "I heard them same two boys killed a feller at a service station in the next county the same night they come in here. If it wasn't for you, I'd be pushing up daisies out there in the boneyard."

"Yeah. I heard the same thing," Clay muttered through his blood-crusted lips. "If I'd known they really meant business, I might have made another door in your back wall getting out of here instead of acting like a fool."

Shorty squinted up at Clay as he washed glasses in a dishpan below the bar. "You ain't fooling me none, Clay McCain. I seen the kind of men who run from a fight, which is most of 'em, and you just ain't got it in you. You enjoyed every minute of looking down that gun barrel."

Clay knew what Shorty said was true. He also knew that it had nothing to do with courage. The feeling that had possessed him that night was one of simply not caring what happened to him. And then there was that feeling like no other when he released the rage burning inside of him, as though someone had turned a pressure valve just before the critical point was reached.

Shorty spoke into his dishpan. "You a sorry sight now if I ever seen one though."

Clay touched his left eye, almost swollen shut. Shorty had cleaned the blood off him and pulled the cut above the eye closed as best he could with adhesive tape. His lips had begun to bleed again as soon as they were cleaned. "I reckon I deserved everything they did to me."

"What did you do—if I'm not meddlin' too much?" Shorty asked hesitantly.

"That's the real pitiful part of this whole mess," Clay laughed bitterly. "I don't even remember."

"Nothing?"

"I said some nasty things to a few people," Clay admitted. "But then I've done that on a pretty regular basis ever since I got back home."

"Maybe you oughta just stay plumb away from parties. I think you're allergic to 'em."

Clay laughed, then stopped abruptly as his lips burned with pain. "I guess you're right."

"Your folks know where you are?" Shorty glanced at the pale amber glow of the Camel Cigarettes clock above the jukebox. "It's past midnight. You better get on home."

"Already been there."

Shorty stepped into the tiny storage room behind the bar, coming directly out with a case of beer.

"Dad kicked me out," Clay continued. "Said he'd had enough of my foolishness."

Shorty began filling the tub with beer.

"I think he's afraid that ol' Hartley's gonna fire him if he sides with me."

"Yeah," Shorty mumbled into his tub, "him and Dobe's big buddies."

Clay stared thoughtfully at the jukebox. "Guess I've got something in common with Ben Logan."

"You mean besides being a war hero?"

"War hero—me?" Clay muttered. "I ain't fit to stand in Ben Logan's shadow."

"They don't give Silver Stars away for door prizes," Shorty objected. "Not in the *Marines* they don't."

Clay shook his head slowly. "Doesn't matter anyway—none of it. What I'm talking about is Ben and I both got dumped by the daughters of the two richest men in town."

Shorty leaned on the bar with both of his milky colored forearms. "That's the gospel truth," he agreed. "But look how Ben come out of it."

"You mean Rachel?"

"Yep. If he'd hooked up with Debbie Lambert—I wouldn't give you two cents for that marriage. But a man couldn't ask for a better wife than Rachel."

Clay continued to stare at the jukebox.

"Same thing could happen to you."

"I wouldn't count on that." Clay ran his hands though his hair and leaned his elbows on the bar.

"Where you stayin' tonight?"

"Beats me."

"I'd ask you over to the house," Shorty hesitated, staring

down at the duckboards resting on the dirt floor. "Well, Edna come back, and it's kinda touch-and-go at the house right now. You know how women are."

"No, I don't think I know much about women at all," Clay mumbled.

"Tell you what." Shorty stepped back and frowned into his storage room. "Nah."

"Nah? What do mean, *Nah?*" Clay leaned over the bar, trying to see what Shorty was looking at.

Shaking his head, Shorty stepped back to the bar. "Want another whiskey?"

"Not now. What were you talking about?"

"I was gonna say you could stay here in the storage room until you found something, but—"

"But nothing, I'll take it," Clay insisted. "It's either that or a bed of pine straw under a tree somewhere."

"It ain't much."

"Good, it'll be perfect for me then," Clay declared bluntly, "'cause I ain't much either."

"You better come around here and take a look before you make your mind up so quick."

Clay walked painfully around behind the bar, stepping to the door of the storage room. Glancing inside he saw cases of beer and whiskey stacked almost to the ceiling in most of the cramped space of the room. Dirt and grime seemed to have taken the place of paint on the parts of the walls that were visible. The low ceiling was rapidly rusting tin that had begun flaking onto the dirt floor and the bare striped ticking of a mattress and pillow.

As he stepped into the cramped confines of the room, Clay heard a rough scratching along the far wall and something heavy banging against the tin roof. Squinting in the dim light, he saw a wood rat that looked as big as a good-sized cat scurry through the opening between the tin and the ceiling joist.

"Maybe sleeping underneath a pine tree won't be all *that* bad," Clay muttered, stepping back out of the tiny room.

"Well, it ain't nothing fancy, but it'll keep you dry if it rains," Shorty offered, touting the room's best feature. "There's a blanket under here somewhere."

While Shorty rummaged around behind some boxes beneath

the bar, Clay glanced back inside the storage room, wondering how his life had come to such a sad state in a little more than two years.

Shorty finished his nightly chores, tucked his cashbox under his arm, and headed for the door. "I won't be here until ten in the morning so don't worry about getting up. I fixed the jukebox so you can play all the songs you want for free."

"Thanks."

"Help yourself to anything you want to drink. I'll bring you some biscuits or something in the morning." With a nod of his head, Shorty walked out into the parking lot.

Clay heard Shorty's pickup grind slowly at first, then faster. Finally the engine sputtered to life. With a creaking of springs and the clanging of scrap metal in the bed, it jounced through the parking lot and onto the highway.

Well, it ain't much, but it's home. Clay surveyed the dimly lighted tavern and hefted a full bottle of whiskey from the shelf. Wandering over to the jukebox, he studied the selections a few minutes before he punched in Tommy Dorsey's "Boogie Woogie," Glenn Miller's "In the Mood" and four other instrumentals. *Nothing with words for me. Keeps down the old memory quotient.*

Raking a chair to him with his foot, Clay sat down and leaned back, crossing his legs on top of the table. *Yes, sir, I gotta, 'Keep gloom down to a minimum.'* He sang to the lyrics of a current pop tune into the gloomy loneliness of the room.

Part 4

THE END
OF THE STORM

13

ROCK BOTTOM

Sunlight streamed through the windows, giving the room a pale gold brilliance that hurt Clay's eyes as he struggled up from a nightmarish darkness. He blinked, his eyes watering in the glare, then sat up, trying to rub the cobwebs of sleep from his eyes. After the light, the first thing he noticed was the fresh clean smell and softness of the sheets and the pale yellow pajamas he had on. He knew they had been dried on a clothesline because he could still smell the sun in them.

Sitting up in the bed, he put a pillow behind him, leaning back against the headboard. A pitcher of water and bottles of patent medicine sat on the nightstand. Furnished with a cherrywood dresser, a cedar chest at the foot of the bed, and a Queen Anne chair, the room was comfortable and inviting.

Noticing a door that led to a tiled bath, Clay eased his legs over the edge of the bed. His head swam and he felt sick at his stomach. When he tried to stand, he felt that the arches of his feet would no longer support his weight. Finally standing up, he had to hold on to the bedpost to maintain his balance.

Walking unsteadily to the bathroom, he flicked on the light and stepped in front of the lavatory. The image in the mirror sent a chill through him. At first he thought it was somehow the reflection of someone behind him, but he quickly realized that was impossible.

Clay saw the dark hollow eyes staring out at him from a gaunt, almost emaciated-looking face. A heavy stubble could not hide the yellow pallor of his skin overlaid with several dark crusty scabs and blotchy ridges that looked like mosquito bites. His teeth appeared coated with a green fungus and his hair, although it had been washed, stuck out in all directions.

163

After washing his face, Clay took a new toothbrush from the medicine cabinet and brushed his teeth. He wet and combed his hair, then rubbed the heavy stubble on his cheeks. He decided he was still too shaky to risk using the safety razor that lay on a glass shelf in the cabinet and walked slowly back to the bed, breathing as though he had run wind sprints.

Still too disoriented and weak to be concerned about where he was, Clay only knew that he somehow felt safe. He had just dozed off when he heard footsteps in the narrow hallway that led to the living area and kitchen. A faint scent of gardenia drifted like a fond memory in the bright air of the room.

Slowly opening his eyes, Clay thought that he was surely lost in a dream. He saw a soft cloud of dark hair and violet eyes that soothed his hurts by their mere presence and a smile that radiated warmth as surely as the sunshine.

"Oh, good, you're awake. I was afraid you were going to sleep twenty years like Rip Van Winkle."

Clay opened his mouth to speak, but only a raspy grunt escaped his dry, scratchy throat.

Angela poured a glass of water from the white ceramic pitcher. "Here, you sound all dried out."

Clay took the glass, turning it up to his mouth and draining it. The water felt like a healing balm as it cooled his throat and stomach. He hadn't realized how very thirsty he was. "Thanks."

Pulling a cushioned chair covered in a striped velvet fabric near the bed, Angela sat down, saying nothing, only gazing at Clay with a pleasant noncommittal expression on her face.

Clay took in her pale green dress made of soft cotton that contoured Angela's body in graceful flowing folds. "How long have I been here?"

"Three days."

"How did I get here?" Clay remembered little since that first night at Shorty's. The days and nights had simply been a blend of morning quiet when he and Shorty had talked, afternoon noise as the tavern grew continually more crowded until closing time, and silent nights, when Clay again found himself alone with only a bottle and a jukebox for company.

His nights on the cot in the storage room had been filled with nightmares and dreams too painful to remember when he had awakened to take several harsh mouthfuls of whiskey and lie down again to stare at rats that were actually in the room with him—and at some that were not.

"Amos found you lying under one of the big pine trees at the back of the property, unconscious." Angela took the glass and poured some more water.

Sipping the water, Clay gazed into Angela's eyes. "I-I can't remember when the party was—the one . . ."

"Ten days ago."

"I have to call home."

"I've already done that," Angela said, her voice hardly above a whisper.

Gradually Clay began to remember the scene at the party with Angela and how badly he had mistreated her. He couldn't hold her eyes as he spoke. "I-I hope you'll forgive me for the way I treated you at the party. It was a terrible thing to do! I don't even know why I acted like that. You've always been nice to me."

Angela smiled, shaking her head slowly. "Don't worry about it. I'm surprised you remember it at all."

"How did I . . ." Clay glanced down at the pajamas.

Angela's quick laugh sounded musical in the stillness of the room. "Amos."

"Who?"

"He's the handyman who's worked here for years. He cleaned you up."

"Where's my uniform?"

"At the cleaners," Angela replied, noticing Clay's modesty. "I'll pick it up later today."

"I guess I'd better get up and get out of here. Don't want to bother you any more."

"I don't think you're strong enough to leave yet." Angela stood up and walked away, stopping at the door. "Just stay in bed. I'll be right back."

"But I can't stay in your house." Clay found himself strangely uneasy in Angela's presence.

"You needn't be concerned about that." Angela laughed again. "This is an apartment above the garage. It's completely separate from the house."

Clay watched Angela disappear down the hall. He felt like a

child again, not only from being so weak, but because he was experiencing the same emotions he had felt as a boy when his mother had taken care of him after he had disobeyed her and gotten into trouble.

Angela appeared in less than a minute carrying a white wicker tray. She walked over to the bedside and placed it in front of Clay, resting the legs on either side of him. "Here you are. Eat as much as you can."

Clay stared down at a large white bowl of vegetable beef soup with crackers and a large glass of milk. Taking a spoonful, he tried it carefully. It tasted rich and nourishing and delicious with just enough seasoning to bring out the flavor of the fresh vegetables. "This is great! Better than my mama used to make, and I thought hers was the best in the world."

"Thank you."

"You made this?"

Angela nodded, never in her wildest dreams believing that she would get such pleasure from watching a man eat. She could almost taste the pleasure that Clay got from every bite, could almost feel the nourishing soup mending his injuries and putting strength back into his malnourished and alcohol-damaged body. "I'm so glad you like it. I never did much cooking before, but lately it's something that I've come to enjoy."

"You oughta open a restaurant," Clay mumbled between mouthfuls. Then, remembering where he was, said apologetically, "But why would you need to, right?"

When Clay had finished, he breathed a deep sigh. "That was the best tasting soup I've ever had."

Angela smiled her thanks again.

"I really gotta get out of here now. How can I ever pay you back for what you've done for me?" Clay set the tray aside and tried to stand up. But the room swam before his eyes, and he carefully lay back down.

"You stay right where you are." Angela took the tray away, returning with a bottle of white pills. Shaking one out, she handed it to Clay along with a glass of water.

"What's this?"

"I don't know. Ollie gave them to me when I told him what condition you were in. He said you should take one three times a day and stay in bed for three or four more days."

"I can't stay here."

"You most certainly *can*."

Clay felt his face grow slightly hot. "But what would people say about you?"

"Nothing they haven't already." Angela took the glass and placed it on the nightstand. Pulling the covers around Clay's chest, she said, "You just rest and let me worry about what people will say. I'll have Amos come up later and help you with your bath. What do you want for supper?"

Clay felt too weak to protest anything that Angela said. "Anything—as long as you cook it."

* * *

"You sho' been a big help to me, Mr. Clay." Amos Chaney leaned on his Kaiser blade, his blue shirt and overalls stained darkly with sweat. Then his face clouded over slightly as he asked, "It ain't none of my business, but I seed that big scar on yo' back and them little un's in yo' chest all week now. What done something like that to you?"

With a bitter smile, Clay pointed to the cluster of jagged white scars beneath his right breastbone. "The Japs gave me these little souvenirs."

"Is all them little bullet holes?"

"Something like that. It's called shrapnel. A mortar round exploded right next to me."

"What about yo' back?"

"The Navy doctor did that taking the Jap souvenirs out."

"I ain't never been to no war. Thank the Lawd for dat," Amos mumbled, his head bowed slightly.

Clay sat down on the pine needles and leaned back against the rough bark of the tree. "This is just what I needed, Amos. Sweat out all that poison I've been putting into my body for the last three or four months."

Amos sat down against a tree next to Clay. "We'll have dis place looking like it ought to in no time wid both of us working at it—sho will."

Clay gazed at the briars and weeds that had grown up in the little glade at the back of Angela's property. "How'd it get away from you like this?"

"Took sick in that last little cold snap back at the end of March. Took me three or fo' months to get shed of whatever it was I got. My chest still burns like fire if I get too winded." Amos smiled at the wild growth in the glade. "Don't take long for wild things to take over if you jes' turn 'em loose on their own."

"How long you been working for the Spains?" Working with Amos took Clay back to the times when he had worked with Cletus Felder at the lumbermill. The satisfying feeling he had was the same—that of any man who gives an honest day's work for his pay. He wondered if he could ever feel at ease with men who didn't earn their living by hard labor.

"Little more'n twenty years." Amos took a white handkerchief from his back pocket and wiped his face. The color of coffee and cream, his skin was freckled with brown spots half the size of dimes. "Mr. Morton never paid no mo' attention to me than he did a stray cat. Never treated me bad neither."

"How about Angela?"

"She wudn't no more than a child when she married Mr. Morton. Jest a pretty little girl," Amos grinned. "She sho' turned into a fine lady this last year though. Couldn't ask for a nicer, kinder lady than she is."

Clay picked up a quart bottle of water that sat against the side of the tree. It was filled with ice cubes and beaded with cool drops of condensation. Turning it up, he drank half of it without taking it from his lips. "Ahhh, that's good. Well, I guess we'd better get on back to work."

Amos drank from his own jar. "How long you reckon you'll be helping me out here?"

"Don't know." Clay picked up the long-handled blade and lay into the high, thick stand of weeds. He swung it exactly as he had his bat, swinging for the fence on a high hard one. Working next to Amos gave Clay a sense of belonging although he didn't understand why.

As he worked, Clay kept Angela's image on the front steps of his mind. He could almost smell her fragrance, almost see the graceful sway of her body as she strolled along next to him on their late afternoon walks beneath the purple shadows of the ancient trees.

Angela had begun to be a part of his very being and the

memory of her face would see him through those hours past midnight when he could almost smell the cordite, could almost hear the clattering of heavy machine guns—when the blood of his friends flowed again onto the blackened earth of Tarawa.

* * *

He certainly seems a kind and gentle man—now that he's no longer drinking. I guess losing baseball was about the worst thing that could have happened to him, even though he never mentions it. As soon as he sets a direction for himself in life he'll make some woman a . . . well, that's none of my business. Angela sat at the big wooden desk in the reception area of the *Journal* typing J.T.'s latest column from his scratchy handwriting.

"Angela, could you step in here for a moment?" Lila peeked around the edge of her frosted-glass door.

"Sure thing." Angela typed a final sentence and entered the office.

"Well, you certainly brighten things up around here," Lila smiled, glancing at Angela's summer dress printed with pale blue and green flowers.

Angela smoothed her dress out as she sat down in a leather chair next to Lila's desk. "It's been so awfully hot lately, seems like the bright colors keep my mind off the heat."

"I just want you to know how much I appreciate your helping out around here." Lila stared at the bright window where a warm breeze stirred the diaphanous curtains.

"Oh, you don't have to thank me," Angela said in mild protest. "This has been one of the best things that's happened to me in a long time. I finally feel like I'm doing something worthwhile."

"That's certainly true," Lila replied with conviction. "I get more calls about J.T.'s articles than anything else. And we both know who's writing them."

"Why—J.T. is."

Lila smiled knowingly at Angela. "I've seen those notes of his that you type from. I have to admit that he knows how to collect some colorful information, but making a coherent news article out of them is an entirely different matter."

Angela blushed slightly.

"J.T.'s great verbally," Lila went on, "but he hasn't got the discipline or the inclination to put in the hard work it takes to get something ready for the presses."

"Well, I certainly couldn't do what he does—just go out there cold to homes and businesses and get people to open up their lives," Angela admitted.

"J.T. *is* good at that all right," Lila agreed. "He's certainly got the gift of gab. But even more than that, he genuinely cares about people—and they can tell."

Lila smoothed her hair and fidgeted with the cameo she wore on her linen jacket.

"What's really on your mind, Lila? It must be pretty serious." Angela had noticed how her brow was knitted with concern when she first entered the office.

"The same thing that's been there all along, I suppose." She gazed through the window at two fox squirrels chasing each other in quick spirals around the thick trunk of the oak. "Having to close down the *Journal.*"

Angela was surprised by her answer. "I thought you were doing much better!"

"Oh, we are," Lila admitted quickly. "But it's still not enough for the paper to make it on its own. I've been making up for the losses all along, but now my savings are exhausted."

"I've got some money!" Angela said ardently. "I'll be glad to help you out!" Then she leaned back in her chair, speaking more softly. "Morton was more than generous. I could never spend all that he left me."

Lila felt the warm flow of friendship, almost a living thing, from Angela. "That's awfully kind of you, Angela, but this is something that I have to do on my own."

"Aren't you selling enough papers?"

"We are under normal circumstances. But Dobe Jackson's offered my people more money than I could ever pay them—just to put me out of business." Lila shook her head slowly. "Of course when the competition's gone, he'll fire them all because he doesn't really need them in the first place. Right now, though, all they can see is that big paycheck."

"There must be *something* we can do."

"If I had another good man or two who knew something about

the newspaper business—layout, running the press, selling advertisements. Dobe's got them all sewn up though." Lila began to sort through some invoices on her desk. "In a couple of weeks, all that will be left is Henry and me."

"We just *can't* let this happen!" Angela assured Lila, her mouth set in determination. "I don't know how, but we've *got* to keep this paper going."

"I didn't expect you to be this upset about it, Angela," Lila remarked, a perplexed look on her face. "I guess I didn't know how much it meant to you."

Angela stood up and walked to the window where the breeze stirred her soft hair. "We're fighting a war for freedom. How can we just stand by and let a man like Dobe Jackson take over like he *owns* this town? You've got as much right to publish a newspaper as he does."

"Maybe you've forgotten something in your fervor for the *Journal*, Angela."

Angela turned to face Lila, a puzzled expression on her face. "What's that?"

"Dobe's got rights, too, which means he can use any *legal* means to put me out of business."

"But that's not fair."

"Yes it is." Lila smiled at Angela's passion to keep her in business. "This nation's economy is based on free enterprise. And I'd much rather see things the way they are than to have the alternative."

"Alternative?"

"Yes—government subsidies, which means government control of our businesses. That's when we truly lose our freedom. The next step would be some federal bureaucrat telling me what I can and can't print."

"I hadn't look at it that way."

That's exactly what happened under Hitler. People depended on government, in the form of der Führer, to be like a big daddy to them—to take care of all their needs. Well the price you pay for that is total loss of freedom."

Again Angela felt like a student in class rather than just a friend of Lila's.

"No sir," Lila continued passionately, "I'll take an old rascal like Dobe Jackson any day over some petty Washington lackey whose head would probably split wide open if an original thought ever got close to it."

"OK," Angela laughed. "We won't let anybody with a cardboard briefcase in the door."

"Agreed." Lila felt much better about the problems she faced now that she had shared them with Angela.

"But," Angela spoke with renewed determination, "we're going to keep this newspaper in business."

* * *

"You've just got to help her out, Clay!" Angela sat with him on the flagstone terrace behind the house. She had returned from the offices of the *Journal* just as the sun had vanished suddenly behind a distant stand of mimosa, leaving the sultry air bathed in a rose-colored glow.

Clay, his hair still wet from his shower, sat across from her drinking a tall glass of lemonade. He wore a clean white T-shirt and faded jeans, his long legs stretched out, bare feet resting on the cool smooth stone. "I don't know, Angela."

"But you already know about the newspaper business, and Dobe Jackson's stolen everybody else away from her." Angela poured herself some lemonade from the heavy glass pitcher she had brought outside.

Clay moved his glass slowly around in front of him, listening to the soft chinking of the ice cubes.

"Well?"

"I wouldn't be any good at it, Angela," Clay protested. "I've messed up at every job I've tried."

Angela stood up, frustrated by Clay's apathetic demeanor. "What are you going to do then? Give up on your whole life at the age of twenty?"

Taking a long swallow of his drink, Clay stared up at a bullbat flitting about erratically in the darkening air. "I just wouldn't want anybody depending on me."

Sitting back down, Angela crossed her legs and folded her arms across her breast. "I, I, I—me, me, me. That pretty well sums up your whole attitude, I guess."

Surprised at Angela's sudden anger, Clay stared at her face, almost lost in shadow. Still, he could see that her eyes held an intense light. "Why are you so mad at me? It's not like I promised to help Lila out of her trouble."

"No . . . you didn't, did you?" Angela stood up again and the last light gleamed in her hair. "I just realized myself why I'm so angry, Clay. Maybe it doesn't even have to do with Lila."

Clay watched Angela's graceful movements as she paced the terrace. "It's because you're a quitter!"

"What are you—"

"You would never have made it with the Red Sox!" Angela snapped. Pausing, she let the words sink in, watching the fire grow in Clay's eyes. "Even if you hadn't been wounded in this war, you'd have found some other excuse—just like you've found one for losing or quitting *all* your jobs."

Clay prepared to strike out at Angela, then he saw tears glistening faintly on her cheeks as she turned away from him.

Angela's voice grew more hushed as she continued to speak. "I'm sorry. It's none of my business what you do with your life." She paused briefly before continuing. "Life is so precious. I've learned that through this war . . . and other things. It just saddens me so to see it wasted."

A solitary crow sailed overhead, silhouetted against the pale sky; its harsh cry rang out across the quiet evening. Beyond the house, the streetlights were winking on one by one.

Angela stood very still for a few moments as though she were waiting to hear her cue in the next line of dialogue. Then she turned toward Clay, saw the emptiness in his face, glanced at the deep shadows beyond him, and hurried up the steps into the house.

Sitting very quietly, Clay tried to assimilate all that Angela had just said, as well as the things she had left unsaid. Now, after she had all but flayed him verbally, he felt for some inexplicable reason closer to her than he had to anyone in his life.

Clay had wanted to get up and take Angela in his arms, kiss her and hold her so close that she would feel like that part of him that he already considered her to be—but he merely sat and sipped his lemonade and watched the last of the rosy light fade into a deep midnight blue.

14

A HELPING HAND

"*F*ive of us and some neighborhood boys on their bicycles. Are we enough to keep the *Journal* going?" Lila lounged on the side of her desk, bumping one foot lazily against it as she spoke.

Henry sat in his chair as erect as a drill sergeant, his hair neatly combed and his black tie knotted tightly. "With a little help from Clay, I can keep the press humming. I won't need him full-time."

"I know I could handle all the commercial and out-of-town deliveries if I just had a truck." Clay sat on the hardwood floor, leaning back against the wall. He wore his Marine combat boots, jeans, and a fatigue shirt.

J.T. stood in the doorway wearing his midsummer outfit, the Harvard sweatshirt with the sleeves cut off and his usual khakis. "I think my old jalopy might do the trick."

"I thought the marshal impounded it a long time ago, J.T." Wearing jeans, a white blouse, and brown penny loafers, Angela sat on the floor next to Clay.

"The judge's order said that *I* can't drive it—didn't say anything about Clay."

"Is that the one parked on the side street next to your office, J.T.?" Lila asked.

"Yep. It's a beauty, ain't it?"

Lila shook her head. "I thought it was an abandoned wreck the town just hadn't gotten around to hauling off."

"Does it run at all, J.T.?" Clay leaned forward, elbows resting on his knees.

"Did when I parked it. At least I *think* it was running. It mighta been towed in. My head was kind of fuzzy that night," J.T. explained. "Now—who knows?"

"Well all it takes is fire and gas to get an engine running if it

175

ain't busted up somewhere." Clay felt encouraged now about the deliveries. "I can handle that part."

Lila gazed around the room at the little group of friends who had gathered to help her save the *Journal*. She felt extremely fortunate in spite of all her problems and realized that she would never trade places with Dobe Jackson. "All right, let's get ourselves organized."

"Take it away, boss lady," J.T. beamed with a quick nod and a wink in Lila's direction.

Lila frowned at him, then continued. "I'll handle the wire services and the government and police beats—they'll have to cooperate with me whether they like me or not since they're public servants."

"If they don't, we'll just put them on the front page. Tell the public they're un-American—trying to sabotage the freedom of the press," J.T. offered with a sly smile. "That's the one thing *all* politicians are afraid of—bad press."

"Will you still take care of the local color articles, J.T.?" Lila asked. "It looks like your idea is becoming the most popular part of the *Journal*."

"Long as Angela keeps typing them." J.T. smiled. "Maybe I oughta just admit it—*writing* them."

"You do all the work, J.T. I just kind of fit it together—like a jigsaw puzzle." Angela smiled.

"Everybody here knows where the *real* work comes in," J.T. admitted, "and since Angela does most of that, I've got plenty of time to sell advertising."

Lila gave him a puzzled look. "I thought you told me you had run out of prospects, J.T."

He scratched his head thoughtfully. "I've been studying on it some since then. Maybe there's a possibility or two that I've overlooked."

"I don't like that gleam in your eyes," Lila admonished. "Just what are you up to?"

"The American way of life, Lila, my love—uh, boss." J.T. cleared his throat, continuing in a more serious vein. "That's what we're fighting this war for, isn't it—democracy and free enterprise, good ol' American ingenuity?"

Lila gave him a level stare over the rim of her glasses. "Just don't do anything that you'd be ashamed of if your mother found out about it."

J.T. thought about that for a moment, rubbing his chin with the knuckle of his forefinger. "Hmm, I think I'd have to stay in bed all day to do that."

"Any other comments?" Lila had to admit that she enjoyed the challenge that lay ahead of her. Dobe Jackson had the power, the money, and the connections, but that just made it all the more interesting.

She thought back to her first days as a fledgling reporter on the Chicago *Tribune* and of how difficult it had been to be taken seriously in a man's world. It had been a long hard fight then, but she had proven herself in the end—and she had done it alone. Now she thought, glancing around the room, *How can I possibly lose when I have friends like these standing with me?*

"I'll be here every day to answer the phone, do the filing and typing—and whatever else you need." Angela had come to feel that Lila was almost like a second mother to her in the months she had been helping out part-time at the office.

Lila merely nodded at Angela, thankful for her friendship and for the changes that she had seen in her life. "Well, if everybody's clear on what they're doing, I guess we'd better get to work. We've got a newspaper to get out."

* * *

"Whadda you mean 'prescription to a newspaper?' I can't even read."

J.T. grinned at the bewildered expression on the sharp, pinched face of Moon Mullins, the local manufacturer and distributor of White Lightning. "It's *sub*scription, Moon, and I don't care whether you read it or not."

Moon perched on a stool in Shorty's Tavern. His whitish hair was slicked back from his low forehead, and his beady eyes and long pointed nose were directed at J.T. "What do I need it for then?"

"So you can do your part to support the war effort," J.T. answered flatly.

Moon tugged at one of his tiny ears and shook his head slowly. "I ain't gettin' this a'tall."

"You can read about the men from Liberty serving in the armed forces. There's an article on one of them in every issue," J.T. explained. "Maybe say a prayer for them."

"Who you kiddin'?" Moon stood up to leave. "I ain't listenin' to no more of this humbug."

As Moon turned toward Shorty, J.T. stared at the back of Moon's head. It looked as though a comb had never touched it although the rest was always slicked down perfectly. Rumor around town had it that Moon was too stupid to know he had hair on the back of his head. "Sit down!"

Surprised at the sharpness of J.T.'s voice, Moon immediately complied.

"Let me pose a question to you, Moon." J.T. frowned at the wail coming from the jukebox as Jimmie Rogers sang one of his songs about loneliness and dying.

"Whut?" Moon asked, his face sullen and sallow-looking in the dim light.

"What do you suppose would happen if the wrong person found out about your," J.T. clasped his hands together, resting his chin on them, "shall we say *clandestine* whiskey business?"

"Clan—whut?"

"Let's say, just for the sake of speculation, that a reporter found out about it and that it made the front page of the newspaper. What do you think would happen?"

"But Dobe . . ."

"I'm not talking about Dobe Jackson." J.T. waved the remark aside. "He'd lose too many of *his* customers if he put you out of business and cut off their supply of hooch."

"Ring wouldn't do nothin' neither," Moon said smugly. "He's in on the whole thing."

"No? I beg to disagree," J.T. said in exaggerated politeness. "I think the good women of Liberty would have our somewhat jaded town marshal tarred and feathered if they found out he was letting you slide because you give him a free bottle now and then. They'd probably do the same thing to anybody else associated with such a shoddy affair. Ring would have you in the calaboose before you could say, 'Still—what still?'"

"Half the town already knows whut's going on," Moon

boasted, grinning slyly at Shorty. "Ain't nobody never done nothin' to stop me yet."

"He's right," Shorty agreed.

"Good point," J.T. admitted, then paused for effect while both men leaned toward him for the finish. "But if it made the papers—the powers that be would *have* to do something about it—and you know it, too."

Moon bared his tiny rodentlike teeth. "This sounds like blackmail to me. I thought that lady that runs the *Journal* was supposed to be such a good Christian woman—churchgoing and all that."

"Oh, she is! Make no doubt about that, Moon," J.T. nodded. "But I'm not!"

"If she's so all-fired righteous how come she ain't done something? It's her newspaper, ain't it?"

"Right again. And if she knew about what you did for a living and how many of Liberty's fair citizens were supporting you, she'd have the whole mess out in the open so fast you wouldn't know what hit you." J.T. stood up, walked over to the jukebox, and unplugged it. The record ground down to a dull growl and stopped.

Moon glanced back at Shorty who shrugged and busied himself rinsing glasses.

"But she *doesn't* know," J.T. continued in the sudden, heavy silence of the tavern as he walked deliberately back over to the bar, "and I don't think you or Ring or a lot of other people want her to find out."

Moon reached into his back pocket and took out his wallet. "How much for one of them prescriptions?"

"It's not quite that simple, Moon."

"Whut?"

"You got forty, maybe fifty regular customers on your route. I think every *one* of 'em needs a *prescription*. All that don't already have one."

"Are you crazy?" Moon glanced over at Shorty as though pleading for help. "I can't make 'em do that!"

"Nothing to it," J.T. grinned. "And since you're such a good friend, I've got it all figured out for you."

Moon lay his head on the edge of the bar, then sat up quickly. "This is the worst day of my life!"

"Oh, come on, Moon," J.T. encouraged. "Think of it as your patriotic duty."

Moon stared at the bright rectangle of the front door as though wishing he could be someplace else.

"All you have to do," J.T. continued in a reassuring voice, "is offer your customers a discount on their whiskey if they'll take the *Journal*. Tell them it's so they can keep up with what's happening with our fighting men from Liberty. Nobody could turn that down—especially when your discount pays for the newspaper."

"That'll ruin me!"

"No it won't, and you know it," J.T. said matter-of-factly, motioning for Shorty to bring him another Coke. "You're making a killing. Besides you can bump the prices up a little in six months or so, and nobody'll know the difference."

Moon stared at the bottle of Coke that Shorty placed on the counter in front of J.T. "That stuff must be doing something bad inside your head, J.T. Never saw a man yet quit drinking and didn't go kindly nuts. Maybe you oughta take it up agin."

"So—how many prescriptions can I count on for you and your customers, Moon?"

"I'll let you know Monday."

"Splendid!" J.T. turned toward Shorty.

"Put me down for one. I'll make Edna read it to me."

*   *   *

After showering, Clay dressed in his faded jeans, white T-shirt and Marine boots with their straps and buckles on the sides. He had always liked their distinctive look, and the boots were the most comfortable footwear he had ever owned. On the way out the door he glanced back at the alarm clock next to his bed. *Midnight—what a time to be going to work!*

Stepping out onto the landing, Clay felt the sultry night air against his skin like a warm, damp cloth. The stars looked hot and white in the sky. Only the moon seemed cold and remote, bathing the world in a bluish light.

Clay stopped in surprise at the bottom of the stairs. Sitting on the back of J.T.'s battered old pickup with her legs dangling over the tailgate, Angela looked dreamlike, her face and bare arms almost luminescent in the pale moonlight.

"What in the world are you doing up?" Clay asked as soon as he found his voice.

"Same as you. Going to work." Angela wearing her work outfit—white tennis shoes, jeans, and a sleeveless cotton blouse—glanced upward. "Isn't this beautiful?"

Clay walked over to the truck. his face dark under the moon. "Angela, I'm afraid you don't know what's in store for you. This is backbreaking work we're talking about."

Angela smiled brightly at him. "You think I'm over the hill at twenty-four?"

"No—you are most *definitely* not over the hill," Clay assured her, glancing at her trim figure. "You're what? Five-three and maybe a hundred and five pounds."

"Close. Maybe you ought to get a job guessing weights at the carnival."

Clay smiled at her. "OK, you win. Let's hope you can keep that sense of humor after tossing those bundles of newspapers around in ninety-five degree heat." He checked the wooden sideframes he had pieced together from scrap lumber and attached to the truck.

They climbed into the cab. Clay touched the starter and the engine roared into life.

"You really do know about engines, don't you?"

"Everybody knows a little something." Clay eased the transmission into first with a clunk. Pulling around from the side of the garage through the portico, he drove down the long driveway to the street.

Angela took a red Thermos bottle from the floorboard, unscrewed the top and poured steaming coffee into a cup. "Here, this ought to get your heart pumping."

Clay took it, sipping the hot coffee carefully. "Mm, that's good! It's strong, but it doesn't have a bite to it—that's a hard formula to come by."

"Eggshells."

"What?"

"I put a spoonful of ground-up eggshell in with the coffee. They cut down on the acid."

Clay leaned on the window ledge with his elbow, letting the

sticky night air cool him as they rode through the quiet, darkened streets. A dog barked in the distance. The streetlights looked misty in the dampness.

"It's got to rain today as hot and sticky as it is already," Clay remarked.

Angela wiped her forehead with a delicate lace-trimmed handkerchief. "I feel like we're riding around underwater."

Noticing the flash of white in Angela's hand, Clay reached down on the floorboard, picked up two fluffy white towels, and dropped them on the seat next to her. "I think you'll find one of these more practical later on."

"I think you're right." Angela took the cup from Clay and sipped the remainder of his coffee. She felt a thrill of excitement at being out in the early darkness, of riding the deserted streets, thinking of all the people still asleep in their beds. It made her feel useful—a necessary part of the town—and important to the lives of the people she worked with. She had longed for this sense of belonging all her life, and the taste of it was like nectar.

Angela glanced over at Clay, who looked relaxed and casual behind the wheel. Somehow he always seemed to maintain that calm exterior even when she knew there was a torrent of emotion raging inside of him. She never failed to notice the tiny crook in his right elbow, thinking of how that slight and barely detectable angle between shoulder and wrist had changed the course of his life.

* * *

"Well, that's the last one." Clay fit the final bale of newspapers securely onto the last stack on the pickup. Tying a rope to the frame, he tossed an end to the other side and started to walk around to secure the papers in place.

"I've got it over here," Angela called out, slipping the rope through the rail and tossing the end back to Clay. "You handle that side."

Clay knew that Angela was already exhausted from helping him load the truck. He had tried to get her to take a break, but she had refused, except to get water. "You keep this up and you might have a real future hauling papers, Mrs. Spain."

Angela's voice was throaty from exertion. "That's not especially

182

funny right now. Why don't you try me after I've had a hot shower and eight hours of sleep?"

"We're just beginning *this* day's fun," Clay taunted. "It's not even three o'clock yet."

Glancing up at the moon's slow drift through its sea of stars, Angela wondered if she had overestimated her endurance. "Don't worry, I'll make it."

After securing the load, Clay vaulted up on the side of the concrete loading dock. Reaching down to Angela, he pulled her up beside him. "You sure you can make it the rest of the day?"

Angela nodded, not wanting to waste her breath.

"Gonna be another hot one!" Henry walked out the open double doors that led onto the dock at the back of the building. As always, with his fresh shave and neatly combed hair, he looked as though he had just stepped out of the shower.

Clay glanced over his shoulder at him, then beyond into the building where the stacked cylinders of newsprint stood in formation like Henry's infantry. "Yep. 'Course it's only three months until October. Don't you ever sleep?"

"On occasion. I try not to make a habit of it though," Henry replied, setting a gallon jug of ice water and two Dixie cups down next to Clay.

"Why come in so early?"

"For one thing, I like to have at least one person around the place all the time. I don't trust our competition to fight fairly." Henry stared off beyond the glare of the loading dock into the night as though expecting an attack. "That Dobe Jackson's got the same gleam in his eyes as Mussolini."

"Oh, come on, Henry," Angela admonished gently. "He can't be *that* bad."

Henry shrugged. "I had to replace some bearings in the press anyway."

"Well, we'd better get on the road." Clay hopped down and offered to help Angela.

She handed him the water jug and cups instead and leaped down herself.

"That's good," Clay encouraged her, walking around to the truck. "I like an independent woman."

"Oh, Clay . . ." Henry called out.

Clay paused, his foot on the truck's running board, the water jug cradled under his arm.

"What time do you think you'll get finished?"

"Oughta be back around ten."

"I'm gonna need your help for two or three hours," Henry said, glancing back into the building at the press, like a mother hen keeping watch over a baby chick.

"Fine."

"You'll still have three or four hours to catch some sleep before you have to be back here to help me with the evening run." Henry grinned. "We don't want you getting bedsores."

"Fat chance."

"And, Angela . . ."

"Yes, Henry, I know," Angela moaned. "Lila needs me to do some typing for her and to try to make some sense out of J.T.'s latest pile of gobbledy-gook."

"Right you are," Henry chirped cheerfully. "I'm so glad we're all volunteers in this outfit."

Angela got through the next few hours on sheer determination. They had visited what seemed to her every business in three counties although they never actually left the Liberty city limits. She felt that she would see shadowed loading ramps and overgrown alleyways in her dreams. She carried bundles of newspapers until her arms ached like fire and felt like lead.

At seven o'clock they finished the town route and headed out into the country. Now the stops would be much farther apart and they'd have time to catch their breath in between them. Angela had never felt so exhausted in her life. She steeled herself for the first stop when she would again slide out of the blessed refuge of the truck seat, take a bundle from Clay after he scrambled up into the truck bed to begin the unloading, and stumble with it to the drop-off point.

They pulled into the graveled parking area in front of Three Corners' Grocery just as the sun climbed above a distant treeline. After leaving three bundles on the benches next to the front door, she climbed wearily back into the truck. Already the air was becoming stifling from the sun's brief appearance.

Clay poured her a cup of water. The remaining ice clinked against the side of the glass jug. "You tired?"

Accepting the water, Angela thought it had the feel of a lead bar as she lifted it to her mouth. "Who me? No, I'm fine. Why do you ask?"

Clay shrugged, started the truck, and pulled out onto the highway. Two minutes later, driving into the red glare of sunlight, he caught a slight movement out of the corner of his eye.

Angela, still holding a half cup of water, had slid quietly down the backrest until her head rested on the seat next to Clay. The water gurgled softly onto the floor of the truck.

Clay gazed at the long dark lashes that curved across the delicate skin beneath her closed eyes. Taking both hands off the steering wheel briefly, he folded the cleanest of the two towels and slipped it beneath her head. With his free hand, he smoothed her hair gently in place.

Three hours later, Angela was still sleeping peacefully as Clay backed the truck up next to the loading ramp behind the *Journal*.

15

A PALE AND
SILVER SHINING

"What a day!" Clay pulled the pickup beneath the portico and leaned on the steering wheel with both elbows.

Angela gave him a tired smile. "Think on the bright side. Henry didn't have any work for you and Lila said that I was all caught up, too—for today."

"You're right," Clay yawned. "Now I can sleep six, maybe even seven hours till I have to go back in and help him with the evening's run."

"J.T.'s doing a great job of getting new subscriptions, but it sure makes our route longer." Angela gazed at Clay's clean profile against the midmorning sun that blazed beyond the shadowed portico. She found herself attracted to his humor, his honesty, and the quiet strength of his ways, but she fought against the warmth that stirred inside her each time they were together. Always the shadow of that fatal and unbearable afternoon fell between them. Guilt bound her as securely as chains.

Clay grinned obliquely at Angela, his teeth white against his tanned face. "That rascal's pulling some kind of shenanigans to sell as many newspapers as he is. I don't know what, but I bet you Lila would skin him if she found out."

Angela gazed through the cracked windshield at the periwinkles growing near the far edge of the terrace. Even in the hot August sunshine, they appeared as cool as early frost. "I think these past few weeks have been some of the best times I've had in my whole life."

Caught off guard, Clay leaned back against the torn seat cover

187

without comment, staring at Angela's flushed face, feeling the almost physical presence of her emotion.

"I never had any close friends before." Quickly she turned away and wiped her face with a towel. Then she glanced over at Clay, her eyes shining with simple happiness. "I've even enjoyed running this miserably hot and tiring route with you. I think I just realized it."

Clay cleared his throat. He wanted to tell her that when he awakened in the hot, hard hours of the night when the protean shapes in the darkness closed in on him that a single thought of her always put his mind as ease and sleep once again became his friend. A dozen thoughts swirled in his mind, but he merely said, "You enjoy this?"

"Strangely enough—I do."

Clay couldn't bring himself to admit that the very best time of the day for him was bounding down the stairs at midnight and catching his first glimpse of her waiting for him on the tailgate of the truck. It made him spring from bed with the first ring of the alarm clock and caused him to sing badly and off-key and with unabandoned joy in the shower. "Well, they say simple pleasures are best. This sure isn't complicated."

"But it's fun."

"If you say so."

"Gets you in shape, too," Angela continued espousing the merits of hard work. "After three weeks of this, I feel better than I ever have, that is when I get a chance to rest."

"If I could teach a mule to drive this truck, you'd have another partner real quick."

Angela laughed softly, stretched lazily, and got out of the truck. Then she turned and leaned back through the window. "You want some breakfast?"

"Sure."

"Good. Let's get cleaned up; I'll see you in the kitchen in thirty minutes."

"It's a date." Clay felt uneasy at the sound of the word, but shrugged it off.

After a quick shower and a fifteen-minute rest, Clay put on jeans and a Marine T-shirt. Heading downstairs in his bare feet, he walked over to the house and knocked on the back door.

"It's open."

Entering the dim, shadowy foyer, he walked down the hall to the kitchen.

"Bacon, eggs over easy, toast, fresh-squeezed orange juice, and plenty of hot coffee. How's that sound?" Angela stood in front of the stove lifting bacon out of a large iron skillet with a fork, her face shiny clean from the shower. She had put on a pink cotton blouse, jeans, and white sandals.

Clay poured a cup of coffee from the big pot on the stove and sat down at the table. "No thanks. I'll just have a cold piece of corn pone."

Angela ignored his corny remark, breaking two eggs into the skillet, which popped and hissed.

"Grease is too hot."

"Really. You want to try it?"

Clay got up and crossed to the stove, where he lifted the skillet off the burner and turned the gas down. After allowing the skillet to cool briefly, he set it back down on the fire and splashed grease gently over both eggs until they turned the color of their shells flecked with bits of bacon.

"Not bad. The edges aren't crispy like when I fry them," Angela admitted.

"Learned it doing KP in the Marines." Just the sound of the word *Marines* took the edge off the pleasant sensation Clay had been experiencing by being with Angela.

Clay finished the cooking and put the food on the table. As they ate at the long table in the shadowed kitchen, he fought against the memories that had surfaced unbidden and unwanted.

Overhead the wooden blades of a fan hanging down from the high ceiling circled slowly, stirring the warm air. Their conversation had slowed down to a trickle and then dried up completely. Down the long hallway a grandfather clock ticked off the minutes with polished precision.

Almost without warning, a thunderhead rolled up from the south, darkening the air as the temperature dropped fifteen degrees in five minutes. Through the tall windows, a white web of lightning flashed against a black wall of clouds. A peal of thunder rolled over the house like a wave of sound, rattling the glass panes in their hardwood frames.

Angela dropped her fork on the plate, jumped up, and ran

over to the open window. In the wind, the long curtains were streaming into the room. "Oh, this is so beautiful!"

Clay watched Angela's hair blow wildly about her face and shoulders. The air seemed charged with the full force of the electrical storm.

Angela sensed Clay's presence before he touched her. Then she felt his lips brushing gently against the pale curve of her neck as he lifted the soft dark mass of hair aside. She remained motionless before the open window as the wind blew a fine cool mist against the warm skin of her face.

Turning to him, Angela lifted up on tiptoe as he kissed her gently, his hand cradling the small of her back. She circled his lean waist with her arms, lost in the urgent demand of his lips. Suddenly a bolt of lighting, popping like the sharp crack of a rifle, snapped off an oak limb. It crashed down with a heavy crunching sound just outside the window.

Angela pulled away, breathless in the sweep of the storm, still lost in the sudden wonder of their embrace. She stared out at the storm, at the gray and misty sheet of rain moving across the wide lawn toward them. Torn between passion and her newfound faith, she trembled before the fury of the storm that raged without and the one that raged within. Even after the miracle of that snowy Christmas in Ollie's Drugstore, she felt burdened by a guilt so dark and heavy that she had told no one about it, but it gnawed at her peace of mind like a furtive rodent.

Taking Clay's hand, Angela felt its strength and its tenderness. She ran her fingertips along a vein that traveled the back of his hand from the knuckle of his ringfinger to the wrist. Without speaking or looking into his face, she turned quickly and left the kitchen, running down the long hall toward her bedroom.

Clay remained at the window, listening to the rain pound flatly on the stone terrace and rush in torrents down the metal gutters. He walked to the hallway and stared after Angela. Then he let himself out through the back door into the cool driving rain.

* * *

In the long refreshing shadows of late afternoon, Angela sat on the terrace. A tall glass of iced tea made a wet ring on the marble-topped table beside her. The storm had left the town wet and glistening in the late sunlight. Leaves and tree limbs lay scattered across the property.

Angela watched a blue jay, its wings glinting like cobalt in the last slanting rays of sunlight, lift from a low branch and sail out of sight beyond the high eaves of the house. She picked up her glass and took a small sip, savoring the sweet, comforting flavor of the iced tea, which she associated with many of her good memories. For half an hour she had been glancing every minute or two at the empty stairs leading up to the garage apartment.

"My, that certainly looks refreshing!" Lila remarked as she came around the corner of the house. Wearing a tan suit and white blouse, she looked the picture of the successful businesswoman.

"It surely is. Here have some." Angela poured her a glass of tea.

Lila glanced at the extra glass near the chair across from Angela. "You're not expecting someone are you?"

Angela couldn't stop herself from taking a quick look at the stairs. "No."

Sitting down, Lila surveyed the littered yard. "That storm made a mess, didn't it?"

"Oh, Amos will have it cleaned up in no time. He's the best worker I know," Angela paused briefly, her eyes growing suddenly dark, "except for Clay."

"He does earn a day's pay, doesn't he?" Lila agreed. "By the way, where is he? I'm surprised he's not having a little refreshment out here with you before he has to go back and help Henry get tonight's run going."

"Resting, I suppose."

"Are you two getting along all right?"

Angela glanced again at the stairs. "Oh, sure. We get along just fine."

"Well, if you don't, you're certainly putting on a good act every time I see you together." Lila could see the uneasiness in Angela's manner but didn't want to interfere with her private life. "You actually seem to enjoy all the hard work."

"I do."

Angela glanced up at Lila, then took a swallow of her drink. "It's so beautiful after the storm. The whole world looks so clean and smells so fresh."

Lila gazed out at the shining wet trees and flowers. "You can almost understand why God destroyed the world once with water. I'm sure the whole earth must have looked brand new after the flood subsided."

Angela nodded, making circles of water on the tabletop with the bottom of her glass.

Lila decided that Angela needed to talk about something, but that she was having difficulty admitting it, even to herself. "Is there something I can do for you, Angela? You seem to have something on your mind."

"Oh, I don't know. Maybe it's the way I'll always be." Angela pushed the glass away from her.

"Is it Clay?"

Angela lifted her eyes, a lingering sadness in their depths. "No, Clay's fine."

"The last thing I want to do is interfere in your life. If I can't help you, I certainly don't want to do anything that would upset you."

Angela knew that Lila respected her privacy. She also knew that she could confide in her, and she suddenly felt the need to do just that.

"Sometimes it helps to talk, but not always. Maybe you'd rather be alone."

"No!" Angela blurted out. "I've been alone quite enough in my life."

Lila sipped her tea, gazing at a fleecy line of clouds just above the horizon. The westering sun had touched their edges with the color of ripe peaches.

"I . . ." Angela started to speak, but couldn't seem to go on. "It's hard to explain."

Lila knew the words would come, and determined that she would put no pressure on Angela.

"I'm a Christian now and I have a peace that could only come from God. But I can't forget what I was in the past, all the times that I . . ."

Lila gave Angela a reassuring nod as Angela glanced up at her, brushing her hair back from her face.

"That afternoon in that awful place when Morton—sometimes I go for a day or two without thinking of it, but it always comes back—especially right before I go to bed." Angela took a swallow of tea, and continued, her voice calmer now. "But after I pray, I just drift right off to sleep."

Lila thought she understood Angela's problem. "Angela, you came under conviction when you accepted Jesus Christ as your Savior. That's why you felt sorry for the things you had done wrong. *That* comes from the Holy Spirit."

"That seems to be just about the way I remember it," Angela nodded with interest.

"But what you're feeling now is guilt about things that you've already confessed, about things that you've already been forgiven for. And that guilt does *not* come from God."

Angela listened attentively, leaning forward on the edge of her chair.

"What you're feeling is just a pack of lies that the devil is telling you to try and tear apart your faith, to rob you of the peace and joy of your new life," Lila continued. "The Bible tells us that Jesus washed us from our sins in his own blood. As far as God is concerned they're gone. So why should *you* worry yourself about them?"

A smile had gradually brightened Angela's face as Lila spoke to her. "You're exactly right. Why *should* I worry?"

"I know it must be especially painful to you when you're around Clay."

Angela nodded.

"You don't have to carry this burden around any longer, Angela."

A bright tear ran quickly down Angela's cheek. She wiped it away, still smiling.

"Just lay it at the foot of the cross."

"I will," Angela whispered.

Lila found as always that when she shared her faith it made her spirit lift within her. "I always like to listen to what Jesus has to say about whatever it is that's bothering us."

Angela felt the heaviness of her guilt lifting as though a weight were being taken off her heart.

Closing her eyes, Lila spoke in a voice that was clear and strong and lilting, "'Come unto me, all ye that labour and are heavy laden, and I will give you rest. Take my yoke upon you, and learn of me; for I am meek and lowly in heart: and ye shall find rest unto your souls.'"

Angela could almost see Jesus in his coarse robes and dusty sandals on a rocky hillside in Galilee, speaking to the multitude of fishermen and farmers and shepherds. Mothers called their children from play, settling them down with the family as they listened to this man who spoke as no man ever had.

Lila, opening her eyes, gazed serenely at Angela. "And then Jesus said, 'For my yoke is easy, and my burden is light.' And it is, it surely is."

The two women sat together, speaking quietly, sharing the ineffable joy of their faith. Then Lila stood up, laying one hand against Angela's forehead and raising the other toward the darkening sky. After a moment Angela stood up. The two of them embraced quickly before Lila walked away down the sidewalk that led around the house.

Ten minutes later, Clay bounded down the steps and ran to the truck.

"Clay . . ."

With his hand on the door, Clay paused. "What is it? I'm running late now."

Angela poured her glass full of tea, added a few half-melted ice cubes, and took it over to the truck. "Thought you might be a little thirsty."

Clay took the tea quickly, drinking half of it without taking the glass from his mouth. "Mm . . . that's just what I needed." He finished the cool liquid and handed the glass back to Angela.

Without any warning, Angela put her arms around his neck and kissed him firmly on the mouth. Pulling away, she smiled up at him. "I thought you might like that, too."

Clay's eyes were wide with surprise; the glass dangled limply in his outstretched hand. "What was that for?"

"Because I enjoyed it."

"But I thought . . ."

Angela took the glass from his hand. "You'd better hurry. Henry's waiting."

"Oh, yeah." Thoroughly confused, Clay slid into the truck and banged the door shut.

"What time do you think you'll be finished tonight?" Angela walked around to the other side of the truck and sat down on the stairs.

"Shouldn't be too long," Clay replied, hardly knowing what to expect next.

"Could you give me a time please?"

"Eight-thirty."

"Good. I don't want the steaks to get cold," Angela smiled wistfully.

"Steaks?"

"You do like porterhouse, don't you?"

"Well, sure, but—"

"Don't be late then."

* * *

The bleachers carried a faint smell of popcorn, chewing gum, and spilled Cokes from the summer baseball season. The storm seemed to have washed the sky so clean that the stars sparkled with a newfound brilliance. With the approach of September, the smell of sweet olive had disappeared from the air, but it lingered still in Clay's memory.

"You aren't much on egg frying, but you sure know what to do with a steak. I'm full as a tick." Clay sat on the second-to-last bleacher, leaning back on his elbows.

Next to him, Angela propped her feet on the weathered plank in front of her, watching the moon rise behind several thin strands of cloud. In its pale and silver shining, they took on the appearance of winter frost.

"Did you hear me?"

Angela turned. "You ate all of yours and half of mine—that's compliment enough."

"I guess it is at that," Clay grinned.

Angela returned to her cloud watching.

Clay leaned forward and took Angela's small hand. His own, hard and tanned, almost completely covered it. "I'm glad you told me about your talk with Lila."

"I am, too," Angela replied softly, still staring out into the night sky.

Clay felt a tenderness toward Angela that he never would have imagined himself capable of. He wanted to spend the rest of his life with her, to keep her safe, to wake each morning and see her next to him. "I didn't mean to upset you this morning in the kitchen, Angela. I just . . ."

Angela patted the top of his hand, then rubbed it gently, feeling the soft texture of the fine sun-bleached hair against her fingertips.

"I hope things are all right between us now."

"It wasn't your fault at all, Clay," Angela assured him, "and things are just fine between us."

Feeling awkward, Clay had no words to express the emotion that rose in his chest. It was almost like the tingling excitement he felt before he walked out to the pitcher's mound at the beginning of a game, but stronger and more enduring. He thought that nothing could ever change it, that Angela must surely feel it pulsing through his hand.

"I'm glad things are going well at the *Journal*," Clay finally said, "for Lila's sake."

In the moonlight, Angela's face looked as placid as the surface of a still woodland pool. "I am too. As hard as she's worked, she surely deserves it."

Clay suddenly realized what Angela had meant about actually enjoying all the hard work. All his life, work had been something necessary, something that was expected and required. It was how you got what you wanted out of life. But somehow the past few weeks had been much different and he finally saw it. "You know you're right."

"About what?"

"About all this hard work we've been doing," Clay continued. "It is fun!"

Angela gave the moon a thoughtful glance. "I think it's because we're almost like a little family—the five of us."

"I think you're right. Even when I was pitching, I don't think I really enjoyed the *game*. I was always thinking of what I could get for myself if I worked hard enough: money, a big expensive car, my name in the newspapers."

"Maybe the difference is who you're working for," Angela suggested.

"And who I'm working *with*," Clay added. He gazed out at the darkened baseball diamond. "Maybe I won't miss it nearly as much as I thought I would."

Angela leaned against him as they sat alone in the bleachers in the silver moonlight.

16

CLOSE TO THE HEART

"Nothing like a good piece of hickory." J.T. twisted the ax handle in both hands, feeling the balance and the smoothly sanded texture of the wood.

Clay sat on the floor, leaning back against a cool steel beam just inside the doors that led to the loading dock. He tapped the end of his bat once on the concrete floor. "You're wrong there, Counselor. Nothing beats ash."

"Well, I hope we don't get the chance to find out which one's best tonight," J.T. admitted.

"You really think they'll come?"

"Who knows?" J.T. stood up and gazed out a back window, sparkling clean thanks to Lila's constant attention to the building.

"Well, if they don't show up tonight, then they won't show at all," Clay muttered. "They know this is the only night the press isn't running."

J.T. glanced at his watch in the anemic light from the window, then sat back down. "I don't usually put much stock in what Shorty picks up from that bunch of pulpwood haulers and out-of-work gas-station attendants that hang around his place, but he said this was the real thing."

"How does he know what the 'real thing' is?" Clay had no confidence at all in the crew from Shorty's, having been one of them himself in the past.

"Volume, I believe," J.T. explained briefly. "Said that *everybody* seemed to know about it."

"Maybe somebody went on a recruiting campaign there," Clay ventured. "Shorty's would be a likely place to find men looking for a quick buck for thirty minutes' work. There's a lot of traffic up and down that highway, men just passing through on their way to who knows where."

* * *

They came at one-thirty-eight. J.T. heard a muffled curse as one of them stumbled over something at the foot of the loading dock. He glanced over at Clay who was dozing, his head slumped down on his shoulder.

J.T. put his hand over Clay's mouth. He motioned for him to be quiet when he awakened with a start, then pointed toward the outside. Clay nodded and stood up.

Easing over to the window, J.T. peered out. In the deep shadows cast by a feeble bulb that hung from a long cord over the loading dock, he saw the three men, dressed in heavy coats with felt hats pulled low over their faces. They lurked near the ramp as though planning their course of action. Then they walked cautiously toward the back door, glancing furtively about. One was a tall brute of a man, the other two short—one slim and the other stocky. All three carried sledgehammers over their shoulders.

J.T. and Clay positioned themselves on either side of the door. Outside, a bolt cutter snapped through the padlock. The door opened slowly, letting a narrow beam of light into the murky darkness. The stocky man appeared first, glancing from side to side then entering the room silently followed by the slim one. Both moved slowly toward the printing press.

Waving Clay off, J.T. shouldered his ax handle. As the big man took his first step inside, J.T. swung the ax handle as hard as he could, cutting the man's legs out from under him. With a terrible roar he landed heavily on the concrete floor. Sprawled in the long, thin rectangle of light, he turned over quickly, his sledgehammer raised above his head.

Clay's bat crashed down on the man's right hand, crushing it with a sound like twigs snapping. The hammer rattled into the darkness as the man bellowed in pain.

J.T. had already turned toward the other two who stood frozen at the edge of the light. Leaving the big man on the floor, writhing and moaning in pain, Clay joined J.T., fanning out to his left in a flanking movement.

The two men, jerking their heads in every direction now looking for a way out, knew their situation as well as J.T. and Clay did. The heavy sledgehammers were perfect for demolishing the printing press but were far too clumsy to wield in hand-to-hand combat against their two opponents who now faced them holding lighter weapons.

In desperation, the stocky man charged Clay, swinging his hammer in a roundhouse motion. Clay easily sidestepped the blow as the hammer swished past his head then slammed his bat against the man's back as he went by. His breath went out of him in a rush as the blow sent him skittering across the concrete floor where he lay gasping for air.

Twenty-five feet away, J.T., holding his ax handle loosely in front of his chest, closed in on the third man.

Suddenly the door to the front office swung open, sending a glare of light into the darkness. Henry stood in front of the opening, squinting through his glasses at the shadowy figures in the cavernous room.

Seeing his only means of escaping the fate of his two fellows, the third man rushed for the lighted door, his heavy hammer held high.

"Get out of his way!" J.T. yelled at Henry. "Let him get past you!"

Confused as well as protective of his printing press, Henry stepped forward in an effort to stop the man. In doing so the neat little printer from Chicago wrote his own epitaph.

The heavy hammer crushed through the layer of bone above Henry's left ear as if it were an eggshell. He crumpled instantly to the floor as the man threw the hammer into the darkness and flashed through the open door to the lighted reception area and out the front door.

J.T. dropped to Henry's side, lifted his head in his arms then looked away, his face ashen.

Clay stood above them. "Is he . . . ?"

J.T.'s expression answered the question.

A frenzy of memories flashed through Clay's mind—of the nights he and Henry had spent running the press for the next day's edition. He pictured the man's intensity as he huddled over his machine.

In a rage, Clay raced out of the building, looking for the man who had robbed him of a friend. He searched several yards and ran to the end of the block, but he had vanished into the darkness.

When Clay returned, he saw J.T. still sitting on the floor, cradling Henry's head in his lap. The other two men, battered by ax handle and bat, had made their escape unnoticed.

* * *

"Remember the time Henry had the press all ready to run the morning edition, and I told him I forgot about picking up those last ten rolls of newsprint down at the depot?" Wearing his black suit with his tie loosened, Clay sat on the couch next to Angela in her huge living room. "You know how he thought the world would end if those papers were a *minute* late coming off the press. I never saw him so mad."

Angela slipped her high heels off and folded her legs under her on the couch, remembering that day, in a time of remembrance the four of them were now sharing. "I never will forget that. Henry picked up a wrench and chased you all the way out to the back fence before you finally showed him those rolls of newsprint in the back of the pickup."

Sipping her coffee from a thin, gold-rimmed cup, Lila spoke in a voice that was little more than a whisper. "If it hadn't been for Henry, I never would have made it with the *Tribune*. He'd come up to the newsroom almost every day to show me the ropes. He'd been with the paper so long, he knew the business inside out. But seeing the finished product rolling off those big presses—that was his one great love."

"What are we gonna do about Dobe Jackson?" J.T. stood at one of the tall windows, watching a mockingbird dive like a fighter plane at a gray squirrel who had climbed the wrong tree. "We *can't* just let him get away with this."

After a momentary silence, Angela spoke for the three of them. "We have to let the law handle it, J.T."

"The law! You mean Ring Clampett?" J.T. turned from the

window, his eyes narrowed in anger. "Ring couldn't find a chicken in a henhouse with a book of instructions. How's he going to find the men who murdered Henry? And that's the *only* way we'll nail Jackson—through them."

"I'm not so sure we could tie him to it even if they *were* caught." Lila turned toward J.T., motioning for him to come sit beside her.

J.T. walked over almost obediently and sat down on the sofa next to her.

"It's an imperfect world, J.T., even in our justice system. But you know that better than any of us." Lila put her hand on his shoulder. "Dobe Jackson's too smart to let himself be directly connected to men like *those* three."

"We all know he was behind it though. He was the only one with a motive." J.T. insisted, his voice rising in anger. "The whole town knows."

"Exactly," Lila said in a level voice.

Angela noticed the portent in Lila's tone. "What are you getting at, Lila?"

"I think the *town's* going to take care of Dobe Jackson," Lila explained. "Oh, they're not going to lock him up or strap him into the electric chair, but a kind of justice *will* be served. I have that much confidence in the people of Liberty."

Clay sat forward on the edge of the sofa. "I still don't understand what you mean."

"It's beginning already." Lila stared at a painting on the opposite wall. It depicted an old man in rough clothes who carried an obviously full bucket up a winding hillside path toward a cabin nestled in the trees. For some reason he reminded her of Henry.

"What's beginning?" J.T. blurted out, growing impatient with Lila's enigmatic answers.

"The supervisor of the *Herald*'s printroom called me about a job."

"He's been there since Jackson took over the newspaper," J.T. remarked in total surprise. "What did you tell him?"

"I told him he had a job."

"That's great!" Clay added. "Now we can keep the press rolling right along."

"You're starting to sound like Henry," Angela grinned.

"Some of the others have called, too." Lila added, still staring at the painting.

J.T. motioned toward Lila with his hand and his head. "They called and . . ."

"I can hire one or two more," Lila continued. "Another reporter maybe and someone to help with the deliveries since Clay's going to be the senior man in the printing section now. But we'll really have to expand to put on many more people."

"Anything else?" J.T. asked.

Angela placed her cup back in the saucer with a soft tinkling sound. "I heard a few people at the funeral say they're canceling their subscriptions to the *Herald*."

"I heard the same thing," J.T. added, "but I didn't think much about it."

"Me, too," Clay put in. "Maybe the town *will* punish Dobe."

"Dobe's had his own way around here for a long time now." J.T. stared at the painting of the old man carrying his bucket. "I guess maybe ordinary people *can* make a difference—if they get a belly full of somebody—and if they stick together."

"I'm speaking almost as an outsider," Lila observed solemnly. "But maybe in a way that gives me an advantage over the three of you. This town's got its share of villains just like every other town, I suppose, but for some reason, I've got confidence that when it comes to something important, like fighting a war against Hitler or uniting against *another* tyrant like Dobe Jackson, the people of Liberty will take charge and put them *both* out of business."

"Can I back up just a little, Lila?" Clay asked, a slight frown on his face.

"Surely."

"Did I hear you say I'd be the senior man in the printing section?"

"That's right," Lila nodded. "The man from the *Herald* will be your assistant."

"But he knows ten times as much as I do about the newspaper business."

"Doesn't matter. You've got seniority on him and you're learning quickly." Lila smiled at Angela. "I've got a feeling that it'll only be a temporary position anyway. If what's happened already is any indication, you'll rise beyond the printing part of the business before long. Just in these last few minutes it seems like I can already see what's going to happen with the *Journal*."

"And what's that?" J.T. asked.

"I just think it's going to grow so fast that none of us will be able to believe it," Lila went on, her face glowing with excitement. "I think Liberty's been ready for a change for a long time now and this last business with Dobe was the final straw."

"A few people quitting, a few more canceling subscriptions . . . I don't recall anything astounding we discussed that would make you believe the *Journal*'s going to take off." J.T. thought Lila had begun to fantasize a little.

"No," Lila agreed, "but I just remembered something I saw at the funeral that makes me *know* it."

J.T. glanced over at Angela and Clay. "You want to let the rest of us in on it, or should we go home and wait for a vision like you had?"

"It wasn't a vision at all," Lila smiled. "But it's a sign almost as certain."

Clay looked at J.T. and shrugged.

"Senator Demerie ignored Dobe Jackson at the funeral today—acted like he didn't even exist."

"Come to think of it, I saw him turn around and walk off when Jackson tried to speak to him," Angela added. "I thought that was kind of strange since he's always been one of the senator's biggest supporters."

"Tyson Demerie is an old-line politician. He's a human weathervane for political winds," Lila explained, staring directly at J.T. "He can smell political *or* economic death on a man like a hyena smells physical death. And for him to treat his biggest contributor in this whole town like he treated Dobe Jackson today, he knows the end is close."

J.T. nodded in agreement. "I don't know why I didn't figure that out myself. Well, even if ol' Dobe has to shut down or sell out, he's got enough money to live like a king for the rest of his life."

"I'm sure that's true," Lila agreed. "Whatever happens though, we're in for some interesting times ahead."

"I can't wait to get back to work," Angela put in. "This is all so exciting!"

In spite of the funeral, Lila felt cheered by Angela's enthusiasm and by the friendship she shared with those who had come together to mourn and remember. "Well, I'm going home to bed. We've go to get the press rolling again tomorrow. The town might overlook one day without a newspaper as a memorial to Henry, but not two days."

After Lila and J.T. had gone, Angela sat next to Clay in front of the tall windows, watching the slanting sunlight fade as purple twilight settled about the town.

Finally Angela broke the silence. "You think you'll keep working at the *Journal?*"

Clay continued to stare out the window, absorbed by the changing colors of the light, remembering the fiery sunsets of the South Pacific. "Probably," he muttered. "Maybe you haven't noticed, but people haven't exactly been standing in line with job offers for me."

"I like working there."

"I know you do." Clay glanced at Angela. "You certainly don't need the money."

"I think there's a real future for you at the *Journal,* Clay. If what Lila was talking about happens, you might take over for her as editor in a year or two. Then she'll be able to spend all her time looking after the business end."

"Maybe. It would sure take some doing to train me as an editor though." Clay replied, taking Angela's hand. "But, whatever happens, I'm glad we've had this time together. Nothing like doing some hard work with a person if you really want to get to know them."

Angela made tiny figure eights on the top of Clay's hand with her fingertip. "Clay . . ."

His eyes narrowed in concern at the tone of Angela's voice. "Something bothering you?"

"If you don't want to talk about it let me know, but sometimes I worry about you."

"Why?"

"It's just that—well sometimes you act like you're off somewhere else, even when you're right here next to me."

Clay felt that Angela knew him better than he had thought. "That's the way I feel sometimes."

Angela squeezed his hand, leaning her head against his shoulder.

"It's almost like I'm living in two places at once," Clay went on, his eyes gazing off into some unknown terrain that only he could see. "When I wake up in the morning I don't know if I'll be here in Liberty or off somewhere in the South Pacific."

The expansive living room was full of shadows now as dusk gave way to night. Out in the hall the grandfather clock punctuated the silence with its metronomic ticking.

After a few moments, Clay continued, speaking as though he were feeling his way through a minefield. "I feel like half a man a lot of the time—like I've only got half a body and half a mind. I can almost see another Clayton McCain still digging into the sand behind a coconut log, trying to get away from the machine gun bullets and the mortars and the artillery."

Angela sat with Clay in the darkness, allowing him to talk it all out, to take some of the pain out of the memories by sharing them with someone else. When he had finished, she kissed him lightly on the cheek. "If it's any comfort to you, Clay, I want you to know that I'll be right here with you—for as long as you want."

Clay leaned forward, rubbing his eyes with both hands. Then he took Angela's hands and kissed her tenderly on the lips. "I think maybe that's enough."

Angela knew that it wasn't, but she also realized that it was something he had to find out for himself.

* * *

"'And him that cometh to me I will in no wise cast out.' Jesus first spoke those words almost two thousand years ago, and they're just as real, just as true today as they were then." As the choir rose to stand behind him, Thad Majors closed his Bible and placed it on the pulpit, stepped down from the platform, and stood in front of his congregation. Beaming his crinkly, genuine smile at his church, he extended his arms. "Come to Jesus. A million years from now you'll still be rejoicing in this day."

> Just as I am, without one plea,
> But that Thy blood was shed for me,
> And that Thou bidd'st me come to Thee,
> O Lamb of God, I come! I come!

Angela knew this was Clay's hour. She had seen it coming for some time now and had been with him at two o'clock this same morning when he had made the decision to give his life to Jesus Christ. She smiled back at him as he patted her hand and rose from the pew. Her eyes shining with tears, she watched him walk purposefully down the aisle of the church toward Majors, who stood waiting like a proud bridegroom.

Majors shook Clay's hand and spoke with him a few minutes, tilting his head forward so he could hear above the singing. Then he introduced him to the church, telling them of Clay's decision. With heartfelt "amens" the church accepted him as a member, then passed by in a long line to welcome him into the church.

As she always would at such times, Angela recalled that bitter cold and snowy Christmas Eve at Ollie's when she had finally seen the light shining in darkness. The noonday sunshine streamed in through the tall stained-glass windows, bathing the church in a rainbow of colors, but Angela saw only Clay's face shining with the joy of a brand-new life.

Angela also knew that something else lay close to the heart of Clay McCain. As they walked the shady sidewalks of Liberty toward home together after the service, he spoke it aloud.

"Angela, there's something I've been wanting to talk to you about," Clay began, as nervous as a boy holding a bat in front of a broken window.

"Yes?" Angela determined that she would enjoy every second of it.

"I don't really know how to begin," Clay mumbled, kicking a fallen twig off the sidewalk.

Angela waved at Ora Peabody, who passed them on the other side of the street. "Offhand, I'd say you should just start right at the beginning."

"Well, it's just that—"

"Yes."

"What?"

"Yes. Oh, for goodness sake, Clay! Yes, I'll marry you." Angela turned to him and, on tiptoe, kissed him full on the lips. "Now, is there anything else?"

Dazed, Clay stared down at her. "You mean you really want to marry me?"

"No, I don't think it's that actually." Angela pursed her lips in mock concentration. "I'm just tired of waiting for you to come down the stairs of that garage apartment every morning, and this is the only way I see out of it."

Clay grinned and took her hand as they continued down the sidewalk. April had come again and with it the fragrance of the sweet olive blossoms. The memories came back, too, and the dreams of glory, but Clay no longer felt the pain. Putting his arm around Angela's waist, he pictured a giant stadium and a young man who looked very much like him on the mound. He saw the familiar windup and the blazing fastball as the last batter went down.

ORDINARY PEOPLE SHARING THE EXTRAORDINARY LOVE OF GOD

A needy child enjoys our Mont Lawn Camp

I SN'T IT reassuring to know that good books are still being published in America? That's the whole idea behind Family Bookshelf ... "Since 1948, The Book Club You Can Trust."

We're proud of this distinction, because it clearly defines the kind of literature we offer — from books that emphasize the importance of family values to self-help, fascinating biographies and exciting fiction. All are written by today's foremost authors. *All of the editions we print are exclusive and not available from any other book club.*

Family Bookshelf is also part of a circle of compassionate ministries which have been reaching out to the poor and needy for more than a century. Our ministries are supported by "ordinary people sharing the extraordinary love of God" — living proof that people can make a real and lasting difference in the lives of others.

Our Christian Herald ministries started in 1878 with a mission to help alcoholic men repair their shattered lives. Today, our care also extends to homeless women and even children. At our new Women's Center in New York City, mothers once caught up in the misery of drugs are regaining their dignity and self-respect through professionally-administered recovery programs.

Our ministries are also a mainstay in the lives of deprived youngsters. Every year, urban children are brought to our Mont Lawn Summer Camp in the serene Poconos of Pennsylvania. Here, far away from the city's vicious streets, they can hike, fish, swim, and enjoy the bountiful beauty of God's great outdoors. It's gratifying to see the smiles on the faces of these small children, and to watch them grow in this nourishing environment. While at the Camp, many discover Christ and feel His love for the first time. And when Camp is over,

most leave with a new and enduring sense of family values.

But our youth ministry doesn't end at Camp. All year long "our kids" and their families receive assistance through a number of programs, including Bible study, holiday meals, tutoring in reading and writing, teen activities and college scholarships.

So you see, Family Bookshelf is much more than just a book club. It's also a ministry of Christian Herald. With a worthy mission to provide the kinds of wholesome books — fiction and non-fiction — which will help develop strong family values and morality. *The proceeds from the book you are holding in your hand – and every book you purchase from Family Bookshelf –help us to fulfill our vital mission.* And we thank you for your support.

If you wish to help even more, you may send a tax-deductible donation, in any amount. Simply make your check or money order payable to The Christian Herald Family Bookshelf. We sincerely appreciate your kindness.

OUR CHAPEL AT FAMILY BOOKSHELF

PLEASE JOIN US IN PRAYER ...

On every Monday morning, Family Bookshelf employees and our ministries staff join together in prayer for the needy. If you have a prayer request for yourself or a loved one, simply write to us or call us at (914) 769-9000.

FULLY ACCREDITED MEMBER OF THE EVANGELICAL COUNCIL FOR FINANCIAL ACCOUNTABILITY
FAMILY BOOKSHELF, 40 OVERLOOK DRIVE, CHAPPAQUA, NY 10514